EMPIRE *of* EXILES

Books of the Usurper: One

ERIN M. EVANS

D0109723

orbit

orbitbooks.net

This book is a work of fiction. Names, characters, places, and incidents are the product of the author's imagination or are used fictitiously. Any resemblance to actual events, locales, or persons, living or dead, is coincidental.

Copyright © 2022 by Erin M. Evans
Excerpt from *Relics of Ruin* copyright © 2022 by Erin M. Evans
Excerpt from *The City of Dusk* copyright © 2022 by T. S. Sim

Cover design by Lisa Marie Pompilio
Map illustrations by Francesca Baerald
Cover images by Shutterstock
Cover copyright © 2022 by Hachette Book Group, Inc.
Author photograph by Kevin Goodier

Hachette Book Group supports the right to free expression and the value of copyright. The purpose of copyright is to encourage writers and artists to produce the creative works that enrich our culture.

The scanning, uploading, and distribution of this book without permission is a theft of the author's intellectual property. If you would like permission to use material from the book (other than for review purposes), please contact permissions@hbgusa.com. Thank you for your support of the author's rights.

Orbit
Hachette Book Group
1290 Avenue of the Americas
New York, NY 10104
orbitbooks.net

First Edition: November 2022

Orbit is an imprint of Hachette Book Group.
The Orbit name and logo are trademarks of Little, Brown Book Group Limited.

The publisher is not responsible for websites (or their content) that are not owned by the publisher.

The Hachette Speakers Bureau provides a wide range of authors for speaking events. To find out more, go to www.hachettespeakersbureau.com or call (866) 376-6591.

Orbit books may be purchased in bulk for business, educational, or promotional use. For information, please contact your local bookseller or the Hachette Book Group Special Markets Department at special.markets@hbgusa.com.

Library of Congress Cataloging-in-Publication Data
Names: Evans, Erin M., author.
Title: Empire of exiles / Erin M. Evans.
Description: First edition. | New York, NY : Orbit, 2022. | Series: Books of
    the usurper ; book 1
Identifiers: LCCN 2022012621 | ISBN 9780316440875 (trade paperback) |
    ISBN 9780316440943 (ebook)
Subjects: LCGFT: Fantasy fiction. | Novels.
Classification: LCC PS3605.V36494 E47 2022 | DDC 813/.6—dc23/eng/20220317
LC record available at https://lccn.loc.gov/2022012621

ISBNs: 9780316440875 (trade paperback), 9780316440943 (ebook)

Printed in the United States of America

LSC-C

Printing 1, 2022

For Susan

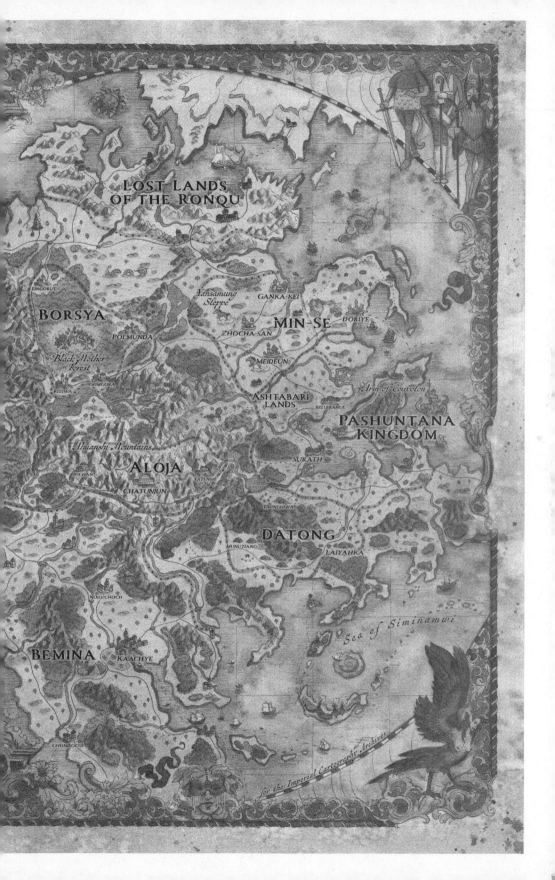

RAGALE

SHADORMA

ARLABECCA

TERZANELLE

GINTANAS

SESTINA

Salt Wall

AUTHORITY·SEATS·FOR
EACH·PROTECTORATE

Arlabecca
Imperial Authority

Khirazj	Sestina
Min-Se	Kiyangga
Orozhand	Maqama
Bemina	Isefa
Rongu	Ragale
Ashtabari	Tornada
Datong	Caesúra
Borsya	Bylina
Aloja	Kiyangga
al-Kual	Arlabecca

SAINT·ASJA·OF·THE·SALT

MARTYR·OF·THE·WALL

DRAMATIS PERSONAE

Ahkerfi of the Copper: a sorcerer of Kuali ancestry

Alletet: the lion-headed Khirazji wisdom goddess; rules over the day

Alomalia of the Bone: an Orozhandi saint whose bones are in the Chapel of the Skeleton Saints

Alzari yula Manco: partner of the yula Manco nest; nest-mother of Tunuk; of Alojan ancestry

Amadea Gintanas: archivist superior of the imperial collections (South Wing); of uncertain ancestry, mostly Semillan

Appolino Ulanitti: "the Fratricide"; a former emperor of Semilla; Clement's second-eldest brother

Asla of the Salt: a martyred sorcerer whose affinity magic helped form the Salt Wall; an Orozhandi saint

Aye-Nam-Wati: the snake-tailed Datongu wisdom goddess

Bayan yula Manco: partner of the yula Manco nest; father of Tunuk; of Alojan ancestry

Beneditta Ulanitti: the Masked Empress of Semilla and Grand Duchess by Custom of Her Protectorates; wife of Ibramo Kirazzi; daughter of Clement

Bijan del Tolube: corundum specialist; married to Stavio Jeudi; of mixed ancestry, Kuali and Beminat

Biorni: a horned rabbit skull

Bishamar Twelve-Spider ul-Hanizan: reza of the ul-Hanizan clan and partial holder of the Orozhandi ducal authority; Nanqii's grandfather; of Orozhandi ancestry

Chiarl: a bodyguard of the Maschano family; of uncertain ancestry
Clement Ulanitti: previous emperor of Semilla; Beneditta's father and target of Redolfo Kirazzi's attempted coup
Clotilda Ulanitti: former empress of Semilla; mother of Clement, Appolino, and Iespero
Corolia: a coffee shop owner of Kuali ancestry

Deilio Maschano: a scrivener of Parem and heir of House Maschano; of mostly Semillan ancestry
Demuth of the Wool: an Orozhandi saint whose bones are kept in the Chapel of the Skeleton Saints
Djacopo Kirazzi: late husband of the former holder of the Khirazji ducal authority; Redolfo and Turon's father
Djaulia Ulannitti: daughter of Empress Beneditta and Consort-Prince Ibramo
Djutubai: a peacock-headed Khirazji wisdom god; rules over the night
Dolitha Sixteen-Tamarisk ul-Benturan: reza of the ul-Benturan clan and partial holder of the Orozhandi ducal authority; Yinii's great-aunt; of Orozhandi ancestry
Donatas Ten-Scarab ul-Benturan: a stonemason of Orozhandi ancestry; Yinii's father

Eschellado Ulanitti: Semillan emperor who reigned during the Salt Wall's sealing

Fastreda of the Glass (Fastreda Korotzma): a sorcerer of Borysan ancestry; coconspirator of Redolfo Kirazzi

Gaspera del Oyofon: retired captain of the Blessed Order of the Saints of Salt and Iron; called the Fox of the Wall and the Penitent Turncoat; joined the Usurper's coup, then betrayed it; of mixed ancestry

Hentara: a day-sister at Gintanas Abbey; of Khirazji ancestry

Hulvia Manche: the Kinship of Vigilant Mother Ayemi's imperial liaison; of Ashtabari ancestry

Ibramo Kirazzi: the consort-prince; son of the Usurper, Redolfo Kirazzi

Iespero Ulanitti: former emperor of Semilla; Clotilda's eldest son; killed with Sestrida and their four children by Appolino; of Semillan ancestry

Iosthe of the Wool: a sorcerer of Ronqu ancestry

Jeqel of the Salt: an Orozhandi saint whose bones are in the Chapel of the Skeleton Saints

Jinjir yula Manco: partner of the yula Manco nest; nest-father of Tunuk; of Alojan ancestry

Joodashir of the Salt: a sorcerer of Minseon ancestry

Karimo del Nanova: a scrivener of Parem; of mixed ancestry

Katucia Ulanitti: Iespero and Sestrida's daughter; killed by Appolino; of Semillan ancestry

Kulum yula Manco: partner of the yula Manco nest; father of Tunuk; of Alojan ancestry

Lamberto Lajonta: Ragaleate Primate of the Order of the Scriveners of Parem; of mixed ancestry; Quill and Karimo's superior

Lireana Ulanitti: daughter of Emperor Iespero and his heir presumptive; presumed murdered by Appolino but claimed to be discovered alive by Redolfo Kirazzi; "the Grave-Spurned Princess."

Lord on the Mountain: the supreme god worshipped in Min-Se, often depicted in a pillar of flames surrounded by his thirteen sage-riders

Maligar of the Wool: an Orozhandi saint whose bones were not safely translated; one of the wooden skeletons in the Chapel of the Skeleton Saints

Melosino Ulanitti: Iespero and Sestrida's infant son; killed by Appolino

Micheleo Ulanitti: son and heir of Empress Beneditta and Consort-Prince Ibramo

Mireia del Atsina: head archivist of the Imperial Archives; of mixed ancestry, predominantly Ronqu

Nanqii Four-Oryx ul-Hanizan: a procurer of questionable goods; of Orozhandi ancestry

Noniva: the Ashtabari mother goddess

Obigen yula Manco: Alojan noble consul; partner of the yula Manco nest; nest-father of Tunuk; of Alojan ancestry

Ophicida: a former empress of Semilla

Oshanna of the Copper: an Orozhandi saint whose bones are in the Chapel of the Skeleton Saints

Pademaki the Source: the Khirazji river god, as well as the name of the river that ran through that ancient kingdom

Palimpsest (Imp): a cat

Pardia Kirazzi: Redolfo's wife, of Khirazji ancestry

Pharas Two-Sand Iris ul-Benturan: Yinii's father's cousin; of Orozhandi ancestry

Phaseran: a beetle-headed Khirazji wisdom god; rules over the twilight hours

Qarabas of the Limestone: an Orozhandi saint whose bones are in the Chapel of the Skeleton Saints

Qilbat of the Cedar: an Orozhandi saint whose bones are in the Chapel of the Skeleton Saints; the maker of the wooden skeletons

Qilphith of the Paint: an Orozhandi saint whose bones are in the Chapel of the Skeleton Saints

Quill (Sesquillio Haigu-lan Seupu-lai): third son of House Seupu-lai and scrivener of Parem; of mixed ancestry, predominantly Minseon

Radir del Sendiri: a generalist of the Imperial Archives; of mixed ancestry

Redolfo Kirazzi: the Usurper; former holder of the Khirazji ducal authority

Richa Langyun: member of the Kinship of Vigilant Mother Ayemi; of mixed ancestry, predominatly Datongu

Ropat of the Sandstone: an Orozhandi saint whose bones are in the Chapel of the Skeleton Saints

Rosangerda Maschano: a lady of a pre-Sealing family; wife of Zaverio Maschano; mother of Deilio Maschano; of mixed ancestry

Senca yula Manco: partner of the yula Manco nest; nest-mother of Tunuk; of Alojan ancestry

Sestrida Pramodia: consort-princess to Iespero; killed by Appolino

Sigrittrice Ulanitti: adviser and seneschal of the Imperial Authority; "the empress's sha-dog"; Beneditta's great-aunt

Stavio Jeudi: a bronze specialist of the Imperial Archives; married to Bijan del Tolube; of Ashtabari ancestry

Toya of the Pottery: an Orozhandi saint whose bones are in the Chapel of the Skeleton Saints

Tunuk yula Manco: a bone specialist of the Imperial Archives; nest-child of Lord Obigen; of Alojan ancestry

Turon Kirazzi: Redolfo's younger brother; of Khirazji ancestry

Uruphi yula Manco: partner of the yula Manco nest; birth-mother of Tunuk; of Alojan ancestry

Vari yula Manco: partner of the yula Manco nest; nest-mother of Tunuk; of Alojan ancestry

Violaria Ulanitti: Iespero and Sestrida's daughter; killed by Appolino

Yanawa of the Gold: an Orozhandi saint whose bones are in the Chapel of the Skeleton Saints

Yinii Six-Owl ul-Benturan: ink specialist of the Imperial Archives; of Orozhandi ancestry; Dolitha's great-niece.

Zara Kirazzi: current holder of the Khirazji ducal authority; Turon's daughter and Ibramo's cousin

Zaverio Maschano: a lord of a pre-Sealing family; husband of Rosangerda; father of Deilio; of Semillan ancestry

Zoifia Kestustis: a bronze specialist of the Imperial Archives; of Borsyan ancestry

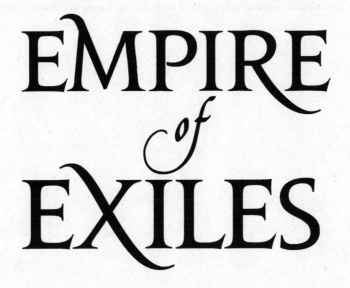

EMPIRE
of
EXILES

I

THE DUKE KIRAZZI

Year Eight of the Reign of Emperor Clement
Palace Sestina

Redolfo, Duke Kirazzi, spends five days in solitude at Sestina, with only the garish birds in the wallpaper for company, before his younger brother finally visits. Redolfo arranges himself on the sofa as if the suit he's wearing isn't his last, isn't stained with sweat, as if he's not been on edge waiting for an answer, an ending—and maybe he hasn't been. Let no one ever say Redolfo, Duke Kirazzi, is an easy man to read.

Enter Turon, the younger Kirazzi, folding his gloves together in one hand. Where Redolfo is arrogant, Turon is cautious. Where Turon is thoughtful, Redolfo is audacious. They might look close to twins—mahogany skin, close-shorn black hair just beginning to pepper to silver, neat goatees in the most current style—but Turon believes himself to be his brother's opposite in every way that matters. Redolfo is like a changeling to his brother, and the daring, the cleverness, perhaps the cruelty glinting in his black eyes only confirm this belief.

This will matter later, more than Turon can appreciate in the moment.

For now, the younger Kirazzi is focused on what lies in front of him. He stands in what was once their father's study, then Redolfo's study, now his brother's final prison, and the one thought that coalesces out of his grief and anger is too inane to speak.

Redolfo smirks. "Let me guess: you still hate this wallpaper."

"No. You like it. It's fine," Turon says, and Redolfo laughs.

"Saints and devils, but you're predictable."

Turon regards his louche brother solemnly—it's all he can manage right now, solemnity. This is goodbye, after all, and it should be solemn.

Redolfo grins back, ready to make it as difficult as possible, and Turon's mouth locks around his solemnity like Redolfo is going to have to break his teeth if he wants to steal *that* from him.

"Do you want a drink?" Redolfo asks. "They wouldn't transfer most of my selection, but there's some fig brandy someone gave me for Salt-Sealing on the sideboard."

"It's the middle of the day."

Redolfo gives him a withering look. "How does that matter at this point? Fetch me some if you're going to be a prig."

Turon crosses to the sideboard, pours a glass of liquor for his brother. Even waiting for the hangman, there's nothing hopeful about Redolfo, nothing fearful either. Just arrogance—gods *above*, his arrogance. It's an old, patient kind of anger that fills up the younger Kirazzi, the sort that's used to being squashed down, waiting for a better time to surge, one that never comes. Turon hands the liquor over, wants it to be a peace offering, but knows Redolfo accepts it as a concession. Whatever Turon wants his brother to be, there's no more time for him to change.

"So," Redolfo says, "have they decided to make a tradition of brothers cutting brothers' throats? Or have you opted to grow some balls and make a daring rescue attempt? What are we doing here?"

Turon bites his tongue. "They thought you'd talk to me. Confess."

Redolfo laughs. "What's there to confess? Did someone miss me at the head of my glass army?"

That anger rises in Turon again—*why you put us in the middle of it, why you raised a coup with your son beside you, a* child *your weapon,*

Pardia is beside herself, Mother's locked herself away, do you even care—before he can press it down. Emperor Clement wants answers and Turon wants a chance to say goodbye, not one last argument.

Though, in this moment, he thinks an argument might be the most fitting goodbye.

"The extent of your conspiracy," he says. "Your motives. What you intended to do. The names of your coconspirators."

Redolfo's eyes *burn*—and Turon knows that look. It's the same look he had when they were boys, when they'd visit Arlabecca and some ruffian or other mistook two weedy boys for easy marks, not the heirs of ancient Khirazj. It's vengeance and fury and *power*, all churning into terrible action. Turon had been afraid, but those older boys, looking for someone to dominate, looking for a war they could win, had instead felt the full force of House Kirazzi brought down on them, and he saw Redolfo had known from the first taunt he would destroy these paltry enemies.

"That's interesting," Redolfo drawls. "Why would I tell you anything? I've already been sentenced and I can't imagine there's anything you can pass along to Clement that will overcome treason."

"We can try."

"'Try.'" Redolfo smiles slyly. He wants to talk; he wants to show off; he wants to rage—Turon knows his brother like no one else does. "They think I'll give you anything they ask for just because we're brothers, but you and I know better. Only one of us is in the business of betrayal."

Turon returns to the liquor arranged on the sideboard. He pours himself a brandy he doesn't want, and it's too sweet, the softness of figs drowning in a sea of sugar.

"You didn't tell me," Turon says, eyes on the liquor.

"Of course not. Did you want to be a traitor?"

"I wanted not to be surprised when my own brother announced he had a pretender to the throne and an army and an intent to stage a coup."

"'Intent' is as lazy a word as 'try.' Like I said, nobody missed my army." He drains the glass of brandy. "Don't be sulky. You didn't want to be a traitor."

Turon sits down opposite Redolfo in a tufted chair upholstered in crimson. "Were you a traitor? That's not the story you told."

"Oh?" Redolfo asks.

"The emperor's killed by his brother. His wife, his children, all die together under the Fratricide's madness. We fight a war—a war in Semilla!—to defeat the murderer, to crown Clement, the least of the brothers. And then you said you found Lireana—you found the daughter of our dead emperor, who should by any right have the throne instead of her uncle, if she survived that massacre. Even Clement would agree to that."

Redolfo makes a lopsided sort of face. "Mm. But he didn't."

"If all that were true," Turon goes on, "then you weren't a traitor, you were a hero, and I don't know how you'd think I wouldn't stand by you." He studies his brother's face. "Which makes me think you're lying about her."

Redolfo snorts. "Is that what Clement wants to know? If she's Lireana?"

"Among other things."

Redolfo grins—maybe he's glad his little brother's come to him or maybe he knows this is all a game. Not an easy man to read, recall. "I'll tell you everything you want to know. All you have to do is ask."

There are ten thousand places to begin, ten thousand paths to the beating heart of Redolfo's rebellion, and as much as Turon Kirazzi wishes for one that leads to his brother contrite and pardonable, five days of grief and rage have made him understand that if this path ever existed, it is lost now.

So Turon begins along the one he thinks will save *someone*, at least. "Start, then," he says, "with the girl."

CHAPTER ONE

Year Eight of the Reign of Empress Beneditta
The Imperial Archives
Arlabecca, the capital of the Imperial Federation of Semillan Protectorates
(Twenty-three years later)

Quill had been hoping, before he came to the Imperial Archives, when all this was just forms and plans and schedules, that Brother Karimo had been exaggerating. But here in the entry hall with the shouts of Primate Lamberto echoing over them, he had to agree: dealing with the Kirazzis made people uncommonly irrational.

Primate Lamberto's voice carried much farther than the head archivist's, but Quill could tell by the way his bellows kept cutting off abruptly that up in her office, the head archivist was giving as good as she got from the formidable primate. Brother Karimo kept looking anxiously up the stairs that led out of the enormous hall.

"I don't *think* she's going to throw us out," Quill said.

Karimo turned back to him and smiled. "You haven't met the head archivist before. It's still a possibility." He glanced once more at the stairs. "Better than when the Dowager Duchess Kirazzi died, though. No one's thrown a punch and I don't *think* anyone's set a fire."

"Saints and devils," Quill said, but Karimo turned back to the stairs.

Quill glanced over at the woman behind the reception desk, a pale, pretty archivist in robes of dark blue with a silver chain running from shoulder to shoulder. Her melting brown eyes fixed on the two scriveners of Parem waiting for their superior in a way that seemed somehow speculative and predatory. Quill gave her a little wave and she frowned.

"Are either of you facilitating those requests?" she demanded. "The Kirazzi ones?"

"Karimo is," Quill said, elbowing the other young man. Karimo jumped and Quill nodded toward the archivist with an expression full of meaning. Karimo often got the attentions of admirers—he was good-looking in a way that a half dozen protectorates would have claimed. Dark curls, golden skin, light, tapered eyes. Unfortunately for those admirers, Quill was usually the one who had to point his dearest friend toward them because he was never paying the least bit of attention.

Karimo followed Quill's gaze and shook his head with a faint smile. "Don't fraternize with clients."

"She's not a client," Quill pointed out.

"She's an *archivist*," Karimo said. Quill gave the young woman an apologetic sort of shrug, but she only continued her speculative study of Karimo.

"Anyway," Karimo went on, "you're the one interested in this place—you should stay."

"If it were up to me, in a heartbeat." The enormous doors to the Imperial Archives dominated the opposite wall, gleaming with their legendary opal mosaics. Symbols and representatives of every protectorate—every culture that shaped the Imperial Federation, every people whose wisdom and treasures had been safely gathered behind those doors—gleamed in a rainbow of shades.

Quill let his gaze drift between them: The elongated Alojan holding a bone flute. The Khirazji woman, adze and compass in hand, her braids picked out by iron banding. The Borsyan man, the curls of his pale, thick beard suggested by the undulating edge of the opals. The Orozhandi holding the horned skull of some ancestor, her own horned head tilted down as if in conversation. The Kuali with her shepherd's crook, the Beminat with a jaguar mask and axe, the Datongu with his ornate basket, the Ashtabari with tentacles clutching a variety of religious icons Quill didn't remember the meanings of. The Minseon man with a drawn bow, his hair sleek and eyes keen, who truly managed to look like Quill's next-eldest brother despite being made of rainbow stones.

A ring of palest white embraced the ten figures: the Salt Wall that surrounded Semilla. Beyond, the jagged edges of a changeling army bristled in more opals of red and green and brown, the force that had appeared as if from nowhere and destroyed all those nations from within, forcing them to flee to Semilla. Eyes and arms and teeth splayed from those strange figures—as if the fearsome shape-shifters were mid-transformation. Or maybe that was what they looked like when they weren't wearing someone else's face—Quill certainly had never seen such a creature, locked away as they were beyond the Salt Wall.

At the center, divided by the doors' split, stood the tenth figure: the Semillan emperor who had reigned during the Salt Wall's sealing, Eschellado, his face the imperial mask of gold instead of more opals.

All the imperial masks were beyond the doors. The archives held the treasures of ancient Semilla and all her protectorates, all those things carried away from the end of the old world that must be kept safe and sure. There was no end to the stories: Whole libraries rescued from kingdoms burning before the changeling army. Intact temples to dead gods. The proclamations of every emperor. The skin of a changeling queen. Diamonds as big as your head. Once, he had heard, a live mammoth, but that was madness—

"You're thinking about all the junk in there right now, aren't you?" Karimo teased.

"You're not even a little curious? I mean, the Kirazzi items aren't that interesting, but they can't stop you looking around while you're standing there. There's *certainly* a collection of Emperor Eschellado's notes about the formation of the protectorate government—if you try to convince me you don't want to see that, I'll call you out as a changeling."

Karimo shook his dark-curled head. "Eyes on the task, brother."

"I've got two eyes," Quill said. "I can do both. Just like you can make sure they find the Kirazzis' things, nice and tidy, *and* ask this girl out for a coffee."

"'Do not be slack in your own business but busy in others'.'"

"I cannot wait until you're through *The Precepts of Bekesa* and on to some other way of lecturing me about how you can't have fun."

Karimo chuckled. But his gaze went up the stairs again.

It would be Karimo who stayed. Brother Karimo had been assisting Primate Lamberto for several years now and had the older man's trust. The primate was highly positioned within the Order of the Scriveners of Parem, the juridical order that managed most of Semilla's legal needs. The primate and his assistants traveled Semilla, spreading the strength and order of the imperial laws and assisting powerful and interesting clients. Assisting the primate was, in all, an excellent position, one Quill's parents found ideal for his station. Even if it didn't suit Quill very well.

Karimo, on the other hand, had his eyes always on the task: the client, the request, the complexities of the law, and the words that made those complexities solid and complete. He prized the duty of the Paremi in a way Quill had always found unsettling in others but somehow right and understandable from Karimo: *The law is what makes us more than beasts, more than the changelings, more than even just ourselves. The law keeps us safe.*

And if Karimo had given Quill a greater appreciation for their duties and their oath, Quill liked to think he'd managed to remind Karimo he could be dedicated and still live a life, deal with "clients" like people sometimes, and look up from his work.

Mostly. Karimo was still watching the staircase.

"Look, she keeps eyeing you," Quill started to say.

But then the door to the office above banged open, and the primate and the head archivist reappeared. Quill and Karimo shot to their feet. The archivist behind the desk only folded her arms over her chest.

The primate came to a stop before them. He was a big man, pale and paunchy, with a fluff of coiled gray hair looped up beneath his miter and half-hooded eyes. Unlike Quill and Karimo, he wore his robes of office instead of traveling robes, and decked in scarlet and gold finery, Primate Lamberto looked very imposing.

And very annoyed.

"The head archivist," he said, "has kindly acceded to our legal and approved requests. Finally."

The head archivist snorted from the foot of the stairs. Mireia del Atsina was an older woman, with a bridge of silver braids framing a narrow, tanned face that suggested at least a little Ronqu blood, and steady gray eyes that declared a Borsyan progenitor or two. She wore the same dark, crisp dress as the girl behind the desk, but hers was accented by a silver chain of office, weighted by the sigil of the imperial crown, a lacquered red cross in the middle of a stylized nest of live branches.

"Next time," she said, "get them approved *properly* and we don't have to do this."

Quill glanced at Karimo, who didn't meet his eye. The whole trip to Arlabecca, Primate Lamberto had been very clear that whatever Quill was used to, this request had its own set of expectations. This was a *highly discreet* undertaking, for a *very important client*, and so there would be *irregularities* that must be set aside because of *expediency and discretion*.

Such as the permissions, signed off not by the empress's secretary but by the Alojan noble consul, Lord Obigen.

"You don't need to bring it up," Primate Lamberto had assured Quill and Karimo. "In fact, until you are within the archives, you don't need to say a solitary word. Your help will please some very powerful people." He hadn't, Quill suspected, thought the issue with the permissions would come up as quickly as the entrance hall, necessitating the long, contentious conference with the head archivist.

"Who gets the bronzes?" the woman behind the desk called out.

Mireia shut her eyes. "Sit *down*, Zoifia."

"It's just a question—"

"Sit down!"

Primate Lamberto grimaced. "I see the Imperial Archives are as . . . *loose* with regard to decorum as ever."

The head archivist regarded him blandly. "Were you introduced to Archivist Kestustis, Most Reverend? She is one of the foremost experts on pre-Sealing cast-bronze works in the entire empire and the possessor of a very strong bronze affinity. When her services are available again, she will find your bronzes and identify them down to the mines their component metals were pulled from. She is twenty-two. The trade is, on occasion, she might offend someone's sense of decorum." Zoifia began to retort but Mireia raised a hand, silencing her. "I assume you're not loitering around yourself this time. Which of them are you leaving to spy?"

Lamberto drew back with a grimace. "Brother Karimo is very experienced, and I will thank you not to besmirch——"

"Most Reverend?" Karimo interrupted. Both Lamberto and Quill looked over at him, startled. Karimo did *not* interrupt the primate.

"If you please," Karimo went on, "I think you should leave Brother Sesquillio behind. He is very interested in the work of the archives—he's been saying so since we left the tower, you know—and beyond that…" Karimo faltered. "Beyond that, you have clients today and tomorrow which I know are difficult matters and which I would feel more comfortable being the one to help you prepare for."

"Or you could leave no one," the head archivist suggested, "and let us get on with our jobs." The primate did not so much as look at her, narrowed eyes on Karimo as if he were trying to find some sleight of hand in the words. Karimo only stared back.

Quill straightened, stinging a bit at the implication that he wasn't capable of scribing for one of Lamberto's clients alone. Besides, while the requests involved the archives, they *came* from the Kirazzi family, and if there were a more complicated client out there, Quill doubted Lamberto would take them on, wealthy or not.

But at the same time, oh how he wanted to lose this argument.

"With all due respect, brother," Quill began.

"Please." Karimo shot a look at Quill, bright with desperation. "Anyway, I think you'll enjoy this assignment. Is it all right, Most Reverend?"

Primate Lamberto studied his two assistants, puzzled, and Quill was certain Karimo's surprising suggestion would be cast aside like a mis-scribed contract.

"It will do," the primate said slowly. "Brother Sesquillio, you... you can accompany the head archivist back to her office. She will apprise you of the limitations the archives insist upon."

"Yes, Most Reverend," Quill said, scooping up his scribe kit and his ledger.

I'll explain later, Karimo mouthed as he passed.

"I'll see you tonight," Quill said, uncertain of what he'd just skimmed the edge of. The archives. The Kirazzis. Or just some tension between the primate and Karimo, some private battle. He glanced back down the stairs as he climbed them, but the other Paremi were already gone.

Whatever it was, Quill reminded himself, Karimo could solve his own problems.

And Quill would get to see the Imperial Archives.

Mireia led him to a room dominated by an enormous wooden desk, dark with age and heavily carved. The light slicing through three windows narrow enough to be arrow loops was somehow sufficient to fill the room and illuminate a wall covered with dark blue satin ropes hanging down from the ceiling, each labeled with a name in delicate script on a cream-colored tag.

"Sit," she said, gesturing at a pair of chairs. Quill did, as she came to stand behind the massive desk. "I assume Lamberto told you not to breathe a word with regard to what this is all about."

Quill made himself smile. "The Kirazzis merely wish to borrow some of their belongings back from the archives."

"Let's skip the things already written on the forms," Mireia said, "and go on to the truth. Which of the Kirazzis hired you?"

Had Primate Lamberto not said even that much? "I...I don't think they want their business aired."

"Let me make this simple: Is your client Ibramo Kirazzi?"

Quill frowned. The empress's consort, the son of Redolfo Kirazzi—but nobody, so far as Quill knew, who was associated with anything approaching mischief. In fact, he'd had the distinct impression that Ibramo Kirazzi held himself apart from anything his family did these days.

"No, no." Quill pulled out his notebook, flipped to the page where he'd written up what he needed to know, copied from the primate's notebook on the road. This had not been a client he or Karimo was allowed to sit down with, and Karimo had been the one to draw up the requests—but Quill had gotten the information down eventually.

"It's . . . the Duchess Kirazzi," he said. "The new one. I think that's his cousin?"

"And the newly crowned duchess wants the Flail of Khirazj? She thinks that's a good idea?"

It was a *terrible* idea, Quill was in full agreement on that much. When Redolfo Kirazzi had ridden against the previous emperor in his attempt to take the throne for the emperor's lost niece, the Grave-Spurned Princess—but really, as everyone knew, for himself—he had always carried the Flail of Khirazj, a symbol of the ancient god-kings the Kirazzi family descended from. A reminder he was greater than what he seemed, a challenge that he was greater than Semilla.

"I cannot say what the duchess thinks is a good idea, esinora," Quill said politely. But then he added, "I hear it's for a Salt-Sealing event. Something in the temple at Palace Sestina."

"And with it she requires . . ." Mireia lifted the requests and read from each page in turn. "One illuminated book, titled *The Maxims of Ab-Kharu*, bound forty years ago with Kirazzi crest on endpapers. One prosthetic arm"—she leveled a sharp gaze at Quill over the papers—"bone and hide, belonging to the late Djacopo Kirazzi. And two bronze statues of Khirazji queens, Bikoro dynasty: one with a headdress of three feathers, one with a scorpion crown. What sort of event is this?"

Quill frowned. His notes only had three items in dispute. Gods and devils, how had he missed one? Had Karimo folded in some other request by mistake? "Statues? Are you sure about those?"

"Am *I* sure?"

Quill shut the book, pushing down the edge of panic with the gesture. Of course Karimo hadn't made an error. Quill had been sloppy and missed an item. *Eyes on the task*, he thought. He could do this. Handling clients was what he was best at.

"It seems my notes are in error. I guess Brother Karimo was correct about my scribing." He smiled winningly at the head archivist. "But to be honest, being graced with a ducal title doesn't necessarily shower good sense on a person. We try not to pry into private matters," he added.

"Even with the Kirazzis?"

Quill took a deep breath and repeated Karimo's words. "The Kirazzi family have paid their debts to society. They make no more mischief than you or I. And legally, while the majority of the items seized in the forfeiture of Redolfo Kirazzi's effects are the possessions of the empire, the Flail of Khirazj remains joint property with the royal bloodline of that preexisting kingdom."

"I understand how the laws work," Mireia said wearily. "But you know as well as I do that the flail is a different beast."

Quill folded his hands. "The requests were approved."

"By Lord Obigen, who will sign any damned request given to him, if he thinks it takes him somewhere politically," Mireia said. "He wants his second wall. Probably wants Duchess Kirazzi to gift him the land around Sestina."

She sighed, then went to the long blue cords, taking three of them in her hands and considering. "While the primate is keen to pretend this is nothing at all, I'm sure the Paremi and the Kirazzi family understand that what you're asking for is akin to kicking a hornet's nest, midwinter," she said. "Maybe nothing, or maybe you're waking something that's going to hurt a lot of people."

"That isn't our intent," Quill said.

But he knew. Everyone knew, including the Kirazzis. No one talked about Redolfo Kirazzi with anything approaching practicality for fear they'd find themselves endorsing treason or worse. And there was no pretending these requests weren't peculiar—the flail, an old hand, and Lord Obigen—but would they be so peculiar from anyone else? A duty was a duty, and ultimately it wasn't Quill's place to say.

"I shall be out from underfoot as soon as possible, esinora."

She snorted. "You assume that because we are the Imperial Archives this is merely a matter of shuffling down a row of boxes and fetching what you want, don't you?"

Quill hesitated. "I don't dare imagine what the archives contain, esinora."

"Hmm," she said. "Sounds like you've heard stories. The mammoth?"

Quill hesitated. "That's *not* true, is it?"

"If it ever was, it's starved by now, but—this is the issue—I cannot say anything for sure. There are centuries of artifacts and writings and more in the archives, the treasures of no less than every Imperial Majesty, every king and queen and duke and warlord and reza and chief, every people that escaped the changelings. Not every Imperial Majesty allowed access. Not every Imperial Majesty had archivists. We are in the middle of a race which we were only allowed to begin halfway, and someone kept flinging pomegranates into our path. You want something from twenty-three years ago. Some of my archivists are still cataloguing things from the Salt-Sealing of the Wall."

Quill could not have hidden his shock, he felt sure. Almost a hundred years had passed since the Salt Wall had been completed. He wondered how much the Kirazzis *were* paying per day. "When... when do you expect to be caught up enough to find Redolfo Kirazzi's effects?"

"Oh, slam the shitting gates," Mireia said. "I'm not going to make you *wait*. They can stop and look—they do it all the time. I mean to say that you all are a nuisance, and you in particular are likely to be underfoot for an uncomfortably long time, but your primate wants his fingers in every pie and he has the right." She looked up, at last, from the three cords. "You never saw Ibramo Kirazzi? Swear it?"

Quill sat a little straighter. "No. Why? Why would it matter?"

Mireia nodded once and gave the center rope three sharp yanks. "I suppose it doesn't," she murmured, "since it's nothing to do with him."

It settled atop the uneasy feeling the strange request had already churned up in his stomach. Quill folded his hands on his knees and

focused instead on how soon he would be within the fabled Imperial
Archives.

The official title given to Amadea Gintanas was "Archivist Superior of the Imperial Collections (South Wing)," which she felt was a
great many words to say "a solver of problems."

Managing the archivists and collections housed in the southern
portion of the Imperial Archives asked for many skills in service to
many problems. Amadea spoke four languages, had a passing famil-
iarity with six more, including several ancient ones from beyond
the Wall, and was, specifically, the one you called when you needed
Early Dynastic Khirazji translated. She knew how to preserve many
treasures against time and the elements. She knew how to date clay-
ware and basket weaves and stone carvings. She knew the faces of
the Orozhandi skeleton saints and the names of the thirteen sage-
riders of Min-Se and the forms of their dresses. She could level a
worktable, repair a torn binding, and fix a Borsyan cold-magic panel
without taking her fingertips off.

Amadea knew how to track the affinity patterns of her specialists, how to talk them down when their magic aligned and overtook
them. She knew how to make a perfect cup of coffee, how to soothe
a heartbreak or the crash that came when an alignment ended, a
burst of anxiety or grief or shame that needed a kind word and a
firm reminder that everything was all right.

Amadea Gintanas did not know what to do about the rabbit skull
sitting on her desk.

"This is the *eighth* time this week he's pulled something like this."
Radir, one of her newest generalists, stood opposite her desk. His
dark, heavily lashed gaze was locked furiously on Amadea. "He put
it under my worktable. I went to sit down and there's this…this
thing snarling up at me."

Amadea considered the skull, the sharp points of its horns and the
fierce arch of its teeth. In the cold-lamps, its shallow orbits glowed
eerily, and the lacy bone of its narrow maxilla filled with shadows.
A flash of gold traced the bone around the horns' bases—an Orozhandi ancestor gift, and a cheap one considering how faint the gold

and how heavy the traces of glue. It wouldn't look friendly in the dark.

"Are you sure it didn't fall?" she said.

"From *where*?" Radir demanded. "You need to assign me elsewhere. I'm done."

Amadea folded her hands in front of her. "Where is Tunuk right now?"

Radir hesitated. "In the Bone Vault."

"Where he is not supposed to be left alone," she noted.

"He seemed fine." Radir rubbed the back of his neck. "He's not in alignment. Bone doesn't come into alignment for four more months."

"He's not in alignment," Amadea agreed, "and how very conscientious of you to keep track."

"Why do you need someone to keep an eye on him if he's not in alignment?"

Amadea smiled. "Because alignment raises the risks of a specialist being caught in an affinity spiral. It doesn't create the risks. You know this."

Radir shook his head. "He wasn't going to go for a walk just because I said so. He *hates* me. I want . . . I want to be here, but I don't know how to keep doing this. Maybe I'm not good enough. He keeps saying he wants you back."

That was when the bell on the wall started jangling. Amadea pressed fingers to her right temple. "You might remind Tunuk that isn't going to happen."

Radir huffed out a breath and said, softer, "I'm worried he might spiral again just so you have to. I don't know how to stop that."

Amadea was beginning to worry about that too. "Tunuk knows that if he does any such thing, he will be sequestered," she said as she came around the desk. "Listen, he has a good heart, but Tunuk is prickly at his best. And a month out from a spiral, he is not at his best." Her own words tugged on Amadea's heart, flooded her thoughts with the memory of Tunuk, a month ago, huddled in the shadows, frozen in place by plaques of bone that clustered over his skin.

"Now, a month is long enough," she continued, telling herself, telling Radir, "that he can probably be left alone with the bones for a bit, and maybe he will appreciate the longer lead. But he needs you."

"He doesn't appreciate anything I do."

"He's not himself right now," Amadea reminded Radir. "And our job is to help the specialists when they can't help themselves. Which they don't always appreciate."

"It's a shit job," Radir said.

"Sometimes it is a *very* shit job. But someone needs to do it." She sighed. "Obviously, the Bone Vault isn't for you. I will work on finding you a replacement, but it will be a while, and right now, even if Tunuk can work alone for a bit, it can't be for long. I'll go talk to him. And if it keeps up, you'll come back to tell me."

The bell on the wall jangled again and she scooped up the rabbit skull. "Go. Take a walk. Buy some cakes or sit and have a coffee or go see that young woman you've been courting. I have to see what Mireia wants and then I'll go return this and talk to Tunuk."

Radir left, and Amadea followed, pausing to check her face in the looking glass that hung over a shelf of figurines. Despite how careful she'd been, fixative gummed her olive temple and the dark streak of her right eyebrow. She licked the corner of her handkerchief and scrubbed at it, noticing as she did the new shaft of silver sprouting from her hairline. Amadea cursed under her breath and pinched the hair out.

You are entirely too old to be vain, she thought, mostly because she ought to hear it. Not because she believed it. She gave the remainder of her part a cursory examination for more traitors before smoothing her hair back down and heading out.

One-handed, Amadea opened the little tin in her pocket and pulled out a knob of scented beeswax. She warmed it in one hand as she walked. An archivist washed well before touching precious things, and old magics kept the archives cool and dry. Good for the artifacts, terrible for the skin. She studied her cracked cuticles a moment, rubbing the beeswax more firmly into them with a thumb, before swapping the skull to her other arm and the beeswax to the other hand.

Vain, vain, vain, she scolded herself as she glanced over the walk-way's edge, through the ornate ironwork grating down at the archives floor below, to the archivists moving among the uncount-able treasures collected there. When civilization had fled the change-ling forces, they brought all manner of precious things to Semilla, and in their subjects, their materials, the names they bore, the shapes they made, lay a map to a world no one living had ever laid eyes on. Beyond the Salt Wall, the remains of those kingdoms and countries lay in ruins, but their traces were treasured and preserved in the Imperial Archives.

Amadea drew another deep breath, full of dust and past and promise, as she came to the foot of the iron stairs that wound down to the main floor. Sometimes it was a shit job, but mostly it was exactly where Amadea belonged.

"Did she call you?" Zoifia demanded as Amadea came into the entry hall, her voice rising and rising. "Do you know if she's giving Stavio my bronzes? Did you know there are Bikoro dynasty bronzes in there that no one's catalogued? I don't know them anyway, and *Stavio*—"

"Good afternoon to you, too. Who is it?"

"A queen consort and a queen regnant, and if they're Bikoro, I think—"

"I mean who is making the requests, not who are the statues." Amadea stopped and eyed Zoifia.

When Amadea had first come to the archives, she had envied the specialists. They had such clear and certain purposes. Not quite sor-cerers out of stories, but born somewhere on the stairs to that plat-form of exaltation and madness, the specialists could connect with worked materials, "speaking" with bone and ink and metals and gems and more. Each material responded to its specialists, grant-ing them information and even limited manipulation, but that skill ebbed and flowed. Sometimes the connection was so thin, so *off*, a specialist could only feel the soft, specific song of their material—*yes, I know this one.*

But when they came into the peak of their power, each turned to each and the magic became greedy and dangerous. A bronze specialist in full alignment could find a pin in a mud puddle, could repair an urn cast a thousand years ago, could even—for the most powerful affinities, at their very deepest depths—coax tin and copper and trace metals together, make something new like a sorcerer could. But each taste, each use, demanded more, and if the specialist wasn't careful, they would begin a spiral of magic that ended only when they were completely merged and entombed by their material, one forever more.

Needless to say, keeping track of alignments and keeping aligned specialists distracted were the greatest of Amadea's problems—and bronze was moving swiftly into alignment. She considered Zoifia's tapping fingers, that too-familiar manic note in her voice, even as she brushed aside anything that wasn't bronze.

"How are you feeling?" Amadea asked.

"I'm *fine*," Zoifia said, tossing her wild curls.

Sometimes Amadea thought it was the prayer of the specialists: I'm fine. *I have lost my sense of self to something inanimate, but* I'm fine. *I've been up all night eating glass and talking to bones, but* I'm fine. *I have smothered myself in gold and drawn trees up through the floorboards, but* I'm fine.

"Did you eat?" Amadea asked, trying to gauge the width of Zoifia's pupils, the color of the irises. She didn't see any bronze flecks there, which was good.

"You'd better hurry," Zoifia retorted. "Mireia wants you to handhold that Paremi. There was a fat old one who thought he could bluster his way in and a young handsome one who was stuffy as a scrivener in a melodrama, but they left. The other young one, a short one with the stupid name, went up with Mireia." She paused, bit her lip a moment. "It's Paremi," she said carefully. "But it's *for* the Kirazzis. You should know."

Amadea's chest squeezed tight around her breath, all her worries about Zoifia suddenly gone. "Oh," she said, and then: "Oh," again, as if that would make anything better.

All she could think of was the letter. *Please never doubt: My love and esteem for you have not changed. There is no force within the Wall that could change them, my darling.*

She cleared her throat. "Well. That's surprising. What do they want?"

"A bunch of junk. And the bronzes. Which, if Mireia gives them to Stavio—" Zoifia stopped herself that time. "I have to assume they said it wasn't Ibramo because Mireia is heartless to *me* but she wouldn't have called you, if it were him."

"It's not anyone but some Paremi," Amadea said. She wondered who had told Zoifia that Ibramo Kirazzi was anyone who mattered, and what exactly they had said.

But love is not enough to withstand the truth of our respective stations, and the dangers of my past are too great to bear. Wedding Beneditta could change all of that . . .

"I bet I could get someone else," Zoifia said. "Some other superior. It doesn't have to be you, right, so I'll go—"

"You have reception duty," Amadea said briskly, brushing the memory aside. "Thank you for your concern, Zoifia, and I'll be sure to remind Mireia you wish to be involved in finding the bronzes when you're up to it. Which is *not* today." She lifted the skull. "Could you keep this for me?"

Zoifia seemed to suddenly notice the horned rabbit skull. "Why do you have *that*?"

"Tunuk." And before Zoifia could be roused to any further kindness, Amadea swept through the entryway and up the stairs to Mireia del Atsina's offices.

Mireia sat at her desk, finishing a request for a specialist. In front of her was what must have been the Paremi—but he was so painfully young that for a moment Amadea couldn't accept that the venerable Paremi came in the form of boys with such guileless eyes. But there he sat, his black, shining hair shaved around his skull, with the top pulled back in an intricate knot at the crown. He smiled eagerly at Amadea, putting her in mind of a puppy. At least Zoifia hadn't destroyed his good mood.

"Amadea, this is Brother Sesquillio," Mireia said. "Quill, this is Amadea Gintanas, one of our superior generalists."

He leapt up from his seat, his dark, tapering eyes sparkling, and grabbed her hand. "Very nice to meet you. I'm so excited to be here."

"It's nice to meet you too." She folded her hands against her skirts, then added to Mireia, "Zoifia mentioned the Kirazzis made the request?"

"The duchess." Mireia handed over the requests to Amadea, eyes full of warning. "But what she's asking for is trouble. You're going to need Yinii, Tunuk, Bijan, and then Zoifia when she's back to herself."

Amadea flipped through the pages, saw the words "the Flail of Khirazj."

She caught her breath, a memory dragged up: *Redolfo, Ibramo's father, flail in hand, looming, looming. Lireana on the floor, on the carpet, the good Alojan carpet, and she's both a million miles away and close enough to hear the beads clink together as the flail swings, before Ibramo shouts—*

Amadea forced herself not to flinch, to ask, "The flail?"

"Apparently, we're not to inquire as to the Duchess Kirazzi's good sense," Mireia said dryly. "Also, Brother Sesquillio has been volunteered to help you, or possibly to make certain we comply to the primate's standards. Or possibly because the primate believes we will make off with the goods, and this one's going to stop us. At any rate, keep him busy so the primate doesn't bother me anymore."

"Right," Amadea said, though it was anything but. She flipped through the request documents as they walked back down into the entry hall. Nothing was ever all right when Redolfo Kirazzi was involved.

Ibramo looking at her, young and fragile, and it scares her. "He's gone to the tombs with her this time. He's going to do something—"

Amadea blew out a breath and the ghost of the memory before it could stir up anything more. A request was a request—what came of it was a question for the officials who reviewed them, not Amadea Gintanas. At the foot of the stairs, she turned and found the Paremi nearly on her heels. "Brother Sesquillio—"

"Quill, please," he said. "No need for formality if I'm helping you."

"Yes." Except there was no task she could think of that she'd be pleased to hand to this untrained young man—maybe someone had a ledger he could check. She considered the requests, calculated how long to find these things, how long she would have to keep this boy—this hostage, this spy—busy to keep peace between Mireia and the primate.

"Perhaps...a tour," she said slowly.

"Oh! That would be *wonderful*." He grinned at her. "The head archivist made it sound like this would be a complicated endeavor. I'm so glad it means there's time to see everything."

Saints and devils, he was so *young*. She sighed. Tours of the archives weren't uncommon—there were public galleries and chapels, but if you had the influence and the interest, and Mireia wasn't annoyed, a tour of the rest of the archives could be arranged. Only, they were arranged months in advance and Amadea's thoughts were full of the many, many things she needed to take care of. Maybe she could find someone else to take him around.

"*Some* things," she corrected. She went to the reception desk and plucked up the rabbit skull. "This way." Amadea heaved one of the great doors open a crack, and she ushered Quill inside.

Amadea tucked the requests under her arm as she mapped the archives in her mind. She narrowed his tour down to the four areas connected to the Kirazzi requests. If Quill met the specialists, perhaps he'd trust them and not worry about hanging around, being in the way. She started up the iron stairs again: The Bone Vault first, where she could collect Tunuk. Then Bijan's workshop. Then Yinii's library; it was close by, and the bronze rooms would be locked for another—

Amadea reached the top of the staircase and stopped. She looked back at Quill. "Did you see Zoifia at her desk?"

He looked startled. "The blond woman? No? Should I have?"

Amadea glanced back at the doors, then up to the third floor, where the bronze collections were. A flash of pale curls appeared between the railings, and Amadea cursed.

"Is something wrong?" Quill said.

"It will be fine," Amadea told him, striding toward the Bone Vault. "But someone else will need to handle your tour. Come with me quickly, please."

CHAPTER TWO

Yinii Six-Owl ul-Benturan had lived in her destiny for five years, but if you were to ask her family, there was still a chance this all might be a misunderstanding.

The day before, the ul-Benturan reza had come to Arlabecca, and Yinii had gone to the home of the far-off cousin the reza was staying with to have dinner with her. Yinii's great-aunt, Dolitha Sixteen-Tamarisk ul-Benturan, had led the families descended from Benturan Canyon for nineteen years now with a pious resolve and a firm hand. Her hair had gone white, her horns now curled around her ears, but still she governed the lives of the ul-Benturans and no one gainsaid her. She was proud, Yinii knew, to have an atnashingyii, "a half-blessed," a specialist, born to ul-Benturan. To the Orozhandi, Yinii's people, affinity magic was a gift from the God Above and the God Below.

Only, Orozhandi were not born with ink affinities, like Yinii had been, and Reza Dolitha was dedicated to finding the key to resolving this little mistake.

"Have they tested you with paints recently?" Reza Dolitha asked, when dinner was finished. Yinii squirmed.

"No, Reza," she said. *There's no need to*, she didn't say. Paint wasn't ink, ink wasn't paint. Dolitha understood that insofar as ink wasn't an Orozhandi affinity, but not in that there could be no mistake.

"Perhaps you should pray to Saint Qilphith," Dolitha said, heavy with meaning. "Perhaps," she added a moment later, "you should consider making *her* your personal saint."

Yinii knotted her hands in her lap and did not touch the amulet dangling from her horn, the crystal of Saint Asla of the Salt, the martyr who created the Salt Wall that saved Semilla and her protectorates from the changeling horde. Saint Qilphith of the Paint was no less revered.

But that wasn't why you chose a saint.

"That is a wisdom, Reza." She cleared her throat. "How long will they have to do without you in Maqama?"

Dolitha sniffed. "I shall return the day after tomorrow. Lord Obigen thinks he's going to sweet-talk me into approving his *blasphemous* plan to knock a hole in the Salt Wall, as if it were inconvenient wreckage left over from the war." She shook her head, her third, parietal eye flinching in involuntary disgust.

"I will attend his repulsive little political maneuver, I will tell him that ul-Benturan will not be quiet *or* cheerful while he disturbs Saint Asla and the Martyrs of Salt and Iron, and if I have any say in it, his 'Second Wall' will be consigned to the rubbish heap of history. Then I will return." She folded her hands and leaned toward Yinii. "Now: I had also considered that perhaps you have only been reacting to *bone* black inks. Has anyone made certain of that? Have you prayed to Saint Alomalia?"

Yinii stayed well into the night, well past the point where the light had faded and Dolitha became a body of warmth to Yinii's dark-eye. She had stayed the night—of course! What sort of reza would send a young girl strolling across this wretched city?—and when Yinii had returned to the archives that morning, it was with orders to pray to six additional saints and to convey a message to a more mundane entity.

She found Tunuk hunched over his worktable in the bone collection, the room they all called "the Bone Vault." All the Borsyan lamps were low, their magical light bluish and dim, and the Alojan archivist's midnight skin was lost in the shadows, his lambent eyes on Yinii as he sorted a tray of beads.

"If Amadea sent you to chastise me," he said in his sonorous voice, "then I want my skull back. Also Radir is a liar and I hate him."

Yinii shut the door, closed her day-eyes, and opened the dark-eye that lay along her hairline, cradled in the swell of her horns. The shift in her sight was like a sudden breath of warm air off a steaming pot. Tunuk was no longer lost in the shadows but a streak of heat, every bit of his enormous, lanky frame outlined.

Yinii crossed to the worktable and sat down opposite him, resting her head in her hands, making the charms wrapped around her horns tinkle. "I'm supposed to tell you to tell your nest-father that he had best prepare for resistance from the ul-Benturan reza tonight."

"I will not," Tunuk said. "Obigen's business is *his* business, and anyway I'm not interested in another lecture about how I need to find some mates and a nest. Apparently," he drawled, "bone speaking is a precious gift I shouldn't squander by living like a hermit."

"I got a similar lecture from the reza about how I should try harder not to have an ink affinity."

"Of course. Because this is all voluntary. We chose this." She heard a bead plink into another container. "*Quartz*," Tunuk sneered. "What are they even paying Radir for?"

"I have to go to the chapel," Yinii said, but she didn't move, head down, stuck in place. She didn't *want* to ask Saint Qilphith or Saint Alomalia for an intervention.

Tunuk sighed, and she heard a piece of paper slide across the table toward her. He took one of her hands, his palm cool and almost gelid against her skin, and slapped it down on the page.

Her nerves leapt over each letter, each lash of ink, as if the words were startled to sense her there.

Sense, see, feel. None of these were quite the right word, but she knew what it was intimately as the ink pulsed over her fingers, memories of the pen and the grinding, the intent and the place. It was a request form, Mireia's sure hand, Amadea's quick notations shivering through the fresh ink. The soot in it muttered of Semilla's rolling hills and vineyards after the frost, prickling her nose with the memory of something like a scent of burning, of grape leaves drying in the sun.

It made her think of the stories of the canyon cities, of the lost catacombs of the saints: a memory she knew intimately, of something she had never seen. Yinii shivered and curled her toes in her shoes, and let her awareness sink deeper into the ink's, felt the words peeling off the page and sneaking over her fingertips, sliding under her nails. Yinii wasn't in alignment, so their edges didn't blur much. She was she, and ink was ink, even if a part of her could imagine their merging, could feel it perfectly. It was safe, even if it wasn't satisfying.

Ink in her mouth, ink in her nose. "If I can't tell you so again, Mother, I love you. But the ink can't. I'm sorry." Yinii lifted her head, took her hand back from the ink, and touched the amulet of Saint Asla again. Satisfying meant addictive, meant dangerous, meant the spiral—though she thought often of Saint Asla's martyrdom, no one would benefit if Yinii ul-Benturan fell into a spiral and drowned herself in ink.

"It's nothing short of *idiocy*," Tunuk declared, "that she thinks you could just *switch*. Just go pester the skeletons into making you anew. The next time she demands you attend her so she can rattle about paint or bone black or sandstone, tell her to fuck off back to the caverns."

Yinii let out a nervous laugh. "I can't do that."

"Then I'll do it for you," Tunuk said savagely. "They can all mind their own business."

Yinii shook her head. It was very like Tunuk. "How are you feeling?"

He snorted. "Are you asking because you care or because you have a ghoulish interest?"

"I ask because I care," Yinii said. "All of us care."

Tunuk lifted his glowing gaze from the beads. "Why? You all stay to your cycles. You don't fall into the spiral out of schedule."

"Well, that's not true. My second spiral was entirely out of alignment, for your information." Yinii swallowed, remembering: *Ink in her mouth, ink in her nose.* Yinii wrapped her arms around herself. "You aren't the only one that...that gets sad and...and desperate." *And lonely and lost*—she thought of the crushing closeness of her family's cavern home, the paucity of books, of ink. It wasn't an Orozhandi affinity. They didn't know what she needed. They didn't know how scared and lonesome she was getting. They didn't know how black the furniture could burn.

After, Reza Dolitha and her parents agreed: as strongly as Yinii's affinity affected her, as unfamiliar as it was, she would be happiest in the Imperial Archives.

"I wasn't *sad*; I was *done*," Tunuk said. He exhaled noisily. "You didn't do it again?"

Yinii shook her head. "I don't like how it feels."

"It's a lot of work," Tunuk said, as if in agreement.

But that wasn't it, not for Yinii. It hadn't been hard to fall into the spiral; it had been incredibly simple. Simple as getting sucked under the tide, simple as drowning. Coming out had been harder, all the will and work her mind and body could handle to climb back into the frenzied, broken world she didn't even want.

"I don't think you want to do it again," she said. "I can't imagine wanting that again."

"I might," Tunuk said diffidently. "You don't know."

"You're right. But I hope you don't."

The door opened, letting in a flash of light that made Yinii open her day-eyes in surprise. "Tunuk!" Amadea shouted. "Are you in here?"

"Yes, and Yinii is too, so you don't get to tell me I—"

"Good," Amadea interrupted, waking the lamps and striding into the Bone Vault, a horned rabbit skull on one hip.

She wasn't alone. A darkblind boy—a human, maybe Minseon—wearing plain robes, with his black hair tied up in a shining loop. He smiled at Yinii, and Yinii touched the amulet of Saint Asla of the Salt again. She didn't say the words to the prayer for guidance and good fortune, but she had to believe, by now, Saint Asla surely knew without words when Yinii was in trouble.

"This is Brother Sesquillio of the Scriveners of Parem," Amadea said, plunking the rabbit skull on the desk and handing Yinii a stack of requests. "He is facilitating a request. He prefers to be called Quill. I am meant to be giving him a tour of the archives, but something has come up."

"What?" Tunuk demanded.

"Zoifia," Amadea said tersely. "There is one page for each of you, and another for Bijan. The last is bronze—it goes on my desk if I'm not back soon. Quill, this is Archivist ul-Benturan and Archivist yula Manco. They will get you started. I will find you when this is sorted. Do *not*," she added to Tunuk, "scare Radir with that skull again."

"It has a name!" Tunuk shouted after her as she raced away. He picked up the rabbit skull, pulled himself upright so he towered over the Paremi, even seated. "I call him Biorni," he told Yinii primly.

"Nice name. It suits him," Quill chimed in. "Manco? Does that mean you're related to Lord Obigen, by chance?" Tunuk's eyes narrowed to slits, and the boy chuckled. "Don't worry. I know the feeling. Everyone knows my family back home too. I'm staying with the yula Mancos is all."

Yinii slipped between them. "I'm Yinii. This is Tunuk."

"Nice to meet you." His smile faltered. "Is Zoifia all right? Archivist Kestustis?"

"My, you're nosy," Tunuk said.

It didn't seem to faze Quill. "I like 'interested.' She seemed fine earlier. She and my friend were eyeing each other," he added in conspiratorial tones.

"Zoifia's, um…" Yinii paused. She was never sure how to best explain alignments and the danger of a spiral. "She's supposed to be on desk duty right now, and not in the archives."

"Nobody can trust her because she's gone insane," Tunuk said dryly. "She's probably trying to seal herself up in a bronze carapace right now."

"Tunuk!" Yinii cried.

"We *all* do it," he drawled.

Yinii flipped through the requests Amadea had shoved in her hands and found the bronze at the bottom. She held it out. "It's this. She was eyeing your friend because she's missing the bronze and she thought she could get him to give her the request. That's her affinity. She's…in alignment."

Quill's brows rose. "Is she going to *spiral*?"

Tunuk snorted, but Yinii blushed. People never understood alignments and spiraling—somehow both too dire and not nearly serious enough. Who knew what he thought that meant? "No, no. Amadea will catch her. She'll talk her down. She's definitely the one you want in a crisis, Amadea."

A dimple flashed in his cheek. "Must be nice to work for someone who takes care of things like that."

"We don't *work* for her," Tunuk said witheringly.

Quill looked around the Bone Vault. "This is... bone and ivory artifacts, right? Does that mean the Chapel of the Skeleton Saints is here? I've always wanted to see that."

"I, um..." Yinii hesitated. She had been told to go pray, and even if she flouted Dolitha, she would have gone to pray just to settle herself, but not with a stranger watching, certainly not with a pretty darkblind boy—

"It's closed," Tunuk intoned. *Lied*, Yinii thought. The chapel didn't *close*. He didn't look at her but snatched his request out of the stack. "And I'm busy. Anyway, that's a terrible place to start, bothering them. Yinii can show you the ceiling or something. Shoo."

It was a kindness Tunuk was offering, Yinii thought as she led Quill up to the top floors, even if it wasn't the sort she needed. You *listened* to the reza, even if she was wrong, even if she misunderstood—and Yinii knew this was no argument she could turn on Tunuk, on any of the archivists who weren't Orozhandi.

Yinii had known since she was thirteen that she would go to the Imperial Archives, hundreds of miles from her family, to live among the most precious documents in the known world, to be their keeper and their guardian—and to be kept and guarded in turn. She found herself surrounded by people who understood what it was to speak a tongue you couldn't explain to others, but not the skeleton saints or the comfort of seeing the pulse of your loved ones in the dark. They cared for her immensely, not in the way you cared for your family, she'd realized. Something deeper—they looked at her and saw themselves, younger, uncertain, dizzied by the voices of the archives—which was precious in its own way.

But not quite enough. She suspected for each archivist, it was *not quite enough*.

Her worries swirled around her, so thick that she reached the last staircase without realizing giving a tour meant she would have to *give a tour.* She turned around, back to the iron railing, and faced Quill.

He was staring up at the great curved ceiling with an awestruck expression. "Saints and devils," he breathed.

Yinii took a deep breath. "There are twelve murals across the ceiling," she said. "One for each protectorate, plus a United Semillan mural, each painted by artists from the...from what would become the protectorates." She searched his face. He *looked* Minseon—but Sesquillio wasn't a Minseon name. And guessing about humans was difficult and fraught. Most of them traced lines back to multiple nations now, and some people cared about their ancestors and some people didn't; some people claimed *these* ancestors but not *those*. If she showed him the Minseon mural of the Lord on the Mountain, he might be elated or insulted.

"What...which one would you like to see?" she asked. "To hear about, I mean. First."

Quill gave her a puzzled sort of smile. "Well, which one is your favorite?"

"All right. Yes," Yinii said. "Um, this way." She led him halfway down the archives, past four other murals of triumphant gods and spirits of knowledge and wisdom. Quill gazed up at them as they walked, and she hoped beyond hope he wouldn't prefer those others.

"*The Martyrdom of Saint Asla,*" she said, pointing up.

Quill stepped up beside her and leaned over the railing to peer up at the painting. Saint Asla, a young Orozhandi woman with loose coppery hair, stood with her arms spread and her three eyes opened wide. Behind her, the gleaming arc of the Salt Wall rose, punctuated by the bodies of other sorcerers, dedicated to salt and iron, and the soldiers who fell defending them from the changelings. Beyond the Wall that would entomb Asla Two-Saint ul-Benturan and the others, the shape of the archives rose, its walls cut away to show the skeleton saints of the Orozhandi, safely translated and decorated with jewels.

Saint Asla's face and hands were left fleshed, but her robes were blown open to display a graceful golden rib cage, trapping a heart of salt within. There were no jewels along her humerus, her delicate spine, the flare of her pelvis—Saint Asla's transmuted flesh became the Wall and so her bones must be beautiful enough alone, even here.

Looking at it made Yinii's throat tight.

"Lord on the Mountain," Quill breathed. "That's beautiful."

Yinii stopped herself from wincing. So he was at least Minseon enough to swear like that. She should have just shown him that panel first. But instead she gestured up at Saint Asla.

"It was the fourth mural begun," she said, "but it was finished sixth because it required more gilt work than some of the others. There were two artists. Both specialists. Gold and paint." She considered explaining how paint was different from ink, but before she could figure out where to start, he spoke.

"That's interesting," Quill said. He looked over at her, thoughtful. "That would have just happened when they painted it. The Salt Wall and everything."

Yinii nodded. "The artists knew her. There's records."

Now Quill swallowed as if his throat were tight. "I can't even imagine it. Having to face the changeling horde. Having to sacrifice myself like that, not knowing if it would make the difference." He paused, then turned to her. "I have a friend, Karimo. He's really smart and he'll talk your ears off about the philosophy of law and the way it makes us sapients, really. But then you look at a moment like this, and...I don't know. There's not a law that stops this, but if you don't have them anyway, what's to say we don't all act like changelings?"

It sent a trill of panic through Yinii. "I don't know. I guess that's why the Vigilant Kinship is around."

He smiled at her. "Yeah that's about what Karimo would say. All the orders—the Kinship, the Paremi, the Golden Oblates, the House of Wisdom, and all the others—if you could make saints of orders, that would be what Karimo believes. That's what keeps us safe and whole and sure." He looked up at the mural. "Is she in the chapel?"

"No," Yinii said. "Saint Asla's, um, in the Wall."

Quill winced. "Oh right."

"I've been to her shrine there," Yinii said. "Twice. She's..." Yinii set her fingers behind the amulet. "We have saints of the canyon, saints of the family, and then a saint for the self. Saint Asla is mine. She was from the same canyon as my family."

Quill smiled. "She sort of looks like you there." And Yinii flushed so suddenly, so deeply, that she could not remember how to make her mouth say "thank you" before he continued.

"Have you ever met a living saint?"

"There aren't any right now," she told him, but because he wasn't Orozhandi, she added, "I did meet a human one if you meant that— a sorcerer? He was Ahkerfi of the Copper. He came to our town when I was a girl. He made me this one." She reached up and laid one of her charms against her fingertips, a seven-petaled copper flower, tiny and intricate, that had bloomed out of the man's fingertips with so little effort he hadn't even blinked.

To the Orozhandi, being born with so much affinity magic was always a gift, these people always saints. But for other peoples, other places, they were isolated and treated as monsters, or leashed and made into weapons. Ahkerfi of the Copper had been a wanderer, never settling, all because he could speak to the copper and it would speak back.

"He called it a gentian," Yinii said. "He didn't seem mad. He didn't talk a lot, but he was nice to me."

Quill peered at the little flower, and Yinii realized he was suddenly very, very close. "That's pretty," he said. Yinii's cheeks burned.

"I know that there are others," she said, too fast. "Iosthe of the Wool, up in the mountains. Joodashir of the Salt is down somewhere on the coast, I think. And Fastreda of the Glass is in Arlabecca, of course—in the Imperial Prison. I've been in the lottery to meet her, but they take so few—"

A screech echoed off the painted vault of the ceiling and Yinii jerked her attention toward the far end of the building. To the hallway that led down to the bronze collections.

"I will tear your *eyes* out!" Zoifia's voice howled from the far passage.

"Oh," Yinii said. "We should...Do you want to see the corundum room or—"

"Sorcha! You can try!" a man's voice bellowed back. *Stavio*, Yinii thought. *Calling Zoifia "witch." Oh no.*

"Um," she said, trying to think of paths to take, ways to rush Quill out of the way, where he wouldn't see two of the archives' specialists at their worst. "We should...not be...here."

But it was too late: Amadea appeared at the mouth of the hallway, pushing Zoifia before her and holding Stavio behind, both at arm's length. Zoifia's blond curls seemed charged, ready to spit sparks, her muscles hard against the edges of her skin.

Stavio seemed less primed to explode, more unstoppable as he pressed forward. From the waist up, Stavio might have been mistaken for a handsome, well-muscled, and thick human, olive-skinned and crowned with shining black curls. But from the waist down, the Ashtabari bronze archivist's body split into eight thick tentacles dappled green and brown. Which were twisting and snapping in an irritated fashion as he moved toward Zoifia.

The pair of them pulled all of Yinii's nerves, as if the magic in her sensed the magic in them, swelling and rising, ready to surge. She tried to peer around the cloud of Zoifia's hair, the thrash of Stavio's tentacles—if she could see the color of their eyes, she might be able to guess how bad it was going to be. She stepped forward—aware that even as she was shielding Quill, she was moving toward the pull of their affinities.

"You think you're clever?" Stavio shouted. "You think you can just sneak in when it's supposed to be locked?"

"Me? *You* were the one trying the door! You were going after the Kirazzi requests. I caught you—you're the sneak!"

"*Neither* of you was supposed to be anywhere near that door." Amadea, caught between them, did not raise her voice. While her two charges looked disheveled, robes askew and faces flushed, Amadea was stern and unshaken, only a lock of her dark hair pulled loose over her face. "It doesn't matter who was there first. It doesn't matter why you were there. It doesn't matter which of you wants the new request—you are both restricted from your workroom until the alignment ends." She looked back over her shoulder at Stavio. "When was the last time I had to sequester you?"

Stavio drew back and Amadea's hand dropped. The power that had been building up between the two bronze archivists ebbed a little. "Nobody needs to be sequestered," he protested.

Zoifia shivered. "You can't sequester me and not him."

"Sorcha," Stavio spat. "You're the one acting like a demon got in her."

Behind Yinii, Quill leaned closer. "Is that a big deal?" he whispered. "Sequestration?"

"Yeah," Yinii answered.

Stavio startled as she spoke, his gaze sweeping over to Yinii and Quill. He scowled. "Hey, you think this is a Datongu melodrama? We're not selling tickets."

"No," Quill said cheerfully. "I'm getting a tour."

"Yinii," Amadea said. "Why don't you show Quill the rest of the murals from the north mezzanine, and I will meet you in your library." She took Stavio by the arm, pulling him forward so the bronze archivists were on either side of her. "You two are going for a walk. With Tunuk. All of you need some air. Once around the square, if you please."

The power ebbed more still, but Zoifia tossed her hair and made a face. "There's bronze out in the world, you know? Loads of it. It's not like I'm some smelter with only enough affinity to clean verdigris."

"I'm well aware," Amadea said, steering them toward the stairs. "I'm also well aware that unless you *do* need sequestration or you've suddenly become a sorcerer, you should be fine encountering bronze where it doesn't fill an entire room."

Yinii watched them go, tension unknotting from her shoulders. She let out a long breath and turned back to Quill, who was still watching Amadea leave.

"That seemed like it was about to go bad," he said.

"Maybe," Yinii admitted. "Probably not. Amadea had it under control. It's just...how it is." If you had come to the archives, your affinity was strong enough that your alignments might always go bad.

Quill considered her a moment. "I don't mean to be presumptuous, but you looked like you were expecting a fight."

Yinii thought back to other bronze alignments—she didn't really understand what made different affinities behave differently, but metallic affinities always seemed to have fast, furious alignments full of fighting and dramatics. When gold and bronze synchronized, it was particularly bad in the southern wing.

"I mean," she said, "that's...possible. It's difficult for them. But Amadea was there. Like I said, she's who you want in a crisis."

"Clearly," Quill said. He looked down the stairs once more, then he smiled back at her. "All right, shall we continue the tour?"

By the time Quill left the Imperial Archives, all requests duly filled and filed, his head spinning with astonishing sights, the sun was edging below the spires of the city, making the light a thick and cozy sort of golden. The late-summer air had a fat humidity after the archives' coolness, and it left Quill simmering with anticipation. He bought a paper cone of fried fish, silvery and slim as his fingers, and ate them as he forged a merry path through the city of Arlabecca to the home of Lord Obigen yula Manco, where he, Karimo, and Primate Lamberto would be staying.

Quill paused beneath a loping red line of an aqueduct so ornate that he craved a name for it, and thought of the way everything in the archives seemed to have a name, a story, a place. After the drama with the bronze archivists, he had learned the details of mural after mural as he walked, Yinii rattling off names and facts as sure as a Paremi advocate in court. After Yinii's library, Amadea had pointed out the sorting facilities down below the first floor, over-looked by the mezzanines, packed with enough treasures he could have understood losing a mammoth. He had met more than a few archivists, including the ones who would be handling the requests, and while Amadea traded forms and permissions, stanched gossip and reminded more than one of them that it did not matter about the flail or the Kirazzis, they had jobs to do—while all that happened, Quill had considered adorned skulls and trays of rubies and more.

For all Karimo's advice to keep his eyes on the task, Quill had enjoyed himself immensely, and it was only now, walking along, thinking of all the things he would tell Karimo about the archives and the archivists, that he began to think about the Kirazzis' involvement. About the oddity of the bronzes. About Ibramo Kirazzi.

He thought of Amadea, and how she had asked about the consort-prince so crisply—so cold it had to be personal, he thought, and what was personal with the empress's husband if you were an archivist? But then he thought of how she'd raced after Zoifia, how Yinii had said everything was fine if Amadea had her, and then how Yinii had spoken of the spiral, like it was the sort of trauma you shut your whole self against the memory of. Whatever secrets or scandals were lurking there, having someone you trusted with something as frightening as that seemed an excellent trade.

An Orozhandi man sat on the street corner, shaking a pot with a few coins in the bottom. He wore the threadbare uniform of one of the wall-walkers, the Blessed Order of the Saints of Salt and Iron. Soldiers who guarded the Wall that sealed the Empire of Semilla off from the wider world and the threat of the changelings. One horn was broken, and his crutch leaned against the wall beside him. In the gloom, his third eye hung blearily open.

Behind him, a Kuali man in hose and an embroidered tunic leaned against the wall of a building, his rust-colored veil draped around a long-stemmed pipe. The sword at his belt was marked with alternating white and blue triangles—another retired wall-walker. He studied Quill carefully over the veil.

Quill dug the change from his purse and added it to the pot. "A good evening to you both, brothers."

"To you as well, and thank you, kind brother," the Orozhandi man said with a salute. "Saints guide you. You know where you're headed?"

"I do, thank you," Quill said. He paused. "Can I ask you something? Can you tell me how to say 'I had a nice time with you' in Orozhandi?"

The man's eyebrows rose. "Depends. Who are you saying it to?"

"A girl I met." He smiled. "Pretty girl I met."

"Hmph. Best you don't, then. Her family might not like her running off with a darkblind boy, you know? Mine wasn't keen on it, and here I am."

"I'm not running off with her," Quill assured him with a laugh. "I only just met her. She was explaining some art to me."

"Mm-hmm. Said much the same."

"You think that was it?" the Kuali man said.

The Orozhandi man sighed and looked skyward. "Mighta been the sandsmut." He squinted at Quill. "All right. You tell your girl, 'Ada-aada, shilukundeh essetii teshi naashishet.' The day before today, I took pleasure in the word you and I had."

Quill brightened. "Ada-aada, shilukundeh essetii teshi naashishet." He repeated it several times, adjusting to the Orozhandi's corrections. He took out his notebook and a bit of lead and wrote out an approximation. "Thank you, I—"

Another man came out of the gloom, swooping close to the beggars and Quill to drop a pair of gold coins in the pan. Quill stepped aside, surprised—and stopped.

The man's gaze caught his.

He was Khirazji, dark-skinned and dark-haired, with a lean dog trotting at his heel, sleek and sharp-faced. A plum cape over his shoulders, a feathered hat low on his brow...a black mask covering his face, revealing only his piercing eyes. Only the imperial family wore masks, especially full masks like this one. There was only one Khirazji man in the imperial family.

The consort-prince, Ibramo Kirazzi.

It was not a strange thing to see the consort-prince in the golden mask of imperial authority, nor in a green mask of personal affairs. But even if you saw him in the black mask, you were to carry on as if you hadn't—the black mask was for secrecy, for privacy and invisibility.

The man nodded once at Quill, as if they'd agreed without words not to speak of it, before stalking off into the night.

"Do you know that man?" he asked the two beggars.

The Orozhandi laughed again and took one of the gold coins from the pot. "I know I like him very well."

"Black mask means you don't see him," the Kuali said. "Those are the rules."

"Blasted mask taboos," the Orozhandi sniffed. "I see what I see."

Quill bade the men good night and continued on, along the red-painted aqueduct glowing in the last of the sunlight, unsettled but unable to say quite why. The Kirazzi requests were irregular, but they were innocuous. And even if they were something more, no one requesting them was Redolfo Kirazzi, back from the grave. No one was Ibramo Kirazzi, stalking through the night not to be noticed yet unable to be ignored. No one was making whatever sort of trouble the archivists feared and Primate Lamberto avoided naming.

When Quill came to Lord Obigen's house, no one was waiting at the door. He knocked, several times, and then several times again, to no avail. Lights blazed through the windows, but it was strangely quiet. He wondered if he ought to let himself in and knocked again.

He thought of Ibramo Kirazzi and tried to put him out of mind.

A scream rang out, chased by a chorus of more screams. Quill did not wait, but pushed through the door, into the long hallway, and then into the great room beside it, now filled with people, all staring down at two bodies lying on the floor.

There was Lord Obigen, his dip-dyed shawl soaked with blood, his eyes no longer shining but flooded red. Beside him lay an elderly Orozhandi woman, crawling away, hand pressed to a bloody forehead. Blood pooled around them both, so much blood.

People were screaming, shouting at Quill to go, to get the vigilants, to do something. Primate Lamberto, clutching his bloody shoulder, shouting at Quill to leave, to go, to run.

Quill could not move. He couldn't look away from the killer, still standing over the bodies: Brother Karimo, staring at the knife in his bloody hand as if he couldn't fathom where it had come from. He met Quill's eyes a moment, still baffled, still blank.

"Karimo!" Quill shouted. "Stop!"

Grief flickered in Karimo's pale gaze, but he only turned to face the screaming party, knife held high.

"Those who sow deception," Karimo called tearfully, "must reap only death." And to a renewed chorus of shrieks, he drew the knife across his own throat, spraying blood everywhere.

CHAPTER THREE

Richa Langyun, of the Kinship of Vigilant Mother Ayemi, stood in the Imperial Archives' entrance hall well after midnight beside a shivering Paremi, turning over the facts of a massacre and wondering if he could catch the owner of the noodle stall on the other side of the Kinship Hall before she shut down for the night.

He'd been up since dawn, on his feet most of the day—running after two robberies, the investigation of a Borsyan street gang, and a small fire in a wine bar—but when he'd returned to the Kinship Hall at the end of his shift, the Paremi boy had shown up, pale and shaking, with bloody hands, and all Richa's thoughts of supper and sleep had fled. He'd sent cadets for fresher vigilants and gone with the Paremi—Quill—along with two more vigilants he'd caught on the way out the door.

He could have sent Quill on. He could have stepped aside and let him continue into the hall, find the vigilants on duty. But Richa hadn't been thinking about any of that. He'd seen the look of horror in the boy's face—a look held in by determination and grief and fear—and just run.

Beside him in the entrance hall, Quill had his arms wrapped around himself as if he were holding in his guts, mouth a pinch, eyes bruised with fatigue and something worse. Poor kid. It was a hard thing, the first time someone you cared for turned into something ugly, something dangerous—like getting the rug yanked out from under your feet just as you were getting your balance, he recalled.

The bodies of Karimo del Nanova and Obigen yula Manco had been removed to the Kinship Hall's mortuary rooms. Dolitha ul-Benturan and Primate Lamberto had been carried off by the hospitalers to the House of Wisdom for surgery and care.

Which had left Quill, desperately trying to get his feet back under him.

"If she doesn't come," Richa said gently, "do you want to go back to the chapter house?"

Quill shook his head tightly. "I can't."

Richa turned back to the doors, determined to keep a light touch. Quill was still shaken—who wouldn't be?—but at least he'd stopped insisting that Karimo couldn't have done this. At least nine witnesses, knife in the good brother's hand, blood all over him, confession out of his own mouth, and *there's no way he would ever have done something like this.*

It was hard, and it was terrible, and Richa wanted so much for Quill to be right, for that young man not to have turned out to be something dangerous. The young ones were the worst, a whole life thrown away by hot blood and bad choices. Richa couldn't help feeling an echo of his own past, when he crossed paths with them— streets and lockpicks and a little extra to get by. Sometimes they had good reasons and bad logic. Sometimes they were in the wrong place at the wrong time. Sometimes the wrong people had made tools out of them. Sometimes he could stop it—he could fulfill the oaths of a vigilant and stop those sparks before they spread and burned those young ones.

But this time: the witnesses, the knife, the blood, the confession.

"I could find a place for you in the Kinship Hall," he offered. "We've got space with the cadets."

"I want to be here," Quill said.

Richa eyed the great doors of the archives with a terrible feeling that what was going to come through them was a freshly woken, panicking young woman who'd have absolutely no idea what to do with her lover all shocked and grief worn.

That's not your problem, he reminded himself. *Especially not at this time of night.* Maybe he could still get Quill back to the Kinship Hall.

Then the doors of the archives parted and a woman burst into the entrance hall.

Oh, Richa thought.

She was not, as he'd feared, young, nor was she panicking. Nor particularly fragile looking. Medium height, he thought, medium build. Natally Semillan, if he had to guess. Late thirties. Black hair, braided. White nightdress, gray robe. Face like Aye-Nam-Wati, knocking down the doors to the Ten Hells, only approachable. Nice eyes.

Saints and devils, he thought, raking a hand through his dark hair. *Be professional.*

"What happened?" she demanded. Quill opened his mouth, fish-like, and shuddered. Richa stepped between them.

"Pardon me, esinora," he said. "Are you Archivist Gintanas?"

"Yes," she said. "What happened?"

"I'm Vigilant Langyun," Richa began.

"I didn't ask your name," the woman snapped. "What happened to Quill? Why are you here?"

"He's dead," Quill said suddenly. "Karimo's dead. He had a knife and…he killed those people. He said he'd tell me, but it wouldn't have been this. It's not who he is. I don't know…I didn't know where to go. I'm not supposed to go to the chapter house. Primate Lamberto said…but I don't know anyone." He looked up at her, imploring, as if she might stop all this. "Yinii said you solve problems. She said everything was fine because you're here. And I don't know where to go or what to do, but I need help, and Richa asked me where I could go and I said here."

So much for secrecy, Richa thought. The fury left Archivist Gintanas's face, and she was still a moment. *Assessing*, Richa thought. She glanced at him then, and he saw that same assessment, like she was trying to decide if she trusted him.

It would be exceedingly helpful if she trusted him. Because he had a lot of questions, and Quill—fragile, shattering, swaying on his feet—was not going to be able to answer them tonight.

Richa could only have been on site for an hour when the Kinship's imperial liaison had arrived at the yula Manco household by carriage. The Ashtabari woman came in the back, keeping her tentacles off the crime scene, and when Richa met her in the library at the rear of the house, Hulvia Manche was not pleased.

"Why are you here, Richa?" she demanded. "You were supposed to be out of the hall two hours ago."

"Good evening to you too. Witness came in just as I was leaving."

"And you didn't pass it along?" Hulvia folded her arms. "Is this an 'I'm always working' thing or a 'favor to a friend' thing?"

"I think you know more of the people here than I do," Richa had said. "Which I assume is why *you're* here. What are we in for?"

To make the matter brief: the murder of a noble consul and the grievous assault of the reza ul-Benturan were serious enough, but that they happened together, at the hand of a Paremi claiming political motives while the senate, the empress, and every fool on the street were arguing about the ethics and economics of Obigen's second wall? Hulvia didn't need to spell out for Richa how quickly and quietly the Imperial Authority needed this to be handled.

"You can hand it off," she had said. Meaning he *should* hand it off—and if he did, he should do it now. But even with the witnesses, the knife, the blood, and the confession…something didn't sit right with Richa about this case. So, regardless of when Richa had been supposed to go home, this case was his to solve and his to contain.

"It's all right, brother," he said to Quill, who was staring blankly up at the opal-decorated doors that led into the archives themselves. "You can…you can talk about it tomorrow." He turned to Amadea. "I need to speak with you, Archivist. In private."

At that, Amadea looked at Richa. Assessment over. She put an arm around the swaying Quill and held him firmly. "Come with me," she said to him. "We'll get you settled for the night. Vigilant…you…you can wait in my office."

Richa followed her into the archives, all silent and sleeping. The Borsyan lamps gave a gloomy light, and the whole place felt more like a tomb for ten nations than a monument to their gifts. She led them both to a room off the second floor on the southern side of the building and ushered Richa inside to a crowded little office. She woke the Borsyan lamps, then crossed the room to a second door at the back, which she shut just as Richa got a glimpse of a bed with sheets thrown back.

"I will be right back," Amadea said. "Make yourself comfortable."

Richa considered the desk covered in stacks of books and papers, the two chairs set before it, and the battered sofa piled with folded quilts at one end. The door behind the desk that led to her living quarters—an arrangement he couldn't say if he envied or recoiled from. This was a person whose work was their highest calling.

Shelves lined two walls from floor to ceiling, mostly filled with trays and boxes, each tacked with papers. Richa peeked in one and saw a polished wooden statue, carved in the shape of a long-necked antlered creature, with forms that said it was to be temporarily loaned to the Duchess del Qualli. Nothing was locked up, he noticed, but there were layers to entering, weren't there? No fear of thieves. If you could get in here, though, you could slip out with something priceless . . .

Directly across from the desk, there were no boxes or trays but, instead, a little gap filled with figurines of glass and wood and stone. Animals, mostly birds. Richa picked up one from the back, a sparrow in yellow-tinted glass, its fine feathers and sharp claws so detailed he couldn't imagine how they'd been shaped. High craft, low materials, a lot of care—there was no dust on the figures on the shelf.

A person whose work was their highest calling, he thought. A touch whimsical, but no-nonsense.

A small mew came from the sofa—a patchy tortoiseshell cat eased out from the blankets. Richa smiled and crouched down to offer her his fingers to smell. The cat gave a delicate sniff, then plunged her whole head into his palm. Richa chuckled and sat down on the sofa beside her, which only made the cat abandon her lair for his lap.

He must have nodded off because the next thing he knew Amadea was standing over him. Assessing again. "Perhaps we should have this conversation at a civilized hour, Vigilant Langyun."

"A civilized hour is a strange concept when we're speaking of a murder," he said dryly. "What did Quill tell you?"

She regarded him silently, expression still, and he adjusted his assessment of her. This was someone used to keeping her emotions in. Maybe someone who'd dealt with the Vigilant Kinship in unhappy circumstances.

"He told me Lord Obigen is dead and possibly the reza ul-Benturan," she said. "That Primate Lamberto is badly hurt. And his friend is possibly the culprit."

"Are you familiar with Lord Obigen and Reza ul-Benturan?" Richa asked.

"Is it true?"

He tilted his head. "Mm. I asked first."

Archivist Gintanas folded her hands together. "I've met both once or twice. Lord Obigen is the Alojan consul. Belongs to the Manco nest of a line that traces back to a valley called Urquna. Currently a topic of general conversation because of his plan to build a saltwater canal beyond the Wall—a second 'wall'—in a bid to expand territory. He thinks we spent too much money in the archives, but he also signed a great many requests that my superior thought were frivolous."

And you don't like him, Richa thought. It glinted between what she said, the hint of an opinion. But the reason? That was harder to guess.

"Reza Dolitha visits the Chapel of the Skeleton Saints," she went on. "She takes a tour of the rest of the archives every fourth time she visits or so. Very pious. Bit insulated. Last time, she complained about our sorting methods. My impression has been that she was the biggest obstacle to Obigen's plans for a wall."

More opinion, less detail. Richa wondered what the reza had done and if it was as bad as Lord Obigen—or maybe Archivist Gintanas was the sort of woman to hold grudges, cling to petty slights. He considered her. It didn't feel right.

But she'd homed in on the Wall, he'd noticed.

"You're very thorough," Richa commented.

"I have a good memory," Amadea said. "Are they dead?"

"Does it matter if you don't really know them?" he asked, smiling at her, teasing at the lie. The wall stayed up. *Oh, you've done this dance before*, he thought.

"It matters," she said sharply, "because Lord Obigen's nest-child is one of my bone specialists. And Dolitha is my ink specialist's reza.

So while it has nothing to do with me, it does impact the work of my specialists. Now: Are they dead?"

That was interesting. He studied her for a moment, that stillness, that fierceness under a coolly proper mask. One thing was for certain, he decided: Amadea Gintanas was very protective of her charges.

"Lord Obigen is dead. They hope Reza Dolitha will recover, but it's... your ink specialist will want to see her. Soon." He scratched the cat under the chin. "We are trying to handle matters as quickly and discreetly as possible given the circumstances. That doesn't entirely account for witnesses in a state of shock, so I'd appreciate you not spreading any rumors."

"I don't spread rumors," she said.

"Good. I thought as much. Do you want to sit down?" he asked, nodding toward the other chair. "I have a few more questions."

"Are you offering me a seat in my own office?" Amadea said tartly. "How kind."

"I'm suggesting you sit before your legs give out," he answered. "Because I need to ask these things, no matter how tired we both are. I trust I'm in the presence of someone quick enough to grasp the ramifications of these deaths. I need to resolve this, and that means exploring all possible connections."

This was the only reason Richa hoped Quill's friend was a simple madman. Each protectorate, each population that descended from the nations that joined Semilla behind the Salt Wall, had their duchies, their elected members of the senate. They also had the noble consuls, those raised up to represent the protectorate as it stood within Semilla directly to the empress. *For we are each and we are one*, as Emperor Eschellado had proclaimed. A nice thought, even if it wasn't always as easy as it should be. Lord Obigen represented the Alojans—had for the last nine years—and was very influential within Empress Beneditta's court. Reza Dolitha ul-Benturan was among the most vocal of the Orozhandi's leaders, who divided their ducal authority. Primate Lamberto was the Ragaleate primate and held a distinct amount of sway over the order.

In other words: three people with a lot of power whose deaths or damage bore a lot of significance.

Amadea seemed to grasp his meaning. She took the seat opposite her desk, turning it toward the couch. "Ask."

"Thank you," he said, aiming for camaraderie and good humor. The wall stayed up. "How do you know Brother Sesquillio?"

"I don't really," she said. "He's not a suspect, is he? Why does it matter?"

He clucked his tongue. "Nope, my turn. Why did he ask to come here and not the chapter house?"

Amadea folded her hands again and shrugged. "I assume what he said in the entry hall. Quill came here yesterday with a request for a client. The primate felt a representative of the Paremi should remain and Quill was keen. While he was here, one of my specialists had some trouble with her affinity, so I left him with a different archivist. I suppose she talked me up."

"Yinii," Richa recalled from what Quill had said in the entry hall. "Orozhandi, right? Is she the one related to Reza Dolitha?"

Amadea hesitated, a flicker of worry. "Yes, Yinii. I don't know what made him think of it. Maybe you ought to ask the Paremi at the chapter house why he can't go there."

"I will. Why do you think he can't go to the chapter house?"

She shook her head. "As I said, I don't really know him."

"Did you meet Karimo del Nanova? He would have come with Primate Lamberto, I assume."

"No," she said. "If he did come, he didn't speak to anyone beyond the reception desk."

"Which doesn't include you?"

She sat back. "Am I a suspect?"

"Right now, you're a mildly hostile person of interest." She bristled at that, and he pressed on. "You have a good memory. Do you know anything about archaeonationalist sects? Separatists? Coups and things?"

She hesitated again, but this time it wasn't concern. It was all wall, all mask. Richa leaned forward, waiting.

"The Imperial Archives has many records of many events," she said quickly, holding his gaze, "including court records. Those are housed in the East Wing, though, and aren't my responsibility."

He shrugged one-shouldered, as if this were the most minor of concerns. As if he didn't notice the distance she'd set between her and those records. "But maybe you've seen some things. Hypothetically. Anyone who says things like 'Those who sow deception must reap only death'?"

That surprised her, shook her from her stillness. "Sorry, what?" He repeated the phrase, watching her closely, and he could see her searching her memories, hunting for the missing piece. "You're sure about separatists?" she asked, frowning to herself. "Any particular sort?"

"I'm wondering," Richa said slowly, "about Alojan separatists. Maybe Orozhandi. Someone who might turn against the reza or Lord Obigen."

Amadea shook her head. "Sowing and reaping sounds like a kingdom based around grain farming—Khirazj or Bemina or maybe the Ronqu's original lands. Aloja was mountainous—they grew tubers, potatoes and things. Orozhandi sayings are mostly around herding or desert dangers. Also, it's not the sort of thing I imagine either sort of separatist would say. An Alojan separatist would be more likely to recite the Jade Sapa's wisdom over Obigen's corpse. And an Orozhandi one would get straight to the point and say 'anathema.'" She paused. "Who said it?"

Richa smiled thinly. "I didn't say anyone said anything."

Archivist Gintanas returned a similarly tight smile. "If you're concerned about people spreading rumors, I think starting with yourself might be sensible. If you're finished?" She clicked to the cat, rubbing her fingers together. The cat regarded her blandly and licked a paw. "Imp," she said firmly, "the vigilant is leaving. Off."

"Imp?" A slow smile curved his mouth. "She's a very cuddly imp."

"It's short for Palimpsest."

"That's . . . a mouthful. What is that?"

Archivist Gintanas pursed her mouth. "It's parchment, or the like, that's been scraped or washed and reused. Because she's patchy."

"That fits a lot better." Richa scratched Imp's orange-patterned jaw before setting her on the floor, standing, and following the archivist back out through the archives. Fresh guards had positioned themselves at the entrance, but it was otherwise deserted in the deep of night. Amadea walked with him outside, past the guards, bundling her robe around her as they stood on the archives' steps. The night air had mostly lost the day's late-summer heat, and a faint clamminess lingered on the air, as if it might start to drizzle.

"Quill will need to come in for an official sealed statement," Richa said. "Tomorrow afternoon. If he's going to stay here, neither of you should leave the city. I might also need to question those two specialists, so tell them the same."

That caught her off guard again, her charges endangered. "They have nothing to do with this. I can assure you of that."

It was as charming as it was frustrating: he saw a kindred spirit in her at the same time he suspected Amadea Gintanas would be as much an obstacle as a source of information in this. "'The map is laid furled before us,'" he said, maybe a little cheeky, "'and who knows where the path may lead.' I follow what I need to follow."

"Don't quote the Vigilant Mother to me, thank you," Archivist Gintanas said. "I'm not your cadet."

"Good guess, but that is from a Datongu story called 'The Thief Outwits the Demon,'" he said. "Little inappropriate. But I think the Vigilant Mother would have accepted its value in this case." He flashed a grin at her. "You should read it."

She considered him a moment. *Assessing*, he thought. "Good night, Vigilant," she said. He made a little bow before heading down the stairs and into the square.

Richa pulled the dark blue half cape of his uniform closed, fastening the silver buttons against the chilly air. The noodle stall would be closed by now, and he was starving. He paused, trying to think of where he could get a bite to eat and thinking of the murder instead.

One dead, two wounded, all of them political targets. One murderer, deceased, whose motive was a mystery—whose motive his closest friend insisted couldn't exist, Karimo wouldn't have done this. A mysterious phrase with no source.

A sound yanked his attention to one of the side alleys, dim in the glow of a Borsyan lamp whose magic had been cut too fine. He glimpsed a man in a plum-colored cape turning the corner, disappearing from view, and relaxed. Just some late-night stroller. He glanced back at the enormous edifice of the Imperial Archives, its windows dark, the statues framing its colonnade lost in shadow. Amadea Gintanas, still standing in the door.

One dead, he thought, starting toward the trade district, where he might find a coffeehouse open, *two wounded*. One murderer, all with some tenuous connection to the Imperial Archives. *To Amadea Gintanas*, he corrected.

Maybe a coincidence, he thought. Maybe not. But he found he had a great many questions for the witnesses that he wouldn't have known to ask before.

＊＊＊

Amadea watched the vigilant head out into the square, watched his attention dart to the alleys and back to the archives. The nightmares his arrival had yanked her from—what had he been chasing after? This didn't touch the archives—it *couldn't*.

Focus, she told herself, as her thoughts began to race. She waited until the vigilant had passed out of sight, then strode back through the doors and turned up the entry-hall stairs, making her way back to the dormitories as quickly as she could. She climbed an extra floor past the one she'd left Quill on, searching her keys with fumbling hands. Everything needed to stay quiet—but she would be damned if she kept this back from the people she cared for.

Especially the one she knew was awake. She came to the door at the top of the hall and knocked.

"Tunuk?" she called. "Are you up?"

"You know I am," came Tunuk's muffled voice. "And I know you're going to come in anyway. I don't know why you pretend it matters if I know."

Amadea let herself in. Tunuk scowled up at her from the floor, where he'd made a nest of blankets around his folded legs. A basket of cold-lamps glowed in the middle of the table, beside a half-eaten bowl of porridge and the skull of Biorni, the horned rabbit.

"Why is Biorni in your rooms?" Amadea asked.

"You have a pet," Tunuk said. "Why can't I? What are you doing in here? It's early."

And suddenly, she didn't know how to tell him. "Something happened," she said softly.

Tunuk unfolded, streaking up to his full height like a shadow beneath a shifting lamp. He snatched the rabbit skull as he stood, tucking it against his narrow chest. "What?" he said, dripping contempt—as if he couldn't fathom being worried, and she knew too well that meant he was terrified. "Did Radir quit? Am I in trouble for making him cry?"

Amadea exhaled. "A vigilant just left. Your nest-father—"

"They sent a *vigilant*!" Tunuk exploded. "This is *madness*! I'm *fine*—"

"Tunuk," Amadea said. She set a hand on his arm. "Obigen is dead."

Tunuk went still as stone. He said nothing for a long moment, only shifted the rabbit skull so that he held it in both hands, as if he and Biorni were going to have a heart-to-heart. "I see," he said finally. "What happened?"

"The vigilants are looking into it," she said carefully. "But he was killed."

Tunuk looked up at her, glowing eyes narrow. "By *who*?"

"The vigilants are looking into it," she said again. "You're safe. The rest of the nest is safe—"

"If you know that, then you know who."

"Tunuk," she said gently, "it won't change it."

Tunuk considered Biorni's lacy fenestrations. "It might."

Amadea set a hand against his arm. "The man who did it is Quill's friend Karimo. They're trying to find out why, but it's difficult. He's dead."

"Quill? The grinning Paremi?"

"Be kind. He lost someone too." She sighed. "Someone he thought he knew very well."

"What do you take me for?" Tunuk demanded. "Some vengeful maniac? I'm not going to hunt *Quill* down."

"I take you for a grieving nest-child," Amadea said, "and one who already hasn't had the best few months of his life."

"I'm also not going to spiral again," Tunuk said, but what little acid he could manage only made him sound fragile. "He made me miserable, didn't he?"

Amadea squeezed his arm. "He was a complicated man," Amadea said. "You can grieve the good parts you've lost and be relieved at the bad being gone." Tunuk just nodded, eyes on the rabbit skull. "We need to be circumspect about this," Amadea went on. "They want to be sure it's all done right. That...people don't take this as a sign."

"So it was *political*," Tunuk said softly. "Of course. What isn't with him?" But then he swallowed, as if it pained him. "Wasn't. Go away now. Biorni and I need to have a drink."

"I will be up to check on you in a few hours," Amadea warned, and left him to the solitude he so clearly needed.

⊷ ⊱⊰ ⊶

Yinii took her breakfast with Stavio and Bijan most mornings, usually with a few others, in the married archivists' larger apartment. She would wake early, sit in the dark with her day-eyes closed, watch with her dark-eye for the traces of heat and movement through the wall that said her neighbors were awake and brewing coffee on the fire, and then wait for someone else to go in first. The morning they found out about the murder and Quill, that had been Zoifia and Radir, but not Tunuk.

"He's mad at me," Radir said gloomily.

"No, no, bedo," Stavio said, leveling a dark gaze over his cup of coffee. "He hates you." He rested with his chest against a leaning chair, a bit of furniture the Ashtabari found more comfortable—his tentacles were still snapping irritably behind him.

"He doesn't hate you," Yinii insisted, as Bijan set a plate in front of her of baigar, little fermented yam pancakes hot with chili and sour with peanut sauce. "He's embarrassed. He spiraled out of cycle and everyone knows it. And now you have to watch after him. Tunuk's proud like that."

"Doesn't mean he has to be a shit," Zoifia said, snatching two of the baigar for her own plate.

"At least Tunuk didn't try and break into the Bone Vault," Stavio retorted.

Zoifia fumed. "Shut up! You were there—"

"Both of you, shut up," Bijan put in calmly. The dark-skinned corundum specialist rubbed his temple, pushed stray braids back over his ears. "You should know better than anybody in this room, right now, that alignment earns people a little extra care."

Both bronze specialists stared daggers at Bijan. Yinii couldn't help noticing both Zoifia's brown eyes and Stavio's hazel were worryingly flecked with bronze that morning. Bijan folded his arms and stared right back. "Eat your breakfast, love. I put in extra onion for you."

Stavio grunted. "If you loved me, you'd make fry bread."

"I hope you're right," Radir said. "About Tunuk, I mean. Otherwise, I'm getting thrown out." He shook his head. "That Kirazzi request—he got a little agitated about looking for the bone hand. Is that something to worry about?"

"He's just excited," Zoifia said dismissively. "It's a request and it's not a stupid request."

"It's *Kirazzis*," Stavio said darkly as he tore his pancakes into pieces. "Nothing good ever came of them. Be worried."

"They're just people," Yinii said.

"People who want the Flail of Khirazj," Stavio said.

"Why is that such a big deal?" Zoifia said. "It's a stick with some beads on it."

"'A stick with some beads on it'?" Stavio repeated. "It's the rallying symbol of the Usurper! The insignia of dissolutionists! Worse: the Kirazzis want it back—that's an *omen*."

"Don't be dramatic," Bijan said.

"Redolfo Kirazzi puts a ten-year-old girl-child in front of a glass army of sorcerer-born soldiers, calls her 'the Grave-Spurned Princess,' and tries to claim the throne for her for five years, and *I'm* dramatic?"

"Right now? Yes, you are being dramatic, love." He gestured to the plate before Stavio, the pancakes torn into little pieces and lined up in a matrix. "That's not eating."

Yinii glanced over at Zoifia's plate, a moment before the other woman guiltily swept pieces of her own breakfast out of a similar pattern and into a pile. She met Yinii's eyes briefly before looking away.

"Do you think she was really Lireana?" Yinii asked Stavio. "Did you ever see her?"

Stavio made a face. "How old you think I am?"

"She wasn't Lireana," Bijan said firmly. "Lireana was killed by the Fratricide and...I'm sure the Grave-Spurned Princess was taken care of."

"Probably strangled in a quiet place," Stavio said. "Get her out of the way. No more questions about whose throne it really is. Or locked up in an oubliette. Maybe if she *was* Lireana, they did that too. Who knows?"

"Dramatic," Bijan said again. "And, really, irrelevant."

"You're *not* giving them the flail, are you?"

"You think I like it? My uncles died in the Usurper's coup. One on each side. But they have the forms, they have rights to the thing." He sat down, his own cup of coffee in hand. "We get a little delay— Amadea pointed out the Paremi forgot the Release of Culturally Significant Artifact for the flail. But I doubt anyone is going to swoop in and stop Duchess Kirazzi. Not with the Paremi fanning her ink and checking her seals, anyway."

Yinii thought of Quill, thought of the way he'd smiled at her, that dimple. Thought of how incredibly stupid she must have sounded, vomiting details about the ceiling paintings.

Zoifia leaned back in her chair, eyeing Bijan speculatively. "What's the story with the Paremi? Do they take vows and things like the Golden Oblates?"

"I mean, you seen his clothes," Stavio started. "He's not taking a lot of coin in."

"No, dummy, I mean are they celibate?"

"Oh!" Yinii said without meaning to.

Bijan eyed her askance, fighting a smile, and her cheeks burned. "A popular question?"

"No!" Yinii said. Then: "Are they?"

"Saints and devils, blessed Noniva!" Stavio said, inching forward on his chair. "Bijan, I told you, I *told* you." He grinned at Yinii, fond and giddy. "It was *all* over your face yesterday."

"They're not celibate," Radir chimed in. "Courted a Paremi

girl a few years back. Definitely not celibate, but *real* wedded to her work."

Yinii blushed. "That's not...It's not..."

"Don't pretend," Stavio said. "You aren't good at it."

"He's right," Bijan said, his smile spreading. "Although that boy, I don't think he can tell."

Zoifia glared at her. "*I* saw him first! You can't just swoop in and say he's yours. I thought we were friends."

"We *are* friends," Yinii protested—and Zoifia was so lovely, and she had been so clumsy. "I didn't say he was anything. If you like him..."

"Zoifia," Bijan interrupted gently, "are you saying you're attracted to Quill?"

"*Maybe.*" Zoifia folded her arms, rolling her shoulders as if she couldn't find a way to make her scapulae sit inside her. "I mean, the other one was better looking, but he doesn't have the requests, now, does he?" She licked her lips. "I think Stavio's right."

"That's new," Bijan said dryly. "What about?"

"The *omen*," she said, sounding far away. "I'll bet they're not empty. I bet they have a void."

"Zoifia?" Yinii said. "Are you all right?"

Stavio snorted. "You are *guessing.*"

"They're *Bikoro dynasty* castings," Zoifia snapped. "Not shitting old swords. I know, you don't. I'm right."

"You're assuming they're late period. They were early, you won't have space for a fart in there!"

"*Bronzes*," Bijan said with sudden understanding.

"*All* Bikoro dynasty castings were done hollow method," Zoifia said. "Which means a void. And if they're late in the period, they're likely full-sized—"

"If, if, if," Stavio said. "Early means tiny and who cares?"

"Why else would the duchess suddenly remember she owns these two statues? We haven't even catalogued them. There's a void, and I'll bet it's not about the statues; it's about what's inside."

"Will you tell *her* she's being dramatic?" Stavio demanded.

"What do you think is in there?" Yinii asked.

Zoifia shrugged, loose and antsy. "Weapons? Messages? Money?"

"Redolfo Kirazzi, shrunk very small," Stavio said. "It doesn't matter. You can't get them."

"It *will* matter," Zoifia said. "I'm right. I'll bet you I'm right—one halvmeta, I'm right. No, five!"

"One halvmeta and *you* have to make breakfast for a week," Stavio said. "Fry bread."

Zoifia's hand shot out, a pale streak to grasp Stavio's own. She grinned, wild, triumphant, and turned to Yinii. "You ought to check your book, too, when you find it. I'll bet it's a pattern—something's in it, too. Kirazzis are trouble."

A knock came at the door. "Come in," Stavio called.

Amadea pushed open the door, and everyone sat a little straighter. "Good morning," she said, and Yinii could hear how tired she was.

"Everything all right?" Bijan asked.

"We have a guest," Amadea said to the room. "And I'm going to need some help from those of you who can spare it. Brother Quill…he witnessed a death last night." She paused. "The vigilants are attending to it, but Quill's going to be staying here for a few days in the meantime."

"Why?" Radir asked. "Don't the Paremi have a place for him?"

"Because he asked to stay here," Amadea said firmly. "The requests are still in effect—"

"Accelerated?" Zoifia asked.

"*No.* You are still restricted. And…" Amadea sighed a heavy breath and said in tones that made panic bloom in Yinii's chest, "Yinii, you need to come with me."

⊷ ≼✦≽ ⊶

Richa Langyun considered the stack of official statements from the witnesses to the murder of Lord Obigen and the grievous assaults on Reza Dolitha Sixteen-Tamarisk ul-Benturan and Primate Lamberto Lajonta, waiting for the final seal of the Paremi that would mark them finished, official, accepted. Closed.

The Paremi who'd taken down the statements, a slim dark-skinned girl with close-shorn hair and a Beminat-style feather collar over her robes, waited, tapping her seal against the table to a distracted rhythm.

"Nice day," she commented, looking out the window behind him, her impatience barely hidden.

Richa blew out a breath. He had eleven witnesses, the murder weapon, a declared motive, and a killer drenched in blood now lying dead on a slab in the basement. This should be simple. Seal the reports and then he could leave early, get a coffee, get some more sleep. The whole case might be ready for the court advocates of Her Imperial Majesty by the end of the week at the very latest.

And yet...

He slid the stack apart, separating the statements by witness. These four were the most prominent of the guests, the ones unrelated to the Alojan noble consul, who hadn't been injured in the attack. If you looked at any one interview, read down the questions he'd asked one by one, checked against the notes he'd taken himself, then everything lined up.

But if you read across, compared each answer against the next, as if all four had sat here across from him at the same time, everything got a lot more complicated. He drummed his stylus against the rightmost stack of papers, against the name written in the Paremi's neat hand: *Nanqii Four-Oryx ul-Hanizan, attending as representation of the reza ul-Hanizan. A merchant.*

Orozhandi drug peddler, he'd written in his own notes. He could picture the silver-haired Orozhandi man in gauzy turquoise and cream as he'd dropped into the chair, horn charms jingling, and gave Richa a lazy smile. "Nice to see you again, Vigilant Langyun." As if to remind Richa how untouchable he was. *Smug bastard, too familiar.*

That was another thing that was too complicated for Richa's liking: Nanqii wasn't the only witness who had trouble with the law applying to him—so to speak. Richa looked down the row of statements. One would be unremarkable. Two would be odd, given the setting and the crime. Four—*five*, he corrected himself—that felt ominous.

Zaverio, Lord Maschano, the next statement declared. A sallow, stocky man in a fur-trimmed violet cloak, holding tight to his cane and his unpleasant expression, demanding to know why they were wasting the empire's funds this way. *Old, pre-Sealing family*, Richa had written. *Impatience and bigotry given skin and entirely too much money.* A court case, here and there, money passed to hush up an embarrassment, but Zaverio Maschano was the sort of man weighing down the empire with all his might to benefit only himself.

Gaspera del Oyofon, Captain, the Blessed Order of the Saints of Salt and Iron (retired). A tall, trim woman in white hose and a blue tunic, with warm skin to match her Beminat name, and fine, spiky cropped hair and tilted eyes from some other protectorates. *Brisk, proud,* Richa had written. *Just enough valor to cover for her villainy.* As "the Fox of the Wall," she'd been a celebrated commander on the Salt Wall. As "the Penitent Turncoat," Gaspera had been one of the highest-placed traitors to side with Redolfo Kirazzi, but the one whose reversion finally broke his coup.

Deilio Maschano, Scrivener of Parem and Heir of House Maschano. A slight, imperious young man who managed to ignore the other Paremi with an intensity that made it clear he was paying attention to only her, as he arranged his scarlet robes around himself. *Saints and devils,* Richa thought but had not written. *You want to talk about wasting funds, Lord Maschano?* The boy was the source of more than a few of those embarrassed payments, all petty and privileged. Someone who had never needed to think about consequences.

Beneath Deilio's name, the Paremi had added neatly, *accompanied by his mother, Lady Rosangerda Maschano (not a witness).*

"It's not necessary for you to be here, esinora. Only your son," Richa had said to the slender, light-skinned woman whose gray gaze speared him intently over a placid smile.

Rosangerda Maschano had raised a pale eyebrow. "And our advocate says it isn't against any laws. This is only an accounting, isn't it?" She laid a protective hand on her son's shoulder. "We have nothing to hide, and quite a full schedule, if you don't mind." *Not a witness,* Richa had written, *and not going to be dissuaded.* Lady Maschano was clearly accustomed to having her way, regardless of the rules.

Sitting at his desk before the statements and the waiting Paremi, Richa rolled the stylus between his fingers. Maybe none of this should bother him, he thought, considering his notes. Terrible people had terrible friends. Wicked ran in a pack, didn't it?

Except: their answers.

Run down the transcribed interviews, and everything was fine. They had been invited to the party the day before—

> **Lord Maschano:** *I assume that Obigen wanted funding for his wall-that's-not-a-wall. I can't imagine why else he'd have had two words to say to me. That or the primate wanted more funds. I pay him enough already.*

None of them had been invited by Lord Obigen. Instead, it had been the primate who had arranged these guests. It was the primate they all knew—

> **Captain del Oyofon:** *I wouldn't say we're friends, Lamberto and I. One attends many gatherings. One looks for friendly faces. One ignores less interesting faces, but sometimes they seek one out regardless. Maybe he'd say we were acquainted, but I wouldn't. You get the idea.*
> **Vigilant Langyun:** *But he's the one who conveyed the invitation?*
> **Captain del Oyofon:** *(A pause) Yes. He knew I had a parcel of land to sell. I assume you can connect the two?*

None of them were particularly acquainted with Karimo del Nonova—

> **Deilio Maschano:** *I met him once or twice. As I said, the primate took a special interest in me. Brother Karimo had been assisting him for some time.*
> **Vigilant Langyun:** *Did he ever indicate any sort of allegiances outside the Paremi? Did you discuss politics?*
> **Deilio Maschano:** *No, I don't do that.*
> **Lady Maschano:** *I hear the boy was an orphan. It's a tragedy but there's no telling what sort of poison people were filling him up with, if he never had a proper parent guiding him.*
> **Vigilant Langyun:** *Again, Lady Maschano, you're not being questioned.*

Nothing was amiss when they arrived—

Nanqii ul-Hanizan: *It was dull. I was surprised to see the reza ul-Benturan there, and that he'd invited that boor Zaverio. I made for the wine. (A pause) That boy, that Karimo, he seemed agitated, but I suppose that's to be expected.*

But then the interviews changed. Richa took the statements and layered them so it was the last question that showed, one atop the next: *Tell me what happened after Brother Karimo pulled the knife.*

At which point the answers were not simply in agreement: They fell into lockstep. The same beats, the same phrases, the same reactions. Gone were the asides and petty bits of gossip. You could splice the answers together as if they were a single witness's point of view.

Deilio Maschano: *I remember looking at the painting over the fireplace. Drinking wine. A moderate amount. Then I heard shouting. An argument. I heard Lord Obigen call out*

Gaspera del Oyofon: *and when I looked over, I saw that boy, that Karimo, stabbing him. It had to be three or four times before I realized what was going on, because I was standing so far away, beside the wall, and then he turned and attacked the reza*

Zaverio Maschano: *stabbed her through the eye before she could make a sound, right in front of God and the empress, as if we were standing in a Tornada alleyway, tramps and doxies. He stabbed the primate when he tried to intervene. Lady Sigrittrice tried to stop him. Then*

Nanqii ul-Hanizan: *that Minseon fellow came barging in and Karimo turned and looked at us all, and said, 'Those who sow deception must reap only death.' And then he cut his own throat.*

The impatient Paremi set her stamp on the desk and sighed. "Is something wrong?"

Richa looked up from the statements. "Couple things. You going to get something to eat?"

"I need to seal them for the court advocates first," she said. "Which it's sounding like you won't be letting me do?"

Richa shook his head. "Something's off. They all have exactly the same memory of the murders." *I heard Lord Obigen call out . . . It had to be three or four times before I realized what was going on . . . right in front of God and the empress . . . Lady Sigrittrice tried to stop him . . .*

"Isn't that a good thing?" the Paremi asked.

"Not like this. It's as if they've all been trained to give the same report."

"They seemed pretty genuine to me," the Paremi said skeptically.

They had, and that's what made it odder still. Richa felt confident, as long as he'd spent mired in a world of criminality, that he could spot the signs of a conspiracy. The half-breath disconnect between a statement and the emotions it stirred. Eyes that darted to check every listener's, or held too tightly to his own gaze, as if daring him to doubt. A particular fidgetiness. A dance through the questions of the interview, trying to avoid the critical or else drive straight for it. Subtle things, important things, that lit up unintended signal fires: *something is hiding here.*

And they'd displayed none of them, not about the murders or the attacks. Only a strange sameness to their words, the same mistakes in their telling. *I heard Lord Obigen call out . . . It had to be three or four times before I realized what was going on . . . right in front of God and the empress . . . Lady Sigrittrice tried to stop him . . .*

"You have to come back this afternoon, don't you?" Richa asked the Paremi. "For the empress and Lady Sigrittrice?"

That was one discontinuity he could resolve easily: neither Beneditta, the Masked Empress of Semilla, nor Sigrittrice Ulanitti, her great-aunt and seneschal, had been at the yula Manco manor when the vigilants arrived—

Zaverio Maschano: *Clearly she didn't want to be associated with this savagery. I can hardly see how that's the empress's fault.*

No one recalled either leaving specifically—

Gaspera del Oyofon: *They must have slipped out the back. What a thing to see or to be found seeing. I can hardly stand it, and I've seen more than enough blood.*

They had been invited, as well as the empress's husband, Consort-Prince Ibramo Kirazzi, who appeared in no one's recollections—

Nanqii ul-Hanizan: *It was very chaotic, and I might have had something that exacerbated that feeling along with the wine.*

But everyone remembered the empress and Sigrittrice at the time of the murders, even though they were nowhere to be found—

Lady Maschano: *Surely you intend to ask the empress herself? Why are you asking my son?*

But in the now empty interview room, the Paremi only gave him a puzzled expression. "I haven't heard anything from the imperial liaison."

Richa frowned. "Hulvia didn't get us in with the empress?"

She shrugged. "I'm to come back for the other Paremi. That's all I know."

Quill. His outside witness.

Or his thread to another question: *How do the Imperial Archives figure into this?* They shouldn't—there was no reason. And yet Lord Obigen's nest-child was a specialist there, and the reza's great-niece. Amadea Gintanas standing between him and that part of the puzzle.

Richa had gone through what files he could find that morning, and discovered nothing of interest about Archivist Gintanas. But he knew how to spot the signs of a conspiracy, and he knew when a person had run afoul of the vigilants. She was hiding something—the only question was, did it matter?

"I'm going to need to expand these before you seal them," he told the Paremi, tapping the statements back into a stack. "Go feed yourself. Back in about an hour?"

She sighed and slipped the seal back into its little pouch. "Anywhere good near here?"

"Noodle house on the corner," Richa suggested. "Or the coffeehouse down the way, Nella's. They have some pastries most afternoons." He paused. "If I got the empress in, could you stay?"

The Paremi gave him another skeptical look. "If you can talk your way past the imperial liaison, I will stay, because I'd like to see a miracle."

Richa held the door open for her. "I would like one of those too."

He might need a couple, as many people as it seemed were lying to him just then.

II

FOUR WOULD-BE
EMPERORS

Year Eight of the Reign of Emperor Clement
Palace Sestina

Redolfo sips his fig brandy and hisses a breath over his tongue. "That's a terrible place to begin. You'll have to be more specific, for one. Which girl?"

"Lireana, of course," Turon says. "Your 'Grave-Spurned Princess.' What other girl could I mean?"

"Well, she's Clement's problem now, isn't she? Do you know what he plans to do with her? Or is that why you're asking?"

Turon doesn't say. He doesn't say that he worries about the young woman, confined to the Kirazzis' ancestral home, always quiet, lost in thought. She does not have her claimed grandmother's commanding presence, her purported father's boisterous laugh. He wonders sometimes if there is something calculating in her, something imperial, that disguises itself as quietness, the way a mantis poses as a leaf. There's no denying she's a danger. There's no denying she's innocent.

"Is she Lireana?" he asks.

"If you care about her," Redolfo says, "then you should let it stay a mystery. So long as she might be Clement's niece, one assumes our honorable emperor won't cut her throat." He pauses. "Or maybe I have that backward—so long as she's some brat I manipulated, she's no threat to his throne. Either way, better to keep the question unanswered."

"She's a *child!*"

Redolfo takes another sip of brandy. "Yes? As I said, that's a terrible place to start. A piece, a detail—she's not the story."

"That you can say that is a greater indictment than anything the noble consuls have against you," Turon returns.

Redolfo smiles. "That I can say that is proof it's *my* fucking story, brother. So you will sit and you will listen, and you will hear it as I tell it, not as you wish it to be. If I tell you the girl doesn't matter, you apologize and ask me what *does* matter."

Turon's hands make fists he's too settled and proper to use, but only just. Only right now. "You don't give orders anymore, Redolfo."

"Then leave," Redolfo says simply, and drinks a little more.

And that's it. It's now or it's never. The noose is waiting, and so Redolfo Kirazzi has no reason to ever stop being exactly himself. Turon holds his gaze, loath to admit it. But his brother is right—this story is his.

"What does matter?" Turon asks.

Redolfo's smile sharpens. "Many things. Consider: Appolino Ulanitti."

Turon frowns. "The Fratricide?"

"What was the agreement our great-grandparents made? We will bend to Semilla's sovereignty because the Ulanittis rule in perfect order. They will hide their faces and reign over us because they were here first. And what happens less than a century on? Well, like all empires, they are imperfect. One brother decides he's due the throne and wipes out the emperor, his consort, their children. The youngest says this cannot stand, and we have a war."

"I know the story," Turon says. "We all lived through it."

"Then you'll agree, the Ulanittis failed in their promises. A war over the throne is the opposite of perfect order. Two emperors, two armies—how is this just?"

"You would be more convincing if you hadn't done the same thing," Turon notes. "It's as you said, like all empires they are imperfect."

"Khirazj did not bow to imperfection," Redolfo says.

"No," Turon says testily. "It bowed to salvation and shelter. Joining the empire saved us all."

"They gather from us everything that is great and claim it for their own. Why should we settle for whatever governance Semilla offers up?"

These aren't unfamiliar words. Every nation that found refuge in Semilla, behind the squeeze of the isthmus where the Salt Wall would swiftly be pulled into being by the sacrifice of sorcerers, born to salt and iron—every nation harbors an undercurrent of separatism, of futures where Semilla could be carved into minor kingdoms of Minseon, Datongu, Alojan, Orozhandi, Borsyan, Kuali, Beminat, Ashtabari, and Khirazji rule. *After all*, they murmur, *we were greater than Semilla once, and what were they? Only lucky to be on the edge of the world.*

But this, Turon thinks, betrays something of their thoughts. Perhaps the empire still calls itself Semilla, perhaps they have had to shed some of what they were to fit inside—but that is true of every protectorate, every people, including the Semillans. The ones who mutter about those great empires forget what strife is. They forget tribulation. They forget every civilization beyond the Wall that did not make it here.

They forget that Semilla, imperfectly gracious, gathered their forebears to its breast and told them they were home, they were themselves, and they were also Semillan—and what that meant would change here and now and as many times as it needed to. And if the path is thorny and broken, then at least it is a path, which Turon believes with all his heart is getting smoother.

Redolfo, he thinks, doesn't notice the path, except where it leads him to glory. "You don't want a New Khirazj," Turon says plainly. "You want to be a god-king, that's all."

Redolfo shrugs. "The emperor earned nothing about his throne. Are you going to argue Clement deserves to rule?"

Turon hesitates—in the agreements that formed the empire as it stands, the Accords of the Protectorates, Semilla had insisted that an emperor, an empress, always an Ulanitti, would be the final arbiter of the empire's laws. The Imperial Majesty declared their heir, and so far as Turon knew, the throne had passed easily and calmly through the long roll of years. Until the empress Clotilda been succeeded by her eldest son, Iespero.

Now, Clement, ensconced in Arlabecca, is not as foolish as his eldest brother. For one, he knows the threat in Redolfo Kirazzi and has him locked away, not waving aside the threat of assassination as silly and unpleasant the way Iespero ignored rumors of his brother's agitation. Clement does not prize art the same way; he does not revel in *culture*. He dotes upon his young family, much as Iespero had, but always with an eye, Turon thinks, to the future, and the throne that will now fall to his nervous eldest, Beneditta.

Clement, decked in velvets and the golden mask of imperial privilege, is not as brutal as his second-eldest brother, Appolino. He is cautious in his executions, and the very notion of the solemn emperor taking a knife to a babe in arms is so outlandish Turon cannot imagine it. Appolino held the throne so briefly, when one considers the long roll of Ulanittis guiding Semilla, that his recklessness, his ill planning, his cruelty, has an aberrance that makes Turon want to sweep it away—even as he knows Redolfo is not wrong; this is the peril of a monarch. Even as he knows Redolfo holds the same perils in himself.

Clement, ever somber, rules in obligation and promise, as far from Redolfo's ambition as ever a man was, and yet if Turon were to assess these four would-be rulers, decide on their values as potential emperors—Iespero, Appolino, Redolfo, Clement—he would choose Clement, albeit by elimination, not virtue, long before he ever set Redolfo's willingness to claim the throne as a deciding point in emperorship.

"That's not how they did it in Khirazj either," Turon points out. "Without the blood of Pademaki, you couldn't rule. It's not different to say only an Ulanitti can rule Semilla."

"First," Redolfo says, "I think the blood of a god trumps the blood of some old chieftain lost in the annals of time. Second, I never claimed Khirazj did it right. Show me where I said Khirazj did it right."

Turon swirls the glass of brandy and draws a steadying breath. This is how arguing with Redolfo goes—a merry chase down whatever path he chooses. But Turon was sent with orders, with a purpose beyond steeping in these last few hours of his brother's time. "You're stalling," he says.

"I'm building the story," Redolfo chides. "Laying groundwork. Without these facts, you won't understand. You might think what I've done is abhorrent."

"I already know what you've done is abhorrent."

Redolfo rolls his eyes. "Are we back to the girl?"

"Beyond that," Turon says, because he has orders and Redolfo does not have time. "We're talking about the changeling blood. We're talking about how many people you poisoned. How did you get it?"

And it has taken thirty-three years, but at last Turon Kirazzi has surprised his brother. Redolfo laughs once. "Well now," he says. "That *does* matter."

Turon doesn't laugh. "They think you made a deal with the changelings."

"Oh, they wouldn't have made any kind of deal with me," Redolfo says. "Because I had the Shrike."

CHAPTER FOUR

Quill wasn't sure if he'd slept, only that at some point, he didn't want to be lying down anymore. He sat up, his back against one wall, staring at the blank space opposite him.

Karimo was dead. Karimo was a killer. Quill shut his eyes tight and tried to wake up from this nightmare. Tried to will the little spare room in the archives to be the narrow bedroom of the Manco house, where Karimo would be already awake and making notes.

Instead, what flashed behind his eyes was Karimo, the moment before he turned, the moment before he cried out, the moment before he put the knife to his throat—

Quill's whole body flinched, like a spasm, and he pulled his knees in tight to his chest. Dug his hands into his hair. The image wouldn't leave. The *sounds*.

He thought about getting up. He thought about finding something to eat. Some other person to talk to. There were archivists he'd met next door, Amadea had said. Yinii was...somewhere. He knew some other people. Zoifia. Tunuk—

Lord Obigen yula Manco lying on the ground, dead, dead, dead.

He flinched again. *Fuck. Just* fuck.

Quill fetched the bag he'd brought with him, a knot of clothes and books and scribe's tools he'd shoved in there, among the vigilants searching the room for any sign of Karimo's...madness, that was what it had to have been. Madness. Why would anyone have thought he was caught up in separatist nonsense?

They'd told him not to touch anything of Karimo's, and Quill had scooped his belongings in haphazardly, unsure if he'd even managed to grab it all. He needed to leave and no part of him wanted to leave. Karimo couldn't be dead, couldn't be a villain, and if he could just prove that—

The sound of Karimo's blood splatting on the ground.

Quill made fists of his hands, pressed them to his eyes.

There were so many stories of the changeling horde—of creatures that took on the form and face and voice of your loved ones, replaced them and wreaked havoc on your life, until all was burning down around you. It was so near to this moment: Karimo couldn't have done this. There was no world where he would have done this. It was as if he were not Karimo at all.

Get up, he told himself. *Be alive. Figure out what happened.*

He dumped out the whole mess of his bag, hunting for a comb and a razor. His crumpled formal robes, spare shirt, penknife, books, inks—all of it came out in a pile on the bed. Karimo was going to make such a face at the mess—

Quill shut his eyes again, cursed again. Grabbed the toilet bag from the pile...and noticed he had two of the same book. Two notebooks, emblazoned with the stylus and tower of the Scriveners of Parem.

In a breath, he realized his error. His own notebook had never left his bag. The one he'd swept from the desktop in his hurry to get out of the vigilants' way had been Karimo's.

"Fuck," he said out loud. The vigilants would most certainly want that. A history of cases, of private thoughts, of payments—a scrivener's notebook contained all manner of information.

Maybe answers.

"I'll explain later," Karimo had said.

Those who sow deception must reap only death, Karimo had said.

Quill opened the book and skimmed the pages, brushing aside the feeling that he was violating Karimo's trust. If there was anything inside that explained what had happened, he wanted to find it first, before the vigilants made accusations, before someone decided his friend was guilty and...

A lump built in Quill's throat. Karimo *was* guilty. He couldn't defend himself. This wasn't going to change that. It was just an answer. A reason.

An explanation for why the person most dedicated—heart and soul—to the laws and accords of the Imperial Federation of Semilla and Her Protectorates had gone and attacked two officials in front of a room full of people, like he'd never expounded for whole afternoons about things like "the natural right of bodily integrity" or "syncretism and plurality of protectorate legal cultures."

He turned through pages marking earlier appointments and cases, until he neared the end. Here were the notes on the cases in Arlabecca. Here were the Kirazzi requests—including the statues Quill had missed. An appointment with a Captain Gaspera del Oyofon to discuss the sale of some land. A meeting with a Nanqii ul-Hanizan to discuss a pending court case. An appointment with Lord Zaverio Maschano to discuss a prior meeting, with the annotation "Deilio." An appointment with Lady Maschano with the same annotation. Nothing that mattered.

Quill flipped through the empty pages, sorrow tearing a new hole in his gut. They would never be filled. Karimo, who filled every page to the corners, wouldn't fill this—

Suddenly, ink bloomed across the reverse of a page, covered in Karimo's tidy scrawl. Names and notes in a neat table. Payments? No. Quill's eyes stopped at the bottom.

Kirazzi—np in Ses
ul-Hanizan, 350—paid to C, F, M. Bribes?
Maschano, 200, mischarged? Kept?
del Oyofon, 120—why?

Shrike? it read. Followed by six hash marks and the number 2,000 beneath a crossed-out *1,400, 1,600, 1,800.*

Quill frowned. What was a shrike? Two thousand what?

He turned forward in the book but found only the careful ledger of expenses Karimo used the end of his notebook for. He turned back to the page full of names and numbers. It looked similar to the ledger, but as if Karimo were tracking Primate Lamberto's payments.

Or rather, irregularities in Primate Lamberto's payments.

Quill's stomach twisted. He had to be reading this wrong. The primate wouldn't do something like that.

Except...

There had been a moment, the night before: in that large, open room, the dead bodies on the ground covered with sheets, the vigilants corralling everyone into more private spaces, Quill beside the primate because someone had to be, because he didn't know where to go and Karimo was under one of those sheets. The hospitalers of the House of Unified Wisdom had come, bound the primate's wounds, and gotten a stretcher under him to carry him out. Lamberto had grabbed Quill with his good arm, pulled him close, before they could.

"You need to get out of here," he had whispered. "Stay away from here, stay away from the chapter house tonight. Get someplace safe."

In the little room in the archives, Quill shuddered. The primate was well respected, well positioned, not at all the sort of man you saw corruption in. But then... he knew something.

And, it seemed, so had Karimo.

Quill managed to venture out into the hallway, where the archives did not vanish into nightmare either. He'd made it most of the way toward where he expected to find the stairs, when Amadea came around the corner, a paper packet in one hand.

"I was just about to look in on you," she said. She turned him swiftly back toward his room and handed over the packet, which was full of brown and steaming buns. "Hungry? They're lamb and pumpkin, and the ones with the black seeds on top are sweet bean and cheese."

Quill numbly pulled out one of the lamb and pumpkin ones and stared at it. He was famished and he couldn't imagine eating. When he looked up, they were back to his room—he stepped free from Amadea. "I need to go see Primate Lamberto," he said. "Where did they take him?"

Amadea folded her hands against her skirt. "There's a House of Unified Wisdom, north of the yula Manco nest. I expect that's where they are."

"They?"

"Primate Lamberto and Reza Dolitha ul-Benturan." She was watching him intently. "Unless you think the primate would have returned to the chapter house. Although you said last night you couldn't go to the chapter house. Why was that?"

"I don't know," Quill lied. "Primate Lamberto...He doesn't like the prelate; probably I was thinking of that."

Amadea paused, as if choosing her words carefully. "I don't know if you're aware of this. But Lord Obigen's nest-child is Tunuk. The bone specialist. And Yinii is ul-Benturan—Dolitha is her reza." She peered at him a moment, as if expecting him to betray some secret knowledge. "It's odd, isn't it? That those two were attacked and they have these ties to the archives. That you have this tie to the archives now."

"Nothing about this isn't odd," he said sharply. "But I doubt an advocate would think it mattered. They're coincidences." He thought again of the secret ledger in Karimo's notebook—*that* was evidence of something.

He considered, for a moment, showing the book to Amadea. But there was something about the way she was probing at him, only thinking about how best to shield the archives. Amadea was good in a crisis—maybe if you were an archivist.

"I'm going to the House of Unified Wisdom," he announced.

"Yinii and I will go with you," she said. "She's waiting in the entry hall."

Quill nearly replied he would rather go himself—but the thought of wandering Arlabecca's unfamiliar streets alone suddenly seemed impossible. He hesitated. "Does...does she know? Does Yinii know that it was Karimo who...?"

Amadea's expression softened. "She does. But she also understands that you're grieving too. I will ask her first, but I strongly suspect she will appreciate the company and understand." She paused. "Are you safe?" she asked quietly.

Quill gave a bitter laugh. "Who would hurt me?" Grief yawning in his gut. *Not Karimo*, he thought. *Not even if he were a changeling of himself, not now.*

Amadea nodded. "Well, you're safe here. I promise that." And Quill's sureness that he should not tell her about the book slipped a little.

In the entry hall, Yinii looked wound in on herself like a cord was wrapped around her. She flashed him a brief, weak smile when he came through the great doors, but as they crossed the city, following the same line of the aqueduct that Quill had the previous night, neither of them spoke a word.

Every time Quill looked over at her, he remembered the reza ul-Benturan, crawling across the floor, blood pouring from her dark-eye down her face. He flinched.

The House of Unified Wisdom in the Necessary Arts sat on the north end of the city, a broad, bright edifice decorated with enormous statues of its founders—the Khirazji physician in an ancient kilt and headcloth, holding a mortar and pestle; the Datongu surgeon, her tattoos carved lines across her chin and cheeks, holding a scalpel; and the Alojan known as the Bone Sapa, with a jar of ointment in one hand and a thin drill in the other. A temple to healing and the art of medicine.

Inside, it was chaos.

"Who are you looking for?" asked the triaging hospitaler, a frazzled-looking woman with dark hair wisping loose of her green wimple.

"Lamberto Lajonta and Dolitha ul-Benturan," Amadea replied.

The hospitaler looked from Amadea to Quill to Yinii. She pointed her chalk at Yinii. "Reza ul-Benturan is on the second floor. She's got a visitor, so don't all pile in. The primate," she added to Amadea and Quill, "is at the end of the same hall, but he's got clients visiting right now, so you have to wait."

"He's just been stabbed," Amadea said, "and he's entertaining a client?"

The hospitaler rolled her eyes. "Let's just say the Maschanos always want their money's worth. Up the stairs, turn right, fourth door for the reza."

"Thank you so much," Amadea said, and steered Quill and Yinii up the stairs. When they reached the reza's door, it was open. An Orozhandi man sat beside the bed, peering out at the three of them. Yinii stopped dead.

"I can't," she said, barely above a whisper.

Amadea took her by the arm. "I'll come with you. Quill? Would you like to wait, or would you like your privacy?"

"I'll...I'll just go now. Thank you," Quill said. The two women went in, and Quill continued on to the end of the hallway, where the last door hung open.

The primate's room overlooked the street behind, and light from its window spilled into the hall. As Quill came closer, he heard a man shouting.

"Don't know what exactly we're paying for if they're letting in madmen and murderers!"

"Zaverio, please," a woman's voice followed, "I'm quite sure the primate had no idea at all his assistant was going to do what he did. Perhaps he could have planned better," she went on tightly. "Thought things through a bit? Sometime before our innocent boy was put into peril?"

"That's a lot of credit to extend," the man snarled.

Quill stopped outside the door.

"Lady Maschano, Lord Maschano," the primate responded, his deep voice subdued, even shaking, "I assure you, I understand better than anyone how...poorly this reflects on the *integrity* of the Paremi. If you wish Brother Deilio to leave the order, there are steps—"

"When did I say I wanted him out?" Zaverio demanded. "I want assurances he's not surrounded by madmen."

"Perhaps you would consider Deilio for an assistant," Lady Maschano said. "It would soothe my nerves, for one."

Anger swelled up in Quill's throat, a defense of Karimo. He stepped into the doorway. The primate sat propped in a bed, his shoulder wrapped tight against his body. Straight-backed and high-chinned, pale and stern, the woman sitting at the foot of the bed turned, her clear, round eyes pinning Quill. He had the urge to apologize and back out of the door at the sight of Lady Maschano.

"Yes?" she said.

At that Zaverio Maschano, the stocky bearded man in a fur-trimmed cloak who had been pacing the short path beside the primate's bed, turned and scowled. And Quill recognized him—he'd been at the party the night before. With a son wearing Paremi robes.

Quill thought of the notebook. Lord Maschano had an appointment for later today; Lady Maschano had had one the day before. Both of them about a "Deilio"—a Brother Deilio they might withdraw from the order. A son. A son they'd paid money for.

Maschano, 200, mischarged? Kept?

"Brother Sesquillio!" the primate snapped. "What are you doing here?"

Quill's mouth worked a moment before he made himself say, "Apologies, Most Reverend. I came to see if you were doing all right."

"I am fine," Lamberto said, "and I am with a client."

A client you've been taking bribes from, Quill thought.

"I think we'd best go," Lady Maschano said, standing. "We've made our point. Most Reverend, we'll send a message with Deilio's decision. I hope your recovery is quick. Zaverio?"

Lord Maschano glowered at his wife. "Maybe you've finished, but I haven't."

She sighed. "Darling. You are simply overextended after the Kinship Hall."

"Fat waste of time when the little mongrel did it," Zaverio growled.

Quill drew back, rage flushing his cheeks. "Don't you—"

"Lord and Lady Maschano," the primate boomed over him, "thank you so much for your understanding and I do hope Deilio is not too overtaken by what happened last night."

Lady Maschano gave the primate a thin smile. "He *is* a delicate boy. Come, Zaverio." She took her husband's arm and dragged him to the door, still scowling.

Quill watched them go, shaking and hot.

"What are you doing here?" the primate hissed. "I told you to stay away."

Quill shut the door. "Apologies again, Most Reverend. You said to stay away that night. And you didn't say why."

"What more do you need to know?" the primate demanded. "I am up to my eyebrows in a political ants' nest. You don't need to be caught in it too! Where are you staying?"

"The Imperial Archives," Quill said, and immediately wondered if he should have said it.

Primate Lamberto made a face. "I have no idea what possessed you to impose upon them, but…never mind. You should return to the tower in Ragale. There's coin in my desk drawer over there. Take it. Go. Don't look back. Forget about all of this."

"I'm not forgetting about Brother Karimo."

The primate flushed scarlet, as if he were about to let loose a bellowing lecture. But he only said, "What happened is a tragedy. It cannot be changed. Take the coin. Go to Ragale. Wait for me there."

The shift unbalanced Quill. He hesitated. "You know Karimo wasn't…he wasn't the sort…"

"Lad," the primate said sadly, "a great many people are 'the sort.'"

A knock came at the door, another green-wimpled hospitaler with a dose of medicine for the primate. While the primate blustered and groused about his arm, Quill went quietly to the desk, taking the price of a carriage to Ragale from the purse he found there.

Beside the primate's own notebook.

Quill paused. Karimo had known something. Had insisted on going with the primate that day. What if he had been confronting Lamberto about what he'd worked out? *That* sounded like Karimo—pull the primate aside and give him a chance to mend his ways before Karimo reported it to the order or the vigilants.

And if Karimo had known something, chances were good he'd begun to discover it in the primate's notebook.

It won't be anything a person could lose their mind over, a little part of Quill said. *It won't change what happened.*

But Quill ignored the thought, plucked up the notebook, and slipped it into his bag.

＋‹‹═‖═›＋

Reza Dolitha looked so small and fragile, propped up on pillows with a smoky glass cap over her dark-eye, bandages wrapping her head. Yinii entered, hands clasped in front of her, Amadea's hand on her shoulder. She offered a polite bow to her father's cousin before introducing Amadea to Pharas Two-Sand Iris ul-Benturan, who watched Yinii, his eyes full of questions.

Yinii kept watching Reza Dolitha. She kept thinking about Saint Qilphith and Saint Alomalia. She touched Saint Asla's salt crystal.

"They've given her a great deal of sedatives," Pharas said. "She can't hear anything but she can't feel the pain either."

Yinii's stomach tightened. She didn't want to be there. She had to be there. Dolitha was the head of her whole canyon-clan, the one who made certain they survived and thrived and didn't lose themselves. What Yinii owed to ul-Benturan she owed most especially to the reza.

But still: even with Reza Dolitha imperiled and asleep, some part of her, small but growing louder, wanted to run. Sometimes the caverns felt like home and sometimes they felt like a tomb.

"Is she another atnashingyii?" Pharas asked, with a nod at Amadea.

"She is not," Amadea answered with a smile. "I work with Yinii."

"She's my superior," Yinii said quickly. That had to count for something. "Do they know if Reza Dolitha will wake?"

"She's strong," Pharas said. "They say the blade hit bone and turned aside rather than penetrate her brain. She will probably lose the eye, though, and her dark-sight with it." He shook his head. "It's what comes of trying to speak sense to the darkblind," he said in Orozhandi.

Yinii bristled. "This had nothing to do with that."

Pharas looked at her sidelong. He was older, and Yinii would owe him deference unquestionably if she weren't atnashingyii. As it stood, no one ever seemed sure how to fit Yinii in—atnashingyii meant status, but ink-blessed was a quandary. At least, it was to ul-Benturan.

"You've been here too long," Pharas said, a sudden gentleness to his voice. "You've lost track of our ways. Reza Dolitha thought so too. She was considering recalling you to Maqama, you know."

Cold horror swept through Yinii.

"I beg your pardon?" Amadea said, alarmed.

Pharas shushed her. "The reza needs to sleep."

Yinii's ears were pounding. *Ink in her mouth, ink in her nose.* "It's not safe for me to live in Maqama," she said quietly. "Reza Dolitha knows that."

Pharas waved dismissively. "Well, that. You've been with the atnashingyii long enough that surely you know the cycles now. You can handle it if you want to."

Yinii shook her head. "I don't spiral like other people. Don't you remember?"

Pharas shrugged. "I know the ul-Shandiians have an atnashingyii who favors stone. They say when he's in alignment he climbs a tree and prays. Like a stylite. You could just stay away from ink, couldn't you?"

Two books in Reza Dolitha's room, the ink gall and iron, a deep grinding rumble of the mines and the mortar thrummed on the edge of her veins. Yinii squeezed her hands into fists. "That didn't go well before," she said tightly. *Calm down*, she told herself.

"Haven't you taught her better control?" Pharas demanded of Amadea. "Yinii, why are you even there, if they're not helping you?"

Yinii bit her tongue. Her family understood traditional alignments, but not ink. Not the way that when she spiraled it was like a maw opening in her chest, like she had to write the whole world into being before it was swallowed up, but she just needed ink to do it. And making ink meant burning things, meant gathering water and oils and alcohols to her. Meant destruction.

When she'd come to the Imperial Archives, she'd tried to describe what happened in her spiral to Mireia, and the head archivist had peered at her. "Hmm. That's a severe one."

"I can manage," Yinii had said, terrified they wouldn't let her stay. "It's worse when I can't... When I haven't..."

"You need the ink," Mireia had said. "We understand that. All right, no tinder, no flints." She'd made a note on Yinii's paperwork, and while it made a difference having her library, having the sequestration protocols to catch her, having Amadea watching over her—Yinii never forgot the feeling of her mouth filling with ink as everything burned around her.

She could not go back to Maqama. But if she could, if she did, would the rest of her life settle and stop feeling so precarious? She would know where she fit and how to act. She would know when she could flirt with a boy, and when she couldn't. Sometimes the caverns were like a tomb, she thought, and sometimes they were only home.

Amadea set a hand on Yinii's shoulder. "I'm sure that's a conversation we can have later. When the reza recovers."

Reza Dolitha slept on, and Yinii blew out a breath. She hadn't recalled Yinii to Maqama yet, and who was to say she would when she woke? Maybe it would all be fine?

"Amadea, do you want to wait in the chapel?" Yinii asked. "I just have to . . . I have to finish here."

"Of course," Amadea said. She squeezed Yinii's shoulder. "You come find me when you're ready."

She left, and Yinii settled in a chair on the opposite side of the reza's bed, memories pouring through her: Reza Dolitha presenting her to Ahkerfi of the Copper. Reza Dolitha catching her peeling ink off the scrolls to Saints Qarabas and Maligar that hung in Yinii's parents' sitting room. Reza Dolitha saying, "This child is half-blessed. What a gift, what a gift."

Reza Dolitha putting paint, dull and dead, before her. Reza Dolitha telling her to pray and pray and pray. Reza Dolitha in hushed consultation, deciding Yinii needed to leave Maqama, needed to go to Arlabecca, Yinii belonged to the archives, where she'd never quite belong. All her feelings were so churned up, she couldn't grab hold of a single one to claim it.

"Who was that darkblind boy you were with?" Pharas asked. "The one that didn't come in?"

"Quill," Yinii said automatically. "He's visiting Primate Lamberto down the hall."

"A Paremi?" Pharas narrowed his eyes. "He's not the one who stabbed the reza, is he?"

"No," Yinii said. Another slippery, awful feeling: That had been Quill's friend, the one he'd spoken so highly of while she showed him the ceiling, and how did you misjudge someone so completely? How should she look at Quill, knowing he idolized the man who'd done *this*?

"You're not *dallying* with him, are you?" Pharas demanded.

"No!" Yinii said, though she felt her cheeks burn. "He's facilitating a request to the archives. He wants a book." Pharas raised an eyebrow. Yinii blushed harder.

"I suppose you know better than to take up with a darkblind boy," Pharas said, offering his prayer beads over the reza's sleeping body.

Yinii touched the salt crystal and took Pharas's prayer beads. *Saint Asla, grant me a measure of your strength, your sureness*, she thought as she began to pray for the reza's recovery.

⋅⋅◄◈►⋅⋅

An hour later, having left Yinii to return to the archives alone, Amadea stood at the end of a long hallway, beneath a towering statue of the Vigilant Mother Ayemi, stern and beneficent in stone. The Kinship had originated in Bemina, a specialized faction of their fabled military, and the statue of Mother Ayemi, the order's ancient founder, bore the archaic leaf-shaped basket shield and spear of the Bemina infantry, their serpent-head helm balanced on one hip. Her short hair was in knots, a style still fashionable among women with the hair to hold them, and her throat swathed with a collar of feathers, an ornamentation extremely popular with young ladies descended from all the protectorates.

The statue was carved in a fashion born of modern Semilla—the detail wrought in marble, the ease of her posture, the soft forms of her features. Amadea thought of the archivists who could pick out the skills of Bemina and Min-Se, Khirazj and Semilla, and probably others she couldn't spy, blending into this lovely piece.

Amadea had studied every inch of it in the time she and Quill had been waiting for a vigilant to take his official statements. And then, hopefully, escort them to the crypt where Karimo waited.

"No one's going to claim him," Quill had said, as if the words were bursting out of him, panicked and frustrated. "He doesn't have family. Just some orphan. He'll just *lie* there, and...and..."

A wiser woman might have told him the Paremi would surely handle it, or the vigilants. His pain was so fresh; he didn't need to do this. But Amadea had taken in the gray shock of his face, the guilt, and said instead, "Do you know I'm an orphan?"

Quill bristled. "I didn't mean—"

"I didn't take it that way," she said. "What I mean is I can tell you from experience that there are two sorts of families: the ones you are born to, and the ones you find and make for yourself. You cared about Karimo. That counts for something. You can make the claim. I can help you arrange matters."

Footfalls echoed in the long hallway. Amadea stood, expecting the promised vigilant.

Instead her gaze found the unmistakable form of Gaspera del Oyofon, striding toward her, near enough to blot out Mother Ayemi.

Amadea froze.

Gaspera was older now—of course she was older—her dark hair silvered, the lines of her face harder, her frame thinner. But she walked the same way, as if she were striding across a battlefield, surveying lines of troops with a callous eye. Amadea watched her, suddenly swamped with panic, drowning in memories of Gaspera del Oyofon, the Fox of the Wall, in midnight conversation at Sestina, she and Rosa, her aide, and Fastreda Korotzma lit by the candlelight. Fastreda looking across the room, a smile like a shard of glass—

Amadea blew out a hard breath, trying to banish the memories before they broke her control. But that only drew Gaspera's attention, her narrow, tilted eyes scowling at the intrusion. Amadea scrambled—what could she say? Here, now, after all these years? Her memories surged again—*Ibramo grabbing her around the shoulders, pulling her out of sight, away from the room. "I don't like when she gets that look in her eye."*

Gaspera eyeing Lireana in her fine armor beside wicked Fastreda. "You're going to get her killed, and then what?" Gaspera years later, medals on her shoulders. Ibramo's father heading for the gallows—

Gaspera turned away, a look of faint distaste and nothing more on her face, to reveal Vigilant Mother Ayemi once more, in stern observance.

Amadea watched her go, silent as a child caught where she shouldn't be.

"Who was that?" Quill asked.

Amadea forced herself to look away, braced for too many questions. "That... that was Captain Gaspera del Oyofon."

But Quill was only watching the retreating woman's back. "She was there. I think. At the party."

"Then I suppose that's what she's doing here." Gaspera hadn't recognized her. And why should she? She was an archivist, a grown woman plucking gray hairs, not a girl haunting the edges of a conspiracy. And even then, there was so much she was sure Gaspera hadn't seen.

Quill frowned. "Do you know her or something?"

"Archivist Gintanas?"

Amadea looked up to find a vigilant—*finally*—striding toward them, hands full of papers. But not just any vigilant. "Vigilant Langyun," she said, folding her hands reflexively. "I trust you're feeling better rested."

"Never," he said, with a quick smile. But his bright brown eyes looked less shadowed, his uniform trim and tidy. "I didn't ask you to come in."

"She came with me," Quill said, and the vigilant seemed to notice him for the first time. "You said I needed to give a statement. I'm here to give a statement."

"Right, sorry." The vigilant looked up at Amadea. "Thank you for bringing him. I'll take it from here."

"No," Quill interrupted. He looked pale again, and shaky. "I want her to come too. That's allowed. I know the law."

"Is that necessary?" the vigilant asked. "She can wait here if you need."

A surge of protectiveness rose in Amadea—as if he were one of her archivists, as if he couldn't stand alone. "He seems to feel it is necessary. I assume you have a spare chair?"

Vigilant Langyun pursed his mouth in a way that suggested the chair was the least of the issues with this, but he escorted the two of them up to a small room and pointed Amadea to a chair in the corner. A woman in Paremi robes and a feathered collar like Mother Ayemi's took a seat at the table in the corner.

"Sesquillio Haigu-lan Seupu-lai," she read off a parchment. "Of the Order of the Scriveners of Parem. Third son of House Seupu-lai. Correct?"

"Correct," Quill said.

Amadea's brows rose. Seupu-lai? Mireia hadn't mentioned *that*. The Seupu-lais were a powerful family with roots deep in the Four Kingdoms of Min-Se.

She listened with one ear as Vigilant Langyun asked Quill questions about the primate, the party guests, the Manco household. Karimo.

"You never talked about politics?" Richa asked.

"We talked about politics," Quill said. "But not like…not like you're thinking. He was really interested in the way imperial law and the accords were structured. The way we rebuilt it and compromised around the protectorates. The places it wouldn't bend." He swallowed. "You ever read about the Pashuntana?"

Amadea looked over. Richa set down his stylus. "They were like the Ashtabari."

"They were the tormentors of the Ashtabari," Quill said. "They had their kingdom on the seashore and they pushed the Ashtabari into the estuaries and the swamps. Enslaved them and kept them as bondsmen. Burned their fields if they felt like they were getting too comfortable. The Ashtabari got here first because they knew when to run, and when the Pashuntana followed, they wanted to keep doing as they had, holding themselves above the Ashtabari. And Emperor Eschellado said that all were Semillan, and Semillans were equal, so they could rethink their ideas or get out.

"Which the Pashuntana disagreed with. So the emperor cast every single one who protested that truth out beyond the Salt Wall and damned them to whatever their superiority might have bought them. Do you know why I know that story?"

"You like history?"

"Karimo." He leaned back in his seat. "You want him to be some kind of maniac who hates Alojans and Orozhandi, but he loved Semilla, the whole teeming mess of it. He loved the bright goals of it and the stupid, broken little corners of it. He loved the places where we have too many rules from too many people, and the places where we're still cobbling together solutions because one rule won't fit. He wasn't a separatist. He wouldn't have done this."

"So why did he?" the vigilant asked softly.

Quill fell silent for a long time.

"Tell me again," Vigilant Langyun said, "what happened that day. Start that morning."

Quill described arriving at the archives, how Karimo had pushed him forward to stay. He told the vigilant about how he'd gone through the archives with first Yinii and then Amadea, leaving around dinnertime and walking across the city. He'd stopped to give some men a few coins and talked a bit. He went quiet.

"What is it?" Vigilant Langyun asked.

"If I hadn't done that," he said, "I would have gotten to the Manco house in time to stop him."

Vigilant Langyun sighed. "I know it's tempting to look back and find something you should have done differently. Some point in history where you could have shifted things and gotten a future that didn't feel so bleak. But you can't."

Quill shut his eyes. "He might still be alive if I were there."

"Maybe. Maybe you could have stopped Karimo. Maybe you would have arrived to see him start attacking. Maybe you would have gotten stabbed like Primate Lamberto. Maybe Karimo would have done it the next morning. None of it turns on when you walk in that door, which is good, because you can't change what happened." Richa folded his hands together. "Do you want to continue?"

Quill recited the rest of his evening in terse sentences and a flat voice. He went to the Manco manor. The door was shut. No one came when he knocked. He heard screaming and went in on his own. He found Karimo. He watched Karimo . . .

Quill stopped. "I forgot something." He looked back at Amadea quickly, as if checking to make sure she was still there. "When I stopped to talk to those men, I saw Ibramo Kirazzi. In the . . . black mask." He faltered—the imperial black mask wasn't meant to be acknowledged. "I think he was walking away from the Manco house, too."

And then Quill turned all the way around to face Amadea. "Why was the head archivist so worried about Ibramo Kirazzi being the one to make the requests? Do you know something? Is he a villain?"

Amadea's heart stuttered, as if her blood had turned to stone, starving it. *Please never doubt: My love and esteem for you have not changed. There is no force within the Wall that could change them, my darling.*

"No," she said. "Nothing...nothing like that." Now Vigilant Langyun considered her, brow creased, and Amadea cursed inwardly.

"What is it, then?" Quill asked.

"The archives don't involve themselves with gossip," she said. "I don't see how this is relevant."

"Maybe...maybe he was there. Before I arrived." He turned back to the vigilant. "Did anyone you talked to see him?"

Vigilant Langyun held up a hand, though his gaze stayed on Amadea. "I think you're getting ahead of yourself."

"He's a Kirazzi. They're up to something with those requests. He was near the party. The archives don't like him!" Quill gestured wildly back at Amadea.

"Quill, the consort-prince is allowed to walk the city," Amadea said, as gently as she could. "Being nearby doesn't make him a murderer any more than it does the men you talked to."

"But why?" Quill demanded. "Why was he *there*?"

"I think we have enough for today," Vigilant Langyun said, standing. "Thank you for your time, Brother Sesquillio. If we have further—"

"These things are connected," Quill said. "Karimo was involved in the dowager duchess's estate—maybe it's about—"

"Quill, I think we should go," Amadea said, crossing to him. "This is a lot to ask of you right now."

He darted from her reach, betrayal in his expression. "*No.* I want to see him. Someone has to claim him. You said you'd help me."

"Karimo?" The vigilant shook his head. "We've been trying to contact family—"

"*I'm* his family," Quill said.

Amadea set a hand on Quill's shoulder. "What he means is, if no one claims Karimo's body, he would like to make arrangements. But also he's having some trouble with...*accepting*—"

"I want to see him," Quill interrupted.

The vigilant hesitated. "You'll excuse me, esinora, he's not exactly in a condition for visitors."

"Cover him, then?" Amadea said crisply. "And make it possible?"

The crypt beneath the Kinship Hall was chilled by the long metal panels positioned against the walls, powered by the magic the Borsyans had spirited out of their forested lands. There were a dozen stone slabs laid out, and on five of them were unclaimed bodies, covered by sheets. Karimo lay on the nearest of these, a sheet folded back from his face, an extra cloth laid across his throat to cover the wound there, a vigilant cadet standing at his head. He looked peaceful, as if he'd been carved like the Vigilant Mother, of some milky stone, dark curls framing his face like a halo.

Quill stood over the other young man a moment. "Hey, Karimo," he said quietly, his voice breaking.

Amadea did not let herself look away. For all it broke her heart, she knew Quill was well out of his depth, and she was the one he'd asked to guide him back. She watched him, trying to spot the moment when he needed retreat, needed escape, needed solace. He was so young—Karimo, too, had been so young.

Then her eyes dropped to Karimo and she went cold.

On his shoulder, pressed half against the table beneath, the skin was purple with a bruise the size of a plum, points radiating, starlike, around it.

Amadea's stomach dropped. Her hands came up of their own volition, pressed to her chest. *"If it doesn't work,"* a voice that shakes her nightmares says, *"then we'll try again. There's a good girl."* The ghost of a needle pierced Amadea's shoulder, and her throat closed up tight.

"I need some air," she heard herself say, her vision closing.

"Archivist?" the vigilant said, sounding far away. "Amadea?"

She felt his hand on her arm, saw the stairs in front of her, heard him say, "Here, sit down," and they were in an office, and a chair was under her.

"I'll get you a coffee," he said, setting papers down. "Are you all right for a moment?"

"I'm fine."

"Put your head down." She did, hands against the edge of the desk, forehead to her knuckles, and he was gone.

It wasn't happening again, surely. She was wrong. She was stirred up by the sight of Gaspera del Oyofon, by the Kirazzi requests. She was as bad as Quill, her imagination running away. Of course Karimo had bruises—he'd killed two people, stabbed another. Someone would have fought him off. It was a different bruise.

No, she thought. That was nothing but a lie.

In the Imperial Archives, Amadea Gintanas was known for her sharp memory, her ability to step in alongside almost any specialist and assist as if she'd always been there, up to her elbows in bones or scrolls, books or coins or ancient weapons. *Amadea*, the archivists joked, *remembers everything.*

She remembered the room, the wallpaper garish with bright silk birds, the heavy curtains drawn closed. One arm wrapped around a pillow—she remembered the fabric of its skin, worn slick. A man's hand wrapped around her upper arm. *"If it doesn't work, then we'll try again. There's a good girl." A dark-eyed boy peering through the crack of the door, frightened and frozen. Shaking her head, because he was going to do something rash. Something dangerous. A different pillow, the rose-patterned one, flies at him and he bolts. And then she remembers the pinch of the needle and the slow burn—*

She lifted her head, looked around the room. *White paper*, she told herself. *Brown chair. Blue coat. Yellow wallpaper.*

Bird wallpaper.

Changeling blood. She flinched against it, heart racing again, and tried to push her mind farther away.

"Changeling" was the Semillan name. The Orozhandi word meant "they walk in the dusk." The Beminat had called them "skin-stealers." The Datongu had said, "the ones that walk the circle backward," said the changelings represented a broken order, a punishment by the gods upon the world. The Ronqu word was "whisper-eaten," because they held that the changelings were the unfortunate progression of an affinity taken too far, as if one could climb from specialist to sorcerer to changeling.

The Alojans called them a name best translated as "very not us" and said they came from another world entirely.

Whatever the truth, wherever they'd come from, everyone agreed on what the changelings did: they took your shape, they replaced you, they made you turn against one another, then they destroyed everything you'd built.

If one laid out maps, tracked time and place against fragments of letters and proclamations and artifacts collected along the path from home to here, it began first in Khirazj, nearly two centuries ago—a burst of imposters, replacements, found and then smothered. The Khirazji Empire held firm along their river, but the civil war was bright and brutal and stretched over a generation.

It was not the end.

The first to break—at least, the first civilization to break and survive to the safety of Semilla—were the Ronqu, once an empire of filigreed tower temples and glittering waterways; they arrived in Semilla hardened, condensed, no time for the stratification of their old ways. They'd been so long running, so long needing each and every one. They were only ten thousand, a fraction, their tales said, of who they'd been when the whisper-eaten began to stop the canals and set the fires.

The Orozhandi came next, by the cover of night, hearing the rumors blowing out of Khirazj, seeing the trickle of refugees already fleeing, already knowing that when someone stopped seeming like themselves, the time for salt and iron was at hand. They carried the skeletons of their saints on their backs through the wide desert, across the gusting plains, gathering up the gems that fell from their bundled bones.

Min-Se shot across the continent, swift as the wind, their children all born to the horse and the bow, their packs stuffed with fermented fish and vegetables and scrolls the archives were still deciphering. Bemina fled slowly, running back to attack the changelings that chased, with iron weapons, and later, when they gathered the Borsyan to their cause, with the peculiar magics brought out of the Black Mother Forest—the cold-lights and the winds-from-nowhere, the plant gift and the animal speech. The Kuali and the Ashtabari, all the world a road, came early, knowing that when land turned bad, it was wisdom to leave it. Khirazj came last, the changelings on their heels once more.

And then the Salt Wall was sealed and the changelings were held back.

What lay beyond the Wall now was only stories—no one alive remembered the old world, no one alive knew how it felt to truly fear your loved ones, your neighbors; your sovereigns weren't what they said they were. People knew the stories, knew that what their ancestors had fled was something terrible, even if the terror was remote and polished smooth by so many years. They knew the changelings persisted—the soldiers on the Salt Wall spotted scouts or travelers now and again—and that, given the chance, they might tear down this last bastion of civilization.

Some spoke of going over the Wall. Few talked of changeling hunting. Amadea only knew of one person who went over the Wall and returned, carrying the blood of slaughtered changelings.

Ancient Khirazj had known that whatever made the change-lings able to take the shapes of other living creatures, to mimic their voices and carry some part of their minds, could slide into a body and make enough space for a memory that never happened.

Rumors said it had been the favored poison of Redolfo Kirazzi, who used it on any soul who might be useful if they believed a little differently...or might need to forget what they'd seen or done. And in the aftermath of the Usurper's crimes, every-one who'd crossed Redolfo Kirazzi's path was left questioning how much he had stolen. Or pretending to question—he'd had many eager followers.

A little bruise was all it left. A little star shape where the needle went in.

Karimo's bruise is too big, Amadea told herself. But at the same time, she remembered Quill's protests about who Karimo was and won-dered whether there was a dose large enough, a memory bad enough to make a person act like a stranger, and how big a mark it would leave.

Amadea looked down at the papers Vigilant Langyun had left behind. Witness statements. If this was because Karimo had been poisoned, someone might have noticed when he changed.

But you'd have to tell them why you thought that, she realized. She glanced at the door. No sign or sound of Richa. Amadea snatched up the pages and read through them as quickly as she could.

I heard Lord Obigen call out . . . and when I looked over, I saw that boy, that Karimo stabbing him . . . It was three or four times before I realized, because I was standing so far away beside the wall . . . and then he turned and attacked the reza . . . stabbed her through the eye before she could make a sound, right in front of the empress . . . Lady Sigrittrice tried to stop him . . .

No, Amadea thought. *No, no, no, no.* Every one of them was the same. Every one of them had the same memory. Same phrases. Same angles. Same words.

It couldn't be happening again.

Vigilant Langyun came in, holding a steaming cup. Amadea shot to her feet and tried to set the papers on the desk, but they slid off, spilling to the floor. He stepped back, surprised.

"I have to go," Amadea blurted out. "Is Quill finished?"

"He's . . . filling out some forms," Richa said. "You should probably sit down. I don't know if you got a glimpse of his injury or if you're just not used to—"

"No, I just felt faint. That's all." Her ears were ringing as she looked down at the mess of papers. "Oh, sorry. Let me—"

"I've got it." Vigilant Langyun set the coffee on his desk and stooped to gather up the witness statements. He watched her, tapping the papers together. "Trying to help with my paperwork?"

"I'm sorry," she said again. "I'm a little shaken up, I suppose. Where's Quill?"

Amadea moved like a sleepwalker through the Kinship Hall, accompanying Quill through several rounds of bureaucracy, several rounds of tears. She was there and she wasn't, and it took all her resolve to keep moving her feet, keep speaking the right words, keep reminding herself that Amadea Gintanas, Archivist Superior of the Imperial Collections, was a solver of problems, and Redolfo Kirazzi was a dead man, a ghost who couldn't haunt her anymore.

First steps taken, forms and applications made, Amadea and Quill wound their way back to the archives, but Amadea's thoughts were still two decades away and she missed two turns and had to walk them back.

"Are you all right?" Quill asked, his eyes still red.

"Of course," Amadea said.

"You didn't seem all right. Even before . . . About Ibramo Kirazzi."

"Nothing," she said. "You just seemed like you were getting upset."

"No," he said irritably. "I want to make sure no one misses what's important. What did you talk about with Richa?"

"Not much," Amadea said. "He got me a coffee."

"Maybe that's it—maybe you should ask him to get a coffee, and then you can convince him not to mark all this down as exactly what it looks like."

"I said he got me a coffee," Amadea repeated. "And you have to give him a chance."

Quill stopped on the edge of archives' square and frowned at her. "I mean," he said, "you ought to go out with him. You're very alike. Also I want someone to make sure he does his job." He studied her a long moment. "Are you sure you're well?"

Amadea blinked at him, the words he was saying so far from anything she'd been thinking that they might as well have been some long-forgotten tongue. Her thoughts scrambled away from murder and monsters and shock-shredded innocence, but they wouldn't take hold on anything related to Vigilant Langyun.

He had nice eyes, she supposed—dark, deep eyes—but that made her suddenly think instead of Ibramo and his thick-lashed gaze beneath the willow tree. She gave her head a little shake.

"I have no idea why you'd say that," she told Quill. "You don't know him. Or me."

Quill rolled his eyes. "I know enough to spot *this*. I used to . . ." He trailed off and looked away from her across the square. She wondered if he was thinking of Karimo.

But then alarm flashed across Quill's face. He bolted across the square, into the milling crowds. Amadea took off after him. He stopped in the middle of the square and she overtook him.

"The consort-prince!" he almost shouted. "He was right there! Watching us!"

Amadea followed where he pointed, to a patch of wall between a bookbinder and the pancake shop Tunuk liked. There was no one there, most especially not Ibramo.

"He took off when I started running," Quill said. "If that's not guilt—"

"Come on," Amadea said, trying to hide the anxiety hammering at her own heart. "Let's get you settled." And while Quill calmed down, she could figure out what to do. Ibramo could wait for the Venom of Changelings.

She left Quill at the entrance to the dormitories and hurried to her office, locking the door behind her. She paused by the shelf of glass animals. *White cat, black raven, red horse, blue monkey, gray sparrow—*

"Little Sparrow, what are you hunting?" Fastreda croons.

A shadow by the willow where Ibramo's meant to be. Holding out a corked skin to Redolfo. "I took three," a voice whispers, too soft to place. "That should last you a while. But don't hesitate to say if you run low." And Redolfo chuckles. "You choose strange sport, my Shrike . . ."

The needle going into her arm—

Amadea fled into her bedroom beyond, Imp sliding out as Amadea slid in, and she locked that door tight behind her, too.

Vigilant Langyun poring over all the details, untangling all the threads—if that bruise was what she thought, who else would be dogged enough to follow it, to find who could have poisoned the young Paremi—perhaps the whole party—with changeling blood? But he wouldn't have reason to if she didn't point him toward it.

What were the books, the scrolls she needed? *A History of Khirazj, Part III* covered the initial changeling invasion. Which had the blood rituals? *The Maxims of Ab-Kharu? The Precepts of Bekesa? The Papyrus of On?* She had to find them, had to find proof.

But the wrong sort of proof would only send him hunting after *her.* Vigilant Langyun, watching her too closely, asking too many questions, and Quill bringing up Ibramo. How to tell him without telling him too much?

Tomorrow, she told herself as she started shaking. *You have to calm down. You can't make it worse. Not now.*

Amadea stripped off her robes, her blouse, her slip, her shoes and stockings and smallclothes, and moved to stand before the long mirror.

It won't be there, she tried to tell herself. *You were nowhere near that party. It won't be there.*

Even so, Amadea turned before the glass slowly, carefully checking every inch of her skin for a starburst bruise that meant all her memories were suspect.

CHAPTER FIVE

Again, Quill did not sleep so much as he worried over the fragments of secrets he'd discovered while lying down. He wrestled with the primate's order to take the carriage to Ragale all through the night: it was wisest, it was simplest, and he'd said he'd do it.

But he wasn't going to do it. When sunlight crept in the edges of his window, he shot up, laid out the three notebooks on the desk: his, Karimo's, and Primate Lamberto's. He couldn't leave Arlabecca, not while nothing made sense about Karimo's death.

He took out his scribe kit and opened his own book, turning to the ribbon-marked page. There was the Orozhandi phrase, still unspoken, from the night of the murder. *Ada-aada, shilukundeh essetii teshi naashishet.*

If he'd just kept walking, if he hadn't stopped to talk, if...

No. Richa was right. There was only moving forward. Quill prepared a stylus and ink, scratching out notes on the clean page.

Check Lamberto's ledger, appointments.
Those who sow deception must reap only death—doesn't sound like Karimo, find source.
Why was the chapter house not safe that night?
Ibramo Kirazzi seen night of murders.

Quill paused, ink pooling at the end of the line. He knew what he'd seen, even if he didn't know the significance of it. But Richa and Amadea had both discounted it. He thought of Amadea's look of alarm when he'd said Ibramo had been there that night.

Find out why Ibramo Kirazzi not welcome in archives, he wrote.

Amadea had been acting strange ever since then, actually. He'd assumed it was the crypt, but then, she'd been adamant she could accompany him knowing perfectly well who and what was down there. Perhaps she was as surprised as he was when she'd had to flee the room. He thought of the distracted way she'd gone through the Kinship Hall. Maybe he'd asked too much.

Or maybe he'd been right before—maybe she was hiding things too. Maybe everyone around him was hiding things.

He lifted the primate's notebook from the row. Like the others, it bore on its cover a burned-in design of a stylus poised atop the tower of Parem at Ragale. He held the book in both hands, feeling nothing short of blasphemous about what he was going to do.

But Primate Lamberto was lying about something. Something that had ended with two deaths and Karimo's name in the mud.

The front half of the notebook was filled with Primate Lamberto's tightly packed shorthand and scattered with dates. Travel from Ragale to Hyangga, to Tornada, to Maqama, to Terzanelle. To the Wall, to Arlabecca, to the Wall again. To the coasts, and Pentina, Prodelision, Shadorma. Contracts and wills and drafting laws. Over and over back to Arlabecca. A hearing, there and again—Primate Lamberto did not argue the law too often in later life, but exceptions were made for old friends, whose initials and small reference numbers swarmed the pages.

Quill flipped toward the end, to where the reference numbers stretched out into tables of payments, records of actions and documents. Primate Lamberto had not kept as busy as a mere scrivener, but he hadn't left his trade aside when he had been elevated.

Quill began to read, with a growing sense of dread knotting his stomach. He opened Karimo's notebook to the page with the annotations.

He found Nanqii ul-Hanizan's name listed repeatedly with only "services rendered" beside it, and sums that varied but never dipped down to the cost of reviewing an agreement or drafting a legal request—nothing that matched the frequency of the payments.

He found Zaverio Maschano—his payments marked as for the

Paremi with the note "son"—and Gaspera del Oyofon, with an annotation about a property dispute in the east, near the Wall. The amount was too high, once more. He did not find Deilio Maschano listed, but a "Rosangerda Maschano" was listed beginning early last winter with a note about a personal matter, and followed later by a cluster with the "son" annotations.

Amid them, over and over, the word "Shrike." A payment received in the amount of two hundred metas—nearly half an initiate scrivener's yearly pay—once a month, going back nearly a year. No annotation—no hint of a job done or a service offered.

Was it something salacious? Blackmail? A bribe? Who would call themselves "Shrike"?

Here, he thought, was the listing that alerted Karimo, but nothing to show it for what it was. He cursed to himself.

Then, on the last page, halfway down the ledger, he found the reference for the Kirazzi requests. Only the name wasn't Duchess Kirazzi's.

The line read: *I. Kirazzi. Facilitation of Official Requests.*

Ibramo Kirazzi, consort-prince of the Masked Empress, son of the Usurper, enemy of the archives, haunter of crossroads near the Manco household—somebody who was not supposed to be involved with the Kirazzi requests at all. Yet here he was, and *there* he'd been, striding away from a party where...

Where two people whose connections to Ibramo Kirazzi Quill could not fathom were stabbed by a third Quill felt sure Ibramo couldn't choose from a crowd. He scowled at the book a moment.

Find out why Ibramo Kirazzi not welcome in archives. That was where he'd start.

Quill went back out into the hall and knocked two doors down, where Amadea had said Yinii lived. If anyone was going to tell him, he thought, it would be her.

"What are you doing?" a deep voice asked.

Quill turned and found Tunuk standing over him, dark as night and nearly as high as the ceiling. Quill smiled up at the Alojan man. "Is Yinii in?"

"She's sad," Tunuk said. "So she's in the chapel bothering the saints or she's in her library bothering the ink. Why do *you* need to bother her?"

"I want to ask her something." Quill swallowed. "I heard about your nest-father. I'm sorry. I only met him briefly, but he was a good host and he seemed well-liked."

Tunuk stared down at him impassively, his large eyes glowing faintly, like underfed Borsyan lamps. "You knew the man who killed him."

"I did," Quill said. *He didn't do it*—it sounded foolish even unspoken. "I was as surprised as anyone. He never gave any sign . . . I would have stopped him if I could have."

Tunuk made a soft, disgusted sound. "Oh good, you wouldn't aid a murderer. I'm so glad. Come on." Tunuk stalked off down the hall.

"Where?" Quill asked.

"Yinii's library, of course. Clearly you'll get lost, and then someone will probably blame me for it."

Quill hurried to catch up with him, thoughts churning. Ibramo Kirazzi vanishing into the dark. Mireia demanding which Kirazzi had *really* made the request. Amadea's expression closing off when he'd asked about the consort-prince, her tripping on her answer, *No. Nothing . . . nothing like that.*

Over them the painted ceiling stretched, the Datongu wisdom goddess Aye-Nam-Wati looking down with her terrible knife and her beatific smile, her lower half a white snake's tail, curling between the clouds as she escaped the clutches of demons with the secret of writing in her swan-drawn chariot. Pulling knowledge from ignorance.

You can do this, he thought, looking up at the goddess. *You're good at talking to people.*

"How long have you worked here?" he asked Tunuk.

Tunuk looked over his shoulder. "A while. Why?"

"Curious," Quill lied. "You don't get a lot of requests from the Kirazzis, do you?"

"*I* don't. Most of *my* requests are to do with the saints."

"Guess that's mostly the Orozhandi?" Tunuk scoffed and Quill readjusted. "Have you worked for Amadea the whole time?"

"I told you before, I don't work *for* her."

"Right," he said, still not sure of the distinction. "Has she ever said why the Kirazzis aren't welcome?"

Tunuk stilled, turned, his lambent eyes narrow. "What a stupid assumption to make."

Quill shrugged, as if it were nothing. "That's the impression I got from everyone else whispering about Ibramo Kirazzi. Including Amadea."

Tunuk's eyes narrowed further somehow, and it gave his shadowy face a menacing look. "'Everyone' does not whisper about it. I, for one, have no idea what you're talking about."

But he did. Quill would have wagered the whole archives on that much. Trouble was he couldn't quite work out what exactly everyone was whispering about. "Maybe Amadea and the head archivist are keeping secrets from you." He said it lightly, testing the idea. "They seemed...flustered when I mentioned Ibramo Kirazzi."

"Well, now I know you're a liar. Amadea is never flustered."

"Maybe 'flustered' is the wrong word," Quill said. He held Tunuk's fierce glare, trying to tease out what he was protecting. He thought of telling Tunuk that Primate Lamberto was the same way—hiding things, teaching virtues with one hand and with the other aiding criminals. *They act like you need to be perfect while they've got all their own flaws.* But that, he could see, would go poorly. He wouldn't admit to the flaws.

"I'm surprised you like her so much," Quill tried. "She makes you work with Radir, right? Don't you hate him?"

"Who said I hate Radir?"

"It's pretty obvious. I've barely been here, and I know it."

"Well, in that case, I hate everyone, so I suppose she has her work cut out for her. And since you insist on the subject," Tunuk said, his words somehow colder, "you should consider carefully that Amadea has many friends in the archives, and to my knowledge, zero enemies. She is one of us, and she has done as much as or more for most of us than anyone else can claim. She's the smartest human I know and entirely unpretentious about it, which is a marvel when you get down to it, the way you all trumpet about. She is *my* friend, and so she's permitted to suggest I do things I hate because she has my best interests at heart, and she will not suffer when I prove her to be wrong, because she'll be *glad* for me. Don't come to me with half gossips and think I will upend that for your wandering curiosity."

Quill held his hands up in a gesture of surrender—too far, and for what? "My mistake."

"Indeed." Tunuk turned back to the path. "Thank the stars you're planning to make your boredom Yinii's problem. Maybe she'll show you the chapel and then I'll tell you all the ways she's being senti-mental and re-bore you with the differences between physical and magical flensing marks. But I've got to go visit my parents, because apparently with my nest-father dead, Amadea's not the only one insisting I talk to people." He made a low, growling sound in his chest. "My birth mother wants to know if you'll come to dinner. After the memorial, I mean."

Quill startled. "Who... which of them is your mother?"

Tunuk glowered back at him. "Uruphi."

Oh. Quill remembered her, in particular. He'd practiced his fum-bly Alojan on her in the library the evening after he and Karimo and Primate Lamberto had arrived. She'd taught him a dozen new words, brought him Ronqu-style lemonade flecked with grated apple, and told him not to say *sapa*, the formal term, anymore, and if he did not mind, she would stop calling him *apprentice*.

"If she wants me there," he said, "I'll be there. If it's all right with you, I mean."

"She does," Tunuk said, taking the narrow iron steps three at a time. "I don't care. She says the day after Salt-Sealing ends. Don't wear that." He huffed. "When are they interring your friend?"

A lump built in Quill's throat. "I don't know. I'm still waiting for... I haven't gotten his ashes." Quill wasn't sure what to do for his friend. The ashes could go in the columbarium of the chapter house in Arlabecca, possibly... in a city where Karimo had never lived, in a place Quill seldom had cause to visit. Or perhaps he could take them back to Ragale, back to the tower, the place Karimo had called home. A place Quill wasn't sure he could return to.

Tunuk stopped outside a door on the top floor. "Well, you have a conflict the day after Salt-Sealing. I'm sorry for your loss, for what it's worth," he went on in an annoyed tone. "I don't like your friend, obviously, but I also didn't much like my nest-father, so I understand where you're at. This is Yinii's library." He shoved open the door and leaned inside. "She's in there. Don't," he added, "make her sadder." And Tunuk strode back the way they'd come.

Quill watched him go a moment, trying to sort out what had just happened and whether it was friendly. He went into the library and found it dark. "Yinii?" he called. "Are you in here?" A faint light glowed beyond the curve of the near shelves, and he walked toward it.

Yinii sat at the foot of more shelves, an array of books spread out before her. Her regular eyes were closed, and the third eye between her horns was open, glinting in the golden light the ink threw as it crawled off the pages and over her hands. Her breathing came, soft and raspy, along a beat he couldn't hear. For a moment, he stood watching her.

And then her eye blinked. The ink flooded off her hands onto the books again, and Yinii shot to her feet as the motes of light went out and the room plunged into darkness. "Oh!" she cried. "Quill! Sorry! I didn't hear you come in. Oh, bother—the lights." He heard her bustle past him, before the Borsyan lamps at the ends of the shelves burst one by one into brightness. She looked back down the row, green eyes open now, midnight eye shut. "Sorry," she said again. "Did you need something?"

"I meant to say yesterday," he said, "that I'm sorry about your aunt. The reza."

Yinii flushed. "Thank you. I'm sorry about...about your friend." She wet her mouth, as if she was going to speak, but Quill pressed on, not wanting to discuss the murder or the attacks, Karimo or any of it. Not now, not with her.

"I had a question." Quill looked around at the shelves and shelves of books. "Maybe two."

"What about?"

"I have to research something," he said slowly, "and I'm not sure how. I need to find out what the phrase 'Those who sow deception must reap only death' comes from. And I'm not sure where to—"

"*The Precepts of Bekesa,*" Yinii answered. She bit her lip. "Sorry. You weren't done. But that's what it's from. I don't know which translation, but we could check. What do you need it for?"

Quill blinked at her. "You . . . you know it?"

She nodded, charms tinkling. "It's an ancient Khirazji instructional text. The original—or, I mean, the oldest one we have—is in the back, in the panel room where we can keep the moisture and temperature right. It's delicate and we don't have a papyrus specialist. You don't need that, right?"

Quill slid into a chair, thoughts rattling with the sense that he had all the pieces to solve this, but they wouldn't go together. *What's there to solve?* he thought. *You don't even know that.*

But *The Precepts of Bekesa* was the book Karimo had been reading, the one he kept quoting at Quill. That had to mean something. "Can I just see the newer one?"

Yinii disappeared into the shelves and came back with a book. "Did you wash? Your hands?" He shook his head. "That's . . . It's fine. Just don't touch the pages, all right?"

She opened the book and leafed through it to a point near the middle, turning it toward him and laying it flat. It was a reproduction of a Khirazji painting. Two men in long robes—leopard skins over their shoulders, star glyphs above their heads—stood on one side of a table, while a woman in a narrow dress stood on the other, the wisdom spirits Djutubai, Alletet, and Phaseran stacked behind her, peacock, lioness, and beetle heads smug and certain as they knotted reeds into a symbol.

On the table between them lay a form that was almost human—almost, in fact, the same as the woman in the narrow dress. But the outline of the body was traced in green, not black, and the eyes were so wide that their pupils did not touch the edges. There were bowls beneath the table brimming with more green. Another bowl of red was in the standing woman's hands.

"These glyphs are the proverb." Yinii tapped a line of pictures inked along the side of the woman's head. " 'Those who sow deception must reap only death, for though Pademaki'—that's the river god, the one they counted kingship through—'for though Pademaki has said you shall not kill the seven-souled, Khirazj is the field you must protect from the fire.'" She wrinkled her nose. "This is from the end of the civil wars they had, if that's not clear. 'Seven-souled' just means people. You're not supposed to murder people—I mean, that's sort of standard."

"What are they doing?" Quill asked, looking at the images.

"Oh, that's meant to be a changeling on the table," Yinii said. "They're bleeding it. The glyph on the bowls says 'blood.'"

"What's the rest of it say?"

Yinii came around beside him where she could read it right side up. "'I have entered into the fire and have come forth from the water, I have set the salt against my tongue and the iron to my hand, and done the same unto the changeling. I have called: Come, Alletet. Come, Djutubai. Come Phaseran. Light your wisdom upon my souls, and unlock the secret here. For the Venom of Khirazj is the trap of the changeling, and the Venom of Changelings is the trap of Khirazj.'"

Quill stared at the men with the stars on their heads. "I don't think this is what I needed. I don't even understand what that last part means."

"It's confusing," Yinii admitted. "For instance, this word. 'Venom.' *Nit.* It can mean a *lot* of things depending on context, and if you're not ancient Khirazji, you don't always know the context."

"What can it mean?"

Yinii ticked words off on her fingers. "Venom, flood, yeast, blood pouring out of a wound, a vase sometimes. Sometimes the ink knows. But *this* one, it's always translated 'venom' in this context, I do know that. The Venom of Changelings is a poison. Do you know it?"

Quill frowned. "That's...Is that the one Redolfo Kirazzi used? Wiped people's minds and things? Is that real?"

"I don't think it wipes minds," Yinii said. "I think it's supposed to make you remember things that aren't real. This is a recipe for that. 'Four parts the root of lotus, pounded in milk, strained well. One-third the salts of copper. Eight parts the...' I guess it's blood here—'the blood of a changeling, dried; boiled in water and cooled; put to the veins directly.'" Yinii pointed at the man. "That's why he has a knife, I suppose. But I don't know for sure if that means *this* says the Venom of Khirazj."

"What...Why is that..." He covered his eyes with one hand. "I don't need a recipe. This is interesting but it's not what I needed."

"Sorry," she said quietly. Then: "Also I did the translation wrong, since you asked for the other bit. *Djaulbashra*—that's the bit that they sometimes translate 'those who sow deception,' which is literal, but it sort of ruins the meter. Also saying 'changeling' is clearer."

Quill looked up, alarmed. "'Those who sow deception' is Khirazji for *changelings*?"

Yinii nodded. "The line is sort of an admonition. That it's a duty to kill changelings, even though there were arguments that they might be people—'seven-souled'—and therefore subject to Pademaki's proscription of murder. Bekesa—he's the priest writing this— argues because of the level of destruction they'd caused in the civil wars, they're exempt. Khirazj got them first," she added. "They... defeated them then, but...obviously it didn't stick."

Quill stared at the picture. Why had Karimo cried out about changelings? Maybe he *had* been mad, thinking Obigen and Dolitha were changelings impersonating those two officials. Quill tried to remember if he'd seen any sign of delusions or fantasies...Could they have *been* changelings?

You are going well off the path, he thought. How could there be changelings wandering about, as if there were no wall of salt and iron and martyrs in the way? And if there were, if that was what Karimo had done, why would he have killed himself?

Before he could say anything, Yinii added, "Amadea took the translated copy this morning. Did she get it for you?"

"Wait," Quill said. "*Amadea* came and took this book? This morning?"

Yinii nodded. "This one and a few more. Someone needed them. Was it you?"

Quill fumbled with the pieces he'd picked up, tried to fit things together: The head archivist's pointed questions before she chose to summon Amadea. Amadea's swift denial during his statement that Ibramo's presence meant anything at all. Amadea, distracted and withdrawn all the rest of the way back. Amadea coming to get a book Quill didn't even know he needed. Tunuk snarling like a guard dog when Quill suggested she might be hiding things.

What did she know? What was he missing?

"Can I trust you?" he blurted.

Surprise and concern overtook Yinii's pretty features. "What's wrong?"

Everything. Everything was wrong. He felt as if he were going mad. Karimo had killed someone and then died shouting about changelings—*why?* Every time Quill thought he found a clue, a hint that there was some reason buried in all this lunacy, it would somehow slip through his fingers, leaving him with nothing but more questions.

Yinii was looking at him, worried and expectant. He couldn't pour all that on her. If he told her—or Tunuk—that he was trying to prove the murderer of their loved ones didn't do it—*somehow*—and he didn't have proof—*proof of what? That they deserved death?*—saints and devils, Lord on the Mountain—

Eyes on the task, brother, he thought. *You* do *have a clue.*

"This might be a little delicate," he said carefully, "but what I want to know is why is everyone so concerned with Ibramo Kirazzi being the one who made the requests?"

Yinii's mouth went small. "What gives you that idea?"

Quill bit back his frustration. "I know they are. People have asked me if it was Ibramo, and no one said why. Is it to do with Amadea?"

Yinii flushed red and pressed her mouth shut briefly, as if she were biting down on the answer. "Does it matter?"

"It might," he said, trying to keep his voice calm. "It might matter a lot: I saw Ibramo Kirazzi the night of the murders. I think he made the requests."

For a long moment, she sat there, biting her lip. The one person he'd trusted in Arlabecca—was Amadea in the middle of all this? He'd never know, he realized, watching Yinii wrestle with her answer. These people would protect Amadea to their dying breath, and everyone would go on thinking Karimo had been a madman and a monster, and Quill would never know *why.*

But then Yinii leaned in. "I *only* know rumors. And even then barely anything. But I know who does know. And I'll bet he'd tell."

＊＊　▆◆▆　＊＊

Yinii had not gone next door for breakfast that morning but instead sat in her room, considering her things and how she might pack them up ready to take west to Maqama, the city that stood over the Orozhandi cavern-towns. Three chests, she thought. Maybe four. The books took up a lot of space.

But thinking of leaving quickly overwhelmed her—she didn't want to go. If the reza made her leave, she couldn't take her library with her. She was supposed to go again to the House of Unified Wisdom that morning, but she'd fled to the library instead, and while she felt guilty for helping Quill instead of praying over Reza Dolitha once more, she told herself this was more pressing.

And, she thought, a little guilty, far more interesting.

As close as Stavio was to the peak of his alignment, there was nowhere he could be except in the dormitory. Bijan was leaving as they approached. He looked exhausted, his dark skin creased beneath his darker eyes.

"If this is about the flail," he said to Quill, "Mireia said she'd have the paperwork later today."

"I don't need it right off," Quill said. "We're looking for Stavio."

Bijan sighed. "He's inside. I'm going to get him some fry bread. 'The good kind.'"

"We can keep him company while you're gone," Yinii offered.

"Saints and devils, yes, please," Bijan said. "I don't know what's going on this time, but it seems like he and Zoifia both are peaking ahead of schedule."

"Are alignments always this hard?" Quill asked as Bijan headed down the hall and Yinii went to open the door. "Or shouldn't I ask that?"

"They...can be," Yinii said. She paused, hand on the doorknob. It was hard to talk about, harder to explain. But all of a sudden she heard herself saying, "It's like...when you're in a bad mood about something. Something's worrying you or making you sad or angry, and everything comes back to that something. Like you keep falling into a hole and you can't get out. Some things that put you in a bad mood are smaller than others. Some things are easier to set aside. And sometimes you just start... digging the hole deeper and bigger because the hole's the only thing that feels right."

Quill was staring at her, and she slipped a guilty hand up to touch Saint Asla's amulet. "It's hard to explain."

"No, it makes sense." He shrugged. "I mean, at least as much sense as I suspect it can make without experiencing it myself."

Stavio wasn't in the front room or the kitchen, and a quick glance showed Bijan had cleared the rooms of anything bronze—candlesticks, a beaded hanging, a big bowl that usually sat next to the fireplace, all missing. All the fixtures were iron in their apartment, of course, but she found herself checking knobs and nails and other bits of metal as she crossed to the small door on the left side of the room. She knocked softly.

"Stavio? It's Yinii. Can I come in?"

A moan answered her. She glanced back at Quill, and pushed in.

This room was small and sparsely appointed. A bed, a table, two chairs—one for sitting and one Ashtabari-style, for leaning on. Stavio was draped across this one, a plate of broken cakes and a goblet on the table before him. He looked up at her, annoyed.

"Odidunu," Stavio said wearily, "little brother, don't you two come in here and tell me you want anything. I'm too tired and everything is so dull." He glowered at the blank wall beside him. "This room is terrible and I don't know why we have it."

"For days like this?" she suggested.

"For *me*. It's not fair. Bijan only has rubies."

"Corundums," Yinii corrected.

"Where's he gonna slap into a ruby?" Stavio went on. "Hm? They all came from over the Wall! Lock the workroom door and stay away from fancy houses. Easy like *that*." He snapped his fingers. "But me? I have to suffer. And *his* only happens once in two years."

"For a month," Yinii reminded him. "Yours is over faster. And if you didn't have it, you couldn't have the bronze."

Stavio scowled at her, his tentacles coiling. "Stop trying to sound like Amadea. What are you doing here, odidunu?"

"We wanted some information," Yinii said.

"Then read a book. I'm busy dying in this *ugly* room and I don't need an audience."

"Gossip," Quill clarified. "Why do you all hate Ibramo Kirazzi?"

Stavio's gaze slid back to Quill, speculative and wary. "Why do you want to know that? Who said 'hate'?"

"Because we're curious," Yinii answered. "I only know the bits Zoifia told me, and I bet you know more."

"I don't talk about us to outsiders."

"He's all right."

Stavio leveled a look at her. "*Really?*"

Yinii's cheeks burned. "This murder. There might be a connection to the Kirazzis. Should we be worried? Should Amadea?"

Stavio regarded each of them, back and forth, as if weighing their story against Amadea's. But the room was dull and his tentacles all snarled against one another as if anxious for motion. He huffed a sharp breath through his nostrils and drew himself up on his elbows.

"All right," Stavio said. "So I know this: you look at Amadea and you think, there's nothing on this side of the Wall or the other that could hurt that woman. 'Unflappable,' that's the word. But that's now. That's not always been true. When she came here, you could tell, I hear. It seeped off her, such sadness. She never wanted to say why, and it's Amadea—no one wants to make her say. But the reason is that duke, no question, so he can lick the Wall."

"How do you know?" Yinii asked.

"*Everybody* knows." Stavio leaned forward, tentacles lashing. Flecks of bronze blazed in his eyes. "You want a story, so shush and let me tell a story. She was a ward of a fancy house. You can tell when she talks, but that much I *know* from Bijan. Some friend of the Kirazzis or cousins maybe—it's not important, she doesn't talk about it. But anyway, here she is, pretty orphan girl, growing up in a fancy highborn house with people who want to have this ornament to their charity, this well-spoken child they *bought*.

"So picture it: She meets little Ibramo Kirazzi. They play, they grow up, then Redolfo Kirazzi dumps devils all over his house and his business and just about ruins everything for all the Kirazzis now until forever and back over the Wall by digging up his Grave-Spurned Princess and building his sorcerer-glass army.

"That family that bought her? They know how it goes. They don't know Redolfo from the fishes anymore, and they don't want her around that boy. But she's Amadea. What's she going to do? Leave him to be miserable and alone? She gives up everything to stay with him. She's in love, and maybe he is a little too.

"But then, oh see, Redolfo hangs. Lireana is gone—I still say they put her in the oubliette. They're old enough to marry, settled enough, things are serious. Maybe they leave all this behind. You can see her, can't you? Being so sure. And then the emperor decides maybe he doesn't want to salt Kirazzi down to the stones. Maybe things can get fixed here, if Ibramo marries his daughter and passes the dukedom to the uncle. Kirazzi bows, bends—just enough—ties itself to Ulanitti so there can be forgiveness and a future for the sons and daughters of the river.

"Except, oh, Ibramo Kirazzi is in love with our sweet Amadea." Stavio pinned Yinii with a prim sort of gaze. "But you can't have Noniva's smile and the sugar dates both.

"So he *drops* her. Like a hot stone. Never looks back. And she comes to the archives, lives like she's sequestered, pretends it never, ever happened. But you notice. You see things not sitting right. A Kirazzi request comes in, everyone's looking at her. The empress retrieves a mask, Amadea is very busy in her office. Ibramo Kirazzi knows better than to ever cross that threshold, and good riddance." He settled back, curled his tentacles in close. "Like I say: he can lick the Wall, that duke."

Yinii hugged both twisted fists close to her chest. "That's awful." Guilt pawed at her like ink begging off the page. She shouldn't have asked.

"And now?" Quill said. "Does she talk to him ever?"

"He's the consort-prince," Stavio said. "And she's got a speck of pride. They don't mix, and they don't need to."

"I've never seen him here," Yinii offered. "I always assumed... Well, like Stavio said, I don't think it ended well."

Beyond the little room, the front door banged open followed by a bellowed, "*Stavio!*"

"Sorcha!" Stavio snarled. "I don't want to talk to you!"

Zoifia appeared in the entrance to the little room. Her blond curls, always full and fine, stuck out like a bramble, crackling with sparks. Her brown eyes looked too golden, too wild. Yinii swept the room again, looking for errant bronze.

"I know where it is," Zoifia said.

"Where what is?" Stavio snapped, one tentacle nearly catching Yinii on the horn.

"I'm winning our bet."

"We don't have a bet," Stavio scoffed.

But they did, Yinii realized. The bet Zoifia had made with Stavio over whether the Kirazzi bronzes were full of something. Zoifia's eyes seemed to glow, like bronze in a crucible. Yinii took a careful step toward her. This was bad, very bad.

"Zoifia?" she said. "Why don't you sit down?"

Zoifia licked her lips, her gaze flicking from Stavio to Yinii to Quill as if they were nothing more than corners of the room. "I figured it out and I figured out what to do, so we're going to find out and I'm getting that halvmeta. Now, are you coming?"

Stavio went still a moment. "Where you going, sorcha? The workroom's all locked up."

Zoifia's fists bunched, once, twice. "Then I won't wait. Not for you. I'll find it. Now. It's fine. I'm fine." She looked at Yinii, her eyes too bronze and too blank. "I have to go."

And she shot off, her long legs launching her far ahead of Yinii's grasping hands and out the door. "Zoifia!"

"She can't get into the bronze room," Stavio said, alarmed.

"The Pit," Yinii said. "She could break into the Pit." And in the jumble of the sorting facility there would be enough bronze for Zoifia to entomb herself completely. Yinii touched her medals, turned to Quill.

"I'll get Amadea," he said.

"No," Yinii said. "Stavio, *you* have to go get Amadea, you can't go in there. Find Amadea and anyone available who can hold Zoifia down. Quill, come with me. Quickly." She grabbed his arm and ran toward the sorting facility, the vast room they affectionately called "the Pit."

The Imperial Archives contained treasures of every nation, every protectorate, every people, both ancient and new. What had begun as a safeguard against time and grief had burgeoned into a massive undertaking. Imperial Majesties came and went and paid the archives no mind or made them into special, precious projects—but regardless the treasures came in, wanting to be preserved and protected. The sorting facilities—always understaffed—became a jungle of past and present, important and trivial. Generalists sorted, did first-level preservation, and sent likely artifacts to individual workshops and specialists, but the project remained overwhelming.

The first door to the Pit, an iron-and-wood gate, hung open on the spiraling staircase, its lock picked. Yinii hurried down and down and down. The second door, at the foot of the stairs—layers of bronze and steel and glass—was open as well. There was a hole through the bronze the size of a fist.

Yinii's pulse sped as she burst in. The Pit was enormous, a room the length of the entire archives, two stories high. Every wall was lined with scaffolding, packed tightly with artifacts and crates and bundled treasures. The open floor between held a score of worktables, every one of them empty. The archivists had stopped work for the day.

Yinii had no sooner entered than the ink noticed her.

If she had to explain it to Quill, she would have said it was like walking into a room and knowing every person in there was trying to say something to her. A hundred little children reaching for her robes. Ten thousand needles *just* touching her skin. A shift of attention and there would be the grapevine withering on the hillside, the char on the kiln, the root pounded fine, and uncountable hands shaking in uncountably personal ways. She couldn't ignore it, and she needed to ignore it.

"There!" Quill shouted, turning her to the right, to the narrow end of the Pit. Zoifia clung to the scaffolding, scaling it like a spider up a wall. Sparks arced off her, burrowing into the collection.

"Zoifia!" Yinii shouted as she started running, as a hiss of plumbago ink sang the song of the mines.

Zoifia hauled herself up over one of the levels, beside something bulbous wrapped in cloth. Yinii saw her arms were already crawling with fluid bronze, bits scavenged off whatever she'd passed.

"Get down!" Yinii called.

"But they're up here," Zoifia said. "I remembered. They're so loud." She disappeared into the crowded scaffolding as Yinii stopped before it.

A lift—Yinii searched the scaffolding for one of the mechanical lifts the Pit archivists used to raise and lower heavy artifacts. But all the ones she could see had been raised to their pulleys and locked flat against the scaffolds. She traced the ropes, looking for an end, but as Quill caught up to her, she gave up. It would take too long.

"She can't touch the bronzes," she told Quill. "She's right on the edge and she's going to do something dangerous, so we have to climb up there, and she *can't touch the bronzes*, understand?"

Quill nodded, looking up at the scaffolds. Without waiting for Yinii, he ran at the scaffold, leaping to catch the second stage and pulling himself up. Yinii grabbed hold of one of the posts, setting her foot against a crate and scaling bit by bit.

A codex nudged against her thoughts with a hundred different hands. The razor-fine whisper of an ink from a squid she had no name for. Yinii squeezed her day-eyes shut and thought about Zoifia. She wasn't going to be fast enough—and Zoifia would be so much faster, full of bronze and promise and with nothing to lose. She had to slow her down.

"How do you know it's Bikoro dynasty?" Yinii shouted.

A heartbeat passed, and Zoifia stuck her head out, frowning down at Yinii as she climbed the scaffold. "They're *bitter* with arsenic."

"What's the arsenic for?" Yinii asked, finding a handhold between two crates.

Zoifia shook her head, almost a tic. "An accident. The Bikoro dynasty, this king, some early king, took a territory...I don't know, somewhere west. And whatever his name was—"

"Shenqare," Yinii supplied automatically.

Zoifia scowled at her. "Why are you asking if you already know?"

"I just know that part!" Yinii protested. "And he took Yojiath."

"Then I guess you can finish it, book-brain."

"What happened in Yojiath?" Quill shouted. "Why arsenic?"

Zoifia's attention snapped to him. "The copper deposits were contaminated. Very rich, but also full of arsenic. You can treat copper with arsenic and pretend it's bronze, which is what *Yojiath* did. Or you can take it home and smelt it right. Khirazj was always swimming in tin, and once they had that copper, they went wild and..." She smiled, manic. "Oh wait. I'll show you."

Quill had nearly reached her, but Zoifia ducked out of sight again. Yinii heard him curse. He pulled himself up to the railing, just as Yinii got her feet onto the boards. He edged quickly down the railing to help haul her over.

"No!" Yinii said. "Grab her, before——"

Behind Yinii, the lift gave a *clunk*, as the platform dropped flat. Zoifia, sparks snapping, bronze oozing over her arms, gave Yinii a wicked grin as she hauled two cloth-wrapped bundles onto it. She wrenched a switch and began dropping toward the floor.

"No!" Yinii lunged for the rope. It skimmed her palm, burning her skin, and she snatched her hand back.

"Here's how you know a Bikoro dynasty bronze," Zoifia called, hauling one of the two bundles off with preternatural strength. "All that copper, all that bronze, you have time to practice. To get *fancy*. So you get *detail*." She let the statue settle and went for the other one.

Yinii looked down the length of the Pit at the door. They needed Amadea.

"I think I can jump," Quill said.

"We're a full story up," Yinii said. "You'll break your ankles. We have to climb again." But she'd no more than gotten her leg over the railing when Zoifia yanked the coverings off, eyes blazing now.

"Well met, babies," she purred.

The statues were a matched set—two kneeling Khirazji queens in high-collared necklaces and heavy curled wigs, their hands in fists hollowed out to hold spears or flags, their knees settled on wide wooden bases. Zoifia had been right—the faces were wonderfully detailed. The right-hand queen's pouting mouth and full cheeks flush with youth and severity, the left-hand's soft smirk and delicately arched brow all wisdom and wit. On the right, she wore a scorpion, the symbol of a queen-consort. On the left, the triple heron feather of a queen regnant.

Quill's eyes went to the rope. "Here." He climbed over Yinii, grabbing hold of it to slide down. Yinii followed his lead, hand over hand down the rope.

"Is that Neveraka?" Yinii asked, trying to distract Zoifia again. "And Ma'aniphis Wersha? Or Ma'aniphis Sherit?

Zoifia scowled up at her. "Stop interrupting! This isn't about you." She grinned at the statues. "Let's find out what's inside."

As Yinii's feet hit the floor, Zoifia slapped a hand to the back of each statue's head and dived into the spiral.

The sparks leaping in her hair became tiny bright bolts of lightning as the bronze softened, lurched up her arms, onto her legs. From the unsorted artifacts came a groaning, a crackling, a thrumming full of energy and heat and life as bits of bronze woke and stirred, calling out to Zoifia. The gathering storm around her began to *pull*, and suddenly the storage stacks were shifting, sliding. A buckle, a shield, a sword, a latch—bits of bronze broke free of slumber and leapt for Zoifia, becoming soft, becoming liquid, sweeping around her like a shroud of metal. Climbing and clawing toward her throat.

Zoifia's eyes blazed bronze now, her expression twitching between ecstasy and terror as the metal surged and grasped and swathed her. She opened her mouth and molten bronze began to pour out, streaming into the remains of the statues and swords and buckles swirling over her, even as more bits of metal broke free of the jumble and plunged into the growing shroud. A desperate sort of whimper echoed oddly from her throat.

"Can we...can we pull her off?" Quill asked.

"Don't touch her!" Yinii cried.

Because Zoifia was the bronze and the bronze was Zoifia and separating them would be like lifting one water-damaged page from another—Zoifia could be split, could be shattered, but they couldn't leave her this way, and in the presence of the spiral, all the ink was roaring like the tide, ready to drag Yinii down, ready to yank open that gaping maw in her chest—

Suddenly, Amadea was there, in front of Zoifia, cupping her cheeks in both hands, carefully avoiding the streak of bronze down her chin.

"Zoifia," she said sharply. "Zoifia, can you hear me?"

Zoifia's voice rang like a great bell as she answered, "Go away. I'm fine."

"I know you are." Amadea moved a hand around the back of Zoifia's head, like she was a newborn child. "You are one of the finest bronze specialists I know. Who could be so fine as you?"

"Go away," Zoifia said. Tunuk crept up behind Zoifia, every inch of him as tense as Yinii. She wondered how many bones were calling in the Pit.

"You're the specialist," Amadea said, calm and steady. "Zoifia Kestustis. Foremost expert on cast bronze works and still so young. What are you going to be next, I wonder? Zoifia?" Amadea's hand moved to squeeze Zoifia's shoulder, daring the molten edge of the bronze that she had no protection against. "What's the tin content of this?"

Zoifia's throat worked. The flow of bronze stopped. "I'm... twelve percent..."

"It's," Amadea said. "It's twelve percent. Say that."

"I don't want to."

"Zoifia? Zoifia? Natlunkuluchik?" Amadea smoothed the sparking curls back. "Doesn't your mother call you that? Little Sparrow?"

Tears of bronze rimmed Zoifia's eyes. "I don't know."

"You told me that once," Amadea said. "Someone called me it once and that's all the Borsyan I knew, and you told me that your mother calls you that, too. Little Sparrow."

"It's just what you call little girls who don't stop twittering," Zoifia said. "We're not alike."

"We're not," Amadea agreed. "There's only one you, Zoifia. Natlunkuluchik. Zoifia. Come back."

"I can't. I don't want to. I'm fine."

Yinii shivered down to her toes and felt her own eyes fill with tears. The inks lost in the Pit whispered to her, and she thought of the feeling of ink in her throat, a tide of black and green and red flooding over her, the fire to make more and the waters all smothering. In the moment, the spiral was so terrifying and so right. Words were hard and people were hard but the ink sang to her and it always made sense. And if you could just fold yourself into it, then everything would be right and sensible and safe. *Sometimes you just start digging the hole deeper because nothing else feels right.*

"You can," Amadea said. "You're stronger than this, Zoifia. Saints and devils, you're stronger than this. And you might not want to, but think about tomorrow. Think about a week from now. Think about the Festival of Salt-Sealing and ringbreads and kaibo and beetroot soup. Think about dancing."

"I don't like beetroot soup," Zoifia murmured, and the bronze ebbed a little more. "Just because I'm Borsyan, you think I like beetroot."

Yinii watched Amadea's shoulders relax, though she didn't let go of Zoifia. "You like shufuan-style buns. Dumplings full of lamb and garlic. You like kaibo and nut wine. You like soured cream on your bread. You love the bronze, but you love Zoifia too—bright and brash and bold. I know you. I know this." She embraced Zoifia, holding her close behind the head, even as the other woman's hands remained lost in the shapeless shimmer of the Khirazji statues. "You can't have all those things and be the bronze. Zoifia. Natlunkuluchik. Come back to us."

Zoifia went stiff as a rod. The bronze in the scaffolds popped and snapped, as if it might all tear free at once, more threads of lightning arcing from her skin.

Then just as suddenly she collapsed, the bronze flowing off her, separating, remembering what it was and what it was supposed to be. Neveraka and Ma'aniphis, still and firm on their bases. The clatter of fallen weapons, the rattle of latches and buckles.

Tunuk lunged forward and grabbed Zoifia, yanking her backward, away from the scatter of metal, wrapping his long shadowy body around her.

"Is she all right?" Yinii looked up at Stavio clutching the railing two floors up, tentacles coiling over the edge as if he might leap over. "Saints and devils, blessed Noniva, *is she all right?*"

"She's all right!" Amadea called back. Zoifia wouldn't meet her gaze. She was paler than ever and shaking. "She's getting sequestered," Amadea said more gently.

Zoifia wrapped her arms around herself. "Tell Stavio," she said softly.

"He knows," Amadea said. "Tunuk, can you carry her up?"

Tunuk gave Amadea a dark look but scooped a shaking Zoifia up without protest. But Zoifia turned, twisted as if she meant to escape. "No, wait!"

"Zoifia, please," Amadea said, and Yinii flinched. When Amadea spoke like that, it didn't matter who it was to, Yinii felt guilty.

"Wait," Zoifia pleaded. "Open it. I won. Tell Stavio."

"Open what?"

"The statue, the base." She gestured at the two queens, now roughly as they'd been before. "There's something inside. I bet Stavio, and I'm right. I felt it. It's nothing good."

Amadea cast a look back at Yinii and Quill, and the statues between them. She gave the slightest of nods.

Yinii approached Neveraka, the queen with the scorpion crown. She set a foot against the base, and both hands against her head. The metal was still warm to the touch with Zoifia's magic. She shoved against the statue's head with all her might—once, twice, three times. *Crack.*

The statue came away from its base. Quill helped Yinii tilt it back, revealing a dark hole at the bottom. There was something in there. She pulled the broken base down farther and reached in, feeling several lumpy paper-wrapped packages. She took one out and unwrapped it to find a cloudy glass jar full of some sort of green powder. Yinii held it up to the light and gave it a little shake.

"What is that?" Quill asked.

"It's blood," Zoifia said, a touch of pride and her earlier mania in her voice. "It's powdered changeling blood."

CHAPTER SIX

Uruphi yula Manco del Urquanaio," the Paremi read. "An astronomer. Partner of the Manco nest."

"Correct." The Alojan woman looked down at Richa from her seat opposite him, her glowing eyes dim, her shadowy skin grayish. She wore a traditional dip-dyed shawl that shaded from bright red to deep garnet to a dark, roasty brown.

"Sapa, thank you for coming in," Richa said with the Alojan honorific. "You have my condolences."

Uruphi inclined her head. "I appreciate that, vigilant. Well, what can I tell you that the others haven't?"

An Alojan family, a nest, consisted of multiple partners and their shared children, who would then go off and join their own partners to form other nests. An Alojan had the mother who birthed them, nest-mothers who raised them, fathers who shared a sort of partible paternity, and nest-fathers who came to the family after their birth. The Manco nest of Arlabecca was eight adults and two children, of whom only Uruphi, Obigen, and one other were present the night of the attacks. Uruphi had been in the room when Obigen died.

And her story essentially repeated the one the guests had recited the day before. Repetitions and all.

Richa fiddled with his stylus. "I'm curious: Why did you stay when your partners left?"

Uruphi sighed. "Obigen's ambition is...was growing intense. Not all of us have the stomach for politics. Jinjir, Senca, and Vari took the children out to buy changeling masks for Salt-Sealing.

Bayan and Alzari went to have dinner out. I think Kulum managed for all of a quarter hour before he couldn't exchange another empty pleasantry. Poor dear," she added. "He's feeling particularly guilty."

Richa had already spoken to Kulum, already seen the poor man's guilt and grief at being upstairs, alone, unaware of what was happening to his partner in the front room. It made Richa think of Quill the day before, trying to pinpoint the moment when he'd made an error that led to Karimo killing these people.

Richa paused, remembering Quill's testimony. Ibramo Kirazzi walking away from the Manco house in the black mask. "When did Ibramo Kirazzi leave the party?"

"You're mistaken," Uruphi said. "The empress came and Lady Sigrittrice, but the consort-prince sent his regrets. He was in Sestina with his cousin, the Duchess Kirazzi, that evening. He said he would not be back until... well, until today."

Richa frowned. "The empress, what color was her mask?"

Uruphi sighed. "The *green*. Obigen was furious it wasn't the gold."

The imperial family had a number of taboos that they'd been following since long before the Wall was sealed, but the masks were the most visible: The gold to be the face of the empire. The green to signal she was only Beneditta Ulanitti.

The black to mark the wearer invisible, to make clear they weren't to be approached or acknowledged. Richa thought of Quill's claim that he'd seen the consort-prince wearing the black mask the night of the murder.

Everyone in the imperial family wore some variant of the mask. If Ibramo Kirazzi wasn't in Arlabecca, then it would be a matter of finding out who among them might be mistaken for the tall Khirazji consort-prince.

Or maybe, he thought, *it's a matter of finding out if Ibramo Kirazzi was lying about where he was that night.* He thought of Amadea's expression when Quill mentioned the consort-prince—a sudden, very intentional stillness. And then that clumsy rebuttal, that twist away from the matter at hand.

"None of the guests said Obigen invited them," Richa went on. "That it was Primate Lamberto."

"That seems obvious, doesn't it?"

"What do you mean?"

"I mean, those people...they're not friends of ours, clearly. They were there to be convinced of Obigen's canal."

"The second wall."

"I refuse to call it that," Uruphi said plainly. "A barrier, I will grant you—*if* it works, because he still needed to find a way to *confirm* seawater has the necessary concentration to repel the changelings. But a waterway is not a wall." She hitched the shoulder of her wrap up higher. "He had interest simmering. He needed land for staging. And money. Why else would we have allowed Zaverio Maschano past the threshold?"

"Why is that?"

"Don't pretend you don't know, Vigilant," Uruphi chided. "False innocence is unbecoming. The Maschanos are bigots, or at least Zaverio is. If his partner isn't, then she is at least someone I am happy to continue being unacquainted with. The son doesn't give me much hope either, and I don't care if you write all of that down."

"Rosangerda Maschano wasn't there. Was she invited?"

Uruphi folded her long hands together. "It's my understanding," she said delicately, "that the Maschanos are even more uncomfortable with each other's company at the moment than the empress and the consort-prince."

Richa's eyebrows rose. "I haven't heard that gossip. About either of them."

Uruphi waved a hand. "Rumor, I suppose. But you'll notice, in neither case did they attend together. For the empress, I get the impression that's been happening a great deal of late, for one reason or another. People talk."

Richa nodded to himself. "Do you think Obigen might have been keeping anything from you?"

"Never."

"People can be surprising."

Uruphi laughed. "Do you think I saw the moon yesterday, Vigilant? Of course people can be surprising, but I shared a nest with Obigen for twenty years. I loved him and I know his shadow and his searing light—he was a proud man, he could be sullen, he could be intractable and cruel with his words when he was afraid. But I know, too, that he was never one to hide things. He had a thought and he spoke it, which gained him more heartache and trouble than any secret ever could."

Richa finished the interview and retreated to his office, to wait for word from the imperial liaison. He had a number of other cases waiting on him, but this one...this one wouldn't settle. He took a little folding knife from his pocket and plucked a twig, nice and straight, from a small box he kept there. With short, slow cuts, he shaved curls from the twig, keeping his anxious hands busy while he thought.

Hulvia had made it clear that she needed answers. Once the palace was involved, she usually did, and he knew it would be hard to argue in this case that he didn't have them—nine witnesses, the weapon, the motive, the killer's body. It was finished before he'd even started.

And yet...

He turned the twig, began a new row. It was hard to argue that Karimo had not been the killer—but just as hard to argue that Richa had the right motive. Maybe Quill's insistence that Karimo wouldn't so much as swat a wasp was colored by their friendship, but Richa had found nothing that explained why he would have stabbed three people and killed himself. His cadets had found no hint that the boy ever held a seditious thought and nothing to make of the strange statement. Not even Archivist Gintanas recognized it.

He paused. Glanced up at the papers on his desk.

A killer with no motive, victims that all tied to the Imperial Archives, and Amadea Gintanas clearly hiding things. *Clearly* searching through his files.

Twice now, the consort-prince had entered into this—here and not here. Testing the iron with his wife, and maybe not. Known to Amadea Gintanas, but maybe not. He considered Uruphi's rumors—maybe Amadea was sleeping with the consort-prince.

Richa frowned at the little tree. That would explain the look on her face, the denial that it could be Ibramo, maybe even the way she'd walled Richa off. But it didn't so much as touch why a young man with his whole future ahead of him would stab three people and then kill himself.

He was cleaning up the little tree's base when Lady Sigrittrice arrived.

He had no idea how long she'd been standing there, utterly silent and watching him flick bits of wood to the floor through a gilt half mask that covered one eye. Sigrittrice Ulanitti, the empress's grand-aunt, had been a fixture of the imperial government since her elder sister had been crowned fifty years ago, and was now Empress Beneditta's closest adviser. She wore her silver hair in a tidy arrangement of braids, her gown simple and black. As Richa looked up, she stepped into the room.

"Vigilant Langyun," Lady Sigrittrice intoned, as he scrambled to his feet and bowed. "Vigilant Manche said you were very busy with the Manco murders." She looked pointedly at the wood shavings on the floor. "I see she was misinformed."

Richa darted a gaze beyond her to where Hulvia Manche stood, face drawn and tentacles curling around the edges of the door. He nodded at her. "Apologies, Lady Sigrittrice. I was thinking. But since you're here," he hurried on, "I need to ask you some questions."

He caught the tiny shake of Hulvia's head from the corner of one eye, the glitter of the comb that was not regulation at all caught in her dark hair: *Don't you dare, Richa.*

Lady Sigrittrice's dark eyes narrowed, and she considered him, unblinking. "I can't imagine what about."

"The party?" Richa said. "The murders? You were there, you and the empress…you tried to—"

Lady Sigrittrice held up a hand. "I will save you the trouble, Vigilant. The empress and I did attend, but we left before any of this savagery began. Neither of us spoke to the boy. That should be enough."

Richa frowned. "That's…Your pardon, lady, I have five people who swear they saw you both when the murders happened."

Her eyes flicked over Richa. "And?"

"Richa," Hulvia said sternly, "Lady Sigrittrice is here for the sealed statements."

He frowned. "They're not finished. And, your ladyship, if you could just—"

"I'm very busy, Vigilant," Sigrittrice said. "As is the empress. If you have five people who say we were there, I think you are better off questioning what happened that might have altered their perceptions." Her dark eyes bored into him. "Given our company at the time, it doesn't seem so very inventive to suggest the Vigilant Kinship look into what sorts of mind-altering substances might have been at play."

"You think people were drugged?"

"I think it makes more sense than calling me a liar, Vigilant." She held out her hand. "The statements, if you please. The empress would prefer this be finished. I will convey them to the Paremi for sealing."

There was nothing Richa could do but hand over the statements. He still had his notes, he thought, as Lady Sigrittrice swept out of his office. He still had questions.

Hulvia's nostrils flared as she slid into the room. "Richa, I swear to Noniva and all the little fishes, do you have any idea what you're fucking around with?"

"No, and neither do you," he said. "Five people say she was there—say she tried to grab the kid when he stabbed the primate. And her answer is that they were all too drugged to know better?"

"Are you sure they weren't?" Hulvia retorted. "Because the burden of proof is pretty damn high if you're going to accuse Lady Sigrittrice of lying, in a case you've got this many witnesses to, plus the killer on the slab."

"A killer with absolutely no motive. The kid had no reason to do this, and every statement I've taken is odd. Doesn't that bother you?" he demanded. "Get *one of them* to talk to me, Hul. You have to."

"You think I want to throw elbows with Lady Sigrittrice?" Hulvia hissed. "You want me to end up chucked over the Salt Wall? I don't like taking no for an answer any more than you, but I will tell you in this particular case, it's an imperial no."

"Don't give me that," he said. "Skip Sigrittrice if you have to, but the damned empress—"

"The damned empress is the damned *empress*," Hulvia said. "Which means if she says it's done, it's done."

"It's not done," Richa said. "And that's not the oath. The oath is we make sure the city's safe, not to make sure we don't ruffle the feathers of the high and mighty."

"Richa," Hulvia said through clenched teeth. "Imperial no. So whatever you think needs to happen, do it fast and *don't tell me*. Maybe you need to hunt down a drug peddler. Maybe you need to talk to the primate about his assistant. There are ways to keep going when you're finished—understand?"

As she left, Richa set the little tree among the forest on the shelf beside his desk, considering his next steps. This case seemed simple, but everything he turned over revealed peculiar complications. A murder might hide a conspiracy. An empress might hide an alibi. An attractive archivist might hide... gods and ancestors only knew what. But he wasn't going to find out if he didn't *look*.

There were a great many things Richa had carried from his previous life to this one—he knew how to be patient; how to watch and to listen and wait for the answers to come to you; how to think about weaknesses and exit points and entries, escape routes and blind spots; how to find the people who bought things, bound wounds, passed messages along, and didn't ask questions; how to look for what lay behind what was in front of you. A murder might hide a conspiracy. A job might hide a trap.

A vigilant might hide a thief.

It had been a long time, and there were a lot of reasons Richa Langyun had left behind a life outside the laws of the empire, a lot of facets of himself he had shed. He could almost convince himself he'd left for noble reasons, for a belief in the empire and the rightness of the Vigilant Mother's aims, but in moments like this, when his oath tested his patience, Richa knew one thing that he would never let go of was a strong distaste for being told to stop asking questions. Regardless of whether the one doing so was a head-breaking thief-lord or the empress herself.

⋯ ⋯

What would Karimo say, Quill thought, if he saw the eight jars of powdered changeling blood on Mireia del Atsina's desk? What bit of dusty wisdom would put perspective on this? What encouragement or admonishment would set Quill's spinning thoughts straight again? He shut his eyes and imagined Karimo beside him, as he'd been in life, looking down at the changeling blood.

This is fucked. That's what he would say. That's what anyone sane would say. Quill himself had said it several times already. Ibramo Kirazzi had engaged the Paremi to recover those statues, looking for changeling blood—and Karimo might have known it. *Those who sow deception must reap only death*, he'd said. *I'll tell you later*, he'd said.

Mireia removed her spectacles, looking up to consider Amadea and Quill instead of the eight jars on the table. "If this was all inside one of the items on the Kirazzi list," she said, "then I assume the vigilants and the castle will have some questions for the Duchess Kirazzi. And I very much doubt she's getting the flail." She fixed her gaze on Quill. "I assume you'll need to contact your client."

"She's not my client," Quill said. He took out Lamberto's ledger and pointed to the pertinent line. "Ibramo Kirazzi requested these things. The primate *lied*."

Mireia sighed. "Of course he did." She gave Amadea a dark look. "Well?"

Amadea cleared her throat and spoke for the first time since they'd entered Mireia's office. "I don't know if we should send for the vigilants just yet."

"*What?*" Quill leapt out of his seat. "How can you say that?"

"We don't know it's changeling blood," Amadea reminded him. "If it is, we don't know if it's related. And dragging the imperial family into this..."

A knock came at the door, and Yinii pushed in with a dish of salt and a pitcher of water. She set both on the table before Mireia. "Here. You mix them and then it should...do things when you add the blood."

"Thank you, dear. Go stand..." She gestured *away*, and poured enough water in to fill the dish of salt halfway. She plucked a stylus from her desk and stirred the mix with its uninked end.

"I'm not saying that we don't need to tell the vigilants at all," Amadea went on, eyes on the head archivist. "I'm saying we don't need to point fingers. *If* it's changeling blood, that doesn't mean anyone knew it was in there. All we know for certain is that these are Redolfo Kirazzi's statues, and there's no need to catch *him* twice with changeling blood."

"A good way to find out is to *ask the consort-prince!*" Quill said.

"Also," Amadea continued to Mireia, as if Quill had never said anything, "we don't have the other artifacts in hand. If this is nefarious, shouldn't we know *how* nefarious?"

"I can't believe I'm hearing this," Quill said. "I would think of all possible things in the archives, short of an actual changeling queen, we should be alarmed most about eight jars of powdered changeling blood. Especially given these murders!"

Now Amadea's attention snapped to him, alarmed and alert, even if she still sounded infuriatingly calm as she replied, "Why do you say that?"

Mireia set the stylus down, the salt water cloudy now. She pulled on a pair of leather gloves and dipped the tip of a spoon into a jar, tapping a small amount of green powder into the dish of salt water.

The green powder hit the liquid with a *pop, pop, pop*. A flash of white light, and then a soft *whoomp* as the blood all caught fire with an eerie greenish flame that quickly went out. A smell that wavered between grass and hot metal filled the office. He heard Amadea draw a sharp breath.

"Well," Mireia said. "That settles that."

"We don't have the other items of the request," Yinii said. "Bijan obviously knows where his is, but I haven't had time to look and neither has Tunuk, not with . . . you know . . . Maybe Amadea's right and we should find everything first."

"If you let them into the archives, they're going to want to search *everything*," Amadea said.

"Then *let them!*" Quill burst out. "You are all acting like this is a nuisance! Like what matters is a bunch of *junk* instead of people *dying!*"

"Everyone *hush*," Mireia said. "This is well outside of the archives' business and it's already caused enough trouble." She set down her spectacles and frowned at the jars again. "Yinii, go and find that book. Tell Tunuk I want the arm too. Quickly."

"You can't *wait*!" Quill couldn't believe he was hearing this. "Ibramo Kirazzi was at that party, he wanted this poison, why are you letting him get away with it?"

"Quill, I know you have a great deal on your mind right now—" Amadea began.

"You're right, I do," Quill shouted. "My best friend killed a man and then himself while saying proverbs about changelings, and everyone wants to pretend like the answer is that I didn't know him—I knew him, I know this wasn't him, and the more we find out, the more everyone pretends all of this makes sense! But now we have a poison that makes people stop being themselves, and you're telling me I'm just stressed!"

Silence filled the little room. None of them spoke.

"Yinii," Amadea said briskly. "Go and tell Tunuk what he needs to know, and try and track down that book." Yinii nodded and hurried from the room, watching Quill as she went.

"Maybe you should go for a walk," Amadea said to him gently.

Quill rounded on her. "Is that all you can say? That's all you do, isn't it? 'Go for a walk.' 'Eat something.' 'Don't pay attention to the clear conspiracy sprouting up around you'!" He heard himself, sounding like a madman, but it was as if he'd lost the reins to his own mouth. "I trusted you. I believed you could fix this. But you're exactly like everyone else: you don't *care* if some orphan gets hurt; you care about keeping powerful people happy." And he stormed from the room, through the entry hall, and out of the Imperial Archives entirely.

He would go for a walk, all right—he would walk right to the Kinship Hall, find Richa, tell him *everything*. Ibramo Kirazzi, plotting some sort of coup, some sort of new rebellion, no doubt. Gathering up changeling blood to make poison and *poison* Karimo. Make him think he was someone else, someone hateful and backward and . . . quoting Khirazji instructional papyri. Quill squeezed his eyes shut. He couldn't stop seeing Karimo dead on the floor.

He couldn't stop seeing Zoifia, slowly swallowed by bronze. If you could talk a person out of the spiral, what else could you talk someone *into*?

Quill stopped, adrift in the middle of a bustling square. He had no proof. None at all. He had pieces, fragments that wouldn't fit together. The Venom of Changelings. Karimo dead on the floor. Karimo quoting Khirazji instructional papyri. Ibramo Kirazzi where he shouldn't be. The bronze statues that weren't on his list. A shrike and the bribes and Primate Lamberto telling him to leave. But he knew. He knew Amadea fit into the middle of it. Hiding *something*.

Maybe two hundred metas worth of something.

This is fucked, he thought. *You are fucked.* No one was listening. No one believed him. They believed Amadea—she'd made him think she cared, but she was using him; she was using so many people to cover this up, whatever it was. *Smearing Karimo's memory just because it's convenient*, he thought. Making Quill look like another maniac. If he went to Richa with this, he'd start talking like Quill was cracking apart. *I think you're getting ahead of yourself.*

Realization crashed down on him like the waters of the fountain falling on the stone heads of the dolphins: he was the only one who knew what Amadea was doing—mostly, almost—and *she* was the only one who would believe him, because she knew it was true. He had to confront her. He had to make her confess. He turned again toward the Imperial Archives. He wasn't crazy; he was fine. Better than fine, even if his chest felt like a yawning hole and his ears buzzed as he walked. He was fine.

<hr />

In the head archivist's office, Amadea watched Quill go with a mounting sense of dread. Mireia waited until the door had closed before she gestured for Amadea to sit down again.

"I find myself concerned," Mireia said, "when my most level-headed archivist is suddenly advocating for extremely foolish things. What are you doing?"

"You know what I'm doing."

"Being willfully naive?"

Amadea had been a generalist for so many years she could count on both hands the number of people she had met in those first days who were still in the archives. She could count on one hand the number of people who knew the secrets she didn't want to face, the sordid tales of Ibramo and Beneditta, of masks and Sestina and Gintanas. Redolfo Kirazzi and memories that she couldn't quite smother.

"Ibramo wouldn't have requested those statues knowing what's inside them," she said firmly.

"Amadea. You don't know *what* he'd do anymore." Mireia folded her hands, looked down her nose at Amadea. "Unless you want to share some reasons for the current gossip that the consort-prince is out of favor?"

"I beg your pardon!"

"Then admit you don't know him anymore. Don't make yourself his shield. This has to go to the vigilants."

"You didn't meet that vigilant—he won't leave anything unexamined," Amadea said. "They start searching, they start asking questions, they find me, find the link back to the Kirazzis—"

"I've never thought you prone to vanity," Mireia said. "But has it occurred to you that no one cares what you did twenty-odd years ago, but they *will* care very much about why we have a trove of changeling blood on our hands? *Especially* when a hotheaded Paremi is shouting about the Venom of Changelings."

"I'm afraid…" Amadea shut her eyes. "I'm afraid he's right. I think. That boy's body, it had a mark on it, the sort of bruise you get from changeling blood. Only it was enormous—someone spent a great deal of poison on him."

Mireia's brows rose. "You told the vigilants? Tell me you told the vigilants."

"I came back to find books to convince the vigilants with," Amadea said defensively. "If I started babbling about changeling blood, why on earth would they take me seriously?" She blew out a breath. "Ibramo wouldn't do this and this *can't* be the source of the poison, but…if it's related?"

They sat in silence a long moment, the stink of the changeling blood clotting the air. "You know the simple way to handle this," Mireia said.

"Give Quill the books to give the vigilants and find a sudden need to be somewhere else," Amadea quipped.

Mireia shrugged. "I suppose there's that. You could leave. Take a pilgrimage to the Salt Wall. Have an urgent letter from a library by the sea. Smooth things out as it does blow over." She regarded Amadea kindly. "But what's that saying of Stavio's? 'You can't have Noniva's smile and the sugar dates both.' That boy doesn't know anything—saints, he's barely got his chin hairs in, and he's the witness to a lot of hideous, confusing violence. Don't dump this on him. He's going to invent answers if he can't find them. Worse, maybe, you don't tell the vigilants yourself and that's going to look all the more suspicious if they do figure it out."

Mireia knew most all of Amadea's secrets and never breathed a one, and more than once, Amadea had turned to the older woman when it was all too much and she needed someone safe to cry to.

But Amadea Gintanas wasn't a girl anymore, and Mireia del Atsina was the head archivist, not merely a seasoned generalist showing a fresh colleague the ways of the archives and a little kindness. And whatever fears were eating her heart, Amadea had a duty to her archivists. She would not break; she would not lose sight of her task; she would not let the past chase her from her duties.

"Let me call the vigilants," Amadea said. "I'll talk to Quill. Make him see sense. I'll...figure out what to tell the vigilants if they ask." There had to be answers that kept her out of trouble, away from heartache. What was Amadea Gintanas for but solving problems and finding answers? She would work this out.

She returned to her office, to the Khirazji books stacked on her desk, and went to pick them up. But as her fingers grazed the leather of the top book, she felt the thread-worn velvet of the pillow instead, the pinch of the needle, the smell of the changeling blood in her nose—hot metal, cut grass—so thick it would never leave, she would smother with that scent in her nose.

The needle goes into the girl's arm with a pop. *"If it doesn't work," he says, "then we'll try again. There's a good girl."*

Ibramo's in the doorway; the girl's shaking her head; he's going to do something rash, dangerous. He can't, he shouldn't. It's dark. It's hot. She's not breathing, or is she? Where is she? The pillow with the roses on it flies through the air, chasing Ibramo off.

"*That does work quicker,*" a voice murmurs. "*Who knew? We have enough for another?*"

"*Patience, my Shrike,*" Redolfo replies.

Amadea yanked her hand back with a stifled cry and a curse she didn't speak. She pressed both hands to her face, then against either shoulder, a reassurance there was no needle, no Redolfo, no Shrike. No need for the panic swelling in her chest, telling her to run, run, run, before all these miseries caught up to her again.

They're already catching up, a little voice in her thoughts whispered. Requests from Ibramo. Redolfo's poisons. Changeling verses. Gaspera—

Gaspera on horseback, eyeing Lireana in her fine armor beside wicked Fastreda.

Gaspera in the Kinship Hall, no sign she had ever stood beside a usurper.

Amadea said that curse and went behind her desk. She sat down and put her head in her hands. *You can't have Noniva's smile and the sugar dates both*, she thought. *You have to tell him at least a little.*

But Amadea sat, longer than she knew, thinking about all these broken pieces and how to reassemble them. The past wasn't a shattered vase, more's the pity, but it didn't stop her from trying.

What stopped her was the door to her office banging open and Quill bursting in. She shot to her feet, ready for a crisis, but there was only the young man, his eyes bruised and red-rimmed, his face pallid. In one hand, he held the ledger he'd shown Mireia, shaking it at her like a sistrum.

"I know what you're doing," he said, eyes wild, voice breaking. "You're hiding things."

A trill of alarm went through Amadea, and she smothered it. "Quill, calm down—"

"Ibramo Kirazzi," he said. "Stavio told me. You were in love, and he broke it off after Redolfo and the Grave-Spurned Princess were executed. Only I don't think he did. I think you and he are still...

still...something. Because he's wrapped up in this and now you're trying to stop anyone looking into it."

Amadea held her hands up, a gesture of calm. "All right, I don't know what Stavio told you, but that's not true."

Quill shook his head, keeping his distance. "He left you to marry the empress. She was supposed to be there that night. Was that the plan? Was it meant to frame Empress Beneditta and it all went wrong?"

Amadea lowered her hands. "You think I conspired with Ibramo Kirazzi to frame the empress for murder so we could be together?" she said, baffled. "She's the empress, Quill. If she murdered someone, that's not just a simple crime. I don't even know if it is a crime."

"Well, it makes sense!"

"Quill," she said gently, "I know you're hurting, and it's obvious you haven't been sleeping—"

"Are you the Shrike?" he demanded.

The word stopped Amadea as suddenly as if he'd punched her in the chest. Panic melted down her whole frame.

"Who told you that name?" she whispered.

He shook the ledger at her again. "Primate Lamberto kept a record. You were paying him off? Because he'd figured out that you...that you and Ibramo Kirazzi were plotting something? Something like *murder*. And then Karimo found out..." His voice broke again, and he was so young, so sad.

So mistaken. And so very in danger.

Amadea plucked the ledger from his hand before he could stop her, turned to the page the ribbon marked. "Saints and devils," she cursed. "And he wrote it down."

When she looked up, Quill had a little penknife in his hand, holding it like she was going to attack him. "Who are you?" he demanded. "What's worth two hundred metas a month?"

"Put that down." She was shaking again, right to her fingertips, and it wouldn't stop. "Slam the shitting gates."

"Answer me," he said, half a threat and half a plea. "What were you and he doing? Why is my...*why is my friend dead?*"

Amadea closed the book and pressed a hand to her mouth a moment. All of it. She had to tell him all of it. That was the solution, the only solution, and if she didn't do it now, she might never manage. She let out one more shuddery breath before she turned and strode swiftly to the door.

"Don't—" Quill began, skittering back, waving the knife.

But he wasn't going to use it, and she knew that. She shut the door and locked it. "Quill," she said, facing him once more. "Listen to me. This is...so much bigger than either of us thought. It's a secret. It's...it's more than a secret. But if he found the Shrike... and he wrote it *down*. If *that's* what Karimo knew..."

Patience, my Shrike. She squeezed her eyes shut once more. "If the Shrike is involved and changeling blood is involved, then we are far beyond the point where I can justify..."

Run, all her nerves urged. *Run, run, run.* She trailed off again, drawing a deep breath that did nothing. No running. No lying.

"I need you to promise it stays a secret," she said.

Quill stared at her, still gripping the little knife. He shook his head. "I'm not promising that. Not without knowing."

"That's wise," she said, her throat tight. "So promise instead that...if it doesn't hurt anyone...if this stays a secret, everyone is safe. If it's spoken, it's dangerous. So you don't tell if you understand it's dangerous, all right? That way we can help each other."

Quill swallowed, his own eyes shining. "They all trust you. Yinii. Zoifia. Tunuk."

"I think you do too," Amadea said.

"Are you the Shrike?" Quill demanded. "Tell me that first."

"No." She set Primate Lamberto's ledger down on the table beside the door, fingers lingering on its leather cover. It stayed leather and didn't drag up memories for her to drown in. A fortunate sign, she thought.

"But you were involved with Ibramo Kirazzi?"

Amadea pursed her lips a moment. "I was a ward of the Kirazzis. After the coup, until...until I came here."

"But not during."

"During was complicated." All her nerves were screaming to run, to lie, to hide again, and she paused to press them down. "I was involved in the coup."

Quill blinked. "Because...you were childhood friends with Ibramo Kirazzi?"

"No," she said. "Because I was Lireana Ulanitti. I was the Grave-Spurned Princess."

III

A LITTLE BIRD WITH A VICIOUS HEART

Year Eight of the Reign of Emperor Clement
Palace Sestina

Redolfo is being abstruse on purpose, Turon knows. "The Shrike" is a play, a bit of bait, an offered detail meant to make Turon follow his brother where he will lead. Turon doesn't chase—not yet. Instead, he thinks.

He knows, too, what a shrike is—a little bird with a vicious heart. It sits on the edge of the forest and snatches up beetles and grasshoppers, crickets and even lizards in its sharp claws. Then it impales them on thorns and brambles and leaves them to die, a meal ready and waiting for the hungry shrike.

It's a hunter. A surprising killer. It's a word that has no business in Redolfo's mouth.

His brother grins at Turon. "You don't know what that means. Clement doesn't have the Shrike, does he?"

"It's obviously a cryptonym for one of your traitors," Turon says, hiding his ignorance in disdain. "Don't you think that's a bit dramatic?"

Redolfo wrinkles his nose. "I didn't have much to do with it, honestly. If that's why you're here," he adds, "you can ask anything you want. But I don't think it will be much help. You don't expect a shrike, you know? They're such little, unobtrusive things. You never think they're so quick. So sharp. So . . . bloodthirsty, really."

He sounds almost angry when he says this, but he only finishes his brandy and holds out the cup as if to ask for another. Turon takes the glass.

"Did you dose him with the blood?" Turon asks. "Is that why it's no help to ask?"

Redolfo laughs like sparks spat from a fire. "There are two sorts of allies. There are those who want something you can get them, and there are those who are utterly devoted to your cause. And then there's the Shrike."

"That would be three sorts," Turon says. "Did you dose him?"

"I have more of the first sort than the second," Redolfo goes on. "They're very useful, though ultimately perishable. You have less time to get ahead of them before they turn." He considers Turon. "Which of them went to Clement?"

"If they haven't told you, I assume there's a reason."

"You know who it is," Redolfo surmises. "I'll bet everyone knows now. I'll bet there's a triumph in the streets for the Hero Who Brought Down Redolfo Kirazzi and the Grave-Spurned Princess."

"Just call her Lireana."

"But you don't have the Shrike," Redolfo goes on. "The Shrike's not the first sort, not really. Otherwise you'd have them in hand when everything came down. Not the second sort either—just a hunter, my shrike, and I provided the prey. That's why you're here, isn't it? Not the girl at all. You want my hunter. I'd help you find them if I could, but I can't."

It's not why he came, but Turon thinks now it's why he's here. If Redolfo's coup isn't finished, if the Shrike is still out there, then they have to be stopped. "Who is the Shrike?" Turon demanded.

"A killer," Redolfo says. "The very worst."

"A name."

"I don't know."

"A face. A description, spirits in the gates! A man, a woman—"

"I don't know." Redolfo's smile still has its edge, but it's frozen and strange, a thing out of place. "But I know the Shrike is no ally of mine. Not now."

Turon's blood turns cold in his veins. "*You* were dosed."

"That I do remember," Redolfo says, "though obviously, there are some...bits missing."

"By the Shrike?"

But Redolfo only blinks at Turon a moment, before nodding at the empty glass in his brother's hand. "I have a lot of enemies, don't I?" he says as a thousand new paths open in Turon's thoughts, leading into ever more dangerous landscapes of betrayals.

CHAPTER SEVEN

*W*ood *table*, Amadea told herself, clinging to the present. *Yellow sunshade. Brown book. Black hair. Cream paper.*

Quill's mouth hung open. "You . . . you're Lireana Ulanitti?"

"I didn't say that. I said Redolfo Kirazzi said that. Obviously," she went on, "this isn't a story I tell, so I'd appreciate—"

"Are you sure?" Quill asked. "I mean, really sure."

"Yes," she lied.

"Then why . . . what were you doing with Redolfo Kirazzi?"

"I was ten when it started." Amadea's mouth felt dry and her grip on her panic was slipping. "What was I supposed to do?"

When Appolino Ulanitti slaughtered Emperor Iespero, Consort-Princess Sestrida, their three daughters, and their infant son, the empire broke into chaos. The Ulanitti family had ruled Semilla for ages, its protectorates for almost a century, with a calm and steady hand, a kind will, and a clever heart. Things like this didn't happen. The War of the Brothers was ferocious as much as it was brief, for if Clement, the youngest brother, inspired only a fraction of the passion that violent Appolino commanded, he made up for it in sheer numbers of people who would not countenance such a ruler, such a blow to the notion of the protectorates. The war remained a scar on the empire's soul regardless, a hint that perhaps the imperial family was not as safe and certain as they hoped.

"I stood there," Amadea said. "I let him point to me. Set me at an army's head. I was too young to think about the damage, at first. And . . ." She struggled to say it. "Well, you can probably guess, I believed it."

Redolfo Kirazzi, Duke of the Khirazji Protectorate, heir of ancient Khirazj and Pademaki the Source—had the changelings not come, he would have ruled like a god over the River Kingdom. Instead, he took a knife to Semilla's scar and broke open a wound that was only half a decade healed. Gathered the protectorates who watched the new emperor with uncertainty. Pointed to the ten-year-old child at his side. *Here is Lireana, stolen back from the grave, hidden in the Abbey of Gintanas, bless Alletet. The throne is hers, not Clement's.*

The throne is *ours*, he might as well have said. The imperial family asked for the girl, but Redolfo claimed they'd only murder her, and the child that people had begun calling the Grave-Spurned Heir shook with nightmares of masked, jeweled Ulanittis strangling her in the dark.

Amadea flinched at the memory. That wouldn't be in the histories.

"What do you mean, you believed it?" Quill said. "You said you were sure."

"Now," Amadea said. "Now I'm sure. But..." She shook her head—that part wasn't the treason or the Kirazzis or the changelings or the Shrike. "It doesn't matter."

"It rather *does*," Quill said. He stopped, stared at her once more in shock. "Wait. You know about changeling blood. You know because he dosed you."

"Yes," she said quietly. "Hence I don't know the Shrike's real name."

"And you don't actually know if you're Lireana."

Amadea shut her eyes. *Amadea remembers everything*, the archivists all said. The truth, the story that wouldn't fit into a history: She didn't know how many times they'd poisoned her. She didn't know which memories were hers and real, and which were sifted into her head. They shifted, broken rocks, suddenly tumbling together in a slide when the wrong thing shook them loose.

She remembered Emperor Iespero, Consort-Princess Sestrida, masked and serene, unmasked and laughing. Playing castles, playing wolf chase by the fire, bright and happy. She remembered Iespero— *my father*—holding her up on a horse. She remembered sisters— Katucia, Violaria—princesses in their nightgowns burning bits of copying practice in the fireplace embers. Remembered lecturing Violaria for shifting her mask to better nervously chew a strand of her hair, remembered hiding her, letting her cry on a shoulder when the empress Clotilda—*when Granny*—mocked her. Remembered Sestrida—*Mother*—lecturing Katucia for trying to steal cloudberry jam, and stealing it for her anyway, it was so bright and sweet and good. Remembered a baby, a brother—Melosino—pink and blank-faced. The way the glue stuck to your eyebrow if you didn't get your mask patch on straight.

Once she'd woken to Imp sleeping pressed against her face, and nearly smothered in the memory of a fur-lined full mask, of being made to stand before an enormous crowd, perfectly still, growing hot and dizzy despite the snow she knew was outside, the air thick with burning tallow and resiny smoke.

She didn't remember the massacre. It seemed as if she should.

She remembered Gintanas, the abbey of the Golden Oblates, an order with its roots deep in Khirazj, and wheatberry porridge with stewed chicken, copying books and digging in a garden. Day-Sister Hentara slipping her candied orange peel and honey dumplings when Amadea was small and scrubbing the tables, then older and helping Day-Sister Hentara cut parchment for the calendars and mix inks. She remembered the cold stone floor under her feet and the rough cloth of her robes. She remembered the altars to Alletet and Djutubai and Phaseran, the smell of incense that wafted through that side of the abbey. She remembered the day-sisters, the night-brothers, the dusk-given; the other orphans, scores of names; the old duchess Kirazzi, with her jewel-tipped braids, and then her son, the dashing duke.

The first time the bells had rung in the workroom she'd been assigned to at the archives, Amadea had been sucked into the memory of the altar of Alletet, the day-sisters striking sistrums against their palms, the lion-headed spirit golden on her plinth. Her mouth had been dry and tasted of thick raisin cake, but she mouthed the words to the chant even if she didn't feel like singing.

She didn't remember Redolfo taking her from the abbey. It seemed as if she should.

"That's how it works," she told Quill, calm and dull and even. "The blood goes in and it lets someone put memories into you. Lets them change you, and the only way to ever tell if it happened or if it's someone's lie is to find a thread that's already pulled loose, a crack in the base. Proof it's not real." The way it worked—a madman stole you out of your childhood, put you in front of a magical army; nothing would sit right in your head for years and years and years.

"But you don't have a crack?" Quill said. "Nothing?"

"I have the memory of being a little girl in the abbey of Gintanas. I have Lady Sigrittrice's personal assurances that I am not Lireana Ulanitti." She had the memory of Redolfo Kirazzi, whispering, *I made you. I built you into this. I can end you just as easily.*

"How do *they* know?" Quill demanded.

"It doesn't matter," she said. "Which is more likely? That Lireana Ulanitti somehow escaped the massacre that killed the rest of her family, was hidden secretly and with no one's knowledge—most especially the Fratricide's—in a wall-abbey for five years and then was miraculously found? Or that Redolfo Kirazzi was a cruel and ambitious man, who didn't care what happened to an abbey brat he thought bore a passing resemblance to a dead princess?"

Quill regarded her sadly, and she wished she could have said nothing at all.

She was a palimpsest, a skin scraped and rescraped, put to uses that half stained her future—but all that mattered was the surface, the present. She was Amadea Gintanas. She knew what she was for.

"It's horrible and it's cruel, but there's nothing to be done about it," she said. "What we can do something about is catching the Shrike and stopping more people from being altered."

For a moment, he looked as if he would keep arguing with her, and she thought surely she would break. But he nodded, put the silly knife into his pocket again. "Who's the Shrike?" he asked. "What even *is* a shrike?"

"The Shrike," she said, slowly, "is a cryptonym. It's a kind of bird—it hunts things, impales them. They were Redolfo's changeling hunter. They were fast, they were thorough, and they were very good at keeping their name secret—with changeling blood, if needed.

The Shrike vanished before Redolfo Kirazzi was captured, and never resurfaced. The only hint they even existed is that nickname in a few people's memories, and the fact he got changeling blood from *some-one*. Redolfo wasn't going over the Wall." She considered the ledger. "Primate Lamberto was getting two hundred metas a month from the Shrike. That sounds a lot like blackmail. If Karimo knew and told either of them so, then he was in extraordinary danger."

Quill squinted at her. "You think Primate Lamberto was black-mailing a legendary assassin? That seems...very foolish. Why wouldn't the Shrike just kill him?"

Amadea shook her head. "They were an assassin twenty-odd years ago. Now? They could be anyone. They could be infirm or promi-nent or trapped. And it isn't as if Lamberto's would be an unre-marked death. Or maybe they were waiting for a chance to make it have an even bigger impact." She pursed her mouth. "Karimo was poisoned. I am almost completely sure of that. He had a bruise on his arm, the mark the blood leaves. That's why I...I needed to catch my breath. I wasn't expecting to see that."

Quill went still. "You think the Shrike was trying to use him to kill Lamberto and...things didn't fall out right?" He paused. "That doesn't explain why Lord Obigen had to die. Or the reza."

"No," Amadea said. "And I don't expect that Lamberto or the reza surviving was an accident. I don't...there is a lot I don't remember about those days, but I am sure if the Shrike wanted them dead, they would be."

"Karimo..." Quill's voice hitched. "I think he had figured it out. That the primate knew and was blackmailing the Shrike rather than turning them in to the Imperial Authority. So...they made sure he died."

"It seems very likely."

"Lord on the Mountain." Quill's voice broke as he swore. "It really wasn't him. It really wasn't. That *bastard*! I...Wait." He took a step toward her. "If Primate Lamberto was blackmailing the Shrike, then he knows who they are."

"And we need to be very careful," Amadea said. "The Shrike is almost certainly watching him closely, making sure no one else has found out the secret he agreed to keep."

Quill sat down on the wine-colored couch. "So what do we do?"

The speed with which she'd gone from enemy to coconspirator would have made Amadea laugh in any other circumstance. Saints and devils, he was so young.

"I don't think we can go to the vigilants without better information. What we have now is only going to send them haring off on dead trails and give the Shrike space to go to ground again." Amadea considered her collection of glass animals. She picked up the smoky gray sparrow. "There are two people I'm sure we can get some information out of for the vigilant." She hesitated. She didn't want to be here, didn't want to do this. "We need to find a way to contact Ibramo," she said quietly.

"Because he's the Shrike," Quill whispered. "That's why he wanted the changeling blood."

"Stop. You are *smarter* than this," Amadea said. "Ibramo was all of eleven when the rebellion started and I don't care how canny you think he is, a child cannot kill a changeling. Don't let your grief and anger make you into a fool."

"But the blood in the statues—"

"He's not the Shrike. Of that I'm completely sure. But I don't think he knows who they are either, and so *why* he requested those items is vitally important. I can't say what the other Kirazzis would or wouldn't do, but Ibramo wouldn't ask for his father's things for sentimental reasons or a silly argument. The *why* is critical." She hesitated. "That's one reason I balked at involving the vigilants. He might tell me. But he might shut them out. They weren't... We both had a lot of questions to answer at the end of it all."

"And the other is they don't know who you are."

Amadea looked away. "I think there are all of five people alive who know, and that's best. Redolfo was... uncommonly ambitious, but I don't think it helps the empress to resurrect doubts about her legitimacy."

"Or to throw her husband into prison."

"Or that," Amadea said.

Quill stared at the rug a long moment. "Are you why they're fighting? The empress and the consort-prince?"

"I am a memory," Amadea said lightly. "I have no idea why

they're fighting. But," she added, "it's probably best if I'm not the one to contact Ibramo. Beneditta...I make the empress uncomfortable and I don't blame her. You need to write him."

Quill frowned. "Why me?"

"Because you have Primate Lamberto's seal. The empress aside... if I...I don't know if Ibramo wants to talk to me—I think it should be me, but I can't be sure he's not..." She stopped herself. "He dealt with Lamberto. He's likely waiting for word of the requests. He'll read a letter from him."

"All right," Quill said. "Who's the second person?"

Amadea blew out a breath. "The Shrike dosed everyone they could to keep their memory quiet, but that's a great deal of memories to correct."

"So you need to find the thread that's pulled loose," Quill said. "The crack in the base."

Amadea nodded. "There are only a few people Redolfo kept that close, and most of them were hanged. But the one who remembered the cryptonym first wasn't. If anyone alive has a clue to who the Shrike is, it will be Fastreda."

Quill's brows shot up. "Fastreda of the Glass?"

She nodded. "Which is another reason we need Ibramo, as there's no way we're getting into the Imperial Prison without him."

⊷⊷ ⋇⬦⋇ ⊷⊷

Yinii sat in her library surrounded by Khirazji texts, painstaking reproductions of scrolls bound neatly into codices. No one had asked for more information about changelings and changeling blood, but the way Quill had pulled the discovery back to the attacks had lit a fire that simmered along her nerves and wouldn't be extinguished. He might need more. The vigilants might need more. And so, without being asked, Yinii set to work making notes.

Lots and lots and lots of notes.

Says Alletet, says Djutubai, says Phaseran: The changeling hides among the Khirazji like a lizard among the leaves of the palm, she wrote out. *When it is still, there is no marking it, but it must move and breathe and continue its small life according to the circle of Al-Duat.*

She made a little note to explain Al-Duat and the circle if needed—not many people observed Khirazji religious customs nowadays. Then another about the invocation, almost a shorthand of declaring the next bit was true and tested. Then another note to explain the metaphor of the lizard, because Khirazji lizards were clearly different from the fat, scaly ones on Semilla's southern coast—but she scratched it out. Even she was sure that was too far.

As the lizard, the changeling will look unto all who view it as a friend, the very form of the person it performs as. But as the lizard is not the leaf, the changeling is not Khirazji, is not seven-souled, is not of the circle. Come Alletet, come Djutubai, come Phaseran, and ink these signs upon your children's hearts that they might know the changeling that walks among them:

The changeling's souls burn cold, my child. To your skin, their touch is the belly of Pademaki, the silt that makes the riverbed.

The changeling's souls, burning cold, demand powerful ("akit" ... wood? burning? fuel, Yinii decided.) *like a fire desperate to start, so they will crave hot and dry things, heavy meats, sweet foods, strong liquors.*

The changeling, being cold, my child, blinks slow, stares long. You may count their blinks and mark the difference.

Yinii frowned at her translation. There was no reason to think that the changeling blood meant *actual* changelings, here, now, on this side of the Wall. So far as she'd ever heard, the only people who ever saw changelings were the Blessed Order of the Saints of Salt and Iron—and even then, these days that was excitable recruits talking about shadows in the forest beyond the Salt Wall, old wall-walkers telling tales in coffeehouses about a lone scout venturing near enough to shoot arrows at. She eyed the dwindling stack of reference books she'd found. Needed or not, it was something to do.

Says Alletet, says Djutubai, says Phaseran: And when the changeling is suspected, when the lizard flicks its tail, the surest sign will be this: the changeling cannot bear the touch of salt or iron. It will blister their skin and boil their blood.

Yinii thought of the strange green fires that erupted over the basin Mireia sprinkled the blood into, and imagined the feeling of that in her veins.

Cold skin, sweet and heavy cravings, not blinking enough, and of course, an aversion to salt and iron. She flipped back through her notes—there was another sign, but it was attested late in a journal from a night-brother in the flight from Khirazj, once they had encountered Borsyan refugees traveling west, and the knowledge that cold could still the changelings into slumber.

Says Alletet, says Djutubai, says Phaseran, Yinii read. *Says the Black Mother Forest and her crow-winged daughters, who bring secrets to these our newest allies: Bring the snow and the silt-belly of the river to the changelings, and they shall sleep like the dead. Coax the wind into the iron and they shall not wake, no matter how you cut them.*

Yinii shuddered and looked around the library, once with her day-eyes, once with her dark-eye. Just in case.

The next book had texts about the blood ritual again, much of it repeating the one she'd read with Quill. A similar picture of a captured changeling being bled. The same recipe. The same invocations to the spirits of wisdom and knowledge. *For the Venom of Khirazj is the trap of the changeling, and the Venom of Changelings is the trap of Khirazj.*

But here, a note, added by the copyist, once in Khirazji, once in Semillan: *This implies second ritual using human? Khirazji? sapient? blood.* Then a name, a title, another book to consider. Yinii skimmed her stack and pulled the proper book from the bottom.

This one was about Khirazji historical medicine, dense with text. She picked her way through until she found the venoms mentioned. There, buried under a long discussion of whether "venom" was the best translation, and a repetition of the features of the changelings she had already noted, she found the recipe from *The Precepts of Bekesa* for the Venom of Changelings. And then a recipe for something else: the Venom of Khirazj.

> *Four parts the root of lotus, pounded in milk, strained well. One part the powder of ksandja. One-quarter the finest filings of silver. Seven parts the blood of annhu, dried. Simmer this, then cool. Place into the veins of Those Who Sow Deception—says Alletet, says Djutubai, says Phaseran—and speak the truth you wish for them. As the Venom of Changelings changes the truth of annhu in the mind, the Venom of Khirazj makes permanent the lie upon the skin of Those Who Sow Deception.*

Yinii sucked in a breath. Changelings were shape-shifters—but this poison would lock them into a particular shape? *Annhu*, she knew, meant "people" but was used like "seven-souled" to mean specifically all people, not only the Khirazji. *Ksandja* she didn't know, but there were plenty of dictionaries.

Yinii went to the shelves and searched for the one she wanted, feeling the hum of the inks within their bindings. She liked to organize the shelves by ink—type and then age—which confused any generalists she was sent but made better sense to Yinii than anything else. The metal salts liked to be closer to the ground, the chars and soots all separated by source—wood, vine, smelting, oil—then the vegetable bases, and the handful of squid inks. Manuscripts with colored inks she set on their own shelves, based on which voice was loudest, in rainbow order. Except in winter, when they seemed more settled if she rearranged them up and down the shelves into thin slices of reds and yellows, greens and purples, and the oil soots wanted to be down low by the metal salts.

She'd stopped trying to explain why she did that to anyone.

But as she reached across the spines of the vine-char inks where she knew she'd find the dictionary with the obscure medical words, her nerves all swooped toward a different book, a book printed with ink made from the soot scraped off the hard stone roof of a smelting oven. The binding was similar to the ones on either side, though. Yinii blinked. Misfiled. *Generalists*, she thought with a sigh.

Yinii pulled the book out, examined it, and found herself holding the Usurper's copy of *The Maxims of Ab-Kharu*. That was why she hadn't been able to find it.

A strange sort of anxiety fluttered through Yinii as she flipped through the pages. Unlike Zoifia's statues, there was nothing within the book that seemed out of the ordinary. It was printed in Khirazji glyphs on the left, Imperial Semillan on the right. There were notes in the margins here and there, but the sort of marginalia you found in *The Maxims of Ab-Kharu*. Agreements, arguments, doodles. Yinii considered a little figuring of a Khirazji king regnant, a knot of four heron feathers on his crown, and realized that the flutter in her stomach wasn't about holding the Usurper's book; it was what it meant.

Quill was that much closer to leaving.

Yinii shut the book and blew out a breath. He was always going to leave, and anyway, what would she be missing? His pretty face? She thought of Reza Dolitha and how much trouble she'd be in if anyone knew she was blushing about a darkblind boy. People intermarried, of course—and that was miles and miles from anywhere Yinii was setting down stakes. But no one in ul-Benturan had done that—at least, no one had done that and stayed ul-Benturan.

Yinii pushed those thoughts far, far away and instead found the forms for the request, the forms that said she was taking the book from the library, and filled them out with a smooth black vine-char ink. She let it dry, then took the forms and the book down to Amadea, where they were supposed to go.

The fluttering worry didn't diminish as she came down the stairs and approached Amadea's office. Before she could reach the door, it opened, and Amadea came out, turning back to speak to someone else.

"No, *don't* ask about Fastreda in the letter," she was saying, and Yinii stopped. Fastreda? *Fastreda of the Glass?* "Just get him to come to the archives—" Amadea looked back over, saw Yinii standing there, and froze.

"You needn't act like I don't know how to write a letter," Quill said, coming out of her office. "It's not..." He, too, fell silent, spotting Yinii. A terrible fear began to swirl in her guts.

"I was bringing you the book," she said, holding up *The Maxims of Ab-Kharu*. "From the Kirazzi requests. And some notes I made about the venom. Well, *venoms*, it turns out—but I don't know what *ksandja* means, so I—"

"It means 'sulfur,'" Amadea said gently.

"Oh." Yinii looked from Amadea to Quill. "Is everything all right?"

"Perfectly fine," Amadea assured her. "Quill, Yinii has some catalogues to check, up in her library. Perhaps when you're finished you could help out?"

Quill frowned at her, as if he couldn't divine the secret meaning in what she was saying. "All...all right? I'll go write this letter and send it off as soon as I'm finished." He studied Amadea another moment before walking away, toward the dormitories. Amadea walked over to Yinii.

"The book?" She took it from Yinii, brushed a hand over the cover. "You know," she said thoughtfully, "I would feel better, for the moment, if this stayed somewhere secure. Would you feel all right if we locked it up in Bijan's workroom, with the flail?"

Yinii frowned. Normally she would have insisted the book stay with her, but Zoifia's warning rang in her ears. "Do you think there's something wrong with it?"

"I don't know," Amadea admitted. "Given the statues...It'll be secure with the flail."

"All right, I'll take it there." Yinii swallowed. "Are you going to see Fastreda of the Glass?"

Amadea kept smiling. "You don't need to worry about it. It's only to do with a client of the primate's."

Yinii thought of Ahkerfi of the Copper and touched the little metal flower and Saint Asla's crystal in turn. A living sorcerer. Nearest thing to a saint on earth. "I'm not worried. I'm curious. I've been in the lottery to meet her for years. How did you manage?"

"Please don't be curious about Fastreda," Amadea said. "I'll walk you to Bijan's. How is the reza?"

Yinii folded herself around the book. "The same."

"Stable," Amadea said. "That's good. It's late. Have you eaten dinner yet?"

Yinii blinked, trying to remember. She'd eaten in the library... sometime. "I don't think I have."

"Well, we'll make sure. Maybe we can pick up some trinkets for Zoifia, to make her sequestration easier?"

Yinii thought of the last time she'd taken sequestration—she always took sequestration if she could—when Zoifia had brought her a new charm, a sack of plums, and a history book. "That would be nice," she said. "But about Fastreda—"

"There's nothing about Fastreda," Amadea said firmly, and started suggesting places to eat. Yinii fell silent, sure for the first time in her life that Amadea was lying to her, but not at all certain why.

CHAPTER EIGHT

Quill went down to the entry hall the next morning to find a runner to take the letter for Ibramo Kirazzi to the Imperial Palace. No one was in the entry hall apart from the door guards, and the morning light slanting low through the windows over the exit made Quill's eyes ache.

The world was not the same as it had been yesterday. Once more, he'd slept poorly, but knowing that Karimo *hadn't* been a monster, knowing he'd been set up, put a manic sort of energy into Quill instead of the dense, looping grief that had kept him awake before. He thought of Zoifia, crackling with fine, spidery lightning—that was the feeling shooting through all his nerves and veins. How could he sleep, knowing so much?

How could he sleep, still knowing so little?

He had gotten up sometime in the small hours of the night, checked the locked door, shaken the cold-lights to wakefulness, and written a new list of questions, hands trembling as if he'd downed a soup bowl full of coffee.

Who is the Shrike?
Why did they not kill Lamberto?
Why did they attack now?
Why kill Obigen?
Why attack (attempt to kill?) Dolitha?
What is going on?

He'd stopped when he'd realized most of the questions could only be answered by an assassin that had hidden themself completely for more than twenty years. This list dwarfed his first set, the questions he'd thought so huge now neatly answered by Amadea's revelation and a little research.

All but one, that was: Quill still didn't know why Primate Lamberto had been so insistent that he could not go to the Paremi chapter house. What was hiding there?

This morning, Quill intended to find out.

In the entry hall of the Imperial Archives, footsteps on the staircase that led to the head archivist's office made him turn.

Yinii stopped, halfway down, dressed to go out in a cloak and gloves. She looked spooked, and everything Quill had said and done the day before, when they'd found the changeling blood, flooded back to him. That was how you watched a madman, he thought. But the world was not the same as it had been yesterday.

He gave her a hesitant smile. "Good morning." He held up the letter. "Do you know where I can find a runner for this?"

Her eyes locked on the letter, brows rising. "Um," she said. "That's... You should..." She blew out a breath. "It's for the palace, right? You can give it to the gate guard if none of ours are around. I can walk you there."

Her gaze broke for the doors, then back to the letter, like a swallow darting around the summer sky, and his stomach clenched. Amadea had been very clear he shouldn't tell anyone what she'd said... but if Yinii knew it was for Ibramo, she knew *something*.

"I'm sorry," he said, as she led him out the doors. "About yesterday. In the head archivist's office. I was..."

"It's hard to lose someone," she interrupted. "It's harder when it doesn't make sense."

"I was acting like a maniac," he said. "And I'm sorry."

"It's all right."

They crossed the square with the dolphin fountains, where Quill had stopped the day before. "Where are you heading?"

"The House of Unified Wisdom," she said, knotting her hands together. "I have to check on Reza Dolitha."

That lightning-sharp energy shot up Quill's spine. The House of Unified Wisdom—where Primate Lamberto was recovering. Recovering, knowing that the Shrike had made all this happen. Knowing who the assassin really was, maybe why they had chosen this moment to strike, those people to die, Karimo to take the blame for it. Lamberto, sending him off, telling him to stop worrying about it—as if Quill should just do what the primate said because he said it. Telling him to stay away from the chapter house, but not why. Not what he was hiding there.

It left his mouth sour, and his nerves all sharp edged.

"Do you mind if I come with you?" he asked as they approached the gates of the Imperial Complex at the center of Arlabecca. "To the House of Unified Wisdom?"

Yinii's knotted fingers tapped against her knuckles fitfully. "I wasn't going to go quite yet," she said slowly. "I was going to... I wanted to walk a little. To think." She hesitated. "Did you have anything else you needed to do first?"

Which was how he brought Yinii to the Paremi chapter house under a somber sky. The tall white-stone building was wedged between a temple of the Kuali wind gods and a wall from the time of Empress Ophicida, when the city of Arlabecca was much, much smaller. In truth, Arlabecca ought to have had a full tower, like Ragale and Caesura did, but land being scarce as it was, the chapter house was made to do.

The front gate had been decorated for the impending festival, hung with red paper tassels and paper masks of changeling faces, twisted versions of humans with lolling tongues. On the street, stalls were being set up for the night market that preceded Salt-Sealing. The world was moving along like nothing had happened, and it stirred something frantic in Quill that he had to stop and press down.

"Who do you need to talk to?" Yinii asked.

"They don't know I'm coming exactly," Quill said. "But the prelate is the one I should talk to."

Quill wasn't sure what the primate might have been hiding here. But he had turned that over and over, sifted it through all the things Amadea had told him the evening before, and come up with one very important possibility: if Lamberto wanted Quill to stay away from the chapter house that night, it suggested there was something unsafe there, either to Quill or to Lamberto.

And if the primate had known the Shrike was the true killer, the most unsafe possibility Quill could conceive of was that the assassin might return to the chapter house that night. Maybe in the hopes of finishing Lamberto off. Maybe in the hopes of finding whatever he was blackmailing them with.

But if the Shrike had returned to the chapter house that night, he reasoned, then there might be some witness, some sign of their passage.

Whatever order and peace existed on the outside, inside the chapter house just after breakfast was a riot of bodies. The building, he knew, was too small for the number of scriveners and adepts it housed, but again, the price of land, the costs of a new building on this site. Primate Lamberto had visited to store his files and make his offerings but had absolutely refused to stay there, insisting to the prelate he could not snub his dear friend Lord Obigen.

"More than two hours in that ape pen and I shall go mad," he had muttered.

The prelate met them in the entryway, a broad-shouldered man with a strangely timid air and such a blend of features even Quill dared not guess where his people had come from. He greeted them warmly. Quill found himself trying to imagine the man, knife in hand, murder in his heart . . . and couldn't.

"Well met, Brother Sesquillio," he said, clasping Quill's hands. "I've been wondering when you would be joining us." He smiled at Yinii politely. "A friend or a supplicant?"

"Oh! Friend," Yinii said, taking his offered hand. "Quill— Brother Sesquillio asked me along."

The prelate's look turned quizzical. "Not to stay, I hope."

Yinii blushed hard, and Quill cursed to himself. "I'm not staying," he told the prelate. "I've come to see about funeral arrangements for Brother Karimo."

"Here?" the prelate said, surprised. "I don't think that's wise."

"Whyever not?" Quill said, cool and calm. A mask to rival Amadea's, he thought. "Karimo was a model Paremi for years, and those of us he was close to deserve a chance to grieve." He considered the prelate a moment, waiting until the man took a breath to speak, and continued. "And of course I would pay for it from family funds."

It had the effect he'd been hoping for, knocking the prelate off-balance. The man snapped his mouth shut, silently calculating how much of the Seupu-lai fortune might find its way into the under-funded chapter house's coffers if only they held a memorial for one notorious murderer.

Quill smiled. "Would you show me to the chapel, please?"

The chapel at the back of the chapter house was narrow and unadorned, prepared for most any faith a scrivener might follow, and truly suited to none. The columns were painted with geometric flower shapes and off to one side was a statue of Father Parem, the founder of the order. At the end there was an altar, for those who needed it. This hour of the day, it was empty.

It put Quill in mind, abruptly, of a tomb, lost and forgotten, and something in his chest plummeted.

"We'd bring in benches for a funeral," the prelate said, his voice echoing. "Some choose to decorate further. And of course, whatever clergy required can be hired, if my humble self doesn't suffice. Was Brother Karimo observant?" The prelate's eyes lit. "Oh! Perhaps the primate?"

Quill stared at the blank altar, his mind suddenly empty. What would Karimo have wanted? These weren't the sorts of conversations they'd had, their whole lives ahead of them. He knew Karimo went to temples—but he didn't pay attention to which ones. Would he want the prelate giving a homily when he'd never met the man? Would he want the primate, knowing he'd been the key to Karimo's death? Would *Quill* want that?

Eyes on the task, brother, Karimo's voice murmured in his thoughts. This wasn't about funeral planning.

"I suspect the primate would be disinclined," Quill managed, and the prelate went a little pale at his mistake. "Do you have a list of residents?" Quill went on. "Scriveners and officials? I want to make sure I don't forget anyone."

"Of course," the prelate said. He cast another quizzical look at Yinii, who stood fidgeting by the door. "There's an evening study room you can wait in. It should be available." Quill agreed, and the prelate gave him directions to the room while he went upstairs to his offices.

"Are you doing all right?" Yinii asked. "This is a lot to handle. On your own. So soon after."

"I'm fine," Quill assured her. He eyed the halls as they passed, wondering which led to the basement and the records rooms, whether the statements from the witnesses, Richa's notes on the case, had made it here yet. But as he passed what was clearly the crowded stairs up to the dormitories, a new pang of grief struck him—it was so like Ragale, so like where he'd started, where Karimo had started and would never return. Doors shutting, paths closing—

"Does Amadea know you're doing this?" Yinii asked. "She could help, I bet. She *would* help. It doesn't matter who he...She would help because you needed it."

"I didn't want to bother her," Quill said, finding at last the door to the study rooms and choosing one at random on the left-hand side of the hallway. How much *did* Yinii know about Amadea, he wondered? How much did any of the archivists suspect?

He thought of Tunuk's full-throated defense of Amadea the day before—if anyone would understand, it would be them. But he saw, too, why Amadea couldn't tell. Why *Quill* couldn't tell. Too many things rested on it—empresses and protectorates, peace and stability that could shatter so easily.

Karimo. He would have told Karimo. Instantly and completely— Karimo would know to keep the truth about the "Grave-Spurned Princess" safe and be able to help him unpick all the rest. But Karimo wasn't here, and he wondered if it was that secret sitting in the hollow of his throat, wanting to be spoken, that was making him so jittery.

Tell Yinii, he thought, as she sat down at the table inside. *Tell her* part *of it*. The breath of the truth wafted over a comfortable lie. Amadea knew enough, had the books, made connections. She could have found the venom's mark, the possibility, the connection to the

Kirazzi uprising. He could manage that. He would manage that, and then he'd feel better.

But before he could say anything, footsteps sounded in the hallway outside.

"Here will suffice," a voice said from the other side of the cracked door. Quill froze, one hand still on the doorknob, as a woman strode past to one of the opposite doors. She was silver-haired, garbed in a fine black gown trailing ribbons, but she moved with such purpose Quill could not have imagined anyone trying to stop her. She paused at the door, turned back to her companion, and Quill saw the dark frame of a black velvet patch pasted around her right eye. An imperial mask—black for secrecy, for privacy, for invisibility.

The scrivener following her was clearly having similar trouble, shoulders tight, hands clasped. The woman spoke to her, assumed her orders would be followed with a quickness, and yet that mask meant that this was all secret. None of this, officially, was happening.

The Paremi was a woman a little older than Quill, dark-skinned, with her hair shorn close to her scalp and big wary eyes. She wore a feathery collar over her robes and the edges of it fluttered as she went into the room. The door closed behind them.

Quill went cold. That was the scrivener who'd taken down his witness statement. And the woman in the mask, that could only be Sigrittrice Ulanitti. He slipped from the room he and Yinii had been sent to wait in, stood close to the door that had closed.

"Where are your notes from Lord Obigen's murder case?" Lady Sigrittrice was saying.

"My notes?" the scrivener said, puzzled. "It was only a transcription, your ladyship. I gave Vigilant Langyun everything I wrote."

"But there are duplicates made for the files kept by the Imperial Archives. Where are *they*?"

"They have to be sealed and signed off by the vigilants, your ladyship. Vigilant Langyun—"

"I have spoken to Vigilant Langyun," Lady Sigrittrice said crisply. "He is finished with the testimonies. Do you have the duplicates prepared?"

"Only drafts." The Paremi cleared her throat. "I beg your pardon,

Lady Sigrittrice, but when I talked to Vigilant Langyun, he didn't seem ready at all to close the case."

Sigrittrice was silent a moment. "What did he tell you? Exactly?"

"Quill?" Yinii tugged on his shoulder, but Quill pushed her back, pressing his ear right against the door that separated him from Lady Sigrittrice.

"Not much," the Paremi said. "That he thought the testimonies seemed off. That they were too similar. I thought that would be a good thing, you know, a clear-cut sort of case, but I don't usually get called in for murders, so what do I know?"

"What do you know?" Sigrittrice demanded.

"Apologies, your ladyship," the Paremi said, sounding flustered. "That's all. It sounded like Vigilant Langyun thought there was more to it than it seemed. The witness from the Paremi," she offered, "his story was different, so maybe Richa—*Vigilant Langyun* changed his mind?"

"Perhaps," Sigrittrice said. Then: "Have you scribed the primate's statement yet?"

"No, your ladyship, he's the last. The hospitalers said he needed rest when we were meant to."

"Ah! There you are!" The prelate came down the hall, bearing a large dusty book, and Quill straightened up from where he'd pressed his ear to the door. "I thought I might transcribe it, but it's a terribly long—"

The door jerked open, and he hardly had time to skip backward, into Yinii, before Lady Sigrittrice filled the entrance, pinning the prelate with a sharp gaze. He dropped into a bow.

"Oh! Your ladyship! I had no idea you were visiting us."

She stood perfectly still and the prelate seemed to realize the mask she wore was not imperial gold or private green but secretive black. He turned pale and flustered. Lady Sigrittrice's steely gaze swept over Quill and Yinii.

"I did not come here for company," Lady Sigrittrice said.

"Of course, of course!" The prelate straightened and bustled Quill and Yinii away, still shaking. He dragged them to a dining hall half full of crates, and brushed crumbs aside before setting the roster open on the table.

"Gracious," he said.

Quill kept his mouth shut, thoughts rattling. What was Lady Sigrittrice doing, asking questions about the murder? In the black mask, of all things—gold would mean this was the Imperial Majesty's request; green might suggest a personal concern. What did she know that merited both interrogating the Paremi who'd scribed the case and wearing the black mask together?

Quill tried to set that aside as he ran a finger down the first page of names. For all it felt as though a small city were crammed into the chapter house, it was fewer than he expected. Five pages of names.

"Is there any way to tell who was here recently?" he asked, his thoughts still buzzing. "To see who will need to be written at their farther stations and who can be contacted here?"

The prelate indicated a column down the side of the name that noted whether they were receiving board, and a second that stacked the dates scriveners who did not stay permanently were in residence over the last quarter. The prelate's head went up as the sound of someone sweeping down the halls passed the room. "Here, brother, please...Please copy what you need. I will be back shortly." And he hurried out, worrying his hands together.

Quill took out his notebook, going down the list of names and writing down the ones who had been in the chapter house the night of the murder. Maybe one of them was the Shrike, or maybe one of them had seen something. There were a handful of officials—no one more senior than the primate—and scores of scriveners. How he was ever going to track all of these down—

He stopped, finger at the bottom of the fourth page. *Deilio Maschano and guard.* Three dates in the column. The last one the night of the murder.

Quill's pulse sped. *And guard*—was that how the Shrike had passed beneath the notice of everyone? Posing as a bodyguard for a rich family, an old family? Or was it the reverse: Had the Shrike slipped in, claiming to be Deilio's guard? He found himself thinking of Lord Maschano's bad leg and wondering what Zaverio had been doing during the coup.

He knew, right then, he should take this to Richa. Except at the same time, he thought of Lady Sigrittrice, of the way she'd said the investigation was finished. Of the way she'd asked what exactly Richa was still so interested in. Telling him about this clue might only mean it got buried, might put Richa under more scrutiny from the Imperial Majesty.

Quill bit his lip. *It's only visiting a fellow scrivener,* he thought. *A brother of the pen.* He could do this. And then maybe he could go to the primate with enough knowledge to pry answers out of him. Was Deilio the reason he needed to stay away from the chapter house?

Quill looked up at Yinii, who was frowning at him, as if he were a torn page she couldn't work out how to paste back together. "I feel like," she said slowly, "you aren't just planning a funeral."

"No," he admitted. "I'm trying to figure out what happened. What *really* happened." He closed up his notebook, and then the roster. Deilio and his guard was the best clue he had.

"If you come with me on another errand before we go to the reza," he told her, "I can explain some of it."

----- ✴✦✴ -----

Richa went to the archives with an official request and a box of the wine goblets and plates from the Manco manor the next morning, only to be told his consultation would remain pending for two more days. Bronze, he was informed, was in alignment. Of the fourteen bronze specialists living in the archives, none could safely handle this request. He could return in two days, when Archivist Jeudi would be made available.

Now he waited in a coffeehouse near the archives, tapping his fingers against the box's wooden side and watching the door. Two days wasn't going to work—not with Lady Sigrittrice looming over him. He'd considered his options, then scribbled a note to Archivist Jeudi, asking to meet at the coffeehouse, and handed it off to one of the young runners who perched in the entry hall, ready to fly off through the archives.

He looked up at the stuccoed wall beside him, painted with a fresco of two lovely Ashtabari women, their long hair falling artfully and strategically over their chests, dancing to the tune of an Alojan playing a bone flute and a Semillan man with a skin drum.

The owner of the coffee shop, a woman named Corolia, came over bearing a small cup of coffee and a square of wild celery jelly. She had long red-stained braids, plump dark skin, and an intricately embroidered apron, and her coffee made Richa bless the Kuali for bringing their seeds into Semilla, the Borsyans for using their forest's magic to induce it to grow hearty in Semilla's climate.

"Thank you very much," Richa said, taking the cup and the treat. "How's things?"

Corolia frowned. "Whatever you're doing, is it about that assassination?"

Richa sipped his coffee—it was very good. "You know I can't talk about my cases."

"People are talking plenty for you," she said dryly. "I've heard it was the Borsyans and I've heard it was the empress's guards. I've heard it was one of his lovers and I've heard it was his stepson and I've heard it was a suicide and you're all covering it up because the Alojan ducal authority is threatening..." She sighed. "To be honest, that fellow wasn't clear about what they might be threatening to do."

"That's a lot of stories," Richa said. "I'm not supposed to talk about it—"

"You're going to need to start," Corolia interrupted. "People don't get an answer, they'll make one up." She nodded back at the half-full coffeehouse. People were watching him surreptitiously. "Rumor's already gone around you're the one looking into it. They *know* that much."

Richa sighed. "How about this? I'm waiting for a materials expert and all of those are wrong." He ate the jelly, its pungent, sugary flavor filling his mouth and its thickness preventing him from saying he had no idea what *was* true.

Archivist Jeudi turned out to be a thickly muscled Ashtabari man with a haughty expression and mottled tentacles.

When he spotted Richa, he eased over, piercing hazel eyes over a hawklike nose. "You the vigilant asking about bronzes?" he said, his words rolling over a thick Ashtabari accent Hulvia would have called "mud farmer."

Richa stood and offered him a hand, introducing himself. The specialist gripped the offered hand aggressively but said, "You call me Stavio," before he settled himself awkwardly into the chair opposite, gaze flicking to the box.

"I'm not supposed to touch it," he said. "So I don't know what you want."

"I won't ask for that," Richa said, trying to keep Stavio at ease. "But I figure, you know the bronze better than anyone else—better than me, for certain—and better than anyone with affinity magic I could hunt up out of the smelters and fabricators. I'm wondering if you can tell me *without* touching it whether there's anything odd about it."

Stavio regarded him curiously. "Odd like how?"

"Odd like a residue. Something that isn't the wine or the food," Richa said. "You can do that, right? With your affinity?"

"Some," Stavio said. He rolled his shoulders, as if his bones weren't sitting right inside him. "Now, yeah, but... it's a danger, you know? I can tell you. I can maybe pull all that residue off, but..." He spread his hands. "Where does it stop?"

Richa tapped a foot. That was exactly what he needed—someone to pull the residue off, separate it so he could see if it was nothing but wine dregs and grease or something worse. Stavio licked his lips, rolled his shoulders the same way, putting Richa in mind of a sandsmut addict. Well, Richa knew how to manage those.

"You want to look at it?" he asked offhandedly. "Just see if you notice anything I didn't?"

Stavio folded his arms across his broad chest. Nodded once. Richa took out one of the goblets and set it on the table between them. A plain single-piece bronze cup, still stained with the deep red wine that had been served in it that night.

Stavio's expression twitched. "That's nice stuff," he said after a moment. "Looks like it's got some zinc in it. Not a lot of patina. New?"

Richa shrugged. He didn't know, but also not knowing might push Stavio to find out. Stavio stared at the goblet, licked his lips again. "Amadea," he muttered, "would sequester me in a heartbeat if she knew I was here."

Richa tilted his head. "You work with Archivist Gintanas?"

Stavio raised his eyes to Richa's—the way the light crossed the table, they suddenly seemed brighter. More golden. "How do you know Amadea?"

"She's helping me with something," Richa answered. *If one keeps a broad definition of the word "helping."*

Stavio clucked his tongue. "You know, she's not gonna be happy with you. Skirting protocols like this."

"You're your own person," Richa said. "I assume you can decide what you do."

"Yeah, that's not how it works." Stavio sighed and looked at the goblet again. "What are you gonna tell her about this?"

"I wasn't planning on telling her anything. Were you?"

Stavio kept staring at the goblet, but he raised an eyebrow at Richa's words. "Maybe I misunderstood, but I'll give you this advice anyway, because if you don't take it, what you've got is a lot of heart-ache coming: don't hide this from her. It's not something you ought to play around with."

"Why's that?"

Stavio's gaze flicked up. "She's not the kind to make a lot of second chances with fellows, you know? You wouldn't be the first man making stupid mistakes with her, but you'd be the first one I knew to keep her fond feelings after."

"Fond feelings?" Richa frowned, startled. "Did she . . . Did she say something?"

Stavio chuckled. "She doesn't do that either."

Before Richa could press him further, Stavio reached for the goblet carefully, like he was trying to pluck a fish from a stream without startling it. Once it was in his hand, he sucked in a long, hissing breath, turning the goblet with little twitching tosses. Little electric crackles spidered over his knuckles. His dark curls seemed to thicken and his eyes glazed. Richa started to rise from his seat, started to reach for Stavio—

Then the archivist dropped the goblet on the table, yanking his hand back to his chest.

"Real nice," he said, his voice flat. "Good bit of zinc definitely, not enough to make it noisy. You can feel the wine on it. Didn't get washed, but I was right, they're pretty new. But it's got...something *waxy* up the side. Like a residue. Nothing anyone put on there purposefully, not like a coating, but enough the metal can't breathe, you know." He nudged the goblet with a fingernail so its open side faced him.

"Any idea what the residue is?" Richa asked, sitting back down.

"It's not beeswax," Stavio said thoughtfully, peering into the cup's depths. "Came from something alive, though. I think." He licked his lips again, then looked up at Richa. "You do me a favor? If it goes up too much, you slap me?"

"If what goes up?" Richa asked.

"It will be fine."

Stavio, smile twitching at his mouth, snatched the cup off the table again, the sparks a sudden cloud around his hand. The goblet turned bright, turned *liquid*—it bulged up over Stavio's hand, twining up his thick wrist like a serpent. Up and up, toward his throat.

Something tiny hit the table with a *pit*.

But then the box on the table started to rattle. Stavio turned to it, eyes shining bronze, but his jaw set hard.

Oh shit, Richa thought, coming to his feet. He lunged toward Stavio, hand raised as ordered, but the other man grabbed his wrist, attention locked on the rattling box. Richa heard the other patrons' voices rising, panic building, chairs clattering on the floor. Corolia shouting at him to get that man under control, and he couldn't pry Stavio's hand open, fingers crushing down to the bone—

Over Stavio's shoulder the door flew open, and Amadea appeared there, followed by a dark-skinned man, his hair in braids. She arrowed through the other patrons to Stavio, sank her fingers into his shoulder, avoiding the snarl of bronze.

"Stavio," she barked, "let it go."

Stavio's nostrils flared, the bronze wrapped up around his throat, flared over his chin. The grip on Richa's wrist tightened, and for a moment, he was afraid Stavio wouldn't listen. The box jumped, once, twice.

"Stavio!" she shouted. "You know better."

Stavio blinked and seized the former goblet, yanked it away from his body. It fell to the table and—as if nothing had happened—landed once more in its initial state.

"There!" Stavio said, too loud, too fast. "There it is, there it is!" He tapped the table beside the small dark wad of something. "That's all the residue, wine and waxy stuff and maybe some of the tarnish. Usually it'll pull that back, but you know—there, that's what you want." He turned to Amadea, the coffeehouse suddenly silent and staring. "I was fine! I . . . was mostly fine."

"Archivists," Corolia spat.

"Go to sequestration," Amadea said tightly.

"I'm *going*." He rubbed his wrists. "Please. Now."

She turned him bodily away from the table, into the arms of the other man, who caught him in an embrace. "Take him. I will be there in a moment."

As they left, as the coffeehouse settled itself, muttering about specialists and affinities and what exactly that had been, Amadea rounded on Richa and hissed, "What the shitting gates do you think you're doing? Do you understand how dangerous that was? How *lucky* you are that the runner told Bijan where you'd gone?"

Richa faltered. *I needed evidence . . . someone to read the bronze . . .* It all sounded so small and frivolous when he thought of the unnatural strength in that grip. "One of the witnesses suggested that the guests were drugged," he said. Then added, "Lady Sigrittrice."

"Lady Sigrittrice?" Amadea's face went blank again, that mask, that wall. She'd made the same face when the consort-prince came up. The consort-prince, and then his wife's seneschal—so many things were tangled up in this case.

He meant to press her on that, but he thought of the way Stavio had pleaded for isolation, the mania in his eyes, again the strength of his grip. "I'm sorry," Richa blurted. "I didn't think."

The mask turned into that Aye-Nam-Wati fury once more, that vengeful goddess. "No, you *didn't*." But then it softened, and she looked down at the goblet, at the crumb of residue sitting on the table. "I suppose you got what you wanted."

"A ball of dried wine," he said. But he picked it up. It was soft in the pinch of his fingers, and when he crushed it, the faint smell of old wine rose off it...old wine and something sweet and pungent under it, a smell like cedarwood and almond flowers.

"Stillwax," he murmured.

Amadea frowned. "What is that?"

"A sedative." He smelled it again. Definitely stillwax. "Off one of the cups from the party."

"Everyone was sedated?" she asked. "How...sedated?"

"That is my next question." He wrapped the waxy bit in a handkerchief and tucked it into a pocket. Nanqii, that's where he needed to go next. He looked up, ready to apologize, ready to thank her for Stavio's time.

She was watching him, worried, hands knotted together.

"I actually need to talk to you," she said, lifting her chin. "Rather soon...now. Now if you're available."

Richa frowned. "Why? Did you find my phrase?"

"I found a lot of things that are going to change your investigation quite a bit," she said carefully. Her dark brown eyes held his, and a small fluttering part of him thought of Stavio's intimations. But it settled when she added, "Please. Would you come back to the archives now?"

CHAPTER NINE

It wasn't difficult to find the Maschanos' manor. While Yinii had stepped inside a baigar stand to get them some of the pancakes, Quill had stopped a woman who was pushing a cart and asked for directions. Her expression was as sour as the baigar at the request, but she directed Quill to the imposing marble house at the end of a street of similarly large marble houses, a uniformed servant a streak of emerald beside the shining black doors.

Looking up at it, Yinii sucked in a breath. "And you're sure? Really sure?"

She'd asked that question at least a dozen times now about a dozen different things: Was he sure that the Venom of Changelings left a mark like that? Was he sure he'd seen the bruise on Karimo? Was he sure Amadea knew? Was he sure Amadea was going to tell the vigilants?

Was he sure this was a good idea, walking into the Maschano manor?

"It's just," she added, "I don't know if I ought to go in. If they'll *let* me go in."

"If they let me in, they'll let you in."

"Maybe." She wove her fingers together, tapping them nervously. "They don't like anyone whose family came from over the Wall, but I hear they don't like, you know, people who aren't humans more."

Quill looked up at the servant beside the door, who was now frowning down at them as if trying to figure out what they were doing there. He could do this himself. He could suggest Yinii go wait in the shade of the trees planted around the fountain down the street. This wasn't dangerous.

You don't know where the Shrike is, a little part of him whispered. *You don't know what's dangerous.* Inside the house, outside the house—his thoughts swirled. He didn't know what the right choice was.

Before Quill could decide—did he go in without Yinii or coax her along?—the door opened and Rosangerda Maschano stepped out, swathed in violet wool and silvery jewelry.

"When Lord Maschano returns, tell him we're adjourning to the solarium," she said to the door guard. "The sun is too pleasant to…" She trailed off, tracing the door guard's gaze down to Quill and Yinii.

For a moment she looked irritated, as if she couldn't fathom why these passersby were taking her servant's attention away from her. But her pale gaze took in Quill and her brows suddenly rose, a smile curving her mouth. "Brother Sesquillio, isn't it? Did the primate send you?"

"No," Quill said. "I was wondering if Brother Deilio was home."

"How fortuitous. You must come in." She started down the stairs. "We were just sitting down. Deilio will be so delighted to see a friend."

"Thank you," Quill managed. He gestured at Yinii. "My friend was just saying she'd retire to the, um, shade, and—"

Rosangerda's attention shifted to Yinii and she blinked. "We do have more than one extra chair, Brother Sesquillio," she said teasingly. "You are both invited in. Zaverio can cope. *If* he ever comes home." She introduced herself to Yinii, smiled, and said, "Ah, Dolitha's girl, lovely," at Yinii's returned introduction. Yinii opened her mouth as if to correct Lady Maschano, but she was already pulling both of them up the stairs.

The entry hall stretched up two stories, the wall over the opposite passageway crowned with a family portrait of Lord and Lady Maschano with a younger Deilio between them. Rosangerda released Yinii but pulled Quill closer as they climbed the stairs and moved toward the back of the house.

"I do hope our goals align," she said in a low voice. "You see, my son…" She sighed. "Deilio is less *determined* than I would like.

He hasn't the focus, the drive, necessary to lead House Maschano—not yet. He's not a strong young man—not for the Wall or the vigilants—we make certain he has a guard on him always. I thought perhaps the mental rigors of the Paremi would make a good fit, but he hasn't applied himself. I thought perhaps hearing encouragement from a *peer*—and one the dear primate clearly thinks so well of—would make the difference."

"Yes," Quill said, thoughts scrambling as his plans came apart and re-formed around this offer. He would get Deilio alone, talk about the order, ask about the chapter house and the guard, find out what he knew. "That sounds like an excellent idea."

Rosangerda let out a sigh of relief. "Thank you. I don't know what we'll do if he quits the order. And all this business with Lord Obigen." She gave him a worried look. "You knew that other boy. Brother Karimo."

Grief surged up in Quill again, but he pushed it aside. "Not as well as I wished."

"How sad." She patted his arm in a motherly way. "It's so difficult to lose someone when you're so young. To find out they're . . . well." Quill glanced back at Yinii as they rounded a mezzanine overlooking the entry hall, but Lady Maschano tugged him closer. "I hear," she said conspiratorially, "the primate held Karimo in high regard. Very close confidences. Perhaps a more advantageous position is open to you now?"

Quill thought of the proof Lamberto had known about the Shrike, had possibly aided the Shrike, had most certainly left Karimo in harm's way. "I'm still deciding."

"Well, maybe Deilio can be spurred to some competition. Ah, here we are." They stopped before a parlor where several liveried servants were carrying platters and chairs away. Deilio stood behind them, wearing formal Paremi vestments and a sour expression, while Gaspera del Oyofon smirked at him over a glass of wine.

Behind Deilio stood an enormous man, his expression unwavering. Quill eyed him—he certainly looked capable of killing changelings or politicians or any sort of nuisance that crossed his employers' path. He was enormously tall and broad-shouldered, with warm skin and a short black beard. He didn't look over as Quill and Yinii entered.

"We have two more," Rosangerda announced. "This is Brother Sesquillio Seupu-lai and his friend, Esinora ul-Benturan."

"Archivist," Yinii corrected.

"Odd," Gaspera drawled. "Wherever did you find them?"

"They came to visit," Rosangerda said brightly. "Deilio, why don't you show Brother Sesquillio the library on our way to the solarium." She transferred her grip to Yinii's upper arm. "I'll escort Esinora ul-Benturan, brother. Off you go."

Deilio considered Quill, annoyed and puzzled. But then his eyes flicked back to Gaspera and he sighed. "Come along." The guard followed behind, at a distance.

"Is that your guard?" Quill asked.

Deilio looked back over his shoulder. "That's Chiarl. My mother thinks I'm going to be murdered any day now. Ignore him. He doesn't like to talk." Chiarl stared, unblinking, over Quill's head.

The library was up a short flight of stairs on the opposite side of the house, a huge airy room with painted shelves on every wall that wasn't a window, soft chairs positioned around a table crowned by Borsyan lamps, and a pair of heavy armchairs beside a fireplace burning hot and bright. The rug was enormous, a field of turquoise patterned with golden lilies. Over the fireplace was a shield emblazoned with the mask of Semilla and the pale stripe of the Salt Wall on a rust-red field. A tasseled helmet as well as two swords—a Minseon-style saber and a thin-bladed rapier, favored by the Imperial Army's officers.

"Was your father on the Wall?" Quill asked, thinking of Zaverio's limp, of the possibility of a successor with that sword.

Deilio made another face. "Of course not. Chiarl, go stand outside."

"Sorry," Quill said, as the guard took up a position outside the door. "I assumed with the sword and the injury—"

"When I was ten he lost his temper with a horse," Deilio said. "He beat it and it kicked him and broke his knee. He'll call it an old injury from the war, but I was there. He never had an oath to anything." He sat down before the fireplace. "I don't know what my mother's put you up to—"

"She wants me to convince you to stay with the Paremi," Quill interrupted. "I suppose she's worried you might want to leave, after what happened? At the party?"

Deilio's expression clouded. "I don't...I don't want to think about that."

Quill's mind filled with Karimo turning, Karimo's anguish, the knife coming up—*Eyes on the task, brother.*

"I can imagine," he made himself say. "I saw enough myself. I bet you were glad to have Chiarl with you then."

Deilio snorted. "Oh, did she tell you to go at me about that too?"

"About what?"

"I didn't take Chiarl. My father *hates* him. He thinks having such a noticeable bodyguard projects weakness. He was already angry that she disagreed with him about selling the land Obigen wanted. He made me leave Chiarl behind, probably to spite her. My mother was *furious* about it. Said I'd nearly died and it would have been on my father's head. I thought maybe they were finally going to get it over with and divorce."

Quill frowned. If the Shrike could change people's memories with the Venom of Changelings, it was possible that Chiarl could have engineered such a web of falsehoods. Maybe. Trying to wrap his thoughts around how many lies would need to be bundled together and set off of each other felt like trying to unpick a particularly dense inheritance decree—his brain shied away from it.

"How long has he worked for you?"

Deilio shrugged. "A few months? My mother turned out the last one. We'd had him for a year and a few months, but then she found out he was letting me go places alone. So now, Chiarl."

He could have come to the Maschanos after deciding to plan this massacre, Quill thought, grasping at answers. But then he considered, too, the quiet guard's dark hair, his unlined face. The Shrike was an accomplished assassin twenty-four years ago. Chiarl didn't look like he could be any older than Amadea. The hot, dry air stung Quill's eyes and he rubbed them.

"Anyway," Deilio said, "I don't have any plans to leave the order. I mean, it's tedious and I hate it, but it's better than getting sent off to the Wall or some other ghastly nonsense." He yanked on the high collar of his vestments. "And it's temporary. Is that all?"

Quill frowned. "What do you mean temporary?"

"My parents will eventually die; I'll inherit their lands and investments and live off the profits," Deilio said simply. "I don't see the point of wasting time with other things. I don't have to. Only, my parents disagree, so I just go along with what they make me do. Which means you can tell my mother you convinced me to stay. But I am not trying for the primate's assistant position. I'm *not* moving out to Ragale." His gaze flicked over Quill. "No offense."

Quill seized the opening. "I mean, Ragale has a tower. You're living in that shabby chapter house."

"I have a *room*," Deilio corrected. "I use it occasionally, for emergencies. I don't recommend it. Saints and devils, it is *stifling* in here."

"Everywhere is stifling in those things," Quill said, nodding at the heavy robes. "What was the emergency the other night?"

"What other night?" Deilio said, returning to fidgeting with his collar.

"The night of the party."

Deilio froze, just for a moment. Just enough for Quill to notice, for the little spark of panic in his chest to start glowing brighter. "Well, I mean, what was I going to do? Come back here?"

Quill studied him. He didn't remember. He was covering up that he didn't remember. "Chiarl didn't go with you," he noted.

"I said that," Deilio said irritably. "He was here and my mother was furious at my father. Despite what she thinks, I'm not actually at risk for being murdered in my bed."

He would have a mark, Quill realized. A mark that meant he wasn't the Shrike, that showed the Shrike had gotten to him too. That might make Richa's job easier and help get them to answers. Proof.

"You should just get rid of the scapular," he said carefully. "Fussing with it is wrinkling the cloth. Anyway, nobody wears the whole thing together except officials. *Old* officials," he added, and was rewarded with a huff from Deilio.

"I don't know why they don't redo the whole habit," Deilio grumbled, unfastening the outer layer of his uniform. "It's horribly dated."

Lord on the Mountain, let him have been marked somewhere clear. If the bruise wasn't beneath the collar and sleeves of the scapular, he'd have to just ask right out or be very presumptuous indeed.

Deilio pulled the scapular off all the way, stared at it a moment, then turned to toss it on the chair beside the fire. "You tell my mother this is how we wear it."

He turned, and Quill saw the edge of a dark, spiky bruise reach up over Deilio's shoulder from under the cassock's wide collar. He sucked in a breath, relief and disappointment together: Deilio wasn't some successor to the Shrike. He had definitely been poisoned.

"I was just wondering if you saw someone there," Quill said, keeping his voice calm. "At the chapter house."

Deilio squinted at him. "Who?"

"I shouldn't say." Quill gave him a significant look. "The primate wouldn't appreciate that."

That caught Deilio's attention, but after a moment's thought, he shook his head, disappointed. "I probably saw the prelate—I must have, since I signed in. And then I remember the next morning, when I was *rudely* hustled out to talk to that vigilant. Whoever woke me wasn't very interesting." He glanced back at the door. "Look, I'm hungry and I want my wine. Are we finished?"

They would have to be—Deilio didn't remember. Deilio bore the mark and he didn't remember why he went to the chapter house dormitory that night or who he went with. Quill imagined the Shrike using Deilio Maschano as a shield, a cover. Get into the chapter house to find... what? Who?

He followed Deilio back to the solarium, trying to pull the truth out of this snarl of threads. Chiarl fell into step behind them, looking distant and bored.

Did he look like someone who would commit murder? Poison people so they all blamed Karimo? Poison Karimo so he blamed himself? Quill realized he couldn't have said. He couldn't imagine what sort of person would do something so vile. When he tried to imagine the Shrike or their motives, it slipped away, gray and vague, as if the assassin had removed those memories from him as well.

The solarium was at the back of the house, with a wall of windows overlooking the walled gardens behind. A variety of potted plants decorated the room, an arrangement of wooden furniture with bright white cushions centered on the tiled floor.

Lady Maschano looked up from her conversation with a languid Gaspera as they entered, Yinii perched between them, silent and tense. "Finished already?" she asked.

"Quick tryst." Gaspera chuckled.

Deilio glowered at Gaspera before answering his mother. "He says the Paremi is an excellent place for me," he lied. "And he complimented the decorations."

Lady Maschano gave him a knowing sort of smile. "You dear boy. Come, both of you. We have refreshments." She suddenly frowned. "Deilio, *what* are you wearing?"

"It's how the younger scriveners wear the robes," Quill supplied. Deilio favored him with a conspiratorial smirk.

"You're the primate's spare, aren't you?" Gaspera asked, considering Quill over her wineglass. "Are you just wandering free while he mopes over that shoulder? Looking for trouble?"

"I'm tending to some business," Quill said, sitting down beside Yinii. If Deilio didn't remember that night because of the venom, would anyone? Did Gaspera have a mark like Deilio's... or could she have been the one dosing people? Did *she* seem like a killer?

"What on this side of the Wall and the other would a stripling clerk be tending to on his own?" Gaspera asked. Her eyes pinned him, bright and beady. "Are you in the same business of rebellion as your friend was?"

Quill's face burned hot. "That's not—"

"Gaspera, hush, and drink your wine," Rosangerda said. "You're not irritated at him."

"I can be irritated at as many people as I please," Gaspera said as she took a sip. "I'm very talented like that." Deilio gave a mighty roll of his eyes.

Quill considered Gaspera's lean, muscular form, the careless way she wore her sword. She could have killed someone, he decided. She could have held Karimo pinned and injected him with the Venom of Changelings. And she'd been a confidant of Redolfo Kirazzi, back in the days of the coup—she would know how the venom worked, where one got it.

Primate Lamberto *loathed* Gaspera del Oyofon, Quill knew that much. *She is a hero in her own head*, he'd said. *A mask of bravery upon a sack of serpents. A very loud and frequently drunk sack of serpents that is very bad with money.*

"Who are you irritated at?" Quill asked. The primate, Lord Obigen, Ibramo Kirazzi...if she told him, he could narrow things down.

Gaspera cocked an eyebrow. "What a presumptuous little clerk you found, Rosa."

"The vigilant," he guessed.

That lit something in her eyes, and even Lady Maschano looked startled. Deilio gave another shudder and picked up his glass of wine.

"The vigilant," Gaspera said smoothly, "has nothing to say to me. All the traitors I've ever consorted with are dead." She looked him up and down. "I suppose we have that much in common, brother?"

Quill forgot to breathe for a moment, that tide of grief suddenly, swiftly pulling him down. "Karimo wasn't a traitor," he managed.

"Gaspera," Lady Maschano warned. "Brother Sesquillio, would you like a cake?"

"You want my advice," Gaspera continued, as Quill's throat knotted up tight, "and mind I'm probably the best person alive to give it—make some daylight between you and that maniac. You didn't know him that well, didn't like him that much. Never talked about any of this. You weren't even there."

Quill tried to press back the guilt, the denial. If he'd walked faster, if he'd insisted Karimo be the one to stay, if he had asked what was going on. *I'll tell you later*, Karimo had promised.

No, Quill thought dizzily. *You won't.*

"I wasn't there," he said to Gaspera.

Gaspera shrugged. "There you are. Go back to Ragale. Don't give it another thought."

"That's what the primate said," Quill murmured, feeling as if he might lift out of his own body, might watch himself wend through this conversation. If he could just somehow *do* those things, if he could slip backward through time, the surging grief said, if he could solve this, then maybe he could go back, they could all go back. He could fix this, he could save Karimo.

No, Quill thought again, squeezing his fingernails into his palms. *You won't.*

"So you've already discussed it," Gaspera said. "Why are you still here?"

"How is the primate faring?" Lady Maschano asked, as if there were any turning this back to polite conversation.

"He's a bastard," Quill said without thinking. He felt Yinii squeeze his arm.

"What in all the gaping gates is going on here?"

Zaverio Maschano stood in the doorway, scowling down at them all. Gaspera and Deilio both sat a little straighter at his voice. "Well?" Lord Maschano demanded.

He could have done it too, Quill thought. Zaverio Maschano had the means to procure the Venom of Changelings, the temper to want it, the hatred to use it. Deilio had said he had no interest in selling his land to Lord Obigen, Yinii had said he had no love for people like the Alojans—maybe he'd been there to engineer a murder.

But his thoughts eeled away to Karimo turning. Karimo setting the knife against his throat.

"Zaverio, you're being rude to our guests," Lady Maschano said. "Brother Sesquillio, perhaps you should lie down with a cold cloth."

"*None* of these people are welcome in my house."

Eyes on the task, Quill told himself, but he couldn't find the words, and he couldn't stop shaking.

"Well, they're welcome in mine," Lady Maschano snapped, "so if you're going to be a boor, I suggest—"

"We're leaving," Yinii blurted, coming to her feet and pulling Quill with her. His head spun as he stood, feeling everyone's eyes on him. "Thank you for your hospitality, but since Quill's had his talk with Brother Deilio, we ought to go. Thank you," she said again, and bulled past Zaverio, down the stairs, out into the sunshine again.

"I hope you found what you went looking for," Yinii said.

Quill tried to apologize, tried to tell her what he'd found. But when he opened his mouth what came out were all his stored-up sobs. There in the middle of that fancy street, in front of the girl he'd thought about impressing just a few days ago, Quill faced the fact that this wasn't a fixable problem.

He thought of when he first met Karimo—how sure he'd been the older boy would try to put him in his place, or maybe suck up to the son of Seupu-lai. But he hadn't—he'd cracked open some sap wine and traded stories with Quill, telling him some of the primate's lesser-known quirks in preparation for the work the next day.

"Oh!" Yinii cried, and her arm went around him suddenly in comfort.

But it only got worse; he couldn't catch his breath. Quill thought of Karimo expounding on legal histories. Of the way he got flustered when Quill pointed out he had an admirer, and was quietly grateful when Quill did half the talking for him. Of how he was going to move into his own practice—how they were going to do so together, maybe in Caesura or even Arlabecca—and of how Karimo would come to Hyangga next Festival of the Dead, it was settled, since he didn't have any family he knew of, and Quill had a cousin he ought to meet; and of how they were going to find a dhoro brewer in the city that another Paremi had said was excellent, especially the peanut dumplings they sold, and how none of these things were ever going to happen.

His head swam and he wanted fiercely to run and run as if he could flee to some other place, some world where Karimo was alive and all was well, and their plans were *plans*, not *lies* they told to pretend they had any control over a cold, uncaring world. But he couldn't move.

Yinii steered him toward the fountain and the shade of the trees. He was shaking when he sat—*What the fuck?* he thought wildly— and she squeezed his hands together in hers.

"You *don't* have to do this," she said, so soft he almost couldn't hear her. "You don't have to do all this alone, you don't have to do it all right now, you *don't*. Karimo would understand."

"You ... didn't know him," Quill pointed out, his breath hitching as he tried to speak.

"I didn't," Yinii agreed. "Maybe nobody did, really? But if he was your friend, and I *know* he was your friend, he wouldn't want this. You have to slow down."

He shook his head. The Shrike was still out there. People still thought Karimo was a murderer. "I really, really can't."

"Well," she said a little strained, "you also really can't run all over the city pretending you're fine. What were you doing in there so long?"

"He had a mark," Quill said. "On his back." He gulped air, tried to slow his pulse. "I have to tell Richa, only I don't know if Richa's going to be investigating anything, after what Lady Sigrittrice said."

"Well, neither are you. You're not a vigilant." She fidgeted with her fingers. "Quill, did you consider the primate might have told you to stay away from the chapter house because this assassin might go after *you* next?"

Quill blinked. "No. Why would they?" But in the same moment he remembered Primate Lamberto's bright panic at the thought that he might go there. And why would it matter if the Shrike were searching for papers or secrets or coconspirators?

Are you safe? Amadea had asked, and Quill realized that he very much wasn't.

"I don't know," Yinii said. "But you don't know what got Karimo killed, and maybe he didn't either. You need to be careful, and I don't think you are."

Quill wanted to protest, but even shaking and washed hollow with grief he could recognize the truth there: What had he just done but make himself known all over again to three people he suspected of being the Shrike? Worse, he'd all but said the vigilants would still be looking.

"Maybe you're ..." The words died in his mouth as he looked over her shoulder. A man was watching them from the corner—*Ibramo*

Kirazzi was watching them. He stood in the shade of the house on the corner, plum cape pulled close, hat tipped low, black mask still hiding half his features. He nodded, as he had that night, and Quill went cold.

"What?" Yinii asked, looking back, in time for a carriage to obstruct her view. When it had passed, the consort-prince was gone. Yinii shook her head.

"I feel like I'm losing my mind," Quill confessed.

"I think you should go back to the archives," she said. "I'll go to the House of Unified Wisdom myself, it's fine. I'll walk you back first. In case."

"Maybe you're right," Quill said, standing. He needed to tell Amadea what he'd discovered, and she'd probably know how to tell Richa that Quill might have compromised his investigation.

But more than that, she needed to know Ibramo Kirazzi was making sure Quill knew he *was* a part of all of this, whatever Amadea insisted.

———— ◆ ————

Amadea kept her face still as Richa surveyed the array of evidence she'd laid out on her desk, trying not to calculate all the places she might have slipped and given him a clue too many, a reference too clear.

Silver buttons, she told herself. *Wood table. Leather binding. Dark eyes.*

Richa looked up at her, started to speak. Stopped himself. Picked up one of the Kirazzi trial transcripts. "This is a lot more than I was asking about."

"Yes, well." She folded her hands together. " 'Who knows where the path may lead.' "

He chuckled. "It's been a while since I read that story, but I don't *think* the thief wound up with powdered changeling blood." He set the paper down, looked as if he might say something again. Stopped.

White parchment, Amadea told herself. *Blue sleeves.*

"I've sent a private message to the consort-prince," Amadea said. "Through Quill."

Richa frowned. "You told him you found his changeling blood?"

"I told him we had it. For all we know, someone's trying to frame him. Do you want to play along with that?"

"For all we know, he's about to follow in his father's footsteps," Richa pointed out. "Word on the street is, the consort-prince is out of favor. Maybe enough for a coup?"

Amadea clenched her jaw once. *Pink nails. Blond wood. Gray uniform.* "I could just as easily see spreading gossip about a discontented imperial couple and then foisting a trove of changeling blood on the consort-prince to secure his downfall." She slid Quill's and Lamberto's ledgers over to Richa from where he'd set them aside. "Quill's list doesn't have the statues. Lamberto's does. They could have been added later."

"By the primate. Handwriting's the same."

"And we're talking about a poison that makes people misremember," Amadea said.

"Or Quill missed the last item, the way people do," Richa said, leaning back in his chair and folding his arms. "You're so sure, why haven't any of your ink specialists checked it?"

"Because I'm not a vigilant," she said, "and I don't think it's wise to involve unnecessary people in half-formed accusations."

But Mireia's admonitions rang in her thoughts. *You don't know* what *he'd do anymore.* And deep down, Amadea had to admit, she didn't want to test that.

"Three of your witnesses come up in the Kirazzi proceedings," Amadea pointed out. "Captain del Oyofon, Lord Maschano, and Nanqii ul-Hanizan." Lord Maschano with minor but suspicious financial entanglements. Nanqii ul-Hanizan fingered as a supplier of various drugs and poisons.

"That," Richa admitted, "was a bit of a surprise. Not Captain del Oyofon, I mean. Everyone knows that." He scowled at the pages again.

Black ink, Amadea recited over her racing pulse. *Red cover. Glass bird. Silver buttons.*

"I can't figure you out," he suddenly said. "Why are you doing this?"

Amadea blinked, sure she'd misheard him. "Why am I helping you find a murderer?"

"That first night," he said, "you fought me every step. In the Kinship Hall, you were hiding things, eeling around the subject—"

"I beg your pardon! I do not 'eel'—"

"And," he finished, "you looked at my files—don't tell me that's not true, I didn't tell you the names of the guests."

"Quill told me," she said. Then: "But yes, I did look."

"I just wish you'd be honest with me."

Amadea looked down at the spread of documents, the shape of her secret life laid bare if one knew how to connect the edges. The transcriptions of Redolfo Kirazzi's trial, scores of witnesses telling the edges of her story. *The Precepts of Bekesa* with Karimo's strange declaration and the recipe for the poison that had ruined both his and her life, a quarter century apart. The primate's ledger, the hints that conspiracy had left seeds, that her secret couldn't stay secret forever.

White pages, she thought. *Black ink.* She sat down opposite him.

"My job," she said, "is to make sure these archives run. But more than that, it's to make sure my archivists are safe. People who have affinity magic in small quantity, they can live their lives out there, but the specialists, they're here because they can't. The affinity won't let them. I make sure they don't hurt themselves, they don't run themselves to threads, they don't forget who they are. And I will stand between the Vigilant Kinship and them if I need to.

"Whatever threats exist in their own powers? Whatever I protect them from? This is so much bigger. I am not the Salt Wall. Whatever my silence and care gain, I can't stop the Shrike or whatever they're aiming for. And I don't know what that is."

Richa considered her a long moment. Amadea made herself hold that gaze, made her thoughts stay still.

"I hate this," he said, gesturing at the papers. "It's madness. But it makes an awful lot of things that refused to make sense fit together." He told her about the witness statements, about the stillwax. "Nanqii ul-Hanizan sells stillwax," he said. "Sells a lot of things, but stillwax I feel confident in. And a sedative in the wine would have made it a lot easier to go around that room injecting people without anyone raising the alarm."

"Do you think he'd kill Obigen?"

"I don't know why anyone would have killed Obigen, least of all an apocryphal assassin." He considered her again, his expression still troubled. "This is the heart of it: Why now? Why Obigen? Why Karimo del Nanova?"

Amadea flipped open the ledger again. "If Lamberto was blackmailing the Shrike and Karimo found out..."

"A chatty blackmailer isn't exactly holding up their end of the deal," Richa finished. "But they killed Karimo, not Lamberto. And they set him up as Obigen's killer—again, not Lamberto." He ran a hand through his hair. "I swear this keeps getting more complicated."

Amadea frowned. "Why were they all at the Manco house?"

"That canal plan. Obigen had enough interest—everyone wants more arable land, it's just the question of making another wall with *maybe* one salt sorcerer available—he needed the practical aspects."

Money. Such an undertaking would take investment from all corners of the protectorates. Money, and labor and tools and land...

Land.

Amadea frowned to herself. "Have you," she asked slowly, "looked at the cadastres?"

"Cadastres? Like tax maps?"

She stood, looking at the documents, finding the edges to another history, another possibility, lying in between them. "They're downstairs," she murmured. "I want to check something."

Amadea led him to one of the documents libraries, on the west side of the archives, requesting the maps from a blue-eyed human generalist she didn't know but who easily recognized her as his own superior's counterpart—all the while feeling as if this idea would tip out of her head if she moved too fast. The room was bright with sunlight and divided by enormous tables. Richa sat down at one of these, while the generalist returned with two books, each half as tall as he was. Amadea thanked him and opened the first map book.

Amadea flipped through the pages, the sections working their way up through the peninsula that made up the Semillan Empire, from Tornada up at the northwesternmost tip, down over the mountains, and up to the Salt Wall at the southeast. She slowed down here, eyes tracing the edge of the wall through map after map until she found *Gintanas* labeled with a small star about a fingertip from the inked line of the Salt Wall and a hand's width from Sestina, the seat of the Kirazzis, along a slim, sliding river.

"Here," she said. "This is the old map." She switched to the current cadastre while he studied it, flipping to a similar page, the ink a little crisper, the hand a little tighter.

Lines swooped over the land, diving into the Kirazzi holdings and cutting pieces out of the great tracts of land.

Maschano. This one said. *Maschano. Maschano.* In bites and gulps, the Kirazzi holdings had been handed over, and all along the Wall, almost up to the star of Gintanas, the name *Maschano* dominated. But the dates of transfer were haphazard—some before Redolfo's execution, some after. Some transferred directly, some marked as seized by the Crown and sold.

"What if," she said, "it's not about the money? What if it's about the land? About what might still be *on* the land. There's catacombs in here. Maybe there's more."

Richa leaned forward, studying the map. He ran a finger along the wall, to an island amid the sea of *Maschanos*—del *Oyofon*. A narrow wriggling plot that looked as if it followed a stream there. "And there's the captain's plot. Odd shape," Richa said. "Do you have the taxation records here?"

Amadea did, but they illuminated little. The Maschano lands were tenanted to farmers and herders, Gaspera's plot listed as a hunting park with water rights shared to the Maschano lands. It had been transferred from the Kirazzis, but the date was missing, suggesting it had happened during the Usurper's coup. The Maschano lands had been dated before and after the coup.

"Nanqii doesn't own land there, according to this," Amadea noted, leaning over the cadastres. She covered *Gintanas* carefully as she rested her palm against the book. "Would that rule him out?"

Richa came to lean over the map as well. "Honestly, that makes me more suspicious. He's not there because he owns land to sell, so why invite him? And I still want to check that stillwax connection." He rocked on his heels. "You know, the worst part of this venom business you've handed me is that it blows my suspect list across the damn field. It could be anyone, if they covered their tracks correctly."

Amadea pursed her mouth. "It would have to be someone who belonged there. It wasn't a public event, right? And they'd have to get close to each person in order to dose them. Moreover, if the empress was there, not just anyone could wander in."

Richa looked up, again with that uncomfortable, restless look to him, as if he wanted to say something but couldn't. Amadea raised an eyebrow. "*Was* the empress there?"

"That depends on who you ask," Richa said carefully. "Because I have people saying she was there and people saying she'd left long before. And I can't figure out what's happening there: Why would the Shrike put the memory in everyone's mind that the empress and Lady Sigrittrice were there if they weren't?"

Amadea blinked. "Lady Sigrittrice?"

The old woman eyeing her. "You're not Lireana, that's for certain"—her voice is so cold—"but a threat? There are people who would take you up for the same symbol as the Usurper did."

Richa stared at her. "You want to tell me something?"

"I doubt you need me to tell you she's a risky person to tell lies about," Amadea said.

"Unless you outrank her," Richa noted. "Do you mind if I join you if the consort-prince deigns to call? Or is that private?"

"That is up to him."

"How do you know him exactly?"

"Childhood acquaintances."

Richa's eyebrows rose. "That's quite a childhood."

Amadea began to retort, but then the door to the library opened, clumsy footsteps ringing on the polished floor. She turned as Quill pulled out the end chair and dropped down into it.

"Did you tell him about the Shrike?" he asked dully.

"Yes."

"Good." He looked up and his eyes were red and raw looking. "Because I might have fucked everything up."

"*Language,*" Amadea said. Then: "What happened?"

He told them of the ill-advised trip to the chapter house, the proof Deilio Maschano had been there, and the belated realization Quill himself might be in danger from the Shrike. He told them

of his encounter with the black-masked Lady Sigrittrice, not acting privately in the slightest, and then of his attempt to investigate
the Maschano link himself, ending in fleeing that house and Yinii
bringing him back to the archives before going to the House of Unified Wisdom to check on her great-aunt.

"I saw him again," he said darkly to Amadea. "The consort-
prince. I think he's following me."

"Interesting," Richa said. "Lady Sigrittrice *and* the consort-prince
sticking their toes in. Are you close enough acquaintances to ask
about that?" he said to Amadea. Before she could respond, he asked
Quill, "You're sure about the mark on Deilio Maschano?"

Quill nodded. "I saw Karimo's. It's pretty distinctive." He sighed.
"I'm sorry. I should have just come to you. But maybe it was for
the best, if what I heard is true and you're not supposed to be
doing anything." He paused, then added, "But you're still going to,
right?"

Richa let out a sharp breath, almost a laugh. "As quick as I can.
Maybe Lady Sigrittrice will be too busy poring over my paperwork
to notice I didn't follow orders." He frowned down at the maps
again. "I assumed she was shutting me down because of the political ramifications of a noble consul being assassinated in front of the
empress. But she's hiding something."

"And she's not someone to make angry," Amadea reminded him.
"Be careful."

A smile tugged at the corner of his mouth, eyes dancing. "Come
rescue me if the demons bundle me away, Aye-Nam-Wati."

Amadea startled, placing the reference to the Datongu goddess
immediately—the Datongu mural on the archives ceiling depicted
the snake-tailed goddess escaping Hell with the demons' secret
knowledge—but not sure at all for a moment why he'd said it. Was
that a compliment?

"I'll scribe for you," Quill suddenly blurted. "You can't use the
Paremi from before—Sigrittrice has warned her off. I'll do it."

Richa exchanged a glance with Amadea. "You should stay here,"
he said. "*Inside* the archives. Behind the door guards."

"If the Shrike is looking for you—" Amadea began.

"I don't mean any offense," Quill said, "but I hardly see how the Hall of the Vigilant Kinship is less safe than the Imperial Archives. And I want to help," he added, quieter. "I need to help. I need to see this through."

Richa's expression softened, as he seemed to make the same calculations Amadea found herself making. "I will come and collect you in the morning. Do *not* leave the archives in the meantime." He stood. "Could you box up that evidence for me? For when we need it?"

Suddenly the door to the library heaved open, and one of the young runners in a turquoise tunic flung himself in. "Archivist Gintanas!" he panted. "You're wanted at the Kinship Hall! Right away!"

"Who?" Amadea shot to her feet, dread filling her as she catalogued all the archivists who could be in trouble. Not Zoifia, not Stavio, not—

"It's Archivist ul-Benturan," he said, and Amadea started running before he repeated, "They want you right away."

CHAPTER TEN

After depositing Quill at the archives, Yinii had gone on alone to the House of Unified Wisdom in the Necessary Arts, stopping briefly at the market to pick up some things for Zoifia. The ink on broadsheets and receipts, the chapbooks she'd bought Zoifia, and the announcements plastered to the walls buzzed at the edges of her thoughts like circling hornets. There could be a killer—here, now, anywhere, really. It made her want to swath herself in ink, to hide under a wave of it, but she pushed the buzzing aside and walked on.

The hospitalers' notes were louder and worse, and Yinii had to stop on the stairs to slow her breath down. Getting wound up always made her affinity stronger, as if the ink knew she needed someone to listen, but listening to the ink—here, *now*—was a terrible plan. She would see the reza, then she would make sure Quill had gone to Amadea, and Amadea would tell him to stay in the archives where it was safe and give the vigilants what they needed.

Reza Dolitha was awake this time, the glass cap still strapped over her damaged eye. As Yinii entered, Dolitha reached absentmindedly for it, and Pharas, at her side, grabbed her hand and pressed it back against the sheets.

"Reza, the hospitalers say you need to leave it," he told her wearily, "if you want any chance of saving the eye."

"Of course," the reza said, a soft slurring to her words. "Of course. I know. Silly boy. This wicked city. Those hospitalers are doing fine, fine, fine, fine... They are a blessing. Yes. But this city." She clucked her tongue and reached for the cap again, only to have Pharas stop her.

"They are going to put you to sleep once more if you don't stop." He looked up at Yinii standing in the door. "Oh look, reza! Yinii's come to visit you." He shot Yinii a frantic plea of a look. "Reza Dolitha has had a *lot* of…medicines," Pharas explained.

"Yinii!" she cried. "Oh, sweet girl, I'm so happy to see you. Where have you been?"

"She came the first day," Pharas said, as Yinii came up to the other side of the bed. "I told you that. You were sleeping."

"Oh, dear Yinii." Reza Dolitha ignored Pharas and took hold of Yinii's hand in her own age-spotted one. "You brave, brave girl, finding your way across this wicked city just to tend to me."

"It's nothing, Reza," Yinii said. "I live here. I pass the House of Wisdom all the time."

"It's very dangerous," Reza Dolitha said, as if she were agreeing with Yinii. "I have always thought so, and you see, this—*this*—is why…how it came…well. I was attacked! Did they tell you?"

"Whatever they've given her," Pharas said carefully, "is meant to help limit the damage to her dark-eye, but—"

"My dark-eye!" the reza wailed. "I was stabbed. I may be blind! Cut off from the God Below! It's a wicked, wicked city, Yinii, and we threw you into it without knowing how wicked."

"The, um, attitude isn't permanent," Pharas said. He looked exhausted. "At least, they say it's not. The knife didn't go into her brain, so."

"That's good," Yinii said.

She suggested Pharas go stretch his legs and find something to eat, while Yinii stayed behind, and her cousin gratefully took the offer. She sat beside her great-aunt, softly reciting prayers for a long while. Her heart ached for Reza Dolitha—from the sound of things, the hope that her third eye would be saved was slim and growing slimmer. A reza who could not see her way through the tunnel-towns would be badly hobbled. She might be no less sharp, no less skilled in leading, but she would be expected to step down. She would not be Orozhandi enough, in a way, and Yinii knew too well how that felt.

But then the reza squeezed her hands again and said something that sorely tested all of Yinii's pity.

"A wicked, wicked city," she said. "It's a very good thing I sent for your father to come and take you home."

Yinii dropped the reza's hands. "What?"

The reza waved a hand. "Before the party, the attack. Thank goodness. You won't be . . . you can't be . . . You'll be safer, you see? In Maqama."

"I don't want to go to Maqama!" Yinii nearly shouted.

When it had been a question, a possibility, Yinii hadn't been sure—Pharas had said the reza thought it best, and the reza was the one they looked to, so who was Yinii to say it wasn't best? Maybe she would be happier at home, less lost, less worried. Maybe the archives weren't her destiny after all, and maybe she was being foolish for thinking that way.

But with the admission that everything had already been decided, that she was being told she *would* go to Maqama and it was too late to change things . . . suddenly, Yinii *knew* exactly what she wanted and it wasn't what Dolitha had planned for her. She would have to try to talk her out if it.

"Reza," she said, "with all due respect, you didn't ask me—"

"A wicked, wicked city."

"*Reza*," Yinii tried again, "if I leave the archives . . . if I leave, then it will happen again—"

"The archives." Reza Dolitha snorted and reached for her injured eye again. Yinii grabbed her hand and yanked it down this time, and Dolitha looked at her, wounded.

"I'm not going back," Yinii said again.

"You've always been a good girl, Yinii. Not like . . . not like . . . It's a shame," she said, her voice growing thick, "that the last thing my dark-eye may ever see is the shape of that woman, right before she . . . with the knife, what she did."

Yinii stopped, her hand still on the reza's wrist. "Reza," she said carefully, "you were stabbed by a man. A human man, from the Paremi? Remember?"

The reza frowned, squinting into the air before her. "Yes," she said slowly. "A man. That boy. Brother Qarabas."

"Karimo," Yinii corrected.

"Like the saint," Dolitha went on dreamily, "but not. A knife and not the hammers. He stabbed me first and then he attacked Obigen. I remember that. A man to the day-eyes but not to the dark. In the dark, he was a woman."

Yinii said nothing, still holding the reza's wrist, cold panic sliding down her shoulders. In the dark, by her third eye, Yinii could tell one body from another—non-Orozhandi didn't always realize the fineness of the details they could pick up from only heat. She had not met Brother Karimo, but she knew well enough that he shouldn't have looked like a different person entirely to Reza Dolitha in the dark-sight.

Unless, of course, someone had used the Venom of Changelings to insert a memory of seeing Karimo attack, and hadn't known enough to correct the memory of the dark-sight. Unless Karimo had not wielded a knife at all—except against himself.

Because he wasn't a killer, Yinii thought. And why would you risk him making errors because he wasn't? The Shrike could take the knife to whomever they pleased and tell Karimo it had been in his hand—tell everyone who saw that it had been in his hand.

But the Shrike had forgotten this one, small detail.

"What did she look like?" Yinii demanded. "The woman in the dark-sight."

"Like a devil," the reza said. "Like a changeling. She was the sandstorm and the blade."

"Did you recognize her? Do you know her name?"

"I knew her name and it was Death," the reza intoned. She sighed, sleepily. "Such a wicked, wicked city. You'll be safer in Maqama."

Yinii shot to her feet. She had to find someone, tell someone. She heard footsteps in the hallway and bolted after them, hoping Pharas was back or a hospitaler was passing by.

The light from the windows at the end of the hallway was dim and pale, the sun easing down behind the city by now. There was no one in the hallway at all; they must have passed the other way—

Yinii froze. The door to Primate Lamberto's room, down at the end of the hall, was open, the room itself dark.

Don't look, Yinii told herself, all the ink on the charts and the books and the journals beyond the doors growing louder, cacophonous as she ignored that little voice in herself and eased down the hallway. He would be in there, sleeping, she told herself, and she would only be doing a favor, closing his forgotten door.

She eased around the corner, ink hissing along all her nerves, expecting a strange, shadowy woman to burst out at her.

Instead, she found the naked body of Primate Lamberto hanging above her, turning slowly in the dim light.

⋯ ▅◆▅ ⋯

Lamberto Lajonta, the Ragaleate primate, had died around sunset, by his own hand, judging by the letter he'd left, enumerating and regretting his many errors. The House of Unified Wisdom in the Necessary Arts was grieved and appalled, and the young woman who had found him was quite shaken.

"Horseshit," Richa had muttered to Amadea upon hearing this. He had hurried off to his own work, while Amadea went to hers, she and Quill going to Yinii in a small interview room where Yinii had been left with a coffee and a blanket around her shoulders.

Yinii nearly leapt from her seat when Amadea entered, as if she expected an assassin. Amadea swept her up and hugged her hard, as if she could reseat Yinii's whole self back into her body. "Are you all right?" she asked.

"I'm fine," Yinii said, sitting back down. She picked the blanket up and folded it. "Quill, I'm so sorry."

Quill did not look shaken. He looked furious—as if he blamed the primate for this too. "I'm just glad you're not hurt."

"I'm fine," she said again, picking up her cup. "I'm...I mean, I didn't want to see that. Obviously."

"Can I ask about what you saw?" Amadea said gently, as she sat down in the opposite chair. "Exactly?"

Yinii swallowed. "He was hanged. He asphyxiated. His face... The blood vessels break when—"

"Not that exactly," Amadea said. "You don't need to go into those details." She tried to think of a way to bring up the possibility of a bruise on the body, and floundered. "You found the letter?"

"On the bed. 'May my death pay the debts of my errors. May those who remain behind find peace.'" She swallowed. "It was fresh. Just written. He was dying while I was talking to the reza."

Amadea glanced at Quill. It didn't *sound* like what he'd said of the primate.

"You don't think he killed himself," Yinii blurted. "I don't think any of us does. So can we not talk like we do?"

Amadea made herself perfectly still. "Why do you say that?"

Yinii's gaze dropped to her coffee. "Quill told me."

Blood flooded into Amadea's face. "Oh, he did?"

"About the Shrike," Quill said firmly. "About the Venom of Changelings."

At that Yinii looked up, squinting at first Quill and then Amadea. "What . . . What else might he have told me?"

"It's not important," Amadea said.

"It's why you were talking about Fastreda of the Glass," Yinii said. Her eyes suddenly widened, the third eye flicking open in reflex. "Does this have to do with the Usurper?"

"Yinii—"

"The changeling blood, the Shrike, Fastreda." She shook her head, tears suddenly springing into her eyes. "He *had* a bruise, if that's what you're trying to get me to say. The size of this"—she tapped the medallion on her left horn—"right on his chest. Shaped like a star— that's it, isn't it? That means it's the Venom of Changelings. *Why* is anyone using the Venom of Changelings? And why did you *know*?"

Green eyes, Amadea recited. *Gold charms. Pink crystal.*

"I think you should tell her," Quill said quietly. "She's in this too."

But before Amadea could protest that she didn't have to be—that she should *not* be—the door opened, and there was no more arguing about how involved in Amadea's secrets they were as the consort-prince stepped into the room, a black mask embroidered with feathers over his eyes, and locked the door behind him.

"Lira?" he said softly.

Calm, Amadea told herself. *Just be calm.* It was twenty years ago. A whole lifetime, she realized. Sesquillio Seupu-lai and Yinii Six-Owl ul-Benturan might well not have existed yet, when she'd fled to the archives.

So long that Amadea had hoped, had *believed*, she realized now, in her very heart of hearts, that if somehow she laid eyes once more upon Ibramo Kirazzi, he would be an entirely different man. That two decades, a wife, a title, a pair of children—all these would mark themselves upon the bone of that lean and soulful boy and offer up someone else.

But then Ibramo reached up and pulled off his black mask and, oh, she was not that lucky.

Ibramo's eyes found hers, and whatever line she'd repeated about the past not mattering crumbled to pieces. Whatever twenty years had stolen away or loaded upon them, those were the eyes of her confidant, her only friend, her first love. Perhaps he was a little leaner, his dark skin a little more lined, the rime of age on his curls and his beard. But the long lines of his body fit precisely in her memory, waking things she'd thought long dead. It undid some chain of tension on her mind. They were both safer together, even now, some part of her was certain. The boy who had known her—no matter her past—the man who had reached to pull her into the future.

But then the gate to that future had slammed shut, and there was nothing either of them could do but be sensible and grieve it.

Please never doubt: My love and esteem for you have not changed, the letter had said. *There is no force within the Wall that could change them, my darling.*

"Lira?" he said again.

"Why is he calling you that?" she heard Yinii ask in the tiniest of voices, but Amadea felt herself standing, responding.

"Ibramo." She should curtsy. She should call him Your Highness, Consort-Prince Ibramo. She should be formal and she shouldn't be crying.

He half smiled at her. "You look very well."

She shouldn't think of kissing him, of hiding under the willow, of slipping into the tombs near Gintanas where they could be undisturbed. She shouldn't think of Sestina, after, before. The realization of what must be happening—

"How...how did you...?"' Amadea began.

He smiled nervously. "The consort is afforded a certain amount of power and information. One of my people told me you were sent for." He tapped the stiff mask against his opposite hand. "And since you finally asked me to come...I thought...I couldn't wait."

When the Kirazzi Rebellion had been quelled, the Grave-Spurned Princess had been kept under lock and key with Ibramo, the would-be Duke Kirazzi, at the Kirazzi palace at Sestina. There were questions, after all, as the adult members of the conspiracy were hung or imprisoned or their property disbursed. How to be sure the rebellion of Kirazzi was truly crushed? How to be sure that the Grave-Spurned Princess was not Lireana?

How to be sure that no one *believed* she was Lireana?

These were not simple questions. They did not take a simple amount of time.

They took long enough for the Grave-Spurned Princess to fall pregnant.

Amadea squeezed her eyes shut, trying to focus. "You're the one who made the request for Redolfo's things."

"I didn't want to trouble you," he said apologetically. "I know... I mean, it's not as if we have a truce? But I know." He stared at her a long moment. "And if Beneditta..." He swallowed. "Are we really doing it this way?"

Amadea made herself swallow. "What way?"

It had been early days, long before the flutter of a soul testing her belly, but the Grave-Spurned Princess and the would-be duke took it as a sign. They hatched a plan to elope, escape, evade their pasts and make a future that had nothing to do with Kirazzi or Ulanitti. Something small and simple. A house, a farm. The two of them, the baby.

Then Emperor Clement and Turon Kirazzi settled on a solution: Beneditta's hand for the would-be duke's abdication. Tie Kirazzi to Ulanitti, make clear there was no ambition to destroy the Imperial Majesty *or* the Khirazji protectorate, and offer a path away from the Usurper's poisonous legacy.

But love is not enough to withstand the truth of our respective stations, and the dangers of my past are too great to bear. Wedding Beneditta could change all of that...

Ibramo stepped toward her, leaving the support of the door. "I have waited so long..." he began. "I... This is a farce, Lira, that's what it is, to stand here and pretend we have nothing to say to each other. No past."

"Please stop calling me that."

"Amadea," he said, but somehow that was worse. It sent a shiver over her skin, as if the name opened a door to her life now, letting Ibramo in. "Amadea," he said again, and she was seventeen, only becoming aware of the precipice she stood on.

She tried to make herself ask about the requests. She tried to bring up the changeling blood. Why was this so hard? It was supposed to be simple. She had closed this door twenty years ago, a whole lifetime ago.

"I got your letter," Ibramo said, the words edged with hurt. "I just hoped it wasn't the end of everything."

Wedding Beneditta could gain back everything your father took from you, while I will only ever drag you back into that mire. If you stay by my side, you would only be the son of the Usurper. Our children would be a threat to the Crown no matter what we did. I cannot do that to you.

The would-be duke refused the first time—no one spoke of that. No one spoke of the fact that, by then, the Kirazzis knew the Grave-Spurned Princess was with child. No one spoke of what the Ulanittis knew, of what Sigrittrice Ulanitti had been told when she arrived at Sestina to examine the young woman and decide if this could be Lireana indeed.

"So do you believe you're my grandniece?" she asked the Grave-Spurned Princess. "Are you Lireana?"

"I don't want the throne," the Grave-Spurned Princess replied, refusing to cry. "Neither does he. Let us go, we'll disappear, I'll never even say that name again. I'm not a threat."

Lady Sigrittrice had studied her with a hawklike eye for long moments. "You're not Lireana, that's for certain. But a threat? There are people who would take you up for the same symbol as the

Usurper did. And if you married the Usurper's son? Had children with him?" Sigrittrice's dark eyes had held the Grave-Spurned Princess's, unblinking. "You would be a very great threat, indeed."

"I had to fix it," Amadea said to Ibramo, hating how her voice shook. "I had to—"

"You didn't." Ibramo stepped closer. "You didn't do anything. You had nothing to atone for."

"That's not... That isn't it."

"Li... Amadea." He said her name like a sigh, and she fought off another shiver. Fought off the feeling that if she just moved closer, she could slip between the past and the present and find what she'd lost. "Don't lie to me," he said. "Not to me. Not about this. It wasn't your fault."

"But I was the one who could fix it."

"And you're the one who can help solve this murder," Quill interrupted. Amadea and Ibramo both startled, and she flushed. She had forgotten about Quill and Yinii.

She looked back at Yinii, who was staring at her, still as a deer with her eyes huge and staring, as if she could not sort through everything she was seeing fast enough. Amadea longed to sit down beside her, to straighten this all out, to fix the trust that had broken when she should have been able to keep it deep and buried.

But not now.

Ibramo's dark eyes watched her for a long moment, as if he wouldn't discuss the murder without finishing their conversation. As if they would have to go back, dig everything up. The emperor's proposal, Sigrittrice's warnings, his mother's weeping.

The miscarriage.

The realization that the Grave-Spurned Princess had to disappear completely, if anything for Ibramo Kirazzi was going to turn out right.

"We need..." She cleared her throat. "We need to know why you asked for those things. Lord Obigen's murder is tangled up in it. And worse."

Ibramo looked away, as if he didn't want to leave their conversation aside, as if this was somehow a whole new betrayal. But he knew as well as she did, what he'd come for was too important.

"About six months ago, I received a package addressed with the Kirazzi seals. I assumed it was from my cousin Zara, since she took the ducal authority after Duke Turon died a year and a half ago. In it were some of my uncle's belongings—books, letters he exchanged with my mother, and...a letter from my father, tucked into an old copy of *The Precepts of Bekesa.*

"In it, my father...admonished Turon for not joining him, but acknowledged his coup was unlikely to end successfully. He described a cache and suggested his work could be continued with what was in it—or at least, Turon would appreciate the breadth of his vision once he saw it."

"That sounds like your father," Amadea said.

"The letter said the map was hidden in the family Book of Gates. That he'd need their father's arm—that it was a key to get in—and the flail to continue the glory of Khirazj or something." He sighed. "That is bad enough—I don't enjoy thinking of my father's schemes waiting to be rekindled—but when I spoke to Zara next and asked why she sent those things, she told me she had no idea what I was talking about. The package wasn't from her."

"But it had the ducal seals on it?" Quill asked.

"Exactly," Ibramo said. "I conferred with the Duchess Kirazzi and we decided it was wisest to gather up those items, to keep them away from whoever was playing this game. And...I won't lie, I couldn't shake the hope I could find it first. Destroy whatever was there before someone else found it."

"And potentially be caught with it," Amadea pointed out. "They might have been setting you up. Why didn't you tell..." She found she could not say "the empress."

Ibramo dropped his gaze. "The possibility exists that the sender is a member of the imperial family and court. They hold copies of the ducal seals in trust, remember."

"What do you think is *in* the vault?" Quill asked.

"An excellent question," Ibramo said.

"Do you think the Shrike knows what's in there?" Quill asked. "Do you think they know where it lies?"

Ibramo stiffened, his gaze darting to Amadea. "How does he know—"

"There are some inconsistencies with Lord Obigen's murder," Amadea said. She explained to him the marks, the matching testimonies, the ledger with the Shrike's name in it.

Ibramo swore and ran a hand over his silvering beard. "If the Shrike is active, they might be the thief. It would have to be someone my father trusted like he did the Shrike."

"Amadea says she doesn't remember anything about them," Quill said. "What about you?"

Ibramo gave a short, bitter laugh. "They liked to make fun of me? I remember the taunts. The Shrike's identity was too precious for them to risk. My father might have died knowing who they were, but everyone else was...wiped clean."

"She forgot something," Yinii said, voice shaking. She told them what Reza Dolitha had seen that night, a woman attacking her with a knife. "I don't see how that could be anyone but the Shrike. That should narrow it down."

"There's another way we can be sure," Amadea said. "Fastreda."

She heard Yinii suck in a breath. Ibramo went very still, very quiet. "Are you asking me to talk to her?"

"No, I'm asking you to let me talk to her," Amadea said crisply. "She liked me...in a manner of speaking."

"'Little Sparrow,'" Ibramo said, making a face. "I remember."

"Get us in to speak to her," Amadea pleaded. "Please. I don't see a way around it. The only women of the right age we're sure were there that night were Gaspera and Lady Sigrittrice. And we need to be certain."

Ibramo frowned, worried. Always worried. "I don't like the idea of you facing her."

"I'm not that keen on it myself," she said, and at least he laughed a little at that. "Please."

He nodded. "For you."

"There are two other issues," Quill said, and again, Amadea felt her heart jerked out of rhythm, as if had been caught in a current of the past and suddenly tangled in reality's net.

"What did I forget?" she asked.

"Well, first," Quill said, "what were the statues for?"

Ibramo's eyes narrowed, confused. "What statues?"

"The fourth item on the list," Quill said. "Two bronze statues of pre-Sealing Khirazji queens. What are they for?"

Ibramo looked from Quill to Amadea and shook his head. "I don't know what you mean. I didn't ask the primate to find those."

"That's what I was afraid of," Quill said, this time to Amadea. "Because the second thing is that he's not the man I've seen following me. Someone else is pretending to be the consort-prince."

IV

A LIZARD AMONG THE LEAVES

Year Eight of the Reign of Emperor Clement
Palace Sestina

Envision a moment, two scions of Kirazzi—two brothers, a year apart: Redolfo and Turon. They have the same parents, the same lessons, the same tutors, the same texts. *The Equations of Sulba*. The Jade Sapa's *Oration and Rhetoric*. Olouluian *Tactics of the Beminat*—all the best wisdom of the imperial federation, grounded in the dictums of ancient Khirazj—*The Maxims of Ab-Kharu*. The *Papyrus of On*. *The Precepts of Bekesa*.

Two brothers, so alike on sight that one is said to be the other's changeling, but such different people, here, now, at the end of that path.

It is *The Precepts of Bekesa* in particular Turon is thinking of, these proscriptions and admonitions and promises from their distant source. The brothers learned the text from the same tutor, a bent old man with a knobby beard like a statue's—in his youth, he had fled Khirazj, *actual Khirazj*, in the retinue of Turon and Redolfo's great-grandfather, seen the Salt Wall formed in a roar of magic and sacrifice. And while he was meant to drill them on Bekesa's philosophy, the order of the world and the rights and responsibilities of the king-ship, what Turon remembers most strongly are the old scribe's words on the changelings. Two boys—ten, eleven—made to drill on these warnings, because, the old tutor insisted, Those Who Sow Deception had laughed in the face of all those other walls.

Here, now, in the study with the garish wallpaper, Redolfo takes the brandy back. "If I knew who the Shrike was, believe me, I'd tell you. I think that life might be worth as much as mine."

"Why is that?"

He grins. "Where do you think the changeling blood came from? The Shrike is the one who went over the Wall and collected it. Shouldn't the emperor worry about *that* running free?"

It's a press, a dare—another distraction. Turon doesn't follow this time—what is Redolfo distracting him from?

The tutor's voice echoes in his thoughts: *The changeling hides among the Khirazji like a lizard among the leaves of the palm. When it is still, there is no marking it, but it must move and breathe and continue its small life according to the circle of Al-Duat.*

"Which of them turned on me?" Redolfo demands. "If it wasn't the Shrike."

"Make a guess," Turon says, trying to put his finger on what is unsettling.

Redolfo downs the rest of his glass. "I have a lot of enemies, don't I?"

The same words again, the same flourish and intonation. The too-sweet brandy drunk glass after glass. Turon hesitates.

"Will you tell me something?" he asks. "A story. About me, when we were young?"

Redolfo laughs once. "I thought you were supposed to be inter-rogating me about Lireana. About the venom and now the Shrike."

"Humor me," Turon says. "A grieving brother."

Redolfo rolls his eyes, sighs. "When you were five, you went to the temple of the Golden Oblates with Father, and you were so worked up you threw up on the statue. Happy?"

Turon holds his brother's steady gaze until his eyes water, and when he blinks, the memory of the ancient tutor is behind his eyes.

The gods have bound you, the old man said. *You were the ones who would lead Khirazj, and so you will lead here as well. And when Those Who Sow Deception come again and take the faces of your neighbors and your ministers and your day-sisters, you will be ready, because Pademaki the Source has declared you will be.*

Turon wouldn't call himself devout, though he wouldn't call himself an unbeliever—not out loud, anyway. He visits the temples in their cycle, prays to the gods that the path of the world continues. But the world he knows is so complex, so wide, so multifaceted. Does a river god in a far-off land really spit out the sun each morning, when Turon knows the horizon never ends?

But what Turon does believe, so deeply it is like instinct, is that he is a man in seven parts—seven souls divided and united, their strengths and weaknesses influencing his whole. If he is torn, now, between grief for his brother and rage for his circumstances and fear for the future of all of Semilla—similarly divided, similarly united—then this is only natural. He is many things pretending to be one.

But from his brother, Turon has never gotten the same sense: Redolfo is a monolith, singular. He is an entity as whole and endless as the river. The idea that Redolfo is tormented or divided is blasphemy.

Except—here, now—with the *Precepts* in Turon's thoughts, he sees cracks. He sees the lizard move among the leaves—the brandy, the repeated phrases, the eyes that do not blink.

And now this: a story where Redolfo did not once mention himself. As petty as that seems, all stories from Redolfo's lips turn around himself, even if he is only the most important spectator.

Come Alletet, come Djutubai, come Phaseran, and ink these signs upon your children's hearts that they might know the changeling that walks among them . . .

This is not his brother before him, at all.

CHAPTER ELEVEN

The next morning, Yinii's nerves still trembled all along her arms, but she was resolved. She practiced what she was going to say all the way up to Bijan's workroom, where she'd been told Amadea was. She tapped the words against her fingertips, alternating with a touch of Saint Asla's crystal for luck. This would work.

In the workroom, Amadea lay on the floor, under the bulk of a small Borsyan cold-magic panel, a steel sheet pocked with small holes, attached by fine copper tubes to a glass-and-steel box lined with a dark fabric that lay open. Bijan and Tunuk stood beside it, both holding objects in careful hands, but Yinii had eyes only for what Bijan held.

The Flail of Khirazj was not made solely from rubies. The staff of it was actually wooden, covered with gold leaf. The beads that dangled from its threshing end were blue glass and jet, gold and those fat teardrop rubies that seemed to glow in the Borsyan lamps of Bijan's workshop, and looking at it, a part of Yinii could see why the corundum specialist who had preceded Bijan had won out when deciding where the Flail of Khirazj would be kept, after the coup collapsed.

Bijan was frowning at the opened safe. "I don't think it's going to fit."

Tunuk held up a prosthetic arm—Djacopo Kirazzi's, Yinii surmised, the last of the Kirazzi requests. Against the midnight stretch of his own limbs, it seemed childlike. She hung back in the doorway, listening to them.

"If it goes in on the diagonal..." Tunuk bent down, peering into the case. "Why is there a book in there?"

"That's *The Maxims of Ab-Kharu*," Amadea said, muffled by the cold-magic panel that kept the vault air ideal for the wood of the flail. "It will fit."

"And they'll all take the same temperature and moisture?" Bijan said, anxiety edging his voice. "You can't mildew the book to keep the flail from splitting."

"I have discussed this with as many specialists as I could find," Amadea said patiently. "Once I adjust the panel, the humidity will be within the right tolerance for all of them." She broke off with a grunt of effort.

"You have all of the things," Tunuk said. "Aren't you supposed to give them to the Paremi now, and let *them* handle the Kirazzis?"

A *clank*. "The vigilant requested we wait."

Bijan huffed. "That vigilant can lick the Wall."

"Which vigilant?" Tunuk asked, turning the arm over.

"The one that nearly killed Stavio. Gate-slapped idiot."

Tunuk looked up, eyes glowing. "Stavio's fine. Who killed Stavio?"

"The one..." Bijan faltered. "Well, it's not important."

"Oh, I see," Tunuk said. "He essentially murdered your husband, but I want to know and..." His eyes narrowed. "It's the one investigating Obigen's murder, isn't it? What did he do?"

Another *clank*, and this time Amadea sat up, holding a rag in one hand and the glass tube that scintillated with a sliver of Borsyan cold-magic in the other. "He made a very stupid decision," she said. "So did Stavio."

"He wanted a bronze specialist to test your parents' house's goblets for poison," Bijan said. "And he didn't want to wait."

"That *is* Stavio being stupid, then," Tunuk said. "Why are all our bronze specialists flinging themselves into the spiral this week?"

"It's been a hard alignment! And people in alignment deserve a little bit more care."

"Yes, I wouldn't know *anything* about that." Tunuk flipped the arm over and held it up before the case. "This isn't going to fit."

Amadea flicked the tube, and the light inside flared a little brighter. "Tunuk, stop it. Bijan, hand me that valve wrench, if you would." Her eyes caught on Yinii standing in the door. "Oh. Yinii. Did you need something?"

The thread of nervousness in her voice was unmistakable, and it made Yinii suddenly angry. All the ink in Bijan's catalogues started muttering, and she pushed it down.

"I needed to ask you something," Yinii said. "It can wait until you're finished." She folded her hands together. "Does it need a fabricator?" The Flail of Khirazj was important enough that its panel was never left to run down. If the wood split while the Kirazzis held it, that was one thing—if it was damaged in the care of the Imperial Archives, it was quite another.

"No," Amadea said, ducking back under the steel plate. "I'm just tuning for the additional materials."

"She *never* calls for the fabricators," Tunuk pointed out.

"The fabricators are very expensive," Amadea returned. "And they keep splitting the cold-magic pieces and pretending they didn't."

"Speaking of that vigilant," Bijan said, "Stavio and Zoifia wanted to know if he took the statues."

"No," Amadea said. "Just the . . . packages."

"Poison," Tunuk corrected.

"They are not any of our problems anymore," Amadea finished. "I will go make sure Zoifia and Stavio know that."

Yinii's temper flared again. That she could say that, knowing the Shrike was out there, knowing the Shrike had *more* Venom of Changelings. But she bit her tongue.

Tunuk tested the arm again, this time with the palm curled down. He snorted. "I *guess* that fits."

"I cannot believe we're sticking a dead man's false arm in with the Flail of Khirazj," Bijan said, putting the flail back. "Why did we take that in the first place?"

"It is an excellent piece of combined Datongu and Alojan bone-craft techniques," Tunuk retorted. "As well as being one of the few examples of a partially articulated prosthetic made for a human we've collected—"

"All right," Bijan said. "Those are reasons."

"Better than 'oh look, a pretty stick with some beads on it.' And it's easy to say 'false' if you don't need—"

"Settle *down*," Amadea said to Tunuk. She took the arm from him, gently. Tunuk wasn't wrong, Yinii thought. While it might have seemed a peculiar inclusion among the treasures of the Imperial Archives, Djacopo Kirazzi's arm was a delicate work of wires and bone, leather and wood. Amadea slipped it in beside the flail and closed the door, locking it with the key on her belt ring.

Tunuk sniffed again, then said, "He's not entirely an idiot, is he? That vigilant? I mean . . . my mothers say all the paperwork is entirely tangled. And then he goes and hands a specialist in alignment a fistful of bronze—"

"It has been less than a week," Amadea reminded him, squeezing his shoulder. "He's making sure nothing slips past. I trust him."

Again, that spark of anger in Yinii. Amadea trusted him—that once meant something. Now Amadea was a liar and a former malcontent, Redolfo Kirazzi's long-dead pretender walking around like that was nothing—and yet she was still Amadea, and Yinii didn't know how to put these things back together.

But Vigilant Langyun also seemed thorough and thoughtful. She had told him what the reza had said, about seeing a woman, and he'd asked all the right questions to make Yinii trust he believed her and he would use this to stop the killer. Somehow.

Amadea left Bijan's workshop, going to one of the small wall fountains to wash her hands thoroughly. Yinii stood beside her, practicing the words in her thoughts.

"You're angry with me," Amadea said quietly. "That's fair."

The words wouldn't leave Yinii's mouth. She was terribly angry . . . and yet she couldn't work out what she thought Amadea should have done differently.

"You could have told us," Yinii said. "You could still tell all of us. It's the past; it doesn't matter who you were."

Amadea sighed and dried her hands. "Then I don't see the point in telling people. I am who I am. What I did is irrelevant to that.

And…if the wrong people knew I was…that people thought I might be…"

"What?" Yinii demanded. "You'd join them?"

"*No,*" Amadea said, and Yinii felt something in her flinch at Amadea's vehemence. "Never again. But it doesn't help the empress to bring up rival claimants to the Imperial Authority—in any form. So I will beg you again for your silence."

It doesn't help the empress either for you and her husband to act like characters in a Datongu melodrama, Yinii thought, but she would never say anything like that, and she blushed thinking it.

That was enough to slow her down, to let Amadea interject, "I need to go and check on Stavio and Zoifia. Do you want to come? If I recall correctly, you had some gifts for her? Why don't you go and get them?"

It was automatic, the way Yinii agreed, scurried back to her rooms to get the package she'd carried back from the House of Unified Wisdom. She met Amadea by her office and followed her up to the sequestration rooms, where the light was soft and the noises of the city distant, trying to get the argument she had been trying to make back to her lips.

She won't go see Fastreda without you, Yinii told herself. *You won't let that happen.*

Not a saint, but a sorcerer—a living sorcerer, in this very city, a blessed woman with a lottery years and years deep just to speak with her. Yinii's reza was incapacitated, Amadea wasn't who she'd said she was, the saints gave Yinii no guidance, the ink whispered and whispered, and Yinii's father was coming to take her from the archives. When Amadea had said in the Kinship Hall that she wanted Ibramo to make it possible for her to speak with Fastreda, Yinii's fears had condensed around this possibility: She was not a saint, but Fastreda might understand. Might know what to do, when no one else could guide her.

Zoifia and Stavio had claimed the bigger room at the end of the otherwise empty hall, the one with space for three specialists. Someone had hauled a tin bathtub up for Stavio to sit in, and Zoifia had made a nest of her blankets on the bed against the wall. When they came in, Zoifia burst into tears, and Yinii's resolve failed again.

The pull of Zoifia's and Stavio's alignments was nothing like it had been when Zoifia had spiraled in the Pit—the haphazard sloshing of a lake stirred by a passing boat, not the sucking whirlpool. But with her fingers on the chapbooks she'd bought earlier, Yinii could feel the ghostly echo of her own power, filling the waves Zoifia's alignment created in the whisper of the ink.

Yinii sat down on the bed, dropping the chapbooks. "It's all right," she said, rubbing Zoifia's back. "It was the alignment."

Zoifia gave a wet sniff. "It is not all right. I was terrible to you. You were being a good friend—a wonderful friend—and I just...I just..." She covered her face with both hands. "I'm sorry."

"She's doing that a lot," Stavio reported, wilting over the edge of the bathtub. Then, gently: "Sorcha, odidunu, nobody blames you." It said a lot about their relationship, Yinii thought, that Stavio would call her "witch" and "baby sister" in the same breath.

Amadea took Zoifia's arm gently, felt the pulse at her wrist, the heat of her neck. "You're coming down quick, aren't you?"

"It's awful," said Zoifia. "It's so lonely. So empty."

"Like those hollowed-out statues," Stavio added.

"They're not hollowed out," Zoifia sniffed. "They were cast like that. You're saying that to annoy me so I stop crying." And she began weeping again.

"You weren't really awful," Yinii assured her. Maybe she was sharp, maybe she was a little mean—maybe the alignment made the roughest parts of you rougher. But Bijan was right: being in alignment earned people a little extra care. She pushed the chapbooks to her along with a packet of sugarplums and wild celery candies. "Here, I brought you some things."

Zoifia took one look at the title on the top—*Rafiel del Sladio and the Changeling Queen*—and burst into tears anew. "You remembered I hate the smart ones!" she howled.

"You do the same for me," Yinii reminded her, handing Stavio another packet of candies. "Last time, you made me coffee and brought buns. You got me the histories and the myths, because I do like the smart ones, and you only told me once they were boring."

It was meant to be a joke, but Zoifia gave a great sniff. "I was going to steal your dopey Paremi just to get the statues. I'm the worst friend."

Yinii blushed. "Oh...He's not...We're not..."

"Odidunu," Stavio said to her, "nobody believes you."

Amadea hugged Zoifia. "But you didn't do anything," she reminded her. "This was a very difficult alignment—"

"Stavio managed not to ruin anyone's life."

"I'm gonna ruin that vigilant's life," Stavio said dully.

"Both of you, stop," Amadea said. "Zoifia, you were unpleasant and you were rude. You had some thoughts that weren't becoming of you, but at the end of all of this, the only person you came close to hurting was you. Stop whipping your own back." She reached into her pocket and took out a little figure of a bronze bird, a Borsyan amulet of sorts, the eagle at watch.

"Here," she said gently. Zoifia stared at the little bird a moment, before hesitantly taking it. She closed her eyes and shivered, and Yinii felt the ghost of her own shivers, watching it. That first touch after the danger had passed—it was something more than pleasure. Like plunging burned skin into cold water and the sudden absence of pain that came with it.

"And you," Amadea said to Stavio, who groaned. "As much as I am angry at the vigilant, I know you know this is firstly your fault and mine."

"It's not *your* fault," Stavio protested, jerking up from his perch.

"It is my job, ultimately, to keep an eye on you during your alignment, and I didn't. I'm sorry. I owe you better, and before your next alignment, I will find you two a generalist."

Both protested she didn't need to, as if they hadn't complained themselves about having to share generalists with the other metallic specialists, and Amadea listened, but she also didn't relent.

This was Amadea, Yinii thought, the Amadea she trusted and remembered—*this* was the Amadea she wanted to keep hold of, not that other, that Amadea who hid things and lied and let Yinii stumble into the middle of danger like a baby calf off a cliff.

"We'll come see you later," Amadea said. Yinii hugged Zoifia again, squeezed Stavio's hand, her thoughts a thousand miles away.

Amadea heaved another sigh as they left. "So," she said. "Let's talk about Quill."

"No, let's talk about Fastreda," Yinii said, seizing her courage. "You lied when I asked before, so I'm asking again. I want to go with you when you see her today."

"Out of the question," Amadea said. "Yinii—"

"First," Yinii continued, "you know this is important to me."

"Fastreda is *dangerous*, Yinii. She's not a saint."

"No, she's maqu'tajii," Yinii said, using the honorific for sorcerers who might not be Orozhandi but still had the fullness of the God Below's blessings. "Which is still holy, so of course I want to meet her. Besides which, for the second point, I have been to the chapel *twice* since I stumbled on a murdered body yesterday, so I think it would be very good for me to be reminded of the order in the world like this." She swallowed. "I *need* this. And you just said, it's your job to take care of me."

Amadea shook her head, over and over. "Yinii, she's *not* a good person."

"She liked you," Yinii shot back. "Isn't that what the consort-prince said? 'Little Sparrow'? Maybe you should talk to *him* about keeping secrets."

Amadea jerked like Yinii had slapped her, and it was all Yinii could do to keep talking, keep explaining her plan. "And that's third: Why are *you* and the consort-prince going to see her? You don't think that's suspicious? You don't think people will notice and start wondering right off?"

"It can't be helped, and I don't—"

"It can, because if you take me, I'm someone who *should* be there. There are lotteries for Orozhandi to meet with Fastreda *because* she's maqu'tajii—I've been in them since I moved here. There's no reason for you, but *I* have a very good reason, so you can use me." Yinii pulled her fidgeting hands apart. "I can be useful."

Amadea's sternness melted at that, into something soft and sad. "You need to be safe. You don't need to be useful."

Yinii drew a deep breath. And something in her own anger softened too. *That* was Amadea, and maybe that was what spurred Amadea's lie—she had to make sure people were safe.

"I will be with you," Yinii said, "so I will be both."

Amadea was due to meet Ibramo shortly, so once it was clear Yinii wasn't budging, she led her down to the entrance. "You cannot give her anything," Amadea said. "And they'll search you—she can't have any glass or any sand."

"I understand," Yinii said, though she also thought of how it would feel to be locked away from the ink, from any hope of the ink.

Amadea glanced back at her as they descended the staircase, as if she could hear those thoughts. "I will tell you again: Fastreda is not like you're expecting."

"I understand," Yinii said again. "She's dangerous. You can be blessed and not be a good person. I know that." But if you were blessed, she thought, surely you understood the world better. Surely you were wise, even if you were a little wicked too.

Amadea sighed and stepped off the staircase—

And nearly collided with the Masked Empress of Semilla.

Beneditta Iboria Clotilda Doromara Ulanitti, Masked Empress of Semilla and Grand Duchess by Custom of Her Protectorates, stumbled back into her retainers, as a pair of guards interposed themselves, weapons out.

The empress was bright as salt, smooth as marble, in a vast, high-collared gown of ivory and gold satins. Her half mask was an airy one, leaving her uncovered from bronze cheekbones to pointed chin, the eyeholes vast around her widening dark eyes. Gold granules crowded into thick lines around the eyeholes, into stripes down the chin. Gold meant imperial business. The pinch of Beneditta's thin mouth said personal distaste, and Stavio's story, everything that happened in the Kinship Hall, felt contained in the purse of her lips.

Amadea froze—half a breath, no more—before dropping into a low curtsy. "My apologies, Your Imperial Majesty," she blurted. "I wasn't looking."

Yinii dropped into her own curtsy, shaken by how shaken Amadea seemed. *You can't have Noniva's smile and the sugar dates both,* she could hear Stavio saying. *She comes to the archives, lives like she's sequestered, pretends it never, ever happened. But you notice. You see things not sitting right.*

In the whisper of the inks, she heard the echo of Ibramo's soft *Lira?*

Mireia stood beside the empress, looking like nothing so much as a hound ready to spring, but with no prey, no command. Behind her were two more masked ladies, one carrying a casket. Retainers coming to retrieve masks for the festival.

"Archivist Gintanas," Mireia began sternly. "Archivist ul-Benturan—"

"It's fine!" Beneditta said, almost shouted. Yinii dared a glance, saw the blush creeping around the edges of the empress's mask as she looked at Amadea with a strange expression Yinii felt she ought to know. The empress looked abruptly up at the winding staircase. "I suspect you have a great many collisions in this particular location."

Yinii peeked up as the empress's attention flicked back to Amadea, her mouth struggling a moment as though she needed to speak but couldn't. "Archivist Gintanas," she said finally, the name brittle as a dead leaf.

"You may recall, Your Imperial Majesty," Mireia said in firm, stately tones, "Archivist Gintanas is one of our superior generalists. She manages a quarter of our archivists. This is Yinii Six-Owl ul-Benturan. She is an ink specialist. She handles the Orozhandi and Khirazji text collections under Archivist Gintanas."

The empress's clear brown eyes turned to Yinii. "I am very pleased to meet you, Archivist ul-Benturan. Your work in the Imperial Archives is of the greatest importance to our empire and its people. Do you enjoy it?"

"Very much, Your Imperial Majesty."

And then suddenly, Amadea spoke. "I was very sorry to hear of the death of Lord Obigen. I'd heard you were there, Your Imperial Majesty."

Beneditta's brows rose. Yinii sucked in a breath. Mireia stared daggers at Amadea, and though Yinii thought she might choke on the words, she couldn't leave Amadea dangling there, trying to help, trying to be brave.

"Oh, how terrible!" she burst out. "It sounds...It sounded *grue-some*. I do hope you didn't have to see any of that!"

But Beneditta only looked puzzled. "Yes, it was very terrible. But don't fret for me, my dear, I left before the poor man was murdered." She hesitated, then added to Amadea, "Thank you for your concern."

Yinii swallowed. "I'm glad, Your Majesty. My friend...my friend saw..."

And her head filled, not with how she imagined Lord Obigen, but with Primate Lamberto, purple-faced and dangling. She closed her mouth around the words that didn't come.

Amadea put her arm around Yinii. "No one would wish such a trauma on anyone, especially Your Imperial Majesty."

"You're very thoughtful, my dear." Beneditta took a ring from her smallest finger, a pearl on a gold band, and handed it to Yinii with a smile. "Here. It should fit over your horn, if you wish it."

Yinii clasped the little ring between her hands, and she curtsied again. "Thank you. Thank you very much, Your Imperial Majesty."

Beneditta clapped her hands together. "Well. Our tasks are complete. Have a pleasant Salt-Sealing, Archivist ul-Benturan." She hesitated, watching Amadea, still with that strange expression. "Archivist Gintanas. You as well."

"Thank you, Your Imperial Majesty."

And then they were sweeping off, a flock of masked ladies and Mireia, down the walkway, sucking the sudden tension away like a whirlwind behind them. Yinii watched them go, eyes on the empress.

Fear, Yinii suddenly realized. That was the look—a worry, a fear of what Amadea was going to do or say. A worry of what Beneditta might say back. Yinii knew that expression far too well, but it had no business being on the Masked Empress of Semilla's face, so she was almost certainly mistaken.

She turned to Amadea, who was staring after the empress with a look of horror. Yinii followed her gaze...to the small dark star peeking out of the slash in the empress's sleeve.

Yinii straightened, shaking. "Amadea," she said softly, "Amadea, is that the mark?"

"Yes," Amadea murmured. "Which means she was there late enough to be injected."

"She's lying?"

"I don't know," Amadea said, still watching the empress walk away.

— ·—·— ·· —

Richa hired a carriage to get Quill from the archives, two other vigilants out of uniform hanging off the back, in case the Shrike struck again. They were as on edge as Richa—the Vigilant Kinship wasn't tasked with many cases like this one, and where the carriage went, onlookers noticed and whispered. He remembered Corolia's rumors and wondered what was simmering under the surface.

Most of a vigilant's dedication was just that—*be vigilant.* Stop the crimes and put out the fires, yes, but foremost watch for the beginnings. A fight, a thief, a rich man spending coin to buy his own way—these were sparks, beginnings, and better to clear the brush they might ignite before a blaze ever caught. People in want, people in need, people with power they shouldn't wield. Is there water, is there food, is the shelter safe—this was what you made certain of, most of a vigilant's day.

Richa had been eight when the first rumblings of the Kirazzi Rebellion reached Caesura, twelve when it raged over most of southern Semilla. He was only in cloths during the Brothers' War. Not his fight, not his problem—but these were the stories cadets heard over and over. *This was a small thing, an ember spat from a fire, but see all this discontent, all this corruption, all these ways the promise of the empire and her protectorates was flouted.* The Vigilant Kinship had failed, that was the most important lesson to take—not that the Imperial Majesty was fallible, not that ambition and greed could warp people and pervert justice, not that words of tradition could be wielded like a weapon one way or another. *Remember this: when we don't clear the brush of injustice, we as good as set the fire ourselves.*

The Shrike, though, was something else. Not a spark, but a bolt of lightning, an evil out of nowhere. Anything might be tinder to this murder, and Richa couldn't shake the feeling he should have stopped this, caught it when it was small and snuffable. Now it was racing ahead of him, catching on to things he didn't realize were ready to burn. *I hear it's the Borsyans, I hear the Alojan ducal authority is threatening, I hear the empress's guards did it.*

Was this the Shrike's goal? This spreading of discord and fear? He didn't for a breath imagine this as a crime of the moment. What did the deaths of Karimo, Obigen, and Primate Lamberto aid? He thought of what Amadea had told him Yinii had discovered and tried to imagine what Gaspera del Oyofon or Sigrittrice Ulanitti might want. What the empress might want.

He thought of the cadastres, the land along the Wall—and it didn't fit right. Oh, he could believe a murder over land—people feeling desperate or angry could find a lot of reasons to kill once they passed a certain point—but why the artifice? If Obigen needed to be stopped, if the Shrike believed the only way to do it was to murder him, why not stage a suicide as she'd done with Lamberto? If Karimo had stumbled on the blackmail scheme, why not simply make him forget it?

And the only reason he could think of was to spark a bigger fire. To make people feel unsafe or angry or emboldened to something. The death of the Alojan noble consul, the maiming of the ul-Benturan reza, the killer dying with a cryptic phrase—it was like a scene from a play. You heard that story, you would infuse that with meaning. People *were* infusing it with meaning.

Richa sighed—that still felt messy. Messy and inexact.

Bringing Quill along to the second round of interviews was, in Richa's opinion, a bad solution to a worse problem. The Kinship Hall was certainly safer than the archives, and Richa felt better about keeping an eye on the young man. But when he went to collect Quill late the next morning, after sending cadets to bring in the four party guests, all Richa could think of was how fragile Quill had been in the wake of Karimo's death, how hard the death of Primate Lamberto might have hammered the young scrivener.

Instead, he found Quill waiting beside the archives guards,

uniform pressed and expression purposeful, his scribe kit packed into a handled wooden box.

"You doing all right?" Richa asked, as he guided Quill into the carriage, eyes on the passersby.

"Fine," Quill said tersely. Then: "You're going to arrest her today?"

"We're going to find out if we've got a 'her' to arrest today," Richa corrected. "Vigilants are just as beholden to the details as the Paremi are."

"Good," Quill said, with a tight smile. "Then I will help with details."

Richa considered him as they trundled through the city. "I'm sorry about the primate."

"I'm only sorry he couldn't confess before he died. I'm only sorry he couldn't tell us who the Shrike was. I'm only sorry he got the incredibly foolish and self-important notion in his head to black-mail a legendary assassin, leading to more people being killed." He looked out the window. "Do you think it was my fault?" he said more quietly. "Because I went into the Maschanos' house, talking about Karimo and the primate? If it's Gaspera—"

"First," Richa said, "slow down. We haven't arrested her yet, even if I'd bet that's where the day winds up. Second, you're right: the primate built the boat that sank him. I don't know if it's foolishness or an obscene pride that makes a man blackmail the Usurper's pet assassin, but it was an obvious mistake he kept going long past the point he could have repaired it. But third...we all make mistakes." And here he could not help but think of Stavio, the unnatural grip, the flash of bronze in his eyes. The fear and the fury in Amadea's.

"We all make mistakes," he said again. "And so you fix it."

Quill looked up, and there in his eyes was an echo of that first night, that boy cut to the bone by grief. "What if you can't fix it?"

"Then you have to learn to live with it," Richa said. "But let's see what we can fix first." He considered Quill in his Paremi robes. "Why'd you swear to the scriveners?"

Quill frowned at him, confused by the shift in conversation. "Why shouldn't I have?"

Richa shrugged. "Most Paremi I've met are fond of rules. Order. Believe in the empire's justness down to their bones. Some are like the primate—using what they know to bend those rules, subvert the law without breaking it. Or maybe without anyone finding out they're breaking it. A few, the real old ones, are jaded about the whole system—they've seen it fail too many times.

"But you, you're too young to be jaded," he went on. "You're clearly not corrupt. And I know that I've only known you for a few days, which I have to imagine are the hardest and strangest test of your life—but given that, you went right off the path. You didn't leave this to the vigilants. You aren't trusting the system. So: Why did you take the oath of the people who shepherd the system?"

"That's how my family is," Quill said. "Eldest child inherits, second takes the priesthood, third is a scholar, after that crafters. Unless you've got an affinity, which I obviously don't."

"I guess that's a reason."

Quill paused. "I like the details. I like the people. I like fitting the people into the details, you know? Before this, I had a circuit, up north. I did things like interpret wills and figure out property disputes. I was better at that. I liked it better, anyhow." He nodded at Richa. "Why'd you swear to the Kinship? You don't seem like you're that keen on following the rules either."

Richa smiled. "I like rules. When they're fair and just and well applied."

"And you don't think Lady Sigrittrice is—"

"I have no idea whether Lady Sigrittrice is fair or just or well applied," Richa said. "But I also think she's acting with a set of information that's not *our* set of information, so we might as well press on."

"And if she finds out?" Quill asked.

"I have it on good authority that she's in conference with the empress this morning," Richa said as the carriage came to a stop before the Kinship Hall. "So, hopefully, she'll find out when we've got a murderer to offer as an apology."

Richa had ferreted out Sigrittrice's schedule from Hulvia, but he had forgotten to consider Hulvia herself. As he steered Quill down to the hallway lined with interview rooms, he came face-to-face with the imperial liaison blocking his way.

"*You* are out of line, *Vigilant*," she whispered, furious.

"Hulvia," he said calmly, "have you met Brother Quill? Quill, this is Vigilant Hulvia Manche, the imperial liaison."

"I asked you one thing—one thing! This is not quiet!"

"Let's hope you're sharper than Lady Sigrittrice," Richa said. "And you know I'm not out of line. This is what we do, Hul."

"The Imperial Majesty—"

"The empress hasn't said a word about this, and I'm not convinced Lady Sigrittrice isn't..." He stopped himself, not wanting to say it out loud. He had another suspect after all. "You know it's not out of line. You know we're not done. And I know you know, because she's not here. No one from the empress's forces is here. You didn't tell them."

"I didn't want *you* ousted either," she said, tentacles curling. "But we're both in the current if she finds out."

"One," Richa said. "One interview. You come with me, you listen, you don't think something bigger's going on, fine—send for Lady Sigrittrice, and I'll take what's coming to me."

Hulvia's face twisted around her frustration. She was the imperial liaison—it *was* her job if she was keeping things from them. But she was also a vigilant, and she knew as well as Richa: we don't let the fires burn.

"One," she agreed. "And, Richa, I swear to Noniva and all the little fishes, this better be *something*."

"Gaspera?" Quill asked.

"No," Richa said. "Nanqii first."

Nanqii ul-Hanizan sat in one of the small interview rooms, attending to his nails with a thin file and a careless demeanor. His silvery pale hair hung loose around his charm-spangled horns. "I would tell you that this room is hideous and uncomfortable, Richa," he said, as the three of them entered, "but I expect you're well aware. Where's my advocate?"

"On their way. Meanwhile, maybe we can chat."

"About what?"

Quill took the desk beside the door to start recording, while Hulvia stood against the opposite wall. Richa sat down and took out the handkerchief folded around the nugget of stillwax Stavio had stripped from the wine goblet. "I've been talking to some of your fellow party guests. One of them suggested that you might have all been drugged."

Nanqii shrugged. "I told you myself. I wasn't sitting through that party in my right mind. I don't think that absolves anyone wielding a knife."

"And did you share with everyone else?"

"I'm not a man inclined to charity," Nanqii said. "And you sound like a man trying to dance around a question."

Richa unfolded the handkerchief, the apple-seed-sized lump in the center, still wafting cedarwood and almond flowers. He gestured to it.

"Stillwax. It's off the goblets from the party. Do you want to tell me why?"

Alarm flickered in Nanqii's expression—just a flash, and then he was wrinkling his nose. "That seems like a waste."

Richa tilted his head. "Why do you say that?"

"Don't play the innocent, Vigilant—maybe you haven't partaken, but you know as well as I do that stillwax is a sedative. Put it in wine and all you get is a good night's sleep. Maybe a headache the next morning. Not much of a party, if you ask me."

Richa folded his hands together on the table. "So why's it in the wine goblets?"

Nanqii met his eyes, held his gaze. "Maybe Lord Obigen had a mind to knock us all out, tell us in the morning that we'd signed over our fortunes for his not-a-wall. How am I supposed to know?"

"Well," Richa said, "to begin with, you deal stillwax. So how about *you* don't play the innocent either."

"It's not illegal to sell stillwax."

"No one said it was," Richa replied. "And no one's ransacking your house for things it *is* illegal to manufacture and sell just yet, so why be coy? Who do you sell stillwax to?"

Nanqii smiled. "Anyone who has trouble sleeping."

Richa drew a breath, studied the Orozhandi's face. "Do you sell to Gaspera del Oyofon?"

Nanqii laughed, but there was something else there, a tightness to his eyes—he was afraid of something, angry about something. "I have. Not *that* much, though."

"How much would you need?" Hulvia interrupted. "In your professional opinion."

"Dose makes the poison, doesn't it? But for a party of nine to be nice and relaxed?" Nanqii asked. "Maybe a fist-sized"—the smallest of pauses—"a lump about that big." He wet his lips. "Have you talked to Gaspera?"

"We will be," Richa said.

"Can I ask something?" Quill had set his stylus down, studying Nanqii just as hard as Richa. "Have you checked him for bruises?"

"Bruises?" Nanqii asked.

"Not yet," Richa replied. "We're still talking."

Quill hesitated, tapping the stylus against his knuckles. His eyes never left Nanqii—it made Richa antsy and agitated, like he might at any moment need to step in. "You have a gap in your memory, don't you?" Quill suddenly asked. "Something about the stillwax. You're hiding something, and I wonder if that's it. If you don't remember who you sold a fist-sized lump of stillwax to."

Nanqii's expression seemed to freeze. He turned back to Richa. "What sort of a bruise?" he demanded in clipped tones.

"The Venom of Changelings leaves a star-shaped bruise where it's injected."

Behind him, Hulvia swore softly. "What the *fuck*, Richa?"

Nanqii set his fingertips together, leaning back in his seat, wary, canny. "Are we seriously speaking of the memory-altering poison purportedly favored by Redolfo Kirazzi? I thought everyone settled on 'what a convenient lie to tell about your sedition' since there was absolutely no evidence."

Richa met his gaze. "Turns out it exists. You deal that?"

"Hai allainaa, man!" Nanqii snapped. "Are you crazy? That sort of thing sends you to the hangman. Besides, if I recall correctly, the first ingredient is changeling blood. I wouldn't know where to get it and I wouldn't know who to sell it to."

He seemed to consider, to weigh something. He stood, unbuttoning his shirt. He turned, baring his pale, narrow back to Richa. There, under his shoulder blade, was a dark blue bruise, the shape of a star.

"A *friend* noted it the other night. I couldn't place it," Nanqii said. "Is that what it is?"

Richa let out a breath. "Yes."

"The other one too," Quill said.

Nanqii whirled around. "*What* other one?"

Quill stood and pulled Nanqii's left arm back a little. He touched the inner edge of his arm there, where another, fainter star bruise marked his skin. Richa's blood turned cold.

"It looks older," Quill said. "Maybe a few days?"

Nanqii's jaw worked a moment. He pulled his shirt back on and dropped into his seat. Touched the medals to his saints dangling from his horns. "Look...look, you said it...I sell stillwax," he said. "I keep track of my supply, I keep my prices stable, and I keep my records immaculate. Now, it seems I am short a quantity...perhaps a fist-sized lump, and my funds are increased in the amount of the missing stillwax's price. But I have no memory at all of selling it, and what's more, no records either."

Put it in the wine, Richa thought, *and everyone drops off long enough to get injected with the venom*. Tidy. Quick. You wouldn't even need an hour. "Did you deal that to anyone at Obigen's gathering? Anyone who might have lifted the stillwax?"

"I have had business arrangements," Nanqii said, "with Gaspera and the primate. Not Zaverio, of course, but I doubt he knows his boy—Doni or whatever it is—tried to buy some sandsmut once. I didn't sell it to him, and he'll probably come right out and tell you the same. Entitled little shit."

"Gaspera buys stillwax. What's was the primate buying from you?"

"Nothing. He worked for me. Cleaning up messes. Making problems go away. All within the bounds of the law, of course." He frowned. "You think one of my clients had something to do with this?"

"Somebody got close enough to you to make sure you didn't remember." Richa folded his hands. "Maybe make you think you want to fund a second wall."

"I wasn't there because I was planning to fund a damned thing," Nanqii said. "I was there because Bishamar Twelve-Spider told me to be, and when the reza says 'scale the cliff,' you ask if he wants anything particular from the top."

"Same reason you dabbled with Redolfo Kirazzi, from the sound of things."

Nanqii's gaze held Richa's. "What can I say? I'm a good boy. Grandbaba wants secrets, I'll find some secrets. You'll recall, however, the Orozhandi—particularly ul-Hanizan, mind—did not throw in with the Usurper on the whole. So really I stopped it from getting worse, when you think about it." He touched his saints' medallions, then leaned forward. "You think it was one of us. You think one of us used the venom and made this happen. You know about Bishamar Twelve-Spider and Duke Kirazzi and me, which means you've been reading the transcripts of the trials. I'll bet I know something that's not in those transcripts."

Richa raised his eyebrows. "Do you want to wait for your advocate?"

"You should be looking at the primate," Nanqii went on. "He's not in those files, is he? Because the Paremi make the files and keep them." He smiled thinly at Quill. "Your master was the Usurper's. Did you know that?"

"No, but I'm not surprised," Quill said. "What did he do?"

Nanqii frowned, a quick flash of annoyance that he hadn't rattled Quill, then turned back to Richa. "It's helpful, if you're planning a coup, it turns out, to have someone on the inside, shifting paperwork. Hiding what you're doing. Erasing what you've done. When you spring the thing, you can be lengths and lengths ahead of your enemies."

"And there's a reason you employ the primate," Richa finished. He paused, thinking. All the guests had been clients of the primate's.

"Primate Lamberto is dead. Hanged himself. Or at least that's what we're meant to think. I hope that wasn't your advocate."

Nanqii's eyes widened, dark-eye flashing open in surprise. "It *wasn't* me," he said, all of his earlier carelessness gone. "I hope you're not thinking anything so stupid. I can't very well inject myself in the middle of my back." He flung his hand toward the door, charms tinkling with the wild motion. "Ask Zaverio, ask Gaspera—if one of them's got the Venom of Changelings and is murdering—"

"Which of them do you think it is?" Hulvia interrupted.

Nanqii shook his head violently. "You think *I* dabbled with Kirazzi? Where do you think Zaverio's money comes from? The Maschano family was almost penniless before that coup, and now he's suddenly as rich as a gold saint? Plus, you think that man wouldn't *delight* in killing an Alojan and an Orozhandi and getting away with it? But Gaspera..." He hesitated, looking back to Richa. "That woman hasn't shown her true face for twenty-three years—maybe more. I think there's a reason she needs help sleeping." He shook his head again, touched the medallions among his horn charms. "What else do you want to know? Richa, I don't want any part of this mess, I hope you know that."

"Thank you for your candor," Richa said. "I'll have someone bring you a coffee, and let you know when your advocate arrives."

Out in the hall, he turned to Hulvia. "Well? Are you going to throw me to Sigrittrice?"

"*No.*" She looked furious, as if she couldn't believe Richa had had the gall to be right. Her mouth worked a moment, before her eyes cut to Quill. "You're a Paremi?"

Quill bristled. "Yes."

"And you came at him just right. What a waste." She returned to Richa. "You should keep your streak of being clever, and poach him."

Richa had to agree—Paremi usually sat silent, only speaking up to clarify statements or verify details. He'd planned to wait until the end to reveal the bruise, but Quill had spotted Nanqii's nerves faster and known to home in on it. "Well done," he said. "Don't get cocky with the next one."

Zaverio was second, utterly unashamed of the state of the interview room as Richa and the others entered. Quill tucked his scribe's kit up on his hip as he pulled the side table up onto its legs again.

"What the *fuck*—" Zaverio began.

"Sit down, Lord Maschano," Richa said. "We have some questions."

The Vigilant Kinship watched over all citizens by their oath, but if Richa were being honest, while he would, for example, put out a fire at the Maschano house, a tiny part of him would wish to let this man's comfort burn. Zaverio swore at them. He threw the chair aside again. He made implications at Hulvia that threatened Richa's patience.

"You are a person of interest in a very serious crime," Richa pointed out. "You have been suggested as a suspect. Perhaps you should take this more seriously."

Zaverio's eyes narrowed. "*Who* 'suggested' me as a suspect? And *where* is the primate?"

"Dead," Quill said simply. "Was he your advocate too?"

Zaverio's head whipped around in surprise. "What the fuck do you mean 'dead'?"

"Lamberto Lajonta died yesterday evening by hanging," Richa said. "We have reason to believe that it's related to the murders of Lord Obigen and Karimo del Nanova."

"Murders?" Zaverio couldn't catch up and it was making him furious. It was making him careless. "That boy killed himself. He killed the Alojan, tried to kill the Orozhandi and the primate, and then he killed himself—I saw it."

"You also assert you saw Lady Sigrittrice try and stop him, but she says no such thing happened," Richa pointed out. "Because as it turns out, all of the party, except for, one presumes, the actual killer, was under the influence of the Venom of Changelings."

"It seems we can end this very quickly if you submit to a physical examination," Hulvia said. "Do you have a star-shaped bruise on your person? If you're only a dupe, you should."

He did. One. At the center of his shoulder blades.

"You want someone up for murder," Zaverio sneered. "I would

think you'd be chasing the drug peddler. Or Gaspera—we all know she's available to stab people in the back."

"That's a funny way to describe giving evidence against a traitor to the empire," Richa said. "By the by, I've read the trial transcripts. You made out well."

Zaverio's face reddened. "Hearsay and rumor."

"And eighteen thousand metas, from the sound of things," Richa said. "If your only reasons for pointing to Nanqii or Captain del Oyofon are personal feelings—"

"To start with, that horned bastard thinks the Salt Wall is sacred. Doesn't want a hole knocked in it for progress. You don't think that's a better motive than some financial exchanges? Bishamar ul-Hanizan wants it shut down and doesn't think old Dolitha's going to manage.

"As for Gaspera, she owes everyone she knows money. She certainly owes Rosangerda enough. I heard Obigen telling her that selling off her land would make them settled. But did she jump to sell? No. She drags it out. So they've all got a better reason than I do to start killing." Zaverio's grip on the chair tightened as if he was going to throw it again. "And you find out which one put that fucking poison in me—"

Richa stood. "Wait here, if you please."

Out in the hallway, chased by Lord Maschano's curses, Quill huffed a frustrated sigh. "You don't believe it's him."

"No," Richa said, thoughts churning. They were pointing fingers fast enough, spreading out each other's lies. But through the sudden proliferation of motives, he could spy a path: Gaspera had sided with the Usurper. Gaspera owned land along the Wall that wasn't used by anyone else, whose ownership dated to the coup. Gaspera had money problems, but *this* she didn't want to part with. Gaspera knew where to find stillwax, possibly how Nanqii kept his records. She had time to gather supplies, proximity to administer them, reasons.

But why? a little part of Richa murmured.

"I *wish* it were him," Hulvia said. "I don't see a blunt weapon like that using the Venom of Changelings—is that *seriously* what we're dealing with, Richa? Actual, verifiable Venom of Changelings. Why the fuck would you hide something like that?"

"I found out *yesterday*," Richa said. Unbidden he thought of Amadea, planning to visit Fastreda of the Glass, and a pang of worry went through him before he could swat it aside. "But yes, that's what we're dealing with and that's why we're doing this, and that's..." He paused, shaping his next words carefully. "I'm wondering if Lady Sigrittrice already knows."

Hulvia's eyes narrowed. "You think she's burying it?"

"She's burying something," Richa said. "And while I believe in the empire, I also know she's been around for two imperial catastrophes."

"And we don't let that happen again," Hulvia said grimly. "Who's next?"

Deilio Maschano was in the room closest to the stairs, perched on the chair with his knees drawn up to his chest. He looked up, alarmed, when they came in, looking from Richa to Quill to Hulvia to Richa. Richa smiled in a way meant to make him relax, but Deilio's gaze just jumped to Quill again.

"Is this about the chapter house?" he demanded, his voice quick and fragile. "Did something happen there? That's why you were asking, that's why you pulled me in here—"

Richa held up a hand. As much as Richa tried to keep the possibility of a second generation of Shrike acting, he doubted it was Deilio Maschano. "Quill says you have a bruise on the back of your neck. Let's start there."

There were two, tucked in close together. Smaller than the others, but no less sharply defined.

Richa considered—the Shrike poisons Deilio once with all the guests, then poisons him a second time to get into the chapter house, possibly looking for the primate's other assistant. "You don't remember everything about that night, do you?"

Deilio hunched back onto the chair, his tunic replaced, and glared at Richa. "It wasn't a very good night."

Richa considered him. Considered what the others had said. The Orozhandi didn't want the Wall. Zaverio didn't want Obigen pressing him about his finances. Gaspera owed money. What would Deilio know?

"How well do you know Gaspera del Oyofon?" he asked.

Deilio wrinkled his nose. "She's my mother's friend. She's atrocious. She's always drunk, and frequently thinks she can do knife tricks when she is." He hesitated. "She's not really my mother's friend, I don't think. They knew each other, in the order, you know, and she's highborn enough it would be rude not to let her visit. But Gaspera cracked under the pressure or something and threw in with Redolfo Kirazzi before she abandoned all that and turned on him. That's common knowledge. Why?" he went on. "Do you think she did this?"

"We're just asking questions," Richa said. He was about to ask him about Zaverio when a clamor outside interrupted.

He went out, followed by Quill, and found the cadets who had been standing guard now warding off a frantic Lady Maschano. She looked a mess—her dressing gown thrown over a half-made outfit, her hair in a rushed pile on her head. Her eyes were red and she clutched her gown close.

"What are you *doing* with my son?" she demanded. Behind her, a huge guard in her house livery loomed, looking uncertain.

Richa closed the door to Deilio's room. "We're just asking questions. We don't have any reason to suspect Deilio—"

"*Suspect!*" she shrieked. "He's a *good* boy! An innocent—how can you—"

"Lady Maschano, you need to calm down and back away. We are conducting an investigation, your son is not in danger—"

"Don't tell me to calm down!"

"Lady Maschano—"

Lady Maschano swung an open hand toward Richa, as if she was going to strike him or shove him back. He saw it, reached up, and plucked her wrist out of the air, pulling it down and across the center of them. In the motion, her robe slipped from her shoulders.

Baring a dark, star-shaped bruise on the back of her arm.

Richa froze.

Lady Maschano hadn't been at the party, hadn't been near the murder. But here she'd been dosed just the same as the others. Once again, the pattern he'd been forming collapsed, the Shrike's motives shifted, dancing out of reach.

"How *dare* you—" she began.

"Lady Maschano, how long have you had that bruise?" Richa interrupted.

"What bruise?" She followed his gaze down to her shoulder. Frowned. "I don't know. How does that matter?"

"Think," he said. It looked fresher, didn't it? He glanced at Quill, now also studying the mark.

"It...it wasn't there yesterday," Lady Maschano said. "Yesterday morning. I don't recall seeing it when I dressed, at least."

"This morning?" Richa asked.

Fury made her nostrils flare again. "Well, your vigilants hardly gave me time to consider my arrangement, so I wouldn't know."

Richa signaled to the vigilant beside the door. "Take Lady Maschano into one of the interview rooms. I'll be there shortly."

"She was there yesterday," Quill said in a low, hurried voice once Lady Maschano had been escorted out of earshot, still shouting about her son. "Gaspera. She was at the house. She might have done it then." He hesitated. "Zaverio too, obviously, I'm not trying to—"

"Come on." Richa left the room with Deilio in it and instead threw open the door that concealed Gaspera del Oyofon.

Captain del Oyofon sat calmly at the little table, her eyes bleary, a tiny cup of coffee in one hand. She raised her eyebrows at Richa, then smirked at Quill. "This, I think," she said dryly, "is the opposite of the advice I gave you, Paremi."

Richa did not sit. Gaspera had the history, the knowledge, the land that might be hiding Redolfo Kirazzi's secrets. She had the temper and the skill to kill a man, and she had spoken to Quill the day of Primate Lamberto's death, when he might have said something to imply he wasn't keeping his end up. She was friends with Rosangerda Maschano—someone she might have let something slip to, someone who might have guessed and needed silencing.

"We have reason to believe that our original assessment of the murder of Lord Obigen has errors in it," Richa said. "It seems someone poisoned the party guests—twice. The second time with the poison they call the Venom of Changelings."

Gaspera's lazy expression froze. "That's not possible."

Hulvia slipped in behind Richa, glowering as he said, "Captain, I assure you it is—"

"I'll tell you what it is," Gaspera said, eyes darting from vigilant to vigilant to scrivener. "This is someone trying to ruin me. I made mistakes. I repented—more truly than any of those other serpents—and I went to prison all the same." She glared at Richa, her mouth tight and fearful. "I want my advocate. Where is the primate?"

That stopped Richa, a curl of panic unfolding in his gut. Either she was a very skilled actress...or Gaspera had no idea the primate was dead. Either she was far more dangerous than he was ready for...or Richa was wrong.

"Your advocate has been sent for," he said carefully. "In the meantime, you may be aware the Venom of Changelings leaves a distinctive mark where it's injected. Our first steps will be to ascertain whether you have such a mark."

Gaspera stilled, holding his gaze as if waiting for him to add some other trap. "Is that all?" she asked in a flat sort of voice.

"Presumably," Richa went on, "whoever administered the poison wouldn't have such a mark."

"That sounds like thin evidence. But this empire trades in that, doesn't it?" Gaspera's eyes cut to Hulvia. "Let's just clear it up now."

Richa and Quill waited outside while Hulvia and a female cadet checked Gaspera for marks. A path led neatly to Gaspera...and broke apart on her demand to speak to the primate.

Everyone lies, he told himself, *and even you get deceived.* Maybe she was covering, but the venom wouldn't lie for her. He was sure she wouldn't have a mark. She couldn't.

But then Hulvia came out, grim as the statue of Mother Ayemi, and the panic in Richa's gut bloomed. "This was your best suspect?" she asked quietly.

There was, indeed, a mark: a purple star against the freckled skin below her left shoulder blade.

"She couldn't do that herself," Hulvia said. "Human arms don't bend like that."

"I know, I have them!" Richa snapped. He raked a hand through his hair. *It's fine, start over. Get it* right. Not Gaspera, not without an accomplice. Which meant that Reza Dolitha hadn't seen what she'd thought, unless—

"Vigilant Langyun. Vigilant Manche."

All Richa's thoughts scattered into curses as Lady Sigrittrice stormed down the hallway toward them, her mask patch gold and her mouth tight. A quartet of guards in imperial tabards, all in thin gold half masks, marched behind her.

"Lady Sigrittrice," Richa made himself say. "How wonderful to see you. Hulvia was just telling me she'd sent for you—"

"Vigilant Manche, you are relieved of duty as imperial liaison. The Kinship elders will let you know where you should report next," Sigrittrice said simply, her gaze sharp as knives. There was a reason they called this old woman "the empress's sha-dog," and Richa knew he had sorely miscalculated.

"Just a moment," Richa said. "Hulvia wasn't—"

"As for you, Vigilant Langyun," she said, "I had thought we were clear. You were finished and the Imperial Majesty was grateful for your diligence. And yet here you are, hauling citizens in for questioning, siccing your pet archivist on the empress."

That knocked Richa back on his heels all over again. "My what?"

"Whether you are digging on your own or whether you are allowing Amadea Gintanas to hand you spades is not my concern. My concern is that you have flouted my orders and assaulted the empress."

"I did no such thing," Richa began, while at the same time his mind slipped around the idea of *Amadea* assaulting the empress.

"You are fortunate," Sigrittrice went on, "that because of your antics here, a small force were able to securely search Captain del Oyofon's household and recover a quantity of the poison known as the Venom of Changelings. Clearly, she needs to be taken into full imperial custody."

"No!" Quill burst out. "We've just questioned her, we've just looked—she has a mark! She was poisoned too."

Sigrittrice seemed to notice him for the first time, and she frowned. "How clever of her," she said at last. "Less clever of you—Vigilant Langyun, I've spoken to the elders of the Kinship. You are formally discharged. May your gaze seek another horizon, or something like that." She waved him off as she turned and went back up the stairs.

It was so quick, a knife out of the dark, and Richa found himself, shocked and still, overcome by the urge to *run*, to dart and dash through the alleys, and knowing he needed to stay calm, stay still, assess and act carefully. Knowing he wasn't some street thief who just had to think about surviving, knowing he held so much more on his shoulders.

"Hul," he said, eyes still on Lady Sigrittrice's back retreating up the stairs. "I'm sorry you got dragged into this."

"Come on," one of the guards said. "Elders want you out."

"It's what we do," Hulvia said, her expression furious, her tentacles twisting. She lunged forward, seized him in an embrace that made Richa tense—he was fairly sure Hulvia never hugged anyone.

"If I can beat her to them, I'm losing your files," she whispered. "Can't be forever, but it'll buy you time. You aren't wrong and I'm not convinced Lady Sigrittrice isn't *something* either."

"Come on," the guard said again. They marched him up to his office, watched as he piled his personal things into a small wooden box, missed when he slipped his notebooks in among them.

You're not wrong, he told himself. Which meant this strange, dangerous case could get stranger and more dangerous still. Sigrittrice had been at the party and lied about it. Sigrittrice had known about the venom without being told. Sigrittrice had seen Quill at the chapter house. Sigrittrice condemned Gaspera when it couldn't be her.

He left his office without so much as a backward glance, his thoughts too full of all these conflicting, slippery facts. These insurmountable problems. Quill met him in the entry hall beneath the statue of Mother Ayemi.

"What are you going to do now?" Quill demanded.

Richa stared down into the box of notes and little trees. "Burden of proof is pretty damned high if a person's going to accuse Lady Sigrittrice of lying," he said, repeating Hulvia's warning.

"All right," Quill said, yanking the box away from Richa. "So good thing we know people in the place full of proof Sigrittrice can't touch. Including anything Fastreda of the Glass has to say." He paused, his eyes on Richa fierce and unforgiving. "Unless you're done?"

The elders of the Vigilant Kinship would say he was done. But Richa wasn't a vigilant because he revered those who came before and outranked him in the order—he was here because he believed this was how you made the world better. He thought of Amadea, of all that evidence she'd secretly gathered, of the way she reached out to a contact she clearly didn't want to risk, of the way she'd been determined to march up to a sorcerer and demand answers. She wasn't afraid; how could he be?

Quill was still watching him, expectantly.

"I'm done when this city is safe," he answered. "Let's go."

CHAPTER TWELVE

Amadea Gintanas didn't fear Fastreda of the Glass—or perhaps it was safer to say that Lira, Lireana, Amadea had had the fear burned out of her, bit by bit. Terrible marvels sprang from Fastreda's affinity—the glass soldiers that shattered only to re-form into shards that erupted from the muddy battlefields, splitting horses and their riders—and if it was glass, Fastreda would shape it, no matter the use. She laughed at the Grave-Spurned Princess's fear and called her pet names, even while she spoke of how the glass soldiers could slice her up like a summer ham.

But in the wooden tower of the Imperial Prison, Fastreda was far from her power and from anyone who would wield her like a weapon. And without a coup, there was no need for glass soldiers and shards. All of it was memory, and Amadea Gintanas did not dwell on memories.

The only danger, really, was Yinii.

"She's not a saint. She's not even like other sorcerers," Amadea told the younger woman as they entered the special tower of the Imperial Prison, following Ibramo in his emerald half mask. "You need to remember that."

Yinii touched the medallions hanging from her horn. "You have reminded me at least eight times. I remember."

Ibramo glanced back as they approached the guard station. "She's terrible. A monster. Regardless of affinities."

Yinii stopped. "Affinities don't make you a better or worse person, Highness."

Ibramo regarded her a moment, then his gaze caught Amadea's. He'd never seen the battlefield up close, but Amadea had told him on those long, terrible nights when they didn't know what the emperor would do with them. About the screaming and the spray of mud and blood, and Fastreda's crowing laughter.

"In Fastreda's case," he said, "I hope you'll agree, Archivist, that they certainly didn't help."

"Sometimes blessings come down on the unworthy, Highness," Yinii said piously. "They are still blessings, still wisdom." Amadea waved at Ibramo to leave it be—he wasn't winning this argument, and starting it up was only going to make Yinii defend Fastreda more stubbornly.

"Shoes, please, esinoras," the guard near the staircase said. She held out a bin of soft slippers. Ibramo was already removing his shoes.

Amadea frowned. "What's this?"

"Fastreda has a carefully measured allotment of materials allowed her each month," Ibramo said. "Too much and she starts getting aggressive; not enough...well, she'll *make* glass. And we are not cruel. Plus, she might be useful to the empress at some point," he added, in a way that suggested he'd rather Fastreda just transmute herself and get it over with.

Sorcerers' bodies transmuted when they died—but if a wound was great enough, it would begin while the sorcerer was still living. She remembered, during one of the last battles, during the retreat, when a cannonball had hit Fastreda's leg, shattering it to pulp and bone shards that tinkled to the ground in a shower of glass. Lireana's ears had been ringing, her vision pulsing. But she'd seen Fastreda shocked, horrified, *human* a moment—and then her eyes had lit, the glass had turned molten and loose, and her leg had rebound itself into a stump of glass.

And the sorcerer had laughed and laughed, overflowing with joy.

Amadea wondered what Fastreda had done when they hadn't given her enough.

"There might be grains of sand in the crevices of your shoes," the guard explained. "It's safest."

"For one or two grains?" Amadea said doubtfully.

"The allotment is carefully calculated," Ibramo said tersely. "A grain or two is nothing, but before we realized she could do it, she saved them up, added it to the allotment, and made a sword. Obviously, sorcerer or not, Fastreda is still an untrained forty-nine-year-old human woman who doesn't get to roam much. A sword is not going to get her past the guards that stand between her and enough glass or sand to make trouble. But that doesn't matter much to the ones she injured. Too much," he repeated, "and she gets aggressive."

Amadea sat down and exchanged her shoes. Ibramo hadn't liked Fastreda in the first place, long before Amadea's battlefield nightmares. Starting the argument would only make him more stubborn, she reminded herself.

"You have nothing glass on your person?" the guard asked. "No sand?"

"None," Amadea said.

The guard hesitated, eyeing Yinii. "Esinora, she cannot have offerings."

"I *know*," Yinii said.

"And I need to check your charms."

Yinii sat and let the guard go through the ornaments of her horns. He had her remove one milky quartz stone, and hesitated on the salt crystal.

"Leave it, please," Amadea said. "That one is safe."

The guard nodded, looked at Yinii again. "She's not a saint, esinora," he said quietly.

Yinii set her jaw and stood. For all Amadea worried about Fastreda, if anyone could manage the company of a sorcerer, Amadea would bet on Yinii.

Those the archives called specialists, the Orozhandi called atnashingyii, "half-blessed." To be born with an affinity was a mark of the gods' trust, and so if specialists were prized and celebrated, sorcerers were to be nigh on deified, their bones once preserved and decorated and kept in the deepest caverns, now held in the Imperial Archives.

But the Orozhandi were uncommon in this regard. A sorcerer was more than a powerful specialist.

If you began with a specialist, began with an affinity for a material worked by intelligent hands: Say their souls rub off on it, say their life bleeds into it—before it had been rock and now it was *something*, something with a voice. The cycles turned and a specialist drifted in and out of closeness to their material, moving into alignments where the "voice" was so clear and sure that they turned from the rest of the world. When, like Zoifia had, the desire to stop being a person and lose yourself in bronze went from a vague whisper to a demand.

A sorcerer lived in constant alignment, always on the edge of a spiral.

It made them powerful, not only pulling information from their material but crafting it, shaping it, controlling it. If the worked materials sang their songs to the specialists, the sorcerers sang it back to the raw, unmade world. Give Fastreda a beach, and she'd make an army, and not care what you did with it, so long as she got to keep shaping and speaking to the glass.

Fluent in glass as she was, it was hard to say if Fastreda understood people anymore. She certainly didn't care.

No. She did care—*the molten glass between Fastreda's fingers, shifting, pulling. "Here, my little sparrow. So you smile," and the glass spreads wings and Redolfo snorts, "This is beneath you, Streda."*

Amadea focused on Ibramo's back. She cared—only in a way that was hard to predict. Or trust in. Or protect yourself from.

They reached a wooden door on a landing several stories up, guarded by a quartet of soldiers who stood a little straighter when they saw Ibramo in his green mask. Ibramo nodded to them, then turned back to Yinii and Amadea.

"You're *certain* you have nothing glass on you?"

"Don't you trust your own guards?" But all the same, she dipped her hands into her empty pockets to be sure. "Open it."

"Highness," Yinii added for her.

The cell beyond would not have been out of place in a fine ducal house. Bright, fringed carpets cushioned the stone floors, ceramic tiles in the shapes of birds and high hills and red banners spangling the walls. An unmade bed, a pair of couches, a bookshelf filled with volumes and volumes—and opposite the door, a brazier, a small table set with wooden cups and a pitcher, papers and ink; and a high-backed chair from which Fastreda of the Glass watched Amadea enter with a crooked, wicked smile.

Age had softened her pale, narrow face, but not that cruel smile. Furs wrapped her shoulders, spread across her lap, revealing one foot in a pointed slipper, and one—the one the cannon had ruined— made of delicate, swirling glass. A scar ripped its way up the right side of her face, right through her eye into her hairline. That eye shone, bluer, sharper than its companion, a replica in glass. More glass filled the scar, sharp glinting crystals all along the crack. The snarl of her hair, pale reddish curls in a fluff like a blown dandelion, tangled around a tuft of spun glass where the scar struck it.

Not enough, Ibramo had said, *well, she'll make glass.* They'd tried to starve her of her affinity, and Fastreda had solved it. Amadea thought of her specialists and was glad there was no way for Stavio or Zoifia to *make* bronze.

The blue eyes—glass and flesh—locked on Amadea. "Well, well," Fastreda said, her voice throaty. "Natlunkuluchik, Little Sparrow, come hunting crumbs."

"Fastreda," Amadea replied, moving into the room. Whatever flickering warmth, flickering terror, tried to ignite itself in her, Amadea smothered it.

Fastreda chuckled, her gaze moving past Amadea to where Ibramo was relocking the door. "Oh, the Little Sparrow *and* the Little Mouse, and...ah, look." She smiled at Yinii, a sudden slice across her mouth. "You brought me a baby goat-girl."

Little Sparrow, Little Mouse—the sound of those endearments, those taunts in Fastreda's voice, sent a ghostly fork of panic through her, as if her body remembered being small and scared, even as Amadea looked coolly down at Fastreda.

"This is Archivist ul-Benturan," Amadea said. "You can call her Archivist ul-Benturan."

"A specialist!" Fastreda's living eye seemed to blaze. "Well, what got you, goat-girl?"

Yinii straightened. "Ink, maqu'tajii. I...I have waited so long to meet you."

Fastreda beckoned her over, turning to the table beside her and pulling a sheet of paper close, and a small wooden inkwell. "Show me," she said, writing a line of words across the page, a string of Borsyan that Amadea couldn't read.

Yinii glanced at Amadea but stepped forward.

Come, Little Sparrow. Let's see what you are in armor. Ibramo was staring at Fastreda, all tense, as if he needed to leap out at her.

Yinii laid her fingers on the still-wet ink, pulled the ink up under her nails, over her knuckles. "It's...fresh. Fairly fresh," she said. "Vine char from the last harvest. Near the mountains."

"Very pretty," Fastreda crooned. "Very neatly done. Have you tasted the spiral?"

"Twice."

"What happens? How does the ink claim you?"

Yinii huffed out a little breath. "It...Fire." She swallowed. "It wants more char. Then water. Starts a flood."

Fastreda laid a hand over Yinii's. "Could drown like that, couldn't you, goat-girl? With your ink so lonely, so hungry. You're lucky, though. Ink's not so difficult. Burn something, get it wet. You could make ink out of anything, really."

Yinii shook her head, small and fast, as if she was going to argue, but Fastreda lifted her small hand off the page and clasped it between her own. "Glass is so fussy. Only sand. *Silica,*" she said, letting it trip off her tongue so the simple sounded exotic. "They made you empty all your pockets and trade your shoes, didn't they?"

"Yes, maqu'tajii."

"So no glass for Fastreda. No sneaky sands." She shrugged, gave a little laugh. Turned to Ibramo. "I don't know why they bother doing that."

She crushed Yinii's hand between hers, and a deep thrum went through the room.

"Did you know even your bones have trace amounts of that silica?" Fastreda whispered. "They can't take that out. But I can."

Amadea lunged forward as Yinii let out a strangled scream. She grabbed Fastreda's wrists and yanked her hands apart enough that Yinii could scramble free. Fastreda's glinting live eye and bright sharp glass eye met hers, and she gave Amadea a wicked smile.

"No," Amadea snapped. "You will not."

Fastreda struggled in her grasp, but Amadea held firm. Fastreda never blinked until she said, "There you are, my Little Sparrow."

"Archivist Gintanas," she corrected, not releasing Fastreda. "You may be a special prisoner of the Imperial Crown, but Archivist ul-Benturan is in my care and if you try to hurt her again, I have no qualms at all about stopping you. I don't even think the consort-prince will mind."

"Little Mouse likes his rules. Maybe you have to fight about it. Maybe I get your bones."

"The amount of silica you could pull from my bones isn't worth the effort, and you know it."

"Neither is the sand in the cracks of your shoes, but they stop that. Can't let Fastreda have any pleasure, can we?"

"You have an allotment," Amadea reminded her. "Ibramo already said."

"So the Mouse can be Ibramo, but you, my sparrow, you have to be 'Archivist Gintanas.'" She clucked her tongue and rubbed the skin of her wrists, still grinning. "Little Sparrow—no, Little *Sparrowhawk*. I *knew* you had it in you."

Amadea didn't ask what she meant, what *it* was, or when it had occurred to Fastreda she might have it. "What I have are questions," she said.

"About what? Is it something in this room? Because I don't know much else these days."

"About the past," Amadea said. "About the Shrike."

And at that Fastreda tilted her head, her smile shifting into that shard-sharp slice again. "Interesting."

"We think she's surfaced again. Someone was blackmailing her, and now that someone is dead. And a few more people too."

"And so the Shrike sleeps once more. That's not so bad."

Amadea shook her head. "We need to find her."

"'Her' is an interesting start. You know something?"

"We have evidence she's a woman. But Ibramo and I were given the changeling blood—we can't remember who the Shrike was. Do you?"

Fastreda laughed, low in her throat, and settled back into her chair. "And what will you give me if I know something?"

"Not glass," Amadea said lightly. "What do you want?"

Fastreda set her fingertips against one another, considering a moment. "You should come talk to me more, Little Sparrow. Do you still have the glass bird I made for you?"

Amadea hesitated. "Yes."

"I thought you might. But then you never come and visit. You never say, 'How are you, Fastreda?' I'm all alone."

"You want me to visit," Amadea said. "I can do that."

That shard-sharp smile. "Then here's what I know," Fastreda said. "I was dosed too. I suspect we all were—maybe not Redolfo. He probably wouldn't have let that happen. Or if it did, he'd deny it."

"But *you* let it happen?" Amadea asked.

Fastreda waved a hand. "What do I care what people do? The Shrike wanted to escape ahead of the hangman; that seems reasonable. I don't think they would have patted their head and said, 'Don't be so wicked next time.'" She chuckled to herself. "I think we are alike in some way, me and the Shrike. Single-minded, you might say. I have the glass, they have their knives, and the people we like best are the ones who ask us to use them and don't cluck their tongues. The Shrike is not just a mercenary; they're a hunter. A scholar, they would say, to test the limits of our knowledge about the changelings. A monster, perhaps. The Shrike is fast, the Shrike is *merciless*, the Shrike doesn't care what it takes.

"But that means," she said, "so fast as it is, the Shrike doesn't notice what it leaves. You remember anything, Little Sparrow?"

Amadea looked away, unsure what was the fault of her own fear and what was the Venom of Changelings. "It's all blurred. I can remember her saying things."

"I remember someone talking to my father about hunting changelings," Ibramo said. "I remember the words, but I can't hear the voice."

"Exactly," Fastreda said. "It's the problem when you get the poison and they don't tell you enough of what to remember. I bet the Shrike said to us, 'Forget me,' because I have that too. Not the face, not the voice, but the words and the shadow. And that's almost forgetting... except the words."

Her blue eyes danced, glass and flesh. "Here's the thing, the secret the Shrike couldn't erase: the shadow calls me Streda. You know who calls me Streda, Little Sparrow? It's not folks I just met, and it's not folks I don't like, and it's not the Black Mother Forest or the saints or the devils down below. My friends can call me Streda and there we stop. And I don't have a great many friends.

"That name, too—the Shrike," Fastreda went on. "That's what I remembered, what slipped through first and woke itself up. It's a bird, a vicious little bird. And let's be honest with ourselves, that's a Borsyan's nickname, and I'm the only one with Borsyan umas to teach her the words who was close enough to Redolfo to give out pet to names to his hunter.

"So I tell you this for certain: I knew the Shrike. I *liked* the Shrike. But they didn't like me so much, maybe, because I don't get visitors from those days. They were right at the heart and then they vanished into someone else after it was all done. But you know that now." She sat back in her chair again. "You have a guess?"

Amadea mentally mapped the catalogues that contained the Kirazzi hearing records. It would be an extraordinary number of people looking over all those names, all those accusations. But only one of them was a woman who was in the Manco manor.

"What about Gaspera del Oyofon?"

Fastreda thought a moment. "No. I *liked* Gaspera. And her, she could call me Streda. But I remember her plenty, and I remember her at times I remember the Shrike speaking. She didn't erase herself. And she had plenty to do, besides, without chasing changelings over the Wall."

"But she left around the same time, didn't she?" Amadea said. "I think... I think I don't remember the Shrike after that." *Patience, my Shrike*, Redolfo's words hissed across her thoughts.

Clear glass, she told herself. *Wooden pitcher. Blue eye.*

Fastreda shrugged. "'Left.' Turned traitor. But she wasn't alone. Those were dark days. The end of an era."

Amadea hesitated. "What about Sigrittrice Ulanitti?"

Ibramo sucked in a startled breath behind her.

Fastreda laughed. "Lady Gritta? Oh, that would be funny, wouldn't it, Mouse? The architect of all your misfortunes, little loves, and maybe she's the architect of everybody's grief too? She's the sort I would like, I give you that, if circumstances were different. I'd like her more if she managed *this*. It would be *interesting*. But I'd eat my own leg if that were true."

"You'd eat your leg if you were bored," Ibramo said.

"Why?" Amadea said. "Why isn't it her?"

Fastreda smirked. "Lady Gritta has all the power in this empire that she could want. She wants to disappear someone, she might be the only one who can do it. Empress is under a glass since her uncle Appolino burned all the goodwill the Ulanittis saved up. Ducal authorities all eyeing each other. Noble consul gets replaced with a shout. But Gritta, she's living in the gaps, in the cracks of this system. She wouldn't want to pull that apart, and if she did, she can do it from the inside."

Sigrittrice's dark eyes on hers, unblinking. "And if you married the Usurper's son? Had children with him? You would be a very great threat, indeed." The twisting pain like a knife in her belly and then the blood. The bitter taste in the back of her throat as she sips coffee and tries not to cry.

Fastreda tilted her head. "Somebody died, didn't they? Died with the venom in them?"

"Yes," Amadea said. The phantom prick in her arm, the feeling someone was about to grab her, the back of her throat bitter. Her chest was getting tight. *Blue eye, red cloth, green jacket.*

"So there you are: Why go to the trouble, the grief, and the expense of making that unholy concoction when you can say 'This person is a threat to the empire' and get them that way, no need to hunt changelings?" She turned her grin on Ibramo. "How's your mother?"

"Dead," Ibramo said. "Just like the last time you asked."

She chuckled. "Oh right. Now I remember."

Amadea's mouth felt dry and thick. The room felt close, the air too thin, and she couldn't stop thinking she was in danger. *Breathe,* she told herself. She took a step back from Fastreda. "I will see about visiting you next week."

"No," Ibramo started.

"I promised," Amadea replied. "We need to go."

He regarded her, worried and fretful, and ready to argue, so Amadea put a hand on his arm to nudge him toward the door.

And the knowledge that she had not touched him in twenty years leapt up her arm like a bolt of lightning, splitting her building panic. He felt it too, she could tell, in the soft inhale, the shift of his gaze. *Push him away,* she told herself.

She couldn't, though—her mind clinging to the willow, to Sparrow and Mouse—so instead she gestured Yinii toward the door. Yinii hesitated and gave Fastreda the swiftest dip of a curtsy, touching her medallions, before hurrying on, driving Ibramo to open the door once more, and out of Amadea's reach. She let out a breath.

"Archivist Gintanas." Amadea turned back to the sorcerer, who was watching her in a speculative sort of way. "You've gotten very brave. You don't need the Mouse anymore, whether you're in armor or not."

"I do what I can."

Fastreda nodded vaguely. "Do remember: Redolfo was happy to sway whoever he could to his cause, however he could. But those of us who were his tools . . . he chose us carefully and honed us special. Only the best, most perfect weapons. Do not underestimate what you're dealing with. Your mouse cannot shield you like his father did."

"I won't again," Amadea said, and left to consider what little they'd learned.

Once she crossed the threshold, Ibramo yanked the door shut, but the sense of looming danger didn't seal off behind it. He cursed under his breath, staring at the door as if he were considering going back in, fighting Fastreda himself.

Amadea turned to Yinii, rubbing her hands together. "Are you all right?"

"I think so." Yinii hugged her arms to her chest and huffed out a breath. "I didn't expect that."

"Did she hurt you?"

"It...No, not that. It's...it's worse than being next to someone in a spiral. Just...pulls on you. Even beyond the...the thing with the bones. I haven't met a sorcerer like that."

Amadea put a comforting arm around her, squeezed Yinii as if the girl could anchor her to this moment and stop her thoughts from skipping back and forth, carrying all the wrong feelings with them. She started down the staircase, pulling Yinii with her.

She tried to remember whom Fastreda had moved in circles with, whom she'd glimpsed the sorcerer talking to, laughing with, drinking with. Gaspera, to be sure, and sometimes other soldiers. Redolfo. She was always in rough company, the sort that found the glass army thrilling or even amusing. Amadea sifted through her memories, glimpses of different women. Gritta, maybe—

Sigrittrice Ulanitti in Sestina, studying Lira, Lireana, Amadea standing on the fine rug in the bird-papered room. Grief and fear and a hope that things would be all right, that she could climb out of the darkness—all dwindling into dust under that gaze. "You would be a very great threat, indeed."

Her pulse started to race away from her, her breath growing shallow. She set her fingertip on the wall, on the corner where the staircase ended. *Gray robes, red cross, pink crystal, green mask.*

Ibramo had turned to her. "I know you promised, but you're not going back there. I can't let you."

"We don't need to discuss this now." *Green mask, black hair.*

"You're going to try," he said. "I know you that well. I don't know why you aren't afraid, but please, believe me, she is too dangerous and you don't owe her anything."

Soldiers shattering before her, shards flying, shards re-forming, sudden blades bursting from the ground—

White shirt, green vest, black jacket. "I don't *want* to discuss it now—you've locked her up, how is it not safe?"

"I'll block your access."

Screaming and screaming and screaming. Soldiers and then children—her sisters? The sistrums, the clink of the beads as the flail rises, the good Alojan carpet—

"You can block me," she agreed, fighting to keep her voice even, as cold washed down her neck, her shoulders, and her ears seemed to vanish, the whole room turned unreal. *Brown skin, brown eyes, saints and devils, I miss you.* "That's well within your powers. Does make you a bit of a tyrant, but you can decide."

Ibramo drew back as if she'd slapped him. He started to retort... but stopped, expression softer. "Amadea, are you all right?"

Amadea shut her eyes, feeling nauseated beyond bearing, and her memories came to life, Redolfo Kirazzi saying to her, as if in her ear, *Lira, Lireana... we found you in Gintanas.* Then overlaid, as her knees began to buckle. *How do you feel, Lira?*

"Fine," she said or had said. The edges of her vision closed in and all she could see was the memory of Redolfo Kirazzi's face.

Patience, my Shrike.

"I have to go," Amadea said, or tried to say. And she was running or stumbling, searching for an exit from the prison, a way away from her racing pulse, her crushed breath, saints and devils, she was going to die, wasn't she? Filled with poison, threatened with glass, alone, alone.

Not alone—Yinii was grabbing hold of her, pulling her back. "Amadea!" she cried, frantic. "*Amadea!*"

A wall, a corner—Amadea let her knees give, dropping to the cobblestones. *You cannot cry,* she told herself. *You cannot break, not here, not now.* She was already crying, though, and she pressed her face to her wrists. She forced herself to breathe, to make her pulse slow. Yinii's hand rubbed her back.

"I don't know," she heard Yinii say an eternity later, her voice shaking. "She won't answer."

"Lira?" Amadea opened her eyes, looked through the lattice of her arms and knees to Ibramo's shoes and cuffs where he crouched before her.

"Don't call me that," she said.

"Amadea," he said. "Look at me?"

"Please be all right," Yinii said.

"I'm all right. I'm all right. I'm sorry. I shouldn't have let…" Amadea heard her own voice shaking and stopped, swallowed. *Not here*, Amadea told herself firmly. *Not now.*

"Hush," Ibramo said, stroking her hair. "Amadea."

Amadea lifted her head, pulled away. "Someone will see."

She'd veered into an alley across from the prison. Ibramo was crouched there, maskless, holding Yinii's and her shoes. Looking back at the entrance, she could see the guard watching them, curious.

"You need to go back," Amadea started.

"No," Ibramo said. "We didn't find the Shrike. We didn't find the person trying to frame me. I need your help and you need me. Please," he added, holding out a hand to her.

The guard was still watching. Amadea stood, one hand pressed to the wall behind her, vertigo overtaking her as if she'd slammed her head into a cloud of it. Yinii ducked in to steady her—Ibramo didn't move. Amadea pulled her shoes back on while Yinii reattached her surrendered charm to her left horn.

"We should go back to the archives," Yinii said. "Quill and Vigilant Langyun might have found something? Also," she added, dropping her voice, "I don't like just standing still out here if…in case…" She trailed off, tapping her medallions, and did not speak the Shrike's name.

The roads back to the archives passed Amadea in a blur of bodies and buildings and bright red hangings for the Festival of Salt-Sealing. No one looked at Ibramo without his mask, and Amadea thought, not for the first time, that the black mask drew more attention to itself than made any sense.

She pulled her thoughts back in as she walked, listening to her breath, anchoring herself on the world around her. She was Amadea Gintanas, solver of problems. Archivist superior of the Imperial Collection, South Wing. She didn't dawdle over memories—or married men. She dealt with what was in front of her, not the past. She knew who she was and who she wasn't, and this was not going to lay her low.

It already laid you low—the thought broke through her litany, true and unignorable as a rock through glass. Facing Fastreda had dragged her right back, into the fear and the pain, the trauma she'd smoothed and soothed away for more than twenty years. It wasn't gone, she knew that much, but Amadea had to admit to herself she'd thought it tamed, pruned back into something she could close a gate around.

And now the gate wouldn't close. All the tricks she'd picked up for settling that panicky feeling, all the little ways she'd redirected her thoughts, they stopped working—they'd been working less and less, she had to admit, since that day she saw Karimo and the first star-shaped bruise.

You are Amadea Gintanas, she told herself. *But maybe you need to admit you have a past.*

Richa and Quill were waiting in the entrance hall, a box between them. Quill leapt to his feet when he saw them. "Did you find anything? Was it Gaspera?"

"No," Ibramo said, eyeing Richa. "Who's this?"

"This is Vigilant Langyun," Amadea said.

"Not anymore," Richa answered. "I got discharged. Lady Sigrittrice stepped in. She arrested Gaspera, but I don't think it's her."

"It's not her," Amadea agreed. "What now?"

Richa shrugged. "I figure now we catch a murderer on our own. Seeing as the Kinship and the Imperial Majesty have bowed out."

Amadea led all of them up to her office—there was nowhere else private enough, even if it wasn't very comfortable with five all together, with Imp scurrying from place to place with her tail low, doing a terrible job of staying out from underfoot.

Amadea sat behind her desk, the bulk of it reassuring and protective. She laced her fingers, considered Richa standing close to the door, Ibramo eyeing her glass animals, Yinii and Quill on the ancient couch. "So," she said briskly, "it can't be Gaspera."

"No," Richa agreed. "She has a mark, right in the middle of her back. She was injected."

"That matches Fastreda," Ibramo said. "She remembered Gaspera and not the Shrike."

Richa drew a deep breath, and all Amadea's nerves lit, dreading what came next if Richa had to steady himself for it. But then:

"Lady Sigrittrice used the fact we'd pulled Captain del Oyofon in to search her house. She says she found Venom of Changelings." He paused, glancing at Ibramo. "I'm inclined to wonder if the Shrike is Lady Sigrittrice."

"It's not Gritta," Ibramo said flatly.

"I don't suggest it *lightly*, Your..." He trailed off, nose wrinkled as if he couldn't decide how to address the consort-prince without a mask. "She's been very involved in this case, and very inclined to shut the Kinship out of it."

"It's not Lady Sigrittrice," Amadea said. "We asked Fastreda that too. She doesn't remember Lady Sigrittrice, but she pointed out there's no motive. Why would she do this, why would she insist she wasn't there while making sure they all remembered she was?"

"She's got as much or more power than anyone within the imperial family," Ibramo said. "If she wanted to get rid of someone, she didn't need to make a scene."

Richa scowled. "She's up to *something*."

"I don't like it either," Ibramo returned. "But it's not her."

"*Everyone* at the party had injection marks," Quill said. "Which means it could be anyone, really."

"Anyone who could seem like they belonged there," Richa said. Then he shook his head. "Wait, Lady Maschano had a mark as well—a new one since yesterday. So someone who could have gotten close to her yesterday."

"When Quill and I went," Yinii spoke up, "she was with Gaspera and her son. Lord Maschano came in later. And there were servants—the door guard, three bringing the tea things...We weren't there that long, so I don't know, maybe...maybe more people came by?"

"There's the guard, Chiarl," Quill said. "But he definitely doesn't match what Reza Dolitha saw, and he's too young to have known Gaspera. Maybe it is Gaspera?" Quill suggested. "I mean, Lady Sigrittrice said it would be clever to inject yourself, and the Shrike *is* clever."

"Clever and unnaturally flexible," Richa reminded him. "She can't hit herself in the middle of the back."

"She could have an accomplice," Yinii pointed out. "Or she might *be* the accomplice?"

But Richa shook his head again. "The part that I can't make fit is the motive. The only reason you would kill people like this is to make a point. I thought at first it had to be separatists or something, but if they were trying to punish the Alojan noble consul or the ul-Benturan reza, then why force the line about changelings? It has to be about the Wall. And Gaspera doesn't care about the Wall."

Yinii muttered a prayer and tapped her medallions, as Quill said, "Lord Maschano said she doesn't want to sell her land."

"So don't sell it and Obigen moves down the border. What she has isn't prime for staging—it's along a creek and too close to the Khirazji ducal tombs."

At that Ibramo froze, dragged a hand down his face. Turned to the glass animals. The letter from his father, Amadea realized. The thing hidden in the tombs.

"You think it's a reza," Yinii said darkly.

"No," Richa said, turning to face her, "because the rezas have a point that's made a lot better by just speaking it—the Salt Wall is a holy site and the accords make it clear: you can't just knock a hole in the Salt Wall any more than you can plow a Khirazji ducal tomb under. Obigen was in for months of negotiations and he knew it."

Ibramo spun around, started to speak, but half a sound out of his mouth and Imp yowled, streaking out from where his foot had come perilously close to her tail. Ibramo stumbled back; Imp leapt up, clawing her way to Richa's cloaked shoulder and clinging there.

Amadea stood, hurrying around, but Richa, wincing, only reached back, curving his hand around Imp's skinny chest and lifting her up so her claws unhooked. "There's a good girl," he crooned. "There's a . . ."

He stopped, froze with Imp dangling from one hand. He looked at Amadea. "Shoulder. She had a mark on her shoulder, just on the back of her shoulder," he said.

"Oh Lord on the Mountain," Quill swore, coming to his feet.

"It would be clever," Richa said. "It *would* be *clever* to inject yourself, to make yourself look like a victim, cross yourself off the list."

"What are you talking about?" Amadea demanded. "Who?"

"Rosangerda Maschano," Quill said, horrified. "You think Rosangerda Maschano is the Shrike?"

But Amadea heard them as echoes in a long, empty hallway, a cavern she needed to run through. *Rosangerda*, she thought, as the crack in the base widened. *Rosa.*

She was Rosa, Amadea thought. The pale aide with the big round eyes, swift and slight and weighed down with two swords. Suddenly her face was falling into memory after memory. Amadea's vision was closing again, her knees buckling, but she couldn't move, couldn't speak.

No, she told herself. *Let it be, let it happen. It can't hurt you. You have to remember.*

"Lady Maschano?" Ibramo repeated, as if he doubted, as if he couldn't remember, wasn't falling into the past.

"I don't like when she gets that look," Ibramo says, and it's Rosa, Rosangerda, the Shrike, that he means. Vicious and quick and hungry for sport. In close conference with Redolfo. "What are they doing in there?" Lira asks—she asks, and Ibramo shakes his head. "It doesn't matter, just stay out of their way."

"She was always there," Richa went on. "Looking like an over-protective mother—"

"She *is* an overprotective mother," Ibramo said. "I know her by reputation. She seems more suited to a salon than a murder—"

"She belonged to the wall-walkers," Richa said. "Whatever she looks like now, she served with Captain del Oyofon in the Order of the Saints of Salt and Iron."

Gaspera on horseback, eyeing Lireana—eyeing me—in her fine armor beside wicked Fastreda. Rosa arranging a scarlet cape around her shoulders. "You're going to get her killed with that," Gaspera says, "and then what?"

Rosa's gray eyes glinting with amusement, like it's the funniest thing she's heard all day. "He says she needs to look the part."

"They have her swords hanging up," Quill said. "Oh Lord on the Mountain, she tried to get me to go in the other room after I said the primate—Saints and devils, did I almost get killed?"

The pillow, the birds, Ibramo in the doorway, and she's shaking her head, while Redolfo's not looking, but Rosa's looking. She throws the rose-patterned pillow at Ibramo. The pinch of the needle, Rosa's pale hand on her arm, the darkness, Redolfo, but it's Rosa who says, "That does work quicker. Who knew? We have enough for another?"

"Patience, my Shrike," Redolfo replies.

Amadea squeezed her eyes shut. She had to tell someone—

No, she had to tell Ibramo. She had to do it *now*, and she had to do it carefully. Cleverly.

She took a step forward, grabbed Ibramo's arm, and fell to the ground as if she'd fainted.

Ibramo dropped down beside her. Beyond she heard shouting, words about coffee, words about cold compresses. Richa going to find a runner. Yinii and Quill craning over the desk.

"Are you all right?" Ibramo whispered.

"I found the thread," she breathed. "Gods and devils, I pulled the thread."

"What?" He moved to help her up, but Amadea was already coming to her feet.

"Rosa. That's the Shrike. I remember, Ibramo, I remember. But *you* have to pretend you do, because Amadea Gintanas wasn't there."

A shadow by the willow where Ibramo's meant to be, but Redolfo made him stay behind this time, and there's Rosa in the mouth of the cave beyond. Holding out a corked skin to Redolfo. Corked skin of blood. "I took three," she whispers, glee in her mist-soft voice. "That should last you a while. But don't hesitate to say if you run low." And Redolfo chuckles. "You choose strange sport, my Shrike . . ."

Amadea squeezed her eyes shut. A cave? Where was there a cave? "There's a cave," she blurted. "It might be the cache. Your father's cache. She knows."

"I don't remember any Rosa," Ibramo whispered, frantic. "He's going to come back and he's going to ask, so what is our—"

"Rosa del Milar, aide to Captain del Oyofon. Blond, gray eyes, she . . ." Amadea shook her head. "Take me with you. I need to go with you. I'll tell you what you need to say."

Ibramo searched her face, as if trying to determine if this was the maddest possible demand she could make. Amadea held his gaze, refusing to budge, knowing down in the core of her this was more about her, her past and her grief, than any practical help she might be.

Richa came back in, panting and holding a cup of water. "They're bringing someone. Are you all right?"

"Fine," Amadea lied, taking the cup. "I stood up too fast."

"I realized, Vigilant," Ibramo said, "that you're right. You are very right. It took a moment, but the name Rosangerda...I remember her. From when my father was alive. I think. But we should go. Find her. Ascertain that she's the right...person." He looked back at Amadea, eyes pleading.

"I should come with you," she said. "In case you find samples of the venom. I can identify it."

Richa frowned. "We're just going to go? I'm not a vigilant anymore. I can't muster anyone."

Ibramo reached into his pocket, pulled out a thin fabric mask embroidered heavily in gold. "Then it's a good thing you have a representative of the empress with you," he said as he tied it over his eyes. "We can call for the Kinship on the way."

— ◄◆►— —

Yinii retreated a step, watching the vigilant, the consort-prince, and the archivist superior lie, argue, and move into action. Like a play, she thought, all of it so strange and distant. How much of that feeling, she wondered, was the story that hid behind it all—the Shrike and the venom and a secret princess? And how much was the fact that Yinii's thoughts still bubbled with Fastreda of the Glass?

"Hang on a minute," Quill said, pushing forward. "Shouldn't we come too?"

"Out of the question," Richa said.

"No," Amadea said, over him. "She is still out there and you are safest in here. There are layers of guards to get into the archives."

"If we need to be in here, don't *you?*"

"Quill," Amadea said sharply, "I have already said why I'm going. As you said, she's already tried to kill you—twice, perhaps. Please stay here."

And that was it. They were gone, and Yinii and Quill were left with Amadea's cat on the battered sofa in her office, and all the ink on piles and piles of papers stacked along her desk. It called to Yinii, beckoned dangerously, and she knew if she reached for it, she might dive past all her safeguards and go mad as Fastreda, and maybe that would be for the best.

After all, no one would take her back to Maqama if she was mad.

"I don't know if Amadea should have gone," Yinii said to Quill, trying to hold on to *here* and *now* and *person*. "You didn't see her, but something happened when we saw Fastreda. She sort of...crumpled." And when they'd said Lady Maschano's name, Yinii saw it happening again—Amadea's blank, blanched look, the way her breathing sped. "I don't know if she should have gone," Yinii said again.

"Well, she wasn't going to listen to us," Quill spat. He sighed. "It's odd to think that's it. They'll find her and then, it's done. What do I do? Go back to Ragale and...then what?"

"Oh!" Yinii said, to stop the "no!" from bursting out. She had no place to complain; she wouldn't even *be* here if Reza Dolitha had her way.

"I'll bet they'd be glad to have you back," she said, guilty that she wished the mystery weren't solved, that he might stay, and then she might stay too. *You only like the look of him*, she told herself.

Anyone could be a liar indeed, she thought, cheeks burning.

He shook his head, unsure, and looked past her, up at the ceiling murals that peeked through the ironwork. "It's a shame. There's so much more I wanted to see."

Yinii remembered him in the Bone Vault that first day, bright with excitement. She thought of how much she wanted to be in the library—how much she didn't feel safe there now. The only other place she felt safe...and how she'd been hiding from it.

She blew out a breath. "Do you want to see the Chapel of the Skeleton Saints? Properly, I mean."

Quill looked over at her, a glint of that early excitement back. "Is that all right? It's still in the archives, so I guess..." He looked at the door. "There's no point waiting, I suppose."

"Of course," she said. "I need to...I should go and make my prayers. But I can tell you about them, if you want. Another tour."

As they came into the Bone Vault, Tunuk and Radir were leaving. "Do you want to eat?" Radir asked her. "Tunuk is taking me to a pancake house he likes."

"The good one," Tunuk said. "Come on."

Yinii started to answer—Amadea had said not to leave—but Quill spoke up. "Oh, that sounds good. Yinii was going to show me the chapel. Could you bring back some?"

"You cannot eat in my vault," Tunuk said. "Or the chapel."

"Right, I don't want to share with the saints," Quill said. "Well, maybe we'll come find you after, then."

"I will be there as long as I'm hungry," Tunuk said. "Or until they are out of pancakes. Here—" He fished a ring of keys from the pocket of his robe and tossed them to Yinii. "Lock the doors when you're through and don't let the saints out of their rooms."

"Don't be profane," Yinii said, but it made her smile.

"Come on," Tunuk said to Radir. "I'm famished and there's not a lot of tables for four." He lurched from the Bone Vault, and Radir, shaking his head, chased after.

Quill turned to Yinii. "I don't understand them."

"Yeah, Tunuk...He takes some getting used to." She swallowed. "Amadea will be upset if we go."

"I'm hoping she comes right back with news that they've caught Lady Maschano and she's absolutely the Shrike." He sighed. "It feels so *simple*, you know. Like we should have figured it out ages ago, and like it can't possibly be right. And it doesn't really solve anything—I knew it wasn't going to bring Karimo or even Primate Lamberto back, but...that confirmation. It's harder than I thought."

"I'm sorry."

He smiled at her. "Show me the saints?"

Yinii led him down the stairs—through two locked doors that she relocked behind them—to the little back entrance of the shrine, tucked alongside the niche that held Saints Oshanna, Alomalia, and Demuth. Yinii ducked her head and said a little apology to those venerable ladies—she always felt bad slipping in past them, as if she were interrupting. The skeletons held their poses of peaceful contemplation, unbothered despite her guilt.

The Chapel of the Skeleton Saints was a marvel of black marble and polished red sandstone. The vault of the ceiling had been inlaid with a mosaic of stars and bright red and white flowers that had never grown in Semilla. A pattern of bent lines, stylized Orozhandi, read out a prayer to God Above and God Below, along the outer edge of the floor. Alcoves budded off the center, each holding the decorated bones of three saints, and the offerings left to them, while further saints were positioned on the pillars between the alcoves. Ornate glass-topped cases held the more fragile remains, arranged in a row down the center.

Quill smiled at her. "Where do we start?"

Yinii darted a nervous glance at Saint Jeqel of the Salt, standing over her with his cupped hands full of white crystals and his eyes full of disapproving rubies behind a sheet of glass.

She cleared her throat. "The chapel and catacomb were constructed alongside the archives with imperial funds as a gift to the Orozhandi. It's held jointly by the shared ducal authority of the Orozhandi and the Imperial Crown. The saints are, of course, unowned. They're listed as honored guests of the empire in the catalogues."

"Are they all in here?" Quill asked in hushed tones.

Yinii shook her head. "Not every canyon made it to Semilla, so there might have been more. There are seventy-one known saints from the canyons that made it, but only fifty-two were carried to Semilla. The others have replicas made by Saint Qilbat." She beckoned him into another alcove, to a reddish skeleton trimmed in rubies and white lace, crowned by a halo of golden rays. On either side of him, the bone skeletons of two other saints were posed.

"Saint Maligar of the Wool. His bones still lie in Benturan Canyon. We couldn't retrieve them. So Saint Qilbat of the Cedar fashioned this out of wood when she reached Semilla."

It was no less holy, Yinii thought, this placeholder skeleton. This tribute to a long-dead peer, crafted out of magic so potent it still stirred her nerves. She wondered if Fastreda's glass soldiers had created the same pull.

"Benturan Canyon," Quill said. "That's where your family came from."

Yinii nodded. "He's... we call it a canyon-saint. My family has an altar to him, and I wear the medal." She brushed it self-consciously. "There are a few ul-Benturan saints. He's just the one that came from our part of the complex, in the old days."

"Like Saint Asla," Quill said. "Is that right? She's ul-Benturan?" Yinii nodded and touched the salt crystal reflexively. "So... her and Qilbat," he asked. "Are they the last saints?"

"There were five from the canyons that crossed the isthmus: Asla of the Salt, Qilbat of the Cedar, Alomalia of the Bone, Ropat of the Sandstone, and Yanawa of the Gold, who was a child when she arrived. After her, there was Saint Demuth of the Wool, who died just after Emperor Iespero was crowned. None since then. But we hope!" she added, with a lift of her shoulders. "I ought to... I ought to make my prayers while I'm here. If you don't mind."

Quill looked around the chapel of decorated skeletons, saying nothing, so Yinii turned instead to Saint Maligar, who stared back out of chatoyant moonstones set into his wooden orbits. She tried to imagine him, living, cloth spilling from his hands with only will to shape it. She tried to imagine speaking to him, the way he would have spoken back.

She kept hearing Fastreda's icy voice. The threat to pull glass from her bones. As if that were the only way she mattered to Fastreda of the Glass.

Yinii drew a deep breath, dropped to her knees, and pressed her forehead to the floor. *O Saint Maligar, Shepherd of the High Plateaus, blessed by God Above and God Below, grant me a measure of your kindness, your patience, the vision of the weaver, the caution of the shepherd.*

Yinii repeated the prayer four times, fighting back the fizzing in her bones, the image of Saint Maligar smiling cruelly—the way Fastreda had—as he drew the hair from Yinii's head into his spindle. She sat up and opened her eyes, brushed the medal on her left horn. *Stop it.*

Quill was waiting patiently, considering Maligar's wooden bones, as she stood again. "I have a question that might be impertinent," he said.

Yinii felt herself flush. "Oh?"

"Why are they skeletons?"

"Oh! Right, um." She pressed her palms together, needing something for her hands to do. "When a saint dies, their hold on their— we usually call it the affinity spiral, but it's got another name in Orozhandi—it's sort of the intensity of their affinity. When they die, it overtakes them and their flesh is transmuted. It falls away, returns to the earth and the God Below."

"And then you...decorate them?"

"Decorating bones is...it's sort of an art for us," she said. "Art and worship, I guess? For the dead, we use bones to call them close, but we cover them in metals or gemstones, and paints. When the decorations fall away or the bones rot, that's because their spirit has taken the gift and gone on. But the saints *are* the gift *and* the ancestor. So we adorn them. Preserve them."

Yinii knew well enough that plenty of other people found it ghoulish, and she braced for Quill to make a face or laugh or worse. At least that would make everything easier, she reasoned.

But he only smiled slightly and tilted his head. "Huh." He looked at Maligar, at Saints Toya and Qilphith beside him. "You must care about them very much."

Yinii shook her head. "More than that. They're...they're like a bond, between the Gods Above and Below and us. A message. A promise." Even saying the words sent a shiver over her skin.

His gaze stayed on Maligar. "In Min-Se," he told her quietly, "sorcerers were the weapons of kings. They turned them on each other, on their enemies. Iron sorcerers were the most precious. But I don't get the impression they were treated much like people."

Yinii wrapped her arms around herself. She thought of Fastreda, clasping her hand so tight that the bones throbbed, the wild look in that single eye. Redolfo Kirazzi had made Fastreda a weapon, or maybe she'd made herself one—and when you knew what had happened to sorcerers in other lands, well, that wasn't so bad. She thought of Ahkerfi of the Copper, always roaming. Fastreda in her tower, trapped and waiting to be of use. Asla, entombed in the Wall.

Saint Maligar stared down at her. "I suppose that's easier to do with iron than with wool," Yinii said softly.

"After... What happened to Zoifia," Quill said. "That's what it's like if you don't control it, isn't it?"

Zoifia vomiting liquid bronze. Tunuk, sulking, shaking, patched with bone that took days to break away. Fastreda, mad-eyed and full of glass, and the fizzing of silica in Yinii's hand bones, the whisper under that sensation that bone black ink had such lovely variations...

Yinii shut her eyes. "It can be."

"I never understood how... really abhorrent what those kings did was. You can't dress someone in silks and shower them in gold, and then drive them insane for your own purposes and still call yourself moral."

Yinii looked over at him, surprised. "That's... that's a good point. Thank you."

Quill lifted his chin with another smile. "Well, it seems plain to me. Are any of them ink sorcerers?" he asked.

She shook her head. "It's not an Orozhandi affinity. We didn't use ink—we wrote with marks on clay. We didn't have the affinity until we got to Semilla." She hesitated. "Until me. That's one reason I ended up at the archives," she added. "No one... None of my family, none of the cavern-town, knew what to do with me. They know wool and wood and limestone and paint and salt—but not ink. There's no traditions to keep... keep me sane. But the archives know how. I'm really happy here."

"You seem happy."

It was too much—too much to say, too much to admit, so she launched on. "I have to go. Over to there. To Saint Qarabas. That's... My family are stonemasons. That's what I was supposed to do, actually. He's a limestone saint. My family saint."

"Right!" he said. "Sorry I'm getting in your way."

"That's not what I meant!" she said. "I don't mind, I like talking to you. I—I just—I mean I like explaining... It's interesting, you know, and..."

Quill chuckled. "All right. Why don't I sit on that bench over there—"

"That's an offering table."

"Against that wall over there," he recovered. "And we'll figure out how to get pancakes when you're done."

Yinii went to the alcove beside the back exit, to Saint Qarabas of the Limestone, laced with silver and pearls and pale blue gems, his hammers just as ornate. She knelt on the ground and fought the urge to bang her head against the tiled floor. Gods Above and Below, she was so bad at talking to Quill. She should finish and escape up to the library and the books.

Or maybe all the way back to Maqama and the caverns, her parents and her cousins, and the silent ease of customs she understood without learning the hard way. Her father was coming anyway, wasn't he? She didn't even have to do anything to make it happen.

Saint Qarabas, Watchful Eye, Who Finds the Secret in the Stone of the Sea, Blessed by God Above and God Below, grant me a measure of your patience, your sureness. The wisdom of the miner, the certain strike of the sculptor.

But with her family she'd be a different sort of alone. Again. Yinii said the prayer four times, sat up, stared at Qarabas as if he might give her some sign, some assurance.

The saint stared back, peaceful and unconcerned.

She'd go back up to her library after this, let him go off to have pancakes with Tunuk and Radir. It was the easiest place to be alone. As soon as she finished.

Every Orozhandi had three saints they venerated above all others—the canyon-saint, the family saint, and their personal saint, the one they chose to guide their heart. But Yinii's personal saint, Saint Asla of the Salt, was not in the chapel, nor was she replicated in wood. In the chapel, the only presence of Saint Asla, entombed within the Salt Wall beside the Blessed Martyrs of Salt and Iron, was a fresco painted on the wall behind the offering table Quill had nearly sat on.

Here, as on the ceiling of the archives, Saint Asla had been rendered with the flesh of her face and her hands intact, but her gleaming bones bared. A gilt halo surrounded her pretty face, her auburn hair, while a quartet of skeletons—their bones white for the salt and black for the iron—framed her. The martyrs' names—there were nine—floated over them, in crimson.

Saint Asla, Great Martyr Who Turned the Changeling Horde, Savior of the Worlds and the Saints of the Canyon, give me a measure of your wisdom, your focus. Bless me with the strength of your heart and mind. The purity of the salt, the sharp edge of the truth. Tell me what to do because, Gods Above and Below, everything is a mess and I don't know what's wrong with me, but I like this boy and I can't stop thinking about that awful sorcerer and I shouldn't think she's awful and what if I'm awful too? He's going to leave and all he'll remember is how scared I am.

Yinii sat a moment, with her forehead resting on the offering table, ashamed of herself, even while she felt—deep down—that Saint Asla *must* understand. She'd been a saint, but she'd only been Yinii's age when she made the Wall and died.

She said the prayer correctly four times. When she sat up, Quill straightened beside the table. "All done?"

Yinii looked up at Saint Asla again and touched the salt crystal. "Yes. We can go." She held out a hand, and he pulled himself to his feet, Yinii's fingers fizzing with a different sort of energy. He held her hand a moment longer, looking thoughtful, and Yinii forgot the disapproving eyes of all the saints.

"Were you leaving?" a man's voice said. "I was hoping we could finally meet properly, Brother Sesquillio." Yinii looked back toward the other exit, the one that led out into the street.

For a moment, she thought the consort-prince stood there—a man in fine clothes and a dark mask, a Khirazji man whose sonorous voice reminded her of Ibramo's. But then all the differences struck her— shorter, more muscular, more confident, more dangerous. A stranger in Ibramo's black mask, dark eyes glittering through the wide holes.

Quill pulled Yinii away from the man. "Who are you?"

He tilted his head, as if behind his mask he was smiling at Quill. Another man stepped out of one the niches behind the first—Chiarl, the Maschanos' stern-faced guard, watching them with unblinking pale eyes.

"Weren't you looking for me?" the masked man asked, walking toward them. The guard followed, picking up speed.

"Quill, the stairs," Yinii said, hardly more than a whisper. "Follow me." If they got into the archives, there would be more people, more alarms and more exits, more doors that could be locked and bolted. If she could unlock the doors fast enough, if she could lock them behind her—

But she'd hardly pulled Quill toward the back exit before Chiarl lunged forward, grabbing for her. Quill leapt in front and shoved him off-balance, but that only changed the big man's target. He steadied himself and seized Quill by the hair, pulling him in close and wrapping his arm around Quill's neck. Quill kicked and thrashed, but the big man didn't let go, didn't stop glaring at Yinii.

"I was hoping this would be easier, brother," the masked man called. "Martyrdom is overrated, whatever Saint Asla says."

Quill was turning purple. Yinii sprinted for the exit alcove. She pulled Tunuk's keys out, but instead of sliding them into the door, she unlocked the case that held the three saints. Hardly thinking, she threw open the door and yanked Saint Qarabas's silver hammers from his bony grip.

"I'm sorry, I'm sorry!" she gasped. She needed a weapon; she needed it now. She couldn't open the path back to the archives fast enough. The saint had to understand, she told herself, as she ran back to the center and swung a hammer hard into Chiarl's skull.

It made a horrible, hollow *crack*, and the man grunted and his grip briefly loosened as he fell, still holding Quill.

"Stay there!" Yinii shouted at the masked man, who only regarded her curiously as she untangled Quill from his attacker. The wooden bones Saint Hazaunu had crafted all hummed and whispered and pulled on her, like a whole library of ink, and she could feel the letters in the masked man's pocket, screaming like trapped birds. She squeezed her eyes shut. *Hush.*

In that brief moment of darkness, she heard movement, heard Quill gasp. Yinii opened her eyes and saw a metal syringe pull free from Quill's neck as the masked man stepped forward to catch him. The poisoner—she barely glimpsed the blond woman in her dark gray suit—swung around Yinii to set a dagger blade to her throat so quickly she didn't even have time to move.

"That wasn't necessary," the masked man told Lady Maschano as he settled Quill against Chiarl's limp form. Quill's muscles were all loose, his gaze unfocused.

"It was faster," she replied, her teasing voice now brusque and cool. "And we'll have plenty of blood."

"So long as everything starts actually going to plan." The man sighed and turned to Yinii. "As I said, martyrdom is overrated. And I dislike wasting resources."

Yinii licked her lips, eyes on the hand, the dagger's hilt by her chin; heart in her ears; ink on the letters screaming through all her nerves. Quill lay slack and staring, and she could not panic. "What do you want?"

"I want Lira. But I notice she left. Unfortunately, time is of the essence, so you're going to carry her a message. Unless," he added, "you want the good brother to suffer, of course?"

V

THE VENOM OF KHIRAZJ

Year Eight of the Reign of Emperor Clement
Palace Sestina

Here is where so many things about Redolfo matter: that he is a changeling to his brother, that he is cruel and clever and not the least repentant, that he is not an easy man to read.

Redolfo, Duke Kirazzi, the man in truth, spends only two days in solitude at Sestina, counting the garish birds on the wallpaper, before a visitor arrives.

Redolfo arranges himself on the sofa as if the suit he's wearing isn't his last, isn't stained with sweat, as if he's not been on edge waiting for an answer, an ending—and maybe he hasn't been. It doesn't suit Redolfo to be simple, especially not now, when everything has gotten too complicated to track.

Redolfo sips the too-sweet fig brandy and resolves to get Turon to bring something else for him. It's really the least Turon can do. He watches the younger Kirazzi enter, watches his brother survey the slick wallpaper patterned with ferns and gilt and turquoise songbirds.

"No," Redolfo says. "I didn't change it. I wasn't sure if you were coming."

"We're brothers, aren't we?" Turon replies, taking off his coat and folding it neatly over the back of a chair before sitting down.

It isn't an answer, but it's so like Turon, it's not worth arguing over. Redolfo holds up his glass. "Do you want some? It's terrible."

Turon sighs and rolls his eyes skyward. "Why are you like this?"

"Why are you here if you're going to be a prig?" Redolfo returns.

Turon stares at him, as if that's going to make Redolfo break. It's tragic, really, that his brother has grown into such a clucking hen. There was fire in Turon, once—still is, if you know how to feed it, how to stoke it.

"So," Redolfo says, "how's Pardia? Furious, I assume."

"You know why I'm here. Let's stop pretending."

"I don't really," Redolfo says. "I can guess, if you like: Maybe they've decided to make a tradition of brothers cutting brothers' throats? Or have you opted to grow some balls and make a daring rescue attempt? Or are you here to simply 'say goodbye' because you can't think of a single thing to do? No, wait, it won't be that one. You'll want to moralize at me first."

"What you've done is abhorrent."

"You only think that because you don't understand."

Turon drinks his glass of brandy in one go—Redolfo's brows rise. Well, then. He's angry all right.

"I understand plenty," Turon says.

Redolfo pauses—angry . . . but not. Turon has always been like the sha-dogs the Kirazzis brought from their ancestral home. Still, calm, poised—unflappable. But then, too far, and he's a rage of teeth and claws and sharp words. It's difficult to make Turon angry—it always takes a certain righteousness to really set him off—but Redolfo has had thirty-three years to make an art of it. If he's angry enough to call Redolfo *abhorrent*, he's angry enough to yell and maybe take a swing.

But he hasn't.

"You want something," Redolfo guesses. Turon stares at him, unblinking. "Or maybe Clement does. Let's see, what does he know a *little* about, but not enough about? Ah." Redolfo grins—the piece he keeps finding new ways to play. "You want to know about Lira."

"Lira can wait," Turon says. "He wants the Shrike."

Redolfo blinks. Well, that's a bit of news. "Shrike's long gone and took all her secrets to ground with her. Didn't even ask how I felt about it. She's not a fool."

"But you know who she is," Turon says. "You know how to find her."

"Maybe," Redolfo says, smiling. "Telling you seems awfully dangerous, though. If Clement knows to look for her, then Clement knows she'll kill me if I turn on her and she gets away. I'd need guarantees."

"This will guarantee your death is swift."

"Oh, I rather think he should stick with beheading," Redolfo said. "Don't tidy this up or anything. I think I can put on a good show."

But it doesn't provoke Turon like it should. No shock or horror or *How can you say that?* "Where is she?" he asks.

Redolfo shrugs. "Like I said: long gone, not a fool." He taps the side of his glass, studying his brother. "Did Clement threaten you?"

"He didn't need to. What you did is abhorrent."

"Yes, you said that. And you meant the Shrike—which, to be technical, I had very little to do with. She was always like that; I just pointed her at a task she found interesting."

Redolfo pauses, waiting for Turon to launch in about the blood, about the poisoning, about needing to know how many memories he's tweaked and replaced and balanced to keep this rebellion running—Redolfo can imagine how many of his former allies and coconspirators and useful idiots will claim the Venom of Changelings made them turn against their emperor when not a needle brushed their tender skin. He can count on both hands how many he ordered dosed.

Though, he acknowledges, that does leave aside Rosa's rather dramatic exit, erasing herself from every possible mind. He wonders if she found the stash in the statues.

But Turon says nothing. "I figured you meant Lira," Redolfo goes on, "which, really, you'd only say if you believed I made it all up. So I wonder if you believe in her, too. Be a nice thing, wouldn't it? If one little princess survived.

"Well," he adds, "nice for everyone but Clement."

Which is when Turon ought to protest—*his* emperor wouldn't discard a child's life, a girl's future, just because the throne he'd claimed was really meant for her. But Turon only stands, goes to the sideboard again. Pours another brandy.

Redolfo stands too, goes to the window where he can watch his brother's reflection in the glass. Most certainly angry. Maybe afraid. Maybe Clement wants the Shrike badly enough to use that imperial power to squeeze the younger Kirazzi against a hard place he can't turn from. Redolfo considers his nephews, his sister-in-law.

Pardia and Ibramo, he thinks. Turon is honorable enough to take a threat to Redolfo's wife and son to heart. Perhaps even Lira. His brother's so easily moved.

And yet: There is no fire. No rage. No grief in him. No moralizing.

Except about the Shrike.

Turon turns, brandy in hand. "I can wait all day. If you don't know where she is, then who does?"

Redolfo studies Turon in the glass, thinking of how carefully he planned everything, how easy it had been to seize the reins of the discontentment that milled beneath the society of Semilla and her protectorates in the aftermath of the Brothers' War. *We are to put our whole trust in the imperial family, we are to put all our allegiance behind them, our very honor in their hands—and here one of their own breaks everything we've helped them build in a fit of envy? This is not the destiny of ancient Khirazj. It is not worth the might of Bemina or the craft of Borsya, the wisdom of the Ronqu or the tenacity of the Ashtabari.*

The changeling blood is, admittedly, a curiosity he expects Clement to pursue. And if the emperor knows of the Shrike, it makes sense to hunt her, too. Redolfo knows they have Fastreda, knows Gaspera has told them all she has been privy to—knows Clement must wonder which dukes and consuls and rezas and chiefs, which merchants and delegates, must be rooted out. Where are the hives of malcontents and stores of information. Where are the supplies he kept stashed all over Semilla. Redolfo doesn't know how many conspirators Clement has, but he knows this much: Clement is not so stupid as to waste Turon on a curiosity, not when he must capture so many traitors. Not when the question of the Grave-Spurned Princess looms large.

Redolfo smiles to himself as an answer rises out of his puzzlement. A notion so strange it teeters on the edge of absurdity. But how interesting. How exciting.

And maybe, a way out.

He turns to his brother. "Give me your hand."

Turon frowns at him. "Whatever for?"

It's almost as good as an answer, but Redolfo strides across the room. "Give me your hand," he says and snatches Turon's hand even as he pulls it away. It's like ice.

Redolfo smiles. That's why he wants the Shrike. Turon holds his gaze for far too long, unblinking—they never remember to blink quite enough. The blinking, the cold hands, the too-sweet brandy gulped down like a tonic.

It thinks Redolfo's trapped.

"You don't want to pray with your brother?" he asks, all sweetness. "You remember Gintanas? How mother and father used to bring us to the chapel for holidays?"

"Of course."

No, you don't, Redolfo thinks, as he slides around Turon, as if to make himself another awful brandy. Turon doesn't stop him. It really does think Redolfo isn't prepared.

"You remember the time we went for Salt-Sealing and you threw up on the statue? I was seven, and I remember you being in absolute fits over the idol of Djutubai—possibly because I told you it would come to life and trek down from Gintanas to pull one tooth for every lie you told. Who knows really? You were so sensitive."

Turon stares at him—doesn't huff, doesn't sigh, doesn't turn away. Confirmation after confirmation. Redolfo bends down, opens the cabinet. "Oh look. I do have some dhoro after all." He pulls out a bottle of the liquor, opaque dark green glass and an elaborate brass base. "Do you want some?"

"I want you to stop stalling."

Gods and spirits, it's bad at this. It's a wonder, Redolfo thinks, that they ever conquered the known world. "Oh, you should try it," Redolfo says. "It's very good." And before Turon can speak again, Redolfo swings the bottle into his brother's face.

A meaty smack, the crunch of cartilage, and Turon drops to the floor, but Redolfo doesn't stop to consider what he's done or how Turon is hurt. He turns the top of the ornate bottle, unscrewing the body from the base. What comes out isn't the heady liquor of groundnuts but a paper-wrapped package.

Redolfo works quickly—he's practiced this, because he *is* prepared, always prepared, eyeing all the strings and paths and tangles. That he's been caught isn't a sign, mind, of sloppiness so much as a sign of how enormous his plans became and how unreliable people are. No matter.

What's in the bottle is all Redolfo—all his clever mind, all his careful planning. There are—in fact—a dozen of the same packages, hidden throughout his homes and bases and even in his traveling bags. Hidden behind floorboards and sewn into linings and disguised as forgotten delicacies at the very back of a dusty, cluttered cabinet.

From the package he pulls two metal syringes, already loaded with salts and herbs and other obscure bits he's paid the right people to find. There's another packet, already full of dried blood to be rehydrated, but Redolfo doesn't have time. He presses his thumb down hard on the flesh of his forearm and jabs the needle into the vein at his elbow, drawing the blood into the tube as fast as he dares.

When you make enemies, he knows, you have to be ready for them to come for you. The Shrike laughed at him for readying the Venom of Khirazj for the day the changelings realized what he was doing, what he already knew, but Redolfo has never cared what lesser minds made of him.

Turon doesn't stay down. But *Turon* doesn't get up.

For all Redolfo's studies, all his daring, all his worldliness, he's never seen a changeling in its own skin. He's not sure anyone has, or how one would even be sure. What's before him won't fit into his mind or words or anything he knows. Imagine a wildfire. Imagine a rockslide. Imagine all the stars pressed together into a skin, twinkling and collapsing and exploding anew. Imagine looking up from the bottom of a river, water rushing over your drowning eyes. Imagine the sound of a flock of starlings, trapped in a net—what it would look like if the sound took a shape of its own, absent feathers and beaks. The changeling is change, quicksilver and inexorable, and it lunges for Redolfo.

Redolfo, Duke Kirazzi, for all his amazement, shakes the syringe in his hand as he leaps to the side, closer to the wall—closer to trapped. Enough time to make the blood mix, to prepare the Venom of Khirazj—and even here, facing his death or his salvation, Redolfo has to chuckle at how ideal that name is with his own blood, the blood of ancient kings, the blood of the river god, making the poison.

"Murderer!" The changeling lunges again, grabs him around the neck, but Redolfo jabs the syringe into the center of its chest and shoves the plunger down. It doesn't take long—eternities when your throat's being squeezed, but really not that long. The changeling's grip loosens. "Murderer," it says slowly, softly. Redolfo pulls the syringe from its chest.

Salvation, then. Excellent.

"You are Redolfo Kirazzi," he tells it as it slides to the ground. "You are the Usurper, imprisoned here for raising a very elegant and thorough rebellion against a halfwit emperor." A face forms from the chaos—mahogany skin, close-shorn black hair just beginning to pepper to silver, neat goatee in the most current style. "You are the smartest man in any room, you are the most daring duke House Kirazzi ever raised." The face settles in a lazy smirk Redolfo knows all too well. He tells the changeling of his strengths, his manners, his family's names—he's not going to do the half-made job that its superiors did. No one can find this one out again. He keeps talking, telling stories that might matter, telling it how to reply when it doesn't matter. Telling the tale of Redolfo Kirazzi.

And it works—he can see it working. Gods, saints, and spirits bless those wily old Khirazji priests. *The Venom of Khirazj is the trap of the changeling.* Pity no one had this in quantity when the changelings were razing everything down to the stones.

He leaves gaps—he knows he does. Redolfo Kirazzi may be the smartest man in any room, but a smart man knows he's not infallible. It will have to do. He takes the other syringe, the packet of blood, in case of another one—because right now he's sure there will be another one. He considers the other kits in caches he can get to, pulls a plan together as he screws the base back on the bottle and returns it to his hiding place absent its precious load.

"In a few days—most likely—your brother, Turon, is going to come here. You don't want to tell him anything in particular." Redolfo pauses. "Be nice. Not too nice. Nicer than I was. He's going to lose us and it will upset him quite a lot."

The changeling's dark eyes are getting harder, more certain, and its mouth is working, but it nods along.

"And who are you?" mutters the changeling who now and for the rest of its short life knows itself only as Redolfo, Duke Kirazzi.

Redolfo takes the folded coat off the back of the chair and shrugs into it, blessing those gods and spirits again for making his brother so closely his twin. *A changeling of his brother*, people always said. Redolfo pulls the collar up.

"Why, I'm Turon Kirazzi," he says, as he reaches for the door. "At least for the next few hours." He grins at the changeling, as the poison finishes its cruel effect. "Last thing, you don't want the blade, you want the noose. You want to give them a show." And stop anyone looking too closely at Redolfo Kirazzi's suddenly greenish blood.

With any luck, though, he'll be far, far away when that happens.

CHAPTER THIRTEEN

Richa looked up at the elaborate marble edifice of the Mascha-nos' residence as he approached. A breeze hissed through the red paper tassels strung over the gate for Salt-Sealing. The changeling masks grimaced back at him, as if daring him to test the doors.

Nothing seemed out of place about the house as they walked up the long street of fine houses. Nobody he'd asked as they approached had seen Lord or Lady Maschano come out since they left that morning. Everyone was too curious about why he was asking, and why was the consort-prince, gleaming in gold, trailing puzzled vigilants up this respectable street?

Nothing seemed out of place—except here was Deilio Maschano, pounding on the door.

"Where are your parents, Brother Deilio?" Richa called out as he climbed the stairs.

Deilio whirled on him, but that imperious young man who'd sneered through their first interview still hadn't returned. He was pale and shaky, a kid in fancy vestments.

"The door's locked," he said plaintively. "No one's answering. Someone *always* answers. They had no plans to travel, not that I know of, anyway, and my mother *always* tells me when she's leaving. She would have made sure I had Chiarl with me at the very least." He clasped his hands together. "She wasn't there when the vigilants let me go. And I can't find Chiarl."

Richa took his arm, guided him from the door and down the stairs to where Amadea stood. "Can you talk to him for a moment, right *there*"—he positioned Deilio where he'd block the view of the vigilants and the consort-prince standing below—"while I check the door?"

Amadea peered at him a moment but moved to the steps leading up to the entrance, adding to the cover as Richa knelt beside the door.

You didn't forget how to pick a lock, even if you put it out of mind, even if you got a little rusty at the edges. Even if you only gave in at times like these, when you could call it *necessary*, all your muscles remembered, and your mind recalled, and as bad as it was, it felt good and right. You didn't rob one of these old noble houses, not because it was tricky to get in, but because it was tricky not to get caught.

But if you'd taken an oath to the Vigilant Kinship, well, then wasn't it good you knew, still, how to coax the tumblers and the fine breath of cold-magic out of the way of the law?

The elders wouldn't see it that way, Richa knew. But as he popped the handle and opened the door, it didn't much matter what the Kinship elders thought anymore.

The smell struck him first. Three steps into the Maschanos' manor, into the wide foyer, under the gaze of a rich portrait of the current Maschano family, and Richa was sure someone was dead. He went back out, brought the other vigilants in, told Deilio to stay where he was. Amadea and the consort-prince came in, and Amadea stopped, staring up at the portrait of the family hanging over the hallway.

"That's . . . that's her?" she said, an odd hitch in her voice, as if she were afraid.

The consort-prince looked back at her, frowned. Back up to the picture. "Yes," he said quickly. "Most definitely."

Richa considered them a moment.

But then the vigilants were fanning out, creeping through the manor, and he followed, room by room, the scent building as Richa moved, his estimates climbing—not someone, a few someones. Several. *Many.*

In the second-floor salon, they found them, laid out in rows, their arms crossed over their chests: ten servants and Lord Zaverio Maschano at their center. The rug was soaked with blood.

You let a skill sit, Richa thought as he entered the room. Because you weren't that person anymore. But then that person—thief or assassin or anything else—was always there, under your skin. Had the Shrike hunted in the last twenty years? Was this the frustrated burst of a killer made to hibernate?

"Someone send a cadet to the hall to get the body haulers apprised," Richa said, "and someone tell the consort-prince." He walked down the line of bodies, keeping his feet out of the blood. All of them had had their throats cut—except Lord Maschano. Lord Maschano alone did not have his arms positioned, and his chest was damned near split open, like someone had been hacking at it with a cleaver.

Lady Maschano was noticeably absent.

His eyes skimmed the rest of the room—not so much as a splinter out of place. Except—

He peered at the wall over the fireplace—there were dim patches in the paint. As if something that had been hanging there was missing. *They have her swords hanging up*, Quill had said.

Back down the stairs, to the wide foyer. To Amadea Gintanas, standing in the doorway, haloed by the light of noon, and the consort-prince beside her, being told of the many dead. Amadea moved toward Richa as he came down the stairs.

"She's running," Richa told her. "And she's armed."

"Vigilant Langyun?" an Alojan cadet called from the door, her dark skin graying briefly as she realized the mistake. "Richa, esinor, there's a girl—an Orozhandi—she's asking for you and for an Archivist Gintanas, but she won't come in the house."

"Yinii." Richa registered the word in the same moment Amadea was bolting from the house. He chased her, nearly colliding with the consort-prince, who'd had the same thought.

Yinii was sitting on the last step of the entrance, staring into the middle distance. Holding a paper in her fist, with the ink all crawling over her hand like ants swarming.

When Richa reached her, Yinii looked up at Amadea, her eyes

fearful and red-rimmed. Wordlessly, she held up the paper, all the
ink retreating back onto the page. "They said I had to give you
this," she told Amadea, her voice hardly more than a creak.

Amadea took the paper—the letter, Richa realized as she
unfolded it—as the consort-prince came to stand behind her. A chill
ran down Richa's spine as he read the letter over her shoulder, like
the cold hand of a demon reaching up from Hell:

*I hope this letter finds you well—better, at least, than Fastreda. I am
returned and I find my household lacking in hospitality, shall we say?*

*I have taken the Paremi and you will not have him alive unless I
am given the Flail of Khirazj as exchange. Bring it and Ibramo to the
tombs outside Gintanas in three days.*

*I cannot say this was my first plan, but when an opportunity unveils
itself it would be folly to pass it by. Think on this, if you please, as you
decide what to do next, and recall, if you will, that the Shrike has a
temper and Brother Sesquillio a tender neck.*

*The girl has told me you are heading to House Maschano. You
should therefore have ample proof of the current circumstances.*

Your benevolent master,
Redolfo, Duke Kirazzi

Quill's memory was hazy when he looked out the carriage window
and recognized the road south of Arlabecca. He frowned at the herd
of goats speeding past the window for a long moment.

"It doesn't feel very pleasant. You have my sympathies." He
jumped at the voice. Rosangerda Maschano sat opposite him, clad
in a dark gray suit and a black cloak. A sword—the saber—lay across
her lap.

"What doesn't?" he asked.

"The Venom of Changelings." She smiled. "I didn't, as it happens, *give* you any memories. That, I can tell you, is significantly worse."

Quill squinted at her, as if some detail of her face would make
all this make sense. He remembered...jewels. And pancakes. And

Yinii ul-Benturan, with a joyful expression, along with the knowledge he would have to ask her to coffee, because it would be very inappropriate to kiss her right then.

He cleared his throat and looked back at the goats. That had to have been ages ago. And had nothing to do with changeling blood. "Why am I here?" he asked.

"Collateral."

"Oh." *No, wait*, he thought. Yinii wasn't joyful. She was scared. Scared and trying to save him from...something? Someone. "Collateral for what?"

Rosangerda chuckled. "The flail, of course. The last piece."

"There were four pieces," Quill said. "No, wait...three." One was the book and one was the arm and one was...the flail. "What do they do?"

"You'll see."

He looked out the window again. Goats. "Where are we going?"

"The vault. Did you forget that part? The Kirazzi vault."

Quill blinked. "The consort-prince doesn't know where that is."

"No," she said. "He doesn't. But we do. We're going to have to walk a bit, but you don't mind."

"I suppose not," Quill said slowly. His thoughts moved like syrup. Pancakes. Tunuk and Radir were going to the pancake shop and he and Yinii weren't supposed to. But they'd gone down into the chapel first. The skeleton saints. The eyes full of jewels. *Disapproving* jeweled gazes. Then she had hammers and she was screaming, *Quill, run!* But the strange man who never blinked, Chiarl, the guard from the Maschanos' house, had him around the throat with his ice-cold hands—

Quill shut his eyes. "Did you take me from the archives?"

Rosangerda sighed. "Are you going to be difficult, Brother Sesquillio? I would hate for you to be difficult." She lifted the sword, its tip rising from her knee like a hound hearing its name. "It's fortuitous, really, that you were there. Of course, you seem throughout this misadventure to be *constantly* there. Asking questions. Poking at answers. Letting me know the primate wasn't keeping his word and the vigilant was nowhere near the track. It's been very helpful."

"The primate," Quill said, still a little slow, but catching up. "He was blackmailing you."

Rosangerda laughed throatily. "Oh, saints and devils, that's what the other one thought too. What was his name?"

"Karimo."

"That one," she said, snapping her fingers. "Came to me that morning all whispers and worries. Thought the primate was black-mailing me—me!—and he would fix it and I shouldn't pay." She gave Quill a dark look. "I was paying partly for silence, I'll grant you both that, but the two of you made very clear I wasn't getting what I paid for."

"Karimo was trying to help you."

"Brother Sesquillio," she said, sounding almost maternal again, "your mind is not altogether with you yet. Lamberto was never blackmailing me. I was paying him."

Quill blinked. "He's your advocate."

Rosangerda laughed. "He was. He was a bit more than that. I made sure he knew who he was dealing with so he knew exactly what would happen if he crossed me. Perhaps he thought that meant he had me in hand—I wouldn't have put it past him. But I hope he never told you he was an innocent in this."

Something salacious. That had been his first thought, he realized. His first thought about the numbers that were swirling in his head now. "What's worth two hundred metas a month?" he asked.

Someone's tongue clucked—a man's voice off to his right said, "That's going too far, now, brother. Mind your business."

"Sorry," Quill said to the man. He looked down at the floor-boards, at a knot in the wood half under his boot. The carriage rattled along, and he stared at the mark, trying to hold his thoughts together. "You didn't have to kill Karimo," he said.

"I didn't," she said. "Obigen, yes. Lamberto, most definitely. The reza, nearly—and I was so close to taking Lady Gritta, but then *you* were knocking at the door, and I had to leave.

"But the boy killed himself. Which—I think we must all admit— was a thing of art, really. I already needed to stop Obigen and his stupid wall. I already had plans in place to make Obigen kill the reza ul-Benturan—no chance of Orozhandi concessions when *that* happens—so it was simple to make a few changes, get rid of my unwanted hero. He was a talker, your friend, inclined to rhapsodize—"

"Like some people I could name," a man said dryly.

"—and my goodness, did he have a lot to say about the Order of Parem and the laws of the protectorates, what we owe our ancestors for what they sacrificed, what they lost when the changelings descended and unmade all of society. He thought he was moving me to make a stand against the primate, but—funnily enough—he was actually giving me the key to destroying him.

"Because if you convince an impressionable young man like that," she went on, growing excited, her pale eyes gleaming, "that he is not what he has always believed, that he is, in fact, a changeling agent of the horde beyond the Salt Wall—that he has just now murdered a noble consul and an Orozhandi reza in order to further the coming destruction, a second calamity, the undoing of all he has dedicated his life to building? He'll take care of business himself. It's like something from a chapbook, don't you think?"

Quill's gorge rose. The man said, "Rosa, you're being macabre."

"That's why you sought me out, isn't it?" She smirked at Quill. "It took a lot of blood, a lot of *art*, let me tell you. But it should have ensured that Lamberto knew whatever he thought his position afforded him, it wasn't safety. Alas. He was never as clever as he thought he was." She grinned. "You're a wiggly one, though. I nearly had you in the manor, and before that, I thought surely you would have gone back to the chapter house that night, but I couldn't find you. Did Lamberto warn you away from me?"

"He didn't tell me anything," Quill said. "I figured it out later." He looked down at his hands, his fingers twitching as he tried to move them. "You planted the poison in Gaspera's house. I thought she was your friend."

Rosangerda shook her head. "You have friends, brother. I don't. I have tools I keep sharp in case I have a need for them. A use, a reason."

A use. A reason. "I'm collateral for the flail." His mouth was so dry. "You... you gave me something." The memory of the needle in his neck, the cold spreading through his muscles, washed up from his drifting mind. *You were given the Venom of Changelings*, he reminded himself. *You're not thinking clearly.* But it didn't stop the words spilling out of his mouth: "Where's Yinii?"

"The Orozhandi girl is conveying our terms to Lireana." Quill turned toward the man's voice at last and saw a Khirazji man he didn't recognize sitting beside him in the carriage.

Or wait...maybe he did. So many things were swimming up out of the darkness in his head and it was so hard to make any of it fit together.

"Why stop the Wall?" he asked—either of them, both of them.

"Let's say, it's better if there aren't people digging around that land at the moment." The man turned a look on Rosangerda. "And hopefully, despite your improvisations, Rosa, we will have our peace and quiet."

She sniffed. "When have you *ever* craved peace and quiet?" The man's eyes glittered with amusement—and that stirred up more memories. A nod, those eyes buried in a black mask, and that plum cape he was wearing now.

"You," Quill said slowly. "You were the man on the street outside Lord Obigen's. And in the square. And outside the Maschanos'."

"Clever and a good memory." He settled back on the seat. "Let's hope Lira appreciates all of that enough to come and get you."

Lira...Amadea. She would. *She's definitely the one you want in a crisis, Amadea.* Quill blinked at the masked man, unmasked. "You're not going to hurt her, are you?"

The man grinned again. "That depends entirely on Lireana, brother."

⊷ ⊶

Amadea stared at the neat handwriting, feeling her mind fracturing and splintering as if she could stay here on these stone steps and still be *there, then* on the good Alojan carpet, a million miles away. She gripped the paper harder, her gaze skipping all around it. Her ears went muffled and distant; only the raucous chorus of a Salt-Sealing song from down the street slid through like a needle. "A crystal of salt to spark the fire! A mouthful of salt to burn them! Look 'em in the eye and take 'em by the hand! With an ingot of iron to turn them!"

Black ink, she told herself. *Cream paper. He doesn't get to win.*

"Shitting devils," Richa swore beside her ear. It pulled her back to the present and she turned to stare at him. He looked abashed. "Sorry. Is this real?"

"I saw him," Yinii said, hands curled in her lap. Amadea shut her eyes, yanked back to the study and the bird wallpaper, the pillow under her arm. "I saw him and Lady Maschano and...and the guard from the day Quill and I came here. I can't remember his name." She faltered. "What's in the house?"

"Vigilant Langyun!" A thin young woman, her thick hair in knots like Mother Ayemi's, stuck her head out the window high up on the third floor. "There's something...There's *something* up here. Under the eaves. You need to come see."

"I have a situation—" Richa started shouting back.

"*Now*," she shouted.

Amadea exhaled. Back to Richa, back to now. He cursed again, milder and under his breath. "Stay here, please. You too, esinora," he added to Yinii, before taking the stairs two at a time back up to the house.

"What do you mean you 'saw him'?" Ibramo asked Yinii. "You can't have seen him—he's *dead*."

"I don't know," Yinii answered. "But Quill...I think this is the man he saw following him, the one he thought was you, Your Highness. And I know what the man told me, and I know what the letter said." She lifted her face to Amadea, somber as a supplicant, and held out her curled hand.

Inked letters seeped between her fingers, over her curled knuckles. *My dear Lireana*—the greeting missing from the letter. "I didn't think you'd want the vigilant to see."

Amadea sat down beside Yinii on the stone steps. The singers were moving up the street draped in red and gold, clanging bells and hoisting rag-pulp changeling puppets on sticks over their heads for the people in their houses to throw coins at. Amadea slid the paper under Yinii's hand.

"Put it back," she said gently. "That's got to be exhausting you."

"It's not bad," Yinii protested, but her hand shook as she turned it over, let the words slip off her fingers, back into the place they'd been set down.

"The face is a mask, the mask is a face!" the singers chanted as they skipped past, chased by children. "A mouthful of salt to burn them! Look 'em in the eye and take 'em by the hand! With an ingot of iron to turn them!"

My dear Lireana, I hope this letter finds you well—better, at least, than Fastreda. I am returned and I find my household lacking in hospitality, shall we say?

"Give it to me," Ibramo said. "I'll take it. I'll deal with it."

"He wants us both to come," Amadea said to Ibramo. "To chase him." The dream of running through a cavern, the memory of Rosa standing in the mouth of a cave. She closed her eyes, tried to hold the image steady instead of pushing it away. "Is the cache underground?"

"I don't know," Ibramo said, an undercurrent of panic in his voice. "Li—*Amadea*, this is what I do. Let me do it."

Amadea didn't look at the red-and-black-trimmed mask— imperial presence, warfare, and shadows—but thought of the rumors of the consort-prince's network of informers. Her mouse. With an army all his own.

"If you go find him, and you don't have me—" she began.

"He will make do."

"Or he'll kill Quill." Amadea gripped the top of the letter and ripped off the salutation in a long strip. "You may be the consort-prince, but that boy is my responsibility. I'm going with you."

Ibramo looked down at the strip of paper. "The vigilant's already seen the letter. He'll know it's..." He blinked at her. "Does he *know*? About you?"

Amadea folded the paper into a tight bundle. "He does not."

"Not that you can't... You could. I just assumed you're keeping it secret and I didn't think you two were..." He cleared his throat. "What did you tell him about us?"

"That we're childhood acquaintances."

A wounded look crossed Ibramo's features, and Amadea felt the lie she'd been passing over time and time again, heavy and sharp-edged, like it was new and fresh. *Acquaintances.*

"I don't want to upend your past either," she said. "He doesn't know. He doesn't need to know, I don't think, but if it's the difference between saving and condemning Quill—"

"Amadea!" Richa was hanging out the same window the previous vigilant had been. "I have something I need you to identify. *Now.*"

Amadea shot to her feet, but Yinii caught her elbow as she did, too afraid to let her go. Amadea pulled her up too. "Come on," she murmured. "You come with me."

Ibramo took her hand as she turned, and instead of pushing him away, Amadea squeezed his hand in her own. "Go," she said, even though it made her voice shake. She pressed the letter into his grasp. "Go, back to the palace. You *have* to tell the empress. And...do what you do now."

Ibramo's soft eyes searched her face, his fingers tight around hers. "And you?"

"I'll do what I do now," Amadea said lightly. "I'll get your requests in order. We'll find the map and the key in the book and the arm. And then we'll go find whatever salt-sucked bastard is pretending to be your father and get there before he's ready for us."

He looked down at the letter and drew a slow breath. He nodded once and let her go. Amadea watched him return to the vigilants, the consort-prince once more.

It couldn't be Redolfo, Amadea thought as she followed the directions of the vigilants, but she knew that handwriting, knew those words. She pressed a hand to Yinii's where she gripped Amadea's elbow as they went up and up, into a tiny room tucked under the eaves at the back of the house. She found Richa there staring at a chair and an assortment of tools with a dark and thoughtful expression.

A chair, belts wrapped around the arms; a table laid with small bowls dusted by the remains of powders and an array of sharp knives; another larger bowl on the floor, stained dark. The smell was faint but still awful—metallic and meaty, with a resinous, bitter burn—and too thick to be blown away by the open windows on each side of the room. She covered her face with her sleeve. "Richa? What is it?"

Richa gestured grimly at the assemblage of bowls and knives. "I don't know. Looks like she was torturing someone. You can identify changeling blood, can you name any of this?"

One bowl was crusted with some sort of mashed vegetable, a milky sap congealing along the bottom. The other held a layer of vibrant blue powder. When she tipped it toward the light, it glittered.

"Chalcanth," Yinii said softly. She reached past Amadea and poked the blue dust with one finger. "Vitriol of copper. It's a mordant in dyes. Sometimes they use it in inks and...oh." She gripped Amadea's arm like she was falling and Amadea realized what she'd recalled. *The salts of copper.*

"Poison?" Richa asked.

Amadea shook her head, answering despite the old panic rising in her again. She pointed to the bowls. "'Four parts the root of lotus, pounded in milk, strained well. One-third the salts of copper.'"

"'Eight parts the blood of a changeling, dried; boiled in water and cooled; put to the veins directly,'" Yinii finished. "She was making it. She was making the poison."

Amadea looked back at the chair, the heavy restraints. The long, shallow dish positioned where the breeze would blow across it. "Worse. Saints and devils."

"What?" Richa said. "What is that?"

"It's the recipe for the Venom of Changelings," Amadea said. "She wasn't using blood she'd saved from the coup—she was bleeding one. She has a live changeling with her."

CHAPTER FOURTEEN

Amadea stood in Bijan's workroom, surrounded by the tall cases of sorted gems and considering the array of artifacts spread over the worktable, but her thoughts kept veering to the cave she suddenly remembered. To Rosa and Redolfo, and what might be behind the willow. She focused her attention on Tunuk and the prosthetic arm and tried to keep the memory from overwhelming her.

"This design is ludicrous," Tunuk huffed, looking at the prosthetic arm of Djacopo Kirazzi with disgust.

"I thought it was 'an excellent piece of combined Datongu and Alojan bonecraft techniques,'" Bijan said mildly, standing a wary guard beside the open case of the Flail of Khirazj. Tunuk glowered at him.

"It *is* when we're talking about prostheses. When we're talking about secret keys..." Tunuk tugged on the fingers again, but they didn't come out.

"Are you sure it's a key?" Richa asked: He stood back from the worktable, arms folded, having been warded off by the archivists standing over their treasures more than once. "Maybe it's just an arm."

"The consort-prince said that his father's letter told Duke Turon that their father's arm was the key to the cache," Amadea said. "It does *something*."

Redolfo Kirazzi wasn't dead. He wasn't dead and he wanted the flail, and he'd taken Quill, and somewhere there was a cave Amadea hadn't remembered for years and years—because of the Venom of Changelings? Because her memories were damaged?

Because it wasn't real? What was more likely? she asked herself. That Redolfo escaped the noose and no one noticed? That she'd forgotten the cave? Or that someone was playing a dangerous trick, and she wasn't reliable enough to manage this?

Ibramo had not returned from talking to Beneditta. Amadea had not yet figured out what they needed and had pulled in her archivists to figure out the clues they had. Amadea Gintanas was a solver of problems, after all, even if she couldn't pin down all the problems before her.

Tunuk turned the arm over, held it by the elbow, and made a low thrumming sound in his throat. "What kind of a lock is it?"

"I have no idea," Amadea said, even as she smelled a cold, mildewy memory, heard the grinding of stone. She'd remembered the catacombs of the Kirazzis before—not sure if it was as an abbey orphan or Ibramo's companion or some other time. Had that been the cave, the cache, the secret remains of Redolfo's rebellion?

She looked at Yinii, bent over an ornate Book of Gates, scanning the pages with tears brimming on all her eyelids. She came to the endpapers and ran a finger down the seams, biting her lip. She shook her head and looked up at Amadea. "It's no use. I know you said there's a map in here—that *he* said there's a map in here—but I can't find it. I can't find anything. I can't fix it."

Amadea sat down beside her, covered Yinii's hand with her own. "This isn't your fault."

Yinii nodded. "It's the Shrike's. But...but next, it's mine. I shouldn't have dawdled. I should have let Quill go have pancakes instead of showing him the chapel—"

"Yinii—"

"I should have grown a *spine*!" Yinii went on. "And fought right off, instead of just *standing* there, like some *useless*—"

Amadea pulled her close, tucked Yinii's head against her shoulder, as she broke into tears. Amadea smoothed Yinii's hair down to the knot at the base of her neck, waved away Tunuk and Bijan as they moved to help. "It's going to be all right," she promised.

"He's going to die, isn't he?" Yinii wept. "It's my fault."

What could Amadea possibly say? There was no telling what the Shrike would do, and whoever had written the letter, they had no qualms about threatening Quill. But in Yinii's words, she heard her own grief, her own fear: *I had to fix it. I was the one who could fix it.* And she hadn't been, she couldn't have been, just the same as Yinii, caught in the wrong place by the worst people, shouldn't be shouldering any of this.

"It is *not* your fault," Amadea said. "You did nothing wrong. You both got unlucky. You crossed paths with a monster—did you ask for that? Did Quill? All this began before you were even born, my dear, and it's not fair, but it's nothing you've done. I don't know why she took him, but if she harms him, rest assured I will do everything in my power to make sure she doesn't go unpunished."

Yinii sat up, wiped her face. Her dark-eye flashed open briefly. "It won't bring him back."

"No," Amadea said. "That will be the cleverness of the archivists, the duty of the vigilants, the minds of the Paremi, and the spine of a girl who stole a saint's hammers to go fight off her friend's attacker."

Yinii turned away, touching the medal of Saint Qarabas in a guilty way. And froze.

"Spine," she breathed.

She snatched up the Book of Gates, turned it upside down, and opened it wide. The binding gapped between the leather cover and the pages. Yinii grabbed her long tweezers from the worktable, scraping at something within. Slowly, carefully, she peeled it up, withdrawing a folded page the length of the book. "I found it!" she gasped. "Asla and the salt, I found it."

Pinched in her tweezers, it looked like a crushed flower, stained and faded, but Amadea eyed the creases, studied the shape. All of her balked at treating it roughly, but then they had no time at all. She plucked it free, pinched the edges, forcing it into bloom again. The paper cracked as she smoothed it, but it was clearly a hand-drawn map. Everyone leaned close.

"A watercourse with a sharp bend northward," she said. "A footpath that crosses over it. Hills, with the remnants of a pre-Sealing stone wall from the look of it." She pressed her mouth tight. A hash mark under a peak—*a cave.*

"Do you want me to get an atlas?" Richa asked. "I don't remember all that land you showed me before."

"No," Amadea said, her finger resting on the marking for the cave. She could picture the footpath that led up into the hills, up from Gintanas to Sestina, along the fields and pastures. The stream that wound up toward the Salt Wall, vanishing beneath the gleaming bulk of it. The willow would be just *there*, where the ground dipped toward the stream.

"I think I know where this is," she said. "This is near Sestina. This is on Gaspera del Oyofon's hunting park."

Tunuk peered down at the drawing. "*Ah.* Khirazji." He lifted the hand again, and this time bent all the fingers back, away from the palm, so that the block of bone there, a soft organic shape, stood out. "It's a *pressure* key. Someone could have said."

"Well done," Bijan offered. He looked at Amadea. "Are you going to take the flail?"

"Yes. Pack it for travel, please."

Bijan's brows knitted. "Are you *sure*?"

This was the problem Amadea had no sense of how to solve. She needed the flail to get Quill back—but she had no idea what it was for, not any more than Ibramo. What kind of dangers would she be unleashing?

"It's just a stick with some beads on it, right?" she said lightly.

"Hardly."

Amadea looked back and saw Ibramo—in the gold again, a crescent-moon-shaped patch pasted around his right eye—standing in the open door to Bijan's workroom, a pair of black-clad guards behind him. The archivists around them bustled to their feet, made their bows, but Amadea only stood.

"Well?" she said. "What did she say?"

"I'll tell you on the way," he said. "Unless you've reconsidered?"

Amadea folded her hands. "I think the request was quite clear." And far beyond that, she needed to know, needed to see Redolfo with her own eyes. Needed to see the cave that yawned in her mind as if it held a cache of lost memories or—she hoped beyond reason—the lack of any such structure.

Ibramo's mouth tightened, the briefest beginnings of a frown quickly banished. He sighed. "Right. I brought a horse for you."

"Did you bring two, Highness?" Richa asked.

Ibramo turned, a real frown this time. "You wish to come as well, Vigilant?"

"I do," Richa said with that disarming grin. "Whatever's happening here, it's my case. And moreover, it's what Lady Sigrittrice had me ejected from the Kinship over. So I would see this to the end, and I would be able to bring back proof myself, to Lady Sigrittrice and the Kinship elders—with Your Highness's permission, of course—so that I can have my damn job back."

Ibramo studied him a moment, before cutting his gaze to Amadea. She nodded. Richa already knew so much, probably suspected more, and . . . she trusted him.

"What about the rest of us?" Tunuk demanded.

"No," Amadea said.

Bijan took Tunuk by the arm. "I'll watch the fort."

Tunuk yanked away. "Since when are you temporary Amadea?"

"Since always, excepting once for a month, every two years," Bijan said dryly.

"And also if Stavio acts stupid with a vigilant."

"Tunuk," Amadea warned. She turned to Yinii last, dreading the young woman's fretful expression.

Nightmares beyond your own powers, problems that would shake your life to its roots without space for you to solve them, unless you squeezed down into nothing, your anchor such a fallible, fragile boy—all of it was fresh as the day the coup had finally collapsed. She knew how Yinii felt, and she had watched long enough to know how the affinity made that so much more difficult.

But none of that would be solved by handing Yinii over to the Shrike. She could not come.

Suddenly, Yinii leapt to her feet, green eyes full of tears. She threw her arms around Amadea. "Be careful," she said. "Please be careful."

"Yinii!" Amadea said in surprise. She put an arm around the girl and squeezed her tight. "Of course. Of course I'll be careful. Promise me," she said releasing her, "that you'll take care of yourself while I'm gone. You're running ragged—"

"I'll go to sequestration." Yinii reached up suddenly and yanked the little pinkish salt crystal she wore, snapping it off the wire wound around her right horn. "Here. Here. It'll keep you safe."

Amadea tried to press it back. "Yinii, no—"

"Please." Yinii swallowed. "I can't go and I can't help, but…Let her watch you? Let me do something? I'll pray. I'll pray for you and pray for everything to go all right. I can do that."

Amadea stopped fighting and closed her hand around the pink crystal. "Thank you," she said. "I'll keep it safe."

"It'll keep you safe," Yinii said. "I'm sure of it."

⁘

Yinii stood with Tunuk and Bijan in the entry hall and watched Amadea and Ibramo and Richa go. The flail was in a case under Richa's arm, the prosthesis folded into a cloth bag over Ibramo's shoulder, the map tucked into Amadea's pocket.

"He's going to throw that on the back of a horse," Bijan muttered. "It's going to shake to pieces and I'll have to rebuild it."

"Please," Tunuk said. "Like you're not salivating over the possibility of that sort of project."

"It's Salt-Sealing," Bijan said. "I don't want to work." He paused. "This is *madness*. I hope they all come back."

Yinii rubbed her arms and looked up at the opaline changeling army framing the door. She wished she'd gone too, but why would she go? What would she possibly contribute? Facts about changelings? Formulae for the Venoms? She didn't even want to ask to come, knowing the only answer would be Amadea's stern expression and a disappointed, *Yinii*.

Besides: her bones still fizzed when she paid attention, and the forms on the reception desk were all whispering to her. She wasn't in a good place to go wandering.

Saint Asla, she prayed, *keep them safe.*

"I'm going to go up and see Zoifia," she said.

Bijan peered at her. "Are you feeling all right?"

"Fine," Yinii lied. She shouldn't go, what good would she be anyway? Just a friendly face when they rescued Quill, *if* they rescued Quill? Amadea could do that. She fought to keep her hands still. "I'm going up. I'll see if I can borrow her chapbooks."

But Tunuk and Bijan followed her up the long marble staircase. "You don't look all right," Bijan said.

She wove her fingers together, clasped them into a fist. "I'm a little...anxious. This is dangerous. That man. That woman. That... It's bad."

Tunuk stepped in front of her as they reached the top of the stairs. "No. You're spiraling out of alignment, aren't you?" Yinii looked away, down into the entry hall below. "Yinii," Tunuk said, almost as sternly as Amadea.

"How long?" Bijan asked. How long had the ink been pulling on her, how long had she been trying not to think of what it wanted, what *she* wanted from it. She reached for Saint Asla's crystal out of habit and found its absence instead.

"I'm fine," she said. "I'm anxious. It's making all the ink anxious. That's it." The door to the street opened, letting in the sounds of the growing Salt-Sealing crowds. "I'm not spiraling; I'm just worried—"

She broke off with a small gasp as she saw who entered the archives, and ducked behind Tunuk, where her father wouldn't see her.

Donatas Ten-Scarab ul-Benturan looked around the entry hall, a russet sunshade held in both hands like a quarterstaff. Yinii couldn't move—part of her wanted to, knew she ought to go down and hug him, greet him, hear him out. The bigger part of her wanted to flee. She could not go home—not now.

"Who is that?" Tunuk demanded. He moved in front of Yinii more, peering down into the entry hall as the archivist on desk duty came back in through the doors.

"That's my father," Yinii whispered.

"Don't you want to talk to him?" Bijan asked, but even as he said it, he was shifting around, helping to block her from sight.

"He's come to take me back to Maqama. Reza Dolitha sent for him." The reza's letter was in his pocket, but not written by her—maybe Pharas, maybe a hospitaler, with that oily brown ink, short, fluid strokes—

Yinii squeezed her eyes shut, her fists tight.

"He can't do *that!*" Tunuk hissed. "You don't *want* to go—"

"I don't," Yinii said, and it was true, so true, no matter what she meant to make herself feel, to listen to the reza because she was the elder, to listen to Amadea, and not want to go along to save Quill—

Bijan grabbed her by the shoulder and steered her across the mezzanine, down the hall, and up to the sequestration quarters. Down to Zoifia and Stavio's room. Zoifia was sitting on the bed, her back against the wall, knees drawn up, with the *Rafiel del Sladio* chapbook draped facedown over them, staring at the little bronze eagle in concentration. Stavio was slumped low in the tub with his eyes closed. Bijan pushed Yinii in, followed by Tunuk. Zoifia sat up, dropped her knees to the side, launching the chapbook across the bed.

"Do you not know how to knock?" she demanded. Her brown eyes turned to Yinii, and alarm overtook her irritation. "What's wrong?"

"Oh, she's *fine*," Tunuk said. "Only the reza has sent her father to collect her back to Maqama and she's so worried about Quill she's going to spiral. That's all."

Stavio sat up with a splash. "*What?*"

Bijan guided her to the bed beside Zoifia while Tunuk launched into an explanation of Quill's kidnapping, of Amadea and the consort-prince and Richa having left, of someone pretending to be Redolfo Kirazzi, and everything he wasn't supposed to say. Yinii couldn't speak to stop him. She didn't look at the chapbook, pulsing iron and the press, slick with oil and egg white. "I'm fine," she said, and flexed her fingers.

Bijan's hands gripped hers. "Yinii, you're not."

Zoifia looked down at her hands. "Are you going back to Maqama?"

No, Yinii's heart said. But *yes, I have to*, said the ink and the grief and the fear all together. "I don't know. I should."

"You don't want to," Tunuk said stubbornly. "That's what you said."

"I should," Yinii repeated, but she shook her head. She touched the gap on her horn where Saint Asla's amulet had hung. "And I shouldn't go with Amadea."

"Why not?" Zoifia said fiercely. "You like that boy—"

"It's obvious," Stavio added.

"And it's *cruel* to make you wait here for news," Zoifia said vehemently. "I think romances are stupid, and even I say that's mean and unnecessary."

"We're not having a romance," Yinii said. But it didn't matter. It was true that she was worried. She felt as if she were being eaten from the inside out with worry, filled with the yawn of the ink. The hot, slick buzz of the chapbook. The greasy slide of the letter. The brittle humming of the note Zoifia had tucked under her pillow— scratching like bird feet, soot scraping, springwater—a note from her mother. Yinii closed her eyes and wove her fingers together.

Zoifia snatched Yinii's hands up in her own. "You are going to worry yourself into a spiral, you dumpling."

"Odidunu," Stavio said, leaning out of the tub farther, "she's right. You're going to make this so much worse for you, if you listen to the *shoulds* and *shoulds* and *shoulds*. You go home, right now, you're going to be out there alone with your baba when you..." He paused. "I don't remember how your spirals go, but it doesn't matter, does it? You don't like it, and we don't like it to happen to you."

Yinii looked up into Bijan's brown eyes. "Maybe I'm not fine," she whispered.

"Nobody's fine," Zoifia said dismissively.

"What do you need to do right now?" Bijan asked.

"Hide," Yinii said, with a mournful laugh.

"Liar," Tunuk said. And he was right; she knew it like the pulse in her veins, the buzz in her bones.

"I want to go after Amadea," she said in a small voice. "I feel like this is...it's not *all* my fault, I know that, but I know I didn't help matters. I feel like if I don't do *something*...But what am I supposed to even do? Against a...an assassin and...maybe a changeling? And whatever else is happening?"

"A *changeling*?" Stavio burst out.

Zoifia shot Tunuk a look over Yinii's head. "What on this side of the Wall and the other—stop having interesting times without us!"

"We'll compare schedules next time," Tunuk said dryly. He crouched down beside the bed, beside Bijan. "We could, you know. Go after Amadea."

A laugh broke free of Yinii, her gaze darting to Bijan's. "No, we can't."

And to her surprise, Bijan—responsible, cautious Bijan—shrugged. "Why not?"

"Because the changeling," Yinii burst out. "The Shrike? All of that?"

"No one is saying march yourself down into battle. You need Amadea right now," Bijan said. "We should have seen that right off. And you want some space to figure out what to tell your father—"

"I can't tell him no," Yinii said.

"But you have to," Bijan said.

"Tell that reza to fuck off, too," Tunuk chimed in. "I said it before, I'll say it again. Maybe she's important to you and maybe we're not, but *you* matter most, and you don't want to go to Maqama, so you *have to* tell your father you're not going to Maqama."

Yinii's throat tightened. "I don't know how," she said in a small voice. Because you didn't defy the reza, and her father was the one carrying out the reza's dictates. Zoifia was still holding her hands. The ink was still muttering. Tunuk's lambent eyes bored into her. Yinii couldn't swallow right. The room was so very small.

"Then it sounds like you need a ride across the countryside," Zoifia said. She pointed her chin at the cast-off chapbook. "Perfect for getting your thoughts in order, according to Esinor del Sladio. That's when they do all the explaining."

Tunuk snorted. "Those books are so stupid."

"Shut up, bone-brain," Zoifia said. "I'm making your point for you."

"Blessed Noniva, can you take the both of them with you?" Stavio said.

Yinii shook her head. "I can't go." Except she needed some time, some space to think through how to tell her father she was defy-ing the reza. And she couldn't do that while she was so worried about Quill that the ink was all trying to crawl up her nerves. She touched her amulets again—Qarabas, Maligar, the gap of Saint Asla's salt crystal. Did Saint Asla always listen to her reza? Had the ul-Benturan reza even known she was going to make the Wall with the other martyrs?

This wasn't the same—Yinii wasn't *blasphemous* enough to claim it was the same—but nevertheless, it put a crack in her sureness. She blew out a breath, reached for the little copper flower on her other horn, the gift of the sorcerer. "I don't know how I'd even get there."

"Well," Bijan said, standing. "I suspect you have a little bit of time here while your father talks to Mireia. You can sneak out while he's busy."

Tunuk flicked a glance at Bijan. "If you took his horse," he said slowly, "you'd have even more time. But I need one too, I don't think you should go alone, and we're the ones who can see in the dark as well as the horses. We might even catch them well before that way."

"We could make a distraction." Zoifia's eyes glittered. "Maybe I'm *not* out of alignment," she suggested. "Maybe I'm about to have a fit so big Mireia won't figure out where you've gone for at least half an hour."

Stavio laughed once. "If I help, maybe a whole hour."

"Gods, if you get involved, we could be all day."

Yinii knotted her hands together. "You shouldn't. I don't want any of you to get in trouble."

"But we will," Zoifia said.

"And anyway, Tunuk is right. You're flirting with the spiral," Stavio said, "so *really* it's better if you find Amadea anyway. This is best for *everyone*."

"And you'll get to stay," Zoifia added, "and maybe kiss that dopey boy when they rescue him."

"If they rescue him," Yinii added, even as she stood, ready to fol-low Tunuk. *You might be chasing your own heartbreak*, she thought, but listening to herself, to her own wants, was safer than listening to the buzz in her bones and the begging of the ink.

"Don't do anything to get into trouble," she said to Zoifia. "Not on my account."

Bijan sighed, pinched the bridge of his nose. "I hate to point this out too often, but they really can't do without us here. We have a much longer lead than you think."

"You are a terrible temporary Amadea and I love it," Tunuk declared.

"Thank you," Yinii said quietly. "Thank you all." She drew another steadying breath, touched the empty place of the salt crystal. *Saint Asla, give me a measure of your bravery, your resolve.* "All right. Let's go, Tunuk."

— ⚜ —

Quill stepped from the carriage in the gray haze of dawn, looking up at Chiarl, who had climbed down from the coachman's seat. A bruise filled half his face where Yinii had brained him, as he glared, unblinking, down at Quill, as if he'd been the one to wield the saint's hammers.

"You know," Quill said, "you're the one who choked *me*."

"He doesn't talk," Rosangerda said as she climbed out of the coach. "But he does run rather quickly, so think before you do anything stupid."

Quill glanced back over his shoulder. There was a castle, a city in the distance, monumental columns limned in cold-light. Sestina, he guessed. It looked like a Khirazji temple from a scroll mixed with the imperial compound's red roofs and high domes. Too far to run to—

The flat of Rosangerda's saber slapped the back of his thigh. "I said don't be stupid," she sang. "Walk."

They left the carriage in a sheltered little grove, following the line of a field of chickpeas, up into rolling hills dotted with sheep. Quill hunted for a shepherd but spotted no one—there had to be someone.

The Khirazji man who was not Ibramo led them over the hills, away from the sheep, the shining length of the Salt Wall rising over the horizon, catching the first rays of the sun. It stretched beyond

Quill's sight in both directions, high as the aqueduct in Arlabecca. They crossed a stream and in the distance Quill saw a little golden stone complex, its many columns painted. *Gintanas Abbey*, he thought.

The hills turned rocky, steeper. They climbed on, losing sight of the little building and at times even the Wall, as they came up against a sheer rock face twice Quill's height and covered with climbing vines. A willow tree dipped its head into the hollow beneath it.

"Here we are," the man who was not Ibramo said. He beckoned to Chiarl and pulled aside the vines to reveal a gap the width of a book. The giant bodyguard seized the stone edge and pulled.

Something gave a hollow *clunk*, a dry *crack*, a scatter of dust, and one of the cracks in the rock released a piece of stone to reveal a handle. The man went over, smug as smug, and hauled on the handle, launching a panel from the rock face. He shoved it to one side along an invisible track, revealing a cave mouth. Cold air, carrying the scent of mildew and something bitter and resinous, flowed out.

Rosangerda narrowed her eyes. "Why do you need the key if the door's unlocked?"

The man gave her a withering look. "I don't need this key. I need to know Ibramo's not an idiot." He fixed his dark eyes on Quill and beckoned him up. "Come along, brother."

Rosangerda swatted Quill's legs again, as Chiarl lit a torch. Quill moved into the cavern, staying within the torch's light as the door was rolled shut again and the group of them walked down into the earth.

"Do you really intend for us to stay in here?" Rosangerda demanded.

"For a few days," the man said. "It's not bad. Presumably, Ibramo and Lira will be along soon; we can get what we need and move on."

"Unless he shows up with the Imperial Guard. Summons up some wall-walkers."

"Oh, Lira wouldn't let him be that foolish. He always listened to her. And he won't tell Beneditta if Lira's coming along."

"He's stubborn and sullen and ten times worse than he was as a boy. Smug, too."

The man laughed. "You forget, dear Shrike, I know people, and

these two I know better than most. Ibramo will come, because at
his core, he is curious. Dangerously curious. He will read the letter
and be so consumed by the mystery of the sender that his stubborn-
ness will ensure he comes no matter what his sour wife says. If he
does so sullenly, then it hardly matters. If Dita knows, it bears no
consideration—he will come. I will assess what he can offer, and
then I will convince him to give it to me."

"And Lira?"

"Lireana will come because she won't leave the Paremi to his fate.
Isn't that right, Brother Sesquillio? She's a noble little thing."

Quill looked back over his shoulder at the smirking man.
He thought Amadea would be much more likely to insist upon
the Imperial Guard and a squadron of soldiers from the Order of
the Saints of Salt and Iron down from the Wall, but he didn't say so.

Rosangerda seemed unconvinced. "I will grant you the boy—he's
your son and all—but what could you possibly intend to do with
Lira now?"

"I'll tell you what I told Brother Sesquillio," the man said loftily.
"Mind your business."

Quill held his breath. They weren't hiding anything, which
didn't bode well for what they planned to do with Quill. But the
things they were saying—*Lira, Ibramo, he's your son*—made no sense.
They were talking like the man was Redolfo Kirazzi, who was over
twenty years dead.

And yet, he knew about the vault and how to access it. He knew
Amadea was Lireana. He wanted the Flail of Khirazj. And he looked
enough like Ibramo to be mistaken for him in low light.

The vigilants will come for you, he thought. *The Imperial Guard will
be here. They'll catch him, they'll try him again. Karimo was right—this is
what the law is for.*

The cave forked, and the man who could not possibly be Redolfo
paused there. "Come this way," he said, breaking to the right. "I
want to check something."

He moved ahead, closely followed by Rosangerda. Quill glanced
at Chiarl, who still stared at Quill, unspeaking. Quill smiled nervously and got nothing in return. It was like the man wasn't even

quite real. Maybe that's what happened if you were dosed excessively with changeling blood?

"Are you all right?" he asked. The man only stared at him, unblinking.

The whole of the vault had been chilly, but at the end of the hall the temperature dropped again, frosting Quill's breath in the torchlight. Rosangerda and Redolfo stood in the middle of the passage, looking at something off to the right: an iron fence that covered another passageway. There was a gate built into it decorated with ornate flourishes of wrought metal but no handle visible. The man reached up and rattled the door with a gloved hand, giving it a satisfied nod, even as his breath clouded on the air.

"Good," he said. "No one's been in. They're still asleep."

Who? Quill wondered. But his focus was already on the cave stretching on into the distance, past the man who could not be Redolfo. The faint breeze that stirred the air coming down it. He tried to picture the land above, the boundaries of the stream and the Salt Wall. "How...big is this cave?" he asked, before he could stop himself.

Before he realized it wasn't a cave, couldn't be a cave. The distance they'd walked, the breeze in the air—

It was a tunnel.

A tunnel running under the Salt Wall.

Chiarl came to a stop between Quill and Redolfo and yelped, veering away from the iron gate where he'd brushed against it. Rosangerda pulled her saber, poised to run the man through. Redolfo had a hand in his jacket, reaching for something Quill couldn't see.

The man stumbled back, dropping the torch. But when he'd retreated a few paces, he reoriented himself. Straightened. Glared at the cave wall as if nothing had happened.

Quill pressed his knuckles into the screams that threatened to burst out of him. Cold hands. Didn't blink. Panicked at the touch of iron. *Changeling!* he thought. *Changeling, changeling, changeling!*

A tunnel under the Salt Wall, a living Redolfo, a changeling right here by him. How many more changelings might be waiting on the other side of that darkness? And what on this side of the Wall and the other was sleeping behind the gate? Whatever danger Quill thought he was in, the empire was in so much more.

You have to get out of here, Quill thought. *You have to warn people.*

Rosangerda sighed and sheathed her sword. "Come along, Brother Sesquillio. Let's make you less of a nuisance."

CHAPTER FIFTEEN

Sestina, the ducal seat of the Khirazji protectorate, lay a day and a half's ride to the southwest of Arlabecca, in sight of the glittering stretch of the Salt Wall. Amadea had not been there in twenty years, but as the traveling party crested a hill to reveal a wide valley along a winding little river, rolling fields of chickpeas, flax, and wheat, orchards of pistachios and Borsyan-blessed coffee bushes—saints and devils, what Amadea wouldn't do for a coffee right now—the bounty of Sestina around the feet of the shining city, she felt a pang of homesickness, quickly overtaken by a deep-rooted terror.

"Two of you go to the castle," Ibramo indicated as the road split. Two of the black-garbed agents, trimmed in red and gold, took off toward Sestina. Amadea glanced back—eight others stood ready for orders.

"It's odd," she'd admitted to Ibramo when they'd stopped in the night, "watching you ordering people around. I mean, it makes sense, but... I suppose my memories of you have to catch up."

Ibramo had smiled wanly at her. "I was thinking the same of you."

They stood beside the stone wall of the relay house, the moon bright as a cold-lamp above in the clear summer sky. The others had scattered—to the stables, to the hostel, to the messenger station—and she'd lost track of Richa. She wished he hadn't come, hadn't brought himself within range of her past. Within range of Redolfo.

Amadea wet her mouth. "Do you think he's still alive? That it's true?"

"I don't know," Ibramo said. "And...I should hope he's dead. That's simplest. That's best for everyone. He's dead, this is the Shrike or some other imposter pulling our strings. But..." He sighed and dropped his voice. "I want him back. It's childish and idiotic, but I want my father back, contrite and loving and willing to change. Willing to be the father he never was—which he can't possibly be, because he was never the sort to stop and consider his failings long enough to repair them. I want it, I can't have it, and that's exactly what they're using to draw me in. And still I go." He shook his head. "The best thing I can say for Redolfo Kirazzi is that I am a better father for having his example to work against. I'm not perfect, but I am not him."

A sudden tightness constricted Amadea's throat, and she coughed as if she could clear everything that brought it on. "How are they? Prince Micheleo and Princess Djaulia?"

"They're well." Ibramo hesitated. "I have to tell you...I didn't actually talk to Beneditta."

Amadea startled. "You what?"

"I left a letter," he said quickly. "She was in conference with Gritta and the consuls. It was going to take hours, and I knew Gritta was going to fight it—fight me. We didn't have time. So I strongly suspect, first, that we will have an army riding perhaps eight hours behind us when all is said and done, and second, that I will likely be in a great deal of disfavor."

"Ibramo, it's going to look like you're siding with your father!"

"Not if I bring his head back on a pike," Ibramo replied. "Not even Gritta could poison me with *that*. I couldn't let her stop me. I couldn't take the chance—not if it's my father, not if that boy's in danger." He looked down at his hands. "You didn't even let me try before. I think about the baby almost every day," he said quietly. "I think about you. We could have found a way."

With the benefit of so many years, Amadea could see paths that might have unfolded to them. Abdications and sworn testimonies, better grooms and distant cottages. Narrow paths, but paths she could have walked.

But not Lira. Not Amadea of seventeen. Only Amadea, silver in her hairline, had that kind of confidence, that kind of knowledge, that kind of resolve. And that Amadea didn't have Ibramo.

"I think about you too," Amadea said. "And her. But we can't run time backward, and I can't imagine you want to. If nothing else, that path means your children are never born. You can't want that."

"You'll find I'm very good at wanting things I know I shouldn't, as well as understanding as much as I want them, I would be heartbroken if they happened. My father, for example," he said, and she smiled. "I wish you and I had the time to talk. The space to say what should be said. Did you marry?"

"I am married to the archives," Amadea said lightly. "It's a very demanding spouse, but it appreciates my strengths and forgives my weaknesses better than most."

Ibramo took her hand in his, smiling, and for a moment, she couldn't even think of all the terrible things she faced. Just this moment, this man, the paths that she'd passed by. The things you wanted, knowing you shouldn't want.

"I wish you were still mine," he said. "But I hate to think of you lonely."

Amadea smiled back at him. "Well, I am never lonely. I have everything I could want." The words flowed out as easily as the truth—and maybe if she said them often enough, they'd become the truth.

But Ibramo's hand had squeezed hers, his expression unmistakable: he had heard the lie and he loved her well enough not to name it.

Now poised between Sestina and their goal, shielded in the mask of the consort-prince, Ibramo cut a ferocious figure, easing down into the foggy valley below. It was disorienting, her past, his present, Quill's future. And Redolfo holding all these things over her head, and demanding she dance for them.

"So," Richa said quietly, coming to walk beside her as they moved down the grassy hillside, "you grew up here."

"Near to," Amadea said, eyeing Sestina, not wanting to think about it. When Khirazj had reached Semilla, the other protectorates had already settled themselves all across the empire, and looking back with a modern eye, one might assume that this rural seat of power was punishment for their late coming, slipping into Semilla just ahead of the war that saw the Salt Wall sealed.

But ancient Khirazj's power had come from three sources: rich mines, brilliant scholars, and agriculture. In point of fact, they wanted the lands that would become Sestina—the meandering creeks were not the Pademaki, the fields were full of strange crops, but here was something approaching home. Here was a place they could regroup and rebuild, pour their wisdom and industry into something that would shape Semilla and the Imperial Protectorates for the better. Sestina had been a fort against the changelings; now it was a palatial compound of hypostyle halls, red clay tiles, and blooming domes enameled in blue stars and lotuses.

A perfect seat of power for the Duke Kirazzi to launch his coup from. A fortress against the armies he'd told her were coming every day.

"Right," Richa said. "'Gintanas'?" He shrugged when she looked at him sidelong, that almost mischievous smile tugging at his mouth. "When you brought out the map, you put your hand directly onto it. Like you were covering something. And it's a bit notable. A place-name from inside the Wall for your surname."

Amadea turned away from Sestina, away from that memory, toward Richa, past Richa—his dark eyes studying her face—pointing to Gintanas, a splash of warm stone against the pale gray wall. The abbey was older than Sestina, the order older—perhaps—than Khirazj, where they came from. The Golden Oblates of the Book of Days had been tracking every sort of calendar when the first god-king climbed out of the river—cycles of crops, cycles of floods, cycles of stars, the moon, the sun, the affinities. You went to a night-brother to chart a sea course. You went to the dusk-given to find out how a gold specialist came into alignment. You went to the day-sisters to plan your crops or track a pregnancy.

Amadea stopped herself from flinching, but only just. "There," she said. "Gintanas Abbey."

"Very charming," Richa said. "Better than my hometown. Caesura's kind of a swamp. So you went from there to Sestina when you're . . . what, seven?"

"I think so." Ibramo had told him she had been a servant in Sestina in her youth, sent back before the coup, and while it was safer, the lie was slick and new and slippery. She didn't know the words to shape it, and she feared saying the wrong ones.

That was all she was doing, this whole endeavor, guessing at the steps. Waiting, biting her tongue, trying not to scream, trying not to let that waiting become freezing. Redolfo could have her, she thought, if he let Quill go.

No, she thought. *Then it all begins again. And there are so many more people in harm's way.* Ibramo had stopped just ahead of them, before the land dipped down toward another trickling stream.

"Two there," she heard Ibramo say, indicating a little grove that overlooked the left-hand approach to the hollow below. Amadea could see the pale head of the willow tree.

"Let's pretend a moment," Richa said softly, "that what's in that letter is all accurate. That the Usurper faked his death and escaped, and here he is. Why's he want the flail so badly?"

"It's the royal symbol of Khirazj," Amadea said, eyes on the willow. "It gives him legitimacy."

"He's not the duke anymore," Richa said. "He's immediately illegitimate." He looked ahead at Ibramo, studying the shape of the land around the creek. "Did you check it for voids or hollows like the statues?"

"It's not big enough for much," Amadea said doubtfully. But now she wondered. Could there be more to the flail than what it symbolized?

The beads clink—despite her resolve to let the memories wash past, she flinched from that one, locked eyes on the yellow grass under her feet.

Richa said nothing for a moment, then, "You sure you don't want to hang back?"

"Absolutely sure," Amadea said.

But then he took her hand, folded it in his own. "You don't have to tell me what's going on. I know there's plenty I'm missing, and I know you can take care of yourself. But if you decide you need someone else to step in, I am ready to do that. And I don't think I'm generally terrible at it."

Amadea smiled, uncertain. "Ibramo will probably handle most of it."

"Probably." He studied her face a moment. "He sure tells you what to do a lot."

"He tries," Amadea said lightly. "Plenty of people *try*."

They came down to the muddy creekside. A bulge of bedrock muscled its way out of the grass there, and behind it, there was the whole of the willow and the wall of rock where the cave had been.

A shadow by the willow where Ibramo's meant to be, and there's Rosa in the mouth of the cave beyond. Amadea sucked in a steadying breath.

Ibramo looked back at her, then up the crest of the hill where they'd descended. "Four up there. Arrows out," he said grimly. "Two with us." Richa stayed beside her, while the others sorted themselves into groups.

Up close, the stone wall seemed impenetrable, her memories of a cave there so clearly false. But it was there; it had to be. The agent pulled aside the hanging vines, and Ibramo peered at the surface, frowning.

"Here," Amadea said, stepping forward. "Get the hand out."

She ran her fingers over the rough edges of the stone—finding the sharp edges with a bit too certain an angle, a bit too artistic a curve. This sort of stonework wasn't done often, even in ancient Khirazj. The scrolls she'd seen reserved it for hiding the tombs of the god-kings. It was a marvel, really, but when you knew what you were hunting—

"Here," she said, planting her finger in the vaguely hexagonal divot. The seams were almost invisible, but with a careful fingernail she tested them. "Give me the hand?"

She took it from Ibramo, folding the fingers back firmly once more the way Tunuk had, and fitted it into the slot. She pushed hard, throwing all her weight behind the peculiar key. A *click*, a muffled *thunk*, and a crack appeared in the stone.

Ibramo pulled his sword. He gestured to the black-garbed agent, a circle of the finger, a point to the left. She nodded and went scouting off in that direction. Ibramo pulled on the revealed door, and with Amadea's help, it slid open, and the cave from her memories yawned wide.

"Now what?" Richa said in a low voice.

"Now we see what monster is inside," Ibramo said. "My father or someone with the unholy pluck to wear his mask."

"You're just going to stroll on in?" Richa asked. "Pardon me, Your Highness, but this could very easily be an assassination in the making."

"He's not going to kill us," Amadea said quietly. "And he has Quill. We go now." She pushed forward, into the darkness, taking the cold-lamp from her pocket and shaking it into brightness.

This wasn't a cavern—someone had built it. Amadea eyed the plumb walls, the places where the ceiling or floor broke cleanly around another piece of bedrock. The Kirazzis and some more traditional Khirazji Semillans still buried their dead, interring them whole in tombs cut into the ground. But this...this went on forever, blank and undecorated.

The path forked, no sign of which way they should go. Amadea stopped, staring at the stone corner. Something in the back of her thoughts stirred, wriggled against her fear. Had she been here? Did she know this place? Was she remembering the tombs at Gintanas or the catacombs of Sestina and mixing them together?

"Which way?" Richa asked.

"Oh, you're fine right there."

Amadea turned, back the way they'd come from, and there was the monster of her nightmares, the threat in all her memories: Redolfo Kirazzi alive and well and smirking at her like he couldn't believe she'd ever thought she would be free of him.

"How nice to see you again, my dear," he said. He nodded to the case Richa still held. "Is that my flail?" A huge hand settled on her shoulder and Amadea glanced back to see a tall bearded man with a bruised face and a blank expression standing behind her.

"Ibramo, your sword? I trust," Redolfo said to her, "that you're ready to listen?"

⚬⚬ ▰◆▰ ⚬⚬

"Look," Tunuk said, pointing off the road where the land dipped toward a wooded stream. "Those are the consort-prince's agents."

Yinii squinted through the low light and the fog and just made out the heads of four men, popping over a hump of land, the red trim on their jackets bright even in the morning gloom. She climbed off her stolen horse and led it to a tree beside the road. Tunuk did the same, tying their reins to a low branch.

Yinii touched the tree and yanked her fingers back as if burned: it filled her with the hiss of char. Everything around her seemed to be filling the place of the ink. She made herself take a deep breath, knotted her fingers together. "This is all right," she said, mostly to herself.

Tunuk snorted. "It's fine. We're going to go down and ask those guards what's happening and if they have Quill yet. They'll tell us where we can stand and maybe we'll end up waiting in a coffeehouse in Sestina. Worst-case scenario."

Yinii could think of a lot of worse cases, but she followed Tunuk down the hill, losing sight of the consort-prince's agents as she descended. Leaving the archives hadn't cleared her mind at all, and she'd ridden through the long night, trying to ignore the way her bones were starting to feel like they didn't fit inside her skin.

No ink, she told herself, crunching up the second rise, thinking about the minerals in the dirt under her feet. *No ink, no ink, and Amadea is here, and Quill will be fine—*

"Yinii!" A cry. An ugly grunt broke through the storm of her thoughts, and as she crested the second slope, she saw all four of the consort-prince's men lying on the ground, red ink soaking the ground under them, the slashes across their throats—

Blood, Yinii forced herself to think. *Not ink.* That was blood and they were dead and Tunuk—

She turned to Tunuk, slumped on the ground, one long hand pressed to the curve of his ribs. Ink, blood, flowing over fingers. He was looking up at her, disbelieving, and even in her busy, jangling mind, Yinii knew she should panic.

"You again," a weary voice said, and she realized the Shrike was standing there. Ignoring Tunuk. Two notes in her pocket, lampblack and water and waxes. Yinii took a step back. The sword came up, touched her under the chin. The Shrike pressed it into her flesh, just hard enough to make the skin break with a *pop*.

"I should kill you too," she said, as if they were just discussing her plans for the day. "We let you go, you stroll back in. Honestly, it's as if you're asking to be murdered. And I am considered such a gracious hostess, really."

Yinii tried to speak, tried to scream. Couldn't stop thinking about the inks in the Shrike's pocket, the gruesome ink pouring out of Tunuk. She had to do *something*.

"Yinii..." Tunuk breathed. "Run."

"Lucky you," the Shrike said, "I'm on a leash. He said before that you get to live. He doesn't like me improvising? He can be responsible for the outcomes." She glanced down at Tunuk. "You are less lucky, but who knows? I don't study Alojan anatomy. Maybe I missed something important. Though the other one wasn't lucky." She laughed as Tunuk's arm buckled, settling him into the mud. She grabbed Yinii by the arm. "Walk."

Yinii kept her eyes on Tunuk, willing him to keep breathing, but soon he was out of sight and they were over another sprawled body, through a wall, and into the Kirazzi vault, plunging into the rock and earth. The soot of years of torches clinging to the ceiling sizzled along the edges of her brain. She tried not to listen, tried not to panic.

With her dark-eye, she found the faint traces of warmth, the signs of people having passed through here, of torches warming the ceiling along the path. The dark stretched on forever ahead with no side passages, and unlike the tunnels of Maqama, it was a cold, empty sort of dark, full only of foreboding and the sound of dripping water. Yinii pressed on, easing her feet over the uneven floor, like she was home again, and trying not to listen to the letters in the Shrike's pocket or the soot on the ceiling or the water dripping down the walls.

"Stop," she whispered.

"What was that?" the Shrike said.

The sword jabbed Yinii's back, and she shook her head. "Talking to myself."

Yinii heard the man first, the voice saying, "I trust that you're ready to listen?"

Then Amadea, blessed, blessed Amadea saying, "We brought you the flail. Where's Quill?" Saint Asla had kept her safe—so far.

Maybe no farther, the soot and the water seemed to hiss.

"You'll see him soon enough," the man said.

The Shrike pushed Yinii forward into the light of the cold-lamp in Amadea's hand, the torch in the speaker's, the man who must be Redolfo. Redolfo, Amadea, Richa, the consort-prince, and Chiarl, Deilio's guard, standing menacingly over them. Ink in Amadea's pocket—the map, she thought automatically. The torch was charred, bad quality, the soot better, fine and—

"Yinii!" Amadea cried. That same shock back into her bones as when Tunuk cried out, and Yinii saw Amadea lunge for her.

But Chiarl grabbed hold of her as she moved, one hand around her throat. At this, Richa whirled, hitting the man in the jaw with a shout. The man released Amadea as a spray of dark blood and saliva spattered her cheek. Richa fell back, clutching his knuckles, cursing—

Rosangerda's rapier erupted from his shoulder, forcing a gasp of pain from Richa. Amadea shouted, bolted forward, but the blank-faced man grabbed her again—by the arm this time—and there was no reaching the vigilant.

"What's directly below my sword right now is the artery pouring blood into your arm," the Shrike said in her conversational way. "Hit it and you'll bleed out very quickly. I didn't miss, Vigilant. Don't be a hero."

"Rosa," Redolfo said severely, "haven't you made enough bodies today? Give yourself a rest." He cast an irritated look at Yinii, still rooted to the floor, trying to ignore the soot and the blood and the water and two letters in the Shrike's pocket. The ink was clearer. More soothing. More *right.*

"What is this?" he demanded of the Shrike. "I told you to take out the guard."

"And I found *her,*" the Shrike said, yanking her rapier out of Richa's shoulder. "The last time I made decisions without your say-so, you were very put out."

"The Ragaleate primate is very different from a spare archivist."

"You're right," the Shrike said sweetly. "But I presume you left her alive the last time for a reason, so if you want her dead, you need to ask me nicely. I'm not about to be chastised like a pupil again for doing my job."

Yinii ought to be afraid. She ought to be screaming—for herself, for Quill, for Amadea, for Tunuk. But it all felt so far away, so lost in the humming of her bones, the hiss of the soot and the water. The green blood on Amadea's cheek.

Oh, Yinii's thoughts churned under the ink, *they have a changeling.* In some distant and receding part of her, she felt panic—for all of them, for Deilio Maschano too, who had been right beside the creature for so long, not knowing what it was. Not knowing what his mother was.

What are any of us? the voice in the ink hissed. Yinii flinched.

"If you hurt her," Amadea shouted, "then I'm not listening to a word. If you want my help, you let her go and you let Quill go too." She held his gaze, savage in a way Yinii knew was strange, that made her think of the watery ink, iron gall and some bitter root, that etched the map in her pocket. "You need me," Amadea reminded him.

A slow, wicked smile curved across Redolfo's face as he turned from Yinii, like the whole world was turning away from her.

"Do I?" he said. "Rosa, why don't you and our friend escort the extra archivist and the vigilant to our 'guest quarters.' Ibramo, pick up the flail and you can both follow me. You'll find it very enlightening, I think."

⊷ ⚬≔⚬ ⊶

Redolfo was smiling at Amadea as Rosangerda led Yinii and Richa away. Amadea wiped her cheek and looked at her hand. The blood wasn't red but greenish black. Changeling blood. She looked up at the blank-faced man, who stared back.

"Go with her," Redolfo told the changeling. "Don't let her do anything too rash. They might be useful after all." He regarded Amadea and Ibramo. "Do think ahead, though. If you try anything clever, she's not going to let you leave alive. But I know you're curious. And unarmed. Come along."

They walked down the right-hand path. "You look well, Ibramo," Redolfo declared. "Though I notice that you remain a consort, not a king. What a pity. How are my grandchildren?"

"You're dead," Ibramo said stiffly.

"Obviously not," Redolfo said. "You were always a boy of such little imagination. It's a shame to see nothing has changed."

"I *watched* you die."

"You watched a farce. The changelings sent one of their own to assassinate me. I let it take my place and escaped."

"To where?"

Redolfo stopped before an ornate iron gate and smiled back at them, all calm and stillness. "Over the Wall, of course. Back to the old lands."

"Through hordes of changelings," Ibramo scoffed.

"Yes, yes—hordes of changelings, ruined cities, death and destruction." Redolfo waved a hand. "Very convenient stories, don't you think? *Stay here. It's not safe out there. Whatever you say, Your Imperial Majesty.*" His eyes burned. "You should see it, Ibramo. You could see it."

Ibramo faltered a moment. Amadea reached over and squeezed his hand. "You should have stayed out there," Ibramo said.

Redolfo's eyes dropped to their intertwined hands. "There's a lot of world, Ibramo. A lot of options." He looked over at Amadea, still smiling. "And you, Lira. We never finished what we started. You could be an empress still. Come with me. Come understand what I've found, and we shall return to Semilla with a glorious army."

"No," Amadea said. "Never."

"Not even with Ibramo at your side? Like it was supposed to be?" He chuckled. "I bet I know what you're thinking: maybe this time you could throw me off. Who knows?"

The rows of glass soldiers glinting in the rising sunlight. The sound of cannons shattering the glass, the screams, Fastreda laughing. People dying.

"Never," Amadea said again.

Redolfo clucked his tongue. "Maybe wait until you see what I have before you decide. The flail?"

Ibramo hesitated, as if considering refusing, considering hitting Redolfo with the case. But this was his father and he'd wanted answers. Amadea couldn't lie, she wanted them too. Ibramo opened the case.

Redolfo lifted the Flail of Khirazj from its nest, holding the weapon with gentle hands. He sighed, and Amadea thought of the ease, the pleasure, that washed over Zoifia's face when she picked up the bronze eagle. "The right of kings," he said. "The gift of the river god."

"What are you going to do with it?" Amadea asked.

"Nothing. I only need this bit at the bottom." Redolfo turned the flail upside down, jeweled beads dangling. He grabbed the rounded gold end of the handle, wiggled it until something cracked. He yanked hard, and a long, thin key pulled free of the priceless Flail of Khirazj, which Redolfo dropped.

"There we are," he said, unlocking the gate. "Leave that, I'll get it later. I want you to see my *real* treasures."

A wave of cold air washed over them. Redolfo woke ancient, stuttering Borsyan lamps as they followed him into a room, long and narrow and freezing. Two huge Borsyan cold-magic panels rose on either side of a set of biers that Redolfo approached.

"Here, Lira," he said. "What do you think?"

There were four bodies on the biers. Four women, with long dark hair, shafts of silver along their brows. Four arched noses, four pairs of eyes that weren't so wrinkled really. Four pairs of high cheekbones scattered with freckles she could never quite cover. Four pairs of lips she had been assured were her best feature.

Four duplicates of Amadea Gintanas.

The slick fabric of the cushion. The cold air of a cave. A man's hand wrapped around her upper arm. "If it doesn't work, then we'll try again. There's a good girl." Amadea was going to be sick, her body was going to be sick—she was a million miles away and falling farther, faster.

"I must admit," Redolfo said, as if from a distance. "I wasn't sure you were alive still. If I had been Clement, I would have elevated you into some dead-end position where I could keep a close eye on you or forgotten you in a dungeon—and the latter seemed much more likely when I arrived."

The pinch of the needle. The slow burn. "That does work quicker. Who knew? We have enough for another?" Amadea couldn't tear her eyes away from the changelings, lying still and cold. Couldn't find the touchstones to calm herself down. *Dark hair. Gray hair. Cold-magic panels. Fuck fuck fuck.*

"But then I saw you. Just a glimpse, leaving the temple of Alletet. You look exactly the same," Redolfo went on. "And I knew I did not come for these"—he gestured at the changelings—"I came for you. You are the missing piece."

"How long have these been here?" she heard herself ask. They looked like her now—not girls of fifteen, sixteen, but women. Had he made them recently? No—he had said this was what he had come back to find. They had they been sleeping here, her cursed sisters, while she moved through the waking world, unsure of who she was.

What she was, Amadea corrected, cold horror around her throat.

"Always," Redolfo said rapturously. "I am always prepared."

Borsyan cold-magic panels, she made herself think. She squeezed her eyes shut and thought of the vessels and the channels: the glass chambers that held the fragments of the Black Mother Forest, the many valves, the tubes full of charged air and water that looped the cold-magic over and over until it frosted or warmed the steel plates, drawing moisture out or pushing it in. These covered nearly as much area as the panels that framed the seed vault, the coldest, driest room in the archives, and their surfaces were lacy with frost.

Bring the snow and the silt-belly of the river to the changelings, Yinii's notes had said, *and they shall sleep like the dead. Coax the wind into the iron and they shall not wake, no matter how you cut them.* The doubles could have been lying here for thirty-seven years, aging lonely in this cave under the trap of the freezing air the Borsyan cold-magic panels could produce, for all Amadea knew.

"I won't say," Redolfo went on, "that this was all for you—I wouldn't dream of it—but the plans did turn on you, on how to draw you out. You do not leave the archives often, and it's very inconvenient. However, there is convenience in Lord Obigen's nest-child being your charge. I think I set a very compelling stage for

Rosa's little performance. The bone specialist, the ink specialist…"
He turned to his son. "And dear Ibramo, all entangled. How could
you not come out?"

*A man's hand wrapped around her upper arm. The blood beading on her
skin. A dark-eyed boy peering through the crack of the door, frightened and
frozen. The glass syringes full of blood, lying in a row. The molten glass
between Fastreda's fingers, shifting, pulling. "Here, my little sparrow. So you
smile."*

"Always someone's champion," Redolfo went on. "Always
someone's shield." He laughed once, looking down at the changelings. "How useful would it be to have a shield that was your
very double? To draw the eyes of those who wish you harm. We
could leave one behind," he said, dropping his voice conspiratorially. "Let her defend against Ulanitti claws. I can tell you from
experience the Imperial Authority isn't very quick at picking out
changelings."

Amadea swallowed, her throat so tight she almost couldn't ask
him, "Will you let them go?" She heard Ibramo's swift sucked-in
breath and Redolfo spread his hands.

"Am I not a gracious lord?"

A neat dodge, a part of her thought. The part that was used to tugging the truth loose from specialists in the grip of their affinities. But
too much of her head was full of the four doubles lying cold on the
bier, of memories of needles and caverns and whispered threats.

This is your fault, it all whispered. *One way or another.* She felt as if
she were a young girl again, utterly at his mercy, unsure of even the
most basic truth about herself.

"Did you find me in Gintanas?" she burst out. "Was any of it
true?"

Redolfo stared at her, unblinking. Puzzled, she realized. Worried.

"Of course it's true," he said, a heartbeat too late. "Why would I
lie to you?"

All of Amadea's whirling thoughts froze.

Amadea, silver in her hairline, knew that expression, that pause
and then bluster. She watched her specialists wear it when she asked
how they were doing. When she pressed Tunuk about Radir's

complaints. When she took Zoifia's hand from the bronze-room door. A flicker when she'd seized Stavio in the coffee shop. On her own face, she was certain, when the lie of Amadea Gintanas brushed too close to the surface. The emptiness, the panic before the lie can be grasped, because admitting you are at a disadvantage when you are weak or frightened or alone is terrifying. When it was her archivists, she took it as the sign she needed to step in, to be the stronger one.

On Redolfo's face, the expression made a crack in the base, a thread to pull loose.

Brown gloves, she told herself. *Violet cape. White teeth. You're not used to being at a disadvantage, are you?*

Redolfo didn't know. He didn't know what she meant. He was the only person in all the lands, within the Salt Wall and beyond it, who knew the answer—to the long-uncertain question of whether she was truly Lireana Ulanitti, to this new horror of whether she might be a changeling—and he had lied. He had not held the answer over her, had not handed her the answer that would appease her, had not threatened to tell the version that would harm her most. Because he didn't know what she meant.

But Redolfo Kirazzi most certainly knew.

This is not Redolfo Kirazzi, she thought, holding his bright, burning gaze.

She has a changeling, Yinii had said. *She has a live changeling with her.* And that was the giant, the blank-faced man they'd called Chiarl, surely.

But what was to say he was alone?

Amadea looked at the doubles on their biers, those perfect tools, and slipped a hand into her pocket and made a fist around the salt crystal of Saint Asla. She didn't know any of the prayers to Yinii's saint.

Keep her safe, she thought instead. *Keep me safe.*

Redolfo Kirazzi watched her. The monster in all her nightmares, the architect of all her woes. He watched her, terrible and calculating as she walked toward him.

"Ibramo," she murmured. "You were right. He's not your father."

And with the salt crystal in her palm, she slapped Redolfo's face, driving the point of it into his skin.

The changeling who wore Redolfo Kirazzi's face screamed, far too loud for a human, but if there were any doubt, the strange green fire that leapt between her palm and his cheek where he bled was more than enough to wipe it away.

CHAPTER SIXTEEN

In the light of a faltering Borsyan lamp, Quill tugged a piece of the rope around his wrists, trying to hold it between the toes of his bound feet. The knot loosened, ever so slightly. He'd made some give around the right wrist and if he folded his hand in on itself and twisted...

He gritted his teeth against the friction and cursed. It was slow going. Very slow going. But no one knew where he was, no one—he was sure—knew about the changeling or the tunnel under the Salt Wall. No one knew about this madman pretending to be Redolfo Kirazzi—being Redolfo Kirazzi? Lord on the Mountain, he couldn't even imagine.

Rosangerda had tied him up and dumped him in what seemed to be the largest of a series of storerooms. There were ancient crates, falling to pieces, but also a chair with bindings on the arms and legs, and a worktable covered in small bowls and metal syringes. He'd spotted the murky green of changeling blood in one jar, half gone, but the rest—blue crystals; mashed goo; silvery and rusty black and sickly yellow powders—he couldn't identify. He brought the ropes to his teeth and tugged on a different piece of the knot, tightening his right wrist, but loosening the left more, just enough, enough to—

He gasped as his hand came out, scraping the skin off his wrist. Bleeding, rushing, he untied his right hand and the ropes around his ankles.

He thought of the path back to the exit, the small storerooms along the way. If he ducked into one, he could hide, until Rosangerda passed to check on him. Make a break for it, run for Sestina—

Think, he told himself. *You have to get the authorities. You have to show them what's here.* He looked around the room—no map, no survey to show the tunnel.

Quill swallowed. He needed to make sure it *was* a tunnel.

You need to knock the cursed thing in, he thought. Except no—evidence needed to be preserved; the empress would decide what to do. This was how things were supposed to go—*a madman takes the law into his own hands*; he could almost hear Karimo saying it.

He grabbed the half-full jar of changeling blood, hoping it was proof enough, and slipped down the corridor. As it turned toward the fork, he saw the dim glow of Borsyan lamps and heard voices.

Quill darted back and ducked into one of the small storage rooms, backing deep into the shadows as the light progressed across the entrance. He saw Richa, clutching his arm against the side of him, and then Yinii, eyes closed, dark-eye open, hands worrying over each other. She looked into the storeroom and her green eyes opened wide.

She shook her head, as if she could read through the shock in his expression, the sudden panic, the certain knowledge that he could not leave her there.

"No," she whispered. "Don't."

A saber swatted Yinii's backside. "Stop talking to yourself, Archivist," Rosangerda snapped. "Walk." And Yinii disappeared from the frame of the door, followed by Rosangerda.

He had to run. Now, while she was busy. Rosangerda was quick and silent, and if he didn't go *now*, he wouldn't get far enough ahead of her to make any kind of a difference.

She's going to kill them, he thought. *Kill them or poison them.* He had the changeling blood, but he remembered Yinii's scrolls, the list of ingredients, and there was no way to be sure Rosangerda hadn't already prepared more of the venom.

His heart hammered in his ears. He looked around the storeroom, the crumbling crates. He pulled off a board, the nailed-down end snapping off in a fringe of splinters. *Don't think about it*, he thought. *Just move.* Tilt the odds. Get them out.

He moved quietly and quickly down the corridor, arriving in time to hear Rosangerda curse.

Don't think about it, he told himself again, and swung the board at the back of her head.

Rosangerda turned as he swung, eyes wide and furious. She stepped *into* his swing. The board missed the fragile back of her skull, slamming into her cheek, her jaw, snapping her head to the side. She stumbled, but she didn't go down.

Quill turned, bolting for the exit. He'd hurt her, made her mad, maybe mad enough to chase him, mad enough to leave Yinii and Richa untied and able to run. Maybe hurt enough to give him a head start—

Just beyond the door, Quill slammed into the chest of Chiarl, who seized him by the shoulders and turned him back toward the storeroom.

Rosangerda was rubbing her jaw, blood streaming from a cut along her cheekbone. "That was very foolish, brother," she said. "I find I'm quite out of patience with you."

⚔

The changeling that was Redolfo struck Amadea in the center of her chest, knocking her off her feet and onto the stone floor. Her hip hit the ground painfully, then her hands, scraping across the rough stone. Redolfo clutched his cheek where it still smoked slightly.

"Well," he panted, his features a snarl. "There's the fault in my plan."

"He's not Redolfo," Amadea said, as Ibramo helped her to her feet. "He's not your father."

"Good," Ibramo said, eyes locked on the changeling as he pushed Amadea behind him. "Then my father died, the traitor he was."

Or not, Amadea thought. After all, where else had this changeling come from, mimicking the Usurper so completely? How could a changeling, after all, gain Redolfo's face, his mannerisms, his written hand, so closely that it fooled even his son? Rosangerda might have made a copy, but only Redolfo, Amadea felt sure, could make *this* copy.

Over the Wall, replaced on the gallows by a changeling assassin. *Did Redolfo go alone?* Amadea wondered. Did he abscond with the few of his faithful who weren't ever captured? He left the Shrike, left

Fastreda, but there were others. And he could make himself an army by doing what the changelings were said to have done: one by one. Catch a changeling, give it the venom. Make it a follower. Grow your numbers until you did, in fact, have a terrible army.

Please let me be wrong, she thought.

The changeling drew his sword, blocking the door. "I have my orders," he said. "You come with me, or I make certain you aren't alive to follow me back. It's your choice."

She searched the room, keeping her eyes off her own eerie doubles. Aside from the sword in the changeling's hand, the nearest possible weapons were the table of tools behind Ibramo—wrenches, gauges, all meant for setting up the cold-magic panels.

The Borsyan cold-magic panels. *Coax the wind into the iron and they shall not wake, no matter how you cut them.*

Amadea Gintanas would deny being all sorts of things. She was not an empress and she was not a great beauty. She was not a killer and she was not a fighter.

But she could fix a Borsyan cold-magic panel, and she knew if you could fix a thing, you could most definitely break it. Amadea snatched a wrench and a gauge.

Ibramo grabbed a mallet off the table behind him, moved in between Amadea and Redolfo. "No, you're going to put that down and let us go. If you're not him, I don't owe you anything."

"Gods in the mud," the changeling said, "you have no idea what you're dealing with. Not even enough to bluster. A softhearted boy, indeed."

The changeling Redolfo shook his head. Suddenly his skin seemed to shiver like heat off a roof in summer, so strange Amadea's eyes refused to see it. And then she was looking at another double of herself, holding a sword, her eyes as intense as Redolfo's had been, her mouth his crooked smirk.

"This was the plan I was meant to follow," she heard herself say, as cold horror poured over her. "I wonder if it would have suited better."

"You know you're a changeling," Ibramo said faintly. "You're not trapped."

"The poison?" the changeling said, and its skin shimmered again, transforming into Redolfo once more. "That's for traitors. Which could include you, if that makes this simpler."

Amadea stepped back and back and back, eyes on the changeling, who was only looking at Ibramo. She had to be quick, she had to be sure. She squeezed behind the nearer cold-magic panel, a great sheet of steel, so big as to be wasteful. Its rear side was a tangle of metal and glass tubing, of flickering globes of the strange magic the Borsyans took from the Black Mother Forest—quite a lot of them. These had clearly been built to be left alone a long time, if needed. Amadea pushed her sleeves up.

"You're nothing but a pawn of his," Ibramo said. "You're no better, really, than I was. But I'm not that boy anymore, and I'm not letting you or anyone hurt Amadea."

"Well, that I'm glad to hear. Speaking of..."

Amadea clamped the gauge on the wide tube that divided into a hundred little probes that fed into the steel panel itself, watched the strange bluish fragment of the forest as she opened valve after valve, the glow of it growing slowly brighter and brighter.

A shout, a scuffle—the clatter of tools and the smack of bodies. She heard Ibramo cry out in pain, and then there was Redolfo, looking behind the panel.

"There you are," he crooned. "Hiding?"

Amadea swung the wrench hard into the valve that slowed the magic's transfer to the gas and the water. A flash, a *pop*—Amadea backed away, around the other side of the Borsyan cold-magic panel, as frost raced across its surface, up the walls.

Ibramo grabbed Redolfo across the shoulders, blood streaming down his own face. The changeling Redolfo pulled the arm down, keeping it off his neck. He reached back with the other hand, grabbing for Ibramo's ear or maybe a fistful of hair, but Ibramo squeezed, held him tight.

As their breaths clouded on the air, his grasping hand faltered. His eyes unfocused, his legs went slack. Redolfo Kirazzi, or what seemed to be him, slid out of his son's arms, to the ground, insensate as the doubles on their biers.

Ibramo leapt over the body, caught Amadea in his arms, held her so tightly she could do nothing but cling to him, both sobbing and bloody. Ibramo cursed and cursed into her hair, but Amadea didn't dare speak. Her heart was pounding in her ears and she was suddenly shaking to her fingertips.

I made you. I built you into this. I can end you just as easily.

The changeling on the floor wasn't Redolfo. But she felt certain it had known him—Redolfo had escaped to meet this changeling, and this changeling had been taking orders from someone. Who else had the guile, the daring, the charm, to win over a changeling?

To win over unnumbered changelings...

"We need to get out of here," Ibramo managed, still clinging to her. "We need to go."

"We need to bury this place," Amadea whispered. "Burn it all down."

"We'll get rid of it," he promised. "No one will ever see it."

Amadea turned her face into his shoulder. The nightmares of her past, magnified, redoubled, and then this, the refuge of yesterday. She took his face in her hands, brushed the blood from his lip.

"I missed you," she admitted, eyes on his mouth. "I—"

Ibramo kissed her. Desperately, passionately, as if they had never left Sestina, as if she'd never broken his heart. She kissed him back, holding hard to the past, to the possibility—

Ibramo pulled away, pressed his forehead to hers. "Please don't go away again."

Amadea closed her eyes. There was no right path, no correct answer. She held him close and wept for them both. The cold-magic panel hissed as its stored-up air vented, and Amadea had no idea at all what to do.

Except she did. Cold-magic panels. She pushed back from Ibramo. "I broke it," she said numbly.

"You saved us."

"No, I *broke* it." She looked back at the duplicate Amadeas lying on the stone biers. "It's overventing. It's going to run out of the charged air soon. They're going to wake up."

—◆—

Richa clutched his arm against his side as he walked down the corridor. Whatever she'd carefully not done, Lady Maschano had managed to light his whole arm up with pain and make his fingers stiff and sluggish. He'd taken a lot of hits before and more than one blade, but he had to admit, the Shrike had earned her reputation.

Not that he was going to let it stop him from trying to get out of here.

Behind him, Yinii kept muttering to herself—"shush, stop it, shush, no"—and Richa's thoughts filled with Stavio, the rattle of the bronze, and that unnaturally strong grip on Richa's wrist.

It wasn't a variable he was ready to deal with. He thought of Amadea, pulled away after her awful old master—get out of here, get to her, get them all somewhere safe. Don't die.

Lady Maschano steered them into a room at the end of the corridor. Old crates and barrels had been stacked up against the walls, two deep, and along one side a worktable stood, arrayed with more of the bowls and knives and syringes, much like the attic room in the Maschanos' manor.

Richa moved closer to it. The knives were all in reach, but they were little scalpels and fineknives, and he'd have to get dangerously close to put those to use.

Yinii stopped beside him, staring at the worktable. "'Four parts the root of lotus, pounded in milk, strained well. One-third the salts of copper. Eight parts the blood of a changeling, dried.'" Yinii looked up at him and blinked. "'Four parts the root of lotus, pounded in milk, strained well. One part the powder of sulfur. One-quarter the finest filings of silver. Seven parts the blood of the seven-souled, dried.' Stop it," she hissed. "Shush."

"Are you all right?" he asked.

"Nit-min-djaulbashra. Nit-min-khirazji," she murmured. "The venoms. Both of them."

"Where on this side of the Wall and the other has he got to?" Lady Maschano snarled.

The recipes, Richa remembered from the notes Amadea had given him. The venoms. Two groups of syringes, ready to use. One to control people...

An ugly crack yanked Richa's attention back to the door. There was Quill, tossing a board aside. There was Lady Maschano with blood streaming down the side of her face. Quill broke into a run—

There, in the door, was the big fellow Richa'd punched. The one who bled green.

The changeling.

He steered Quill back into the room. Lady Maschano was rubbing her jaw, smearing blood over her fingers. "That was very foolish, brother," she said. "I find I'm quite out of patience with you." She nodded to the changeling. "Put him in the chair. You two," she said to Richa and Yinii, "against the wall. Now."

Richa backed up, beside the worktable, eyeing the chair with the straps that Quill was being muscled into. The knives, then. Unless...

One was to control people...

"Shush," Yinii whispered. "Shush, I have to think."

"Your problem, Brother Sesquillio," Lady Maschano said, sword still bare, "is that you lack patience. Discipline. Really, you ought to be grateful for what I'm going to do to you, but instead, I will be the one to thank you."

"Why's that?" Quill spat.

One was to control changelings...

"Thank you, Brother Sesquillio," Lady Maschano said with infinite grace, "for giving your friends here an object lesson in what happens when you cross me."

Richa dropped his injured arm and leapt forward, snatching up the syringe set beside the jar of black powder. He saw Lady Maschano move—away from Quill, right to Richa—but before she could reach him, Richa plunged the syringe into the changeling's back, pushing all the venom into its skin, and speaking the lie that would change its nature.

"You hate Rosangerda Maschano," he told it, as fast as he could. "That woman right there. You hate her with all your being. You need to kill her. You need to stop her."

The rapier slashed his arm, cutting a long ugly line across his shoulder, and Lady Maschano slammed into him, knocking the syringe from his hand and crashing him into the worktable. Richa ducked, rolled as he fell, but she was quick, nearly on top of him when he stopped, bruised and bleeding.

But she was not as quick as the changeling.

Even with death looming over him, Richa could not take his eyes from the changeling. Even as his whole mind screamed that this *should not be*, he couldn't stop watching. The man began to shimmer, to melt, and it was as if the whole of him were made of the stars that crowded the edges of your vision as you lost consciousness. That starry strangeness whirled on Rosangerda as she stood over Richa and lunged.

"You are the monster," it said in a voice that slipped through and around Richa's attempts to place it. "It is you we have come for."

"More...fool you," Lady Maschano managed, as the changeling gripped her throat. She fumbled at the knives on the table.

"Oh! Quill!" Yinii cried, the first moment Richa felt sure she'd seen what was happening. As Lady Maschano struggled with the changeling, Richa scrambled to his feet and pushed Yinii toward the exit. Then he limped toward Quill, who was trying to undo the bindings on his wrists. Richa's right hand was still aching and prickling, fighting his efforts.

"Just *go*!" Quill shouted. "Get her out of here!"

"Push your fucking wrist up and hold it still!" Richa snapped, grabbing a knife. "The Wall's got enough martyrs!"

One wrist free, then the next—then suddenly a roar like a rockslide overtook the room. Quill leapt to his feet, but Lady Maschano had managed to reach a scalpel and plunged it into the changeling's chest over and over. It released its grip on her throat, swiping at her with scintillating claws that spread from its strange edgeless skin.

Richa pulled Quill with his good arm, skirting the cargo, cursing a steady streak to himself. He pushed the boy around, toward the exit. "Go!"

Lady Maschano held her ground and sliced the creature's throat, cutting so deeply into the shivering skin the head flopped backward as it fell.

Bloodied, gasping, drenched in greenish blood, Lady Maschano plucked up her sword where it had fallen and darted in front of Richa, blocking the exit.

"I," she panted, "had *plans* for that!" She lunged with the rapier, aiming for Richa's middle, driving him into the crates. Lady Maschano pulled back her sword for a slashing strike.

A small hand seized her arm, stopping it with unexpected strength. Yinii ul-Benturan stood beside the Shrike.

Black swirled across Yinii's eyes, tinting them from lid to lid until all three were like pools of ink. Her lips parted as she gasped for breath, the inside of her mouth as black as her eyes.

"Oh fuck," Richa breathed.

⋅⋅ ▰◆▰ ⋅⋅

Yinii could feel herself coming apart, mind sliding between one moment and the next. She begged the soot and the stone and the water to be quiet, to stop whispering of ink-to-be so she could think about danger and Quill and the Shrike and the vigilant, and poor Tunuk who no one knew was dying out there.

She watched Richa turn the changeling, watched the changeling fight the Shrike, and knew she should run, fast and far, only everything was going so fast—except for Quill, except for Richa, caught on buckles and boards, and then so much green ink—no. *Blood.*

Quill stumbled toward her, like he was falling through water—time seemed to stretch out, but still the Shrike moved so impossibly fast.

She'll kill Richa, Yinii thought. *And then she'll kill us.*

The Shrike had killed Karimo and Lamberto and maybe Tunuk. She'd stabbed Reza Dolitha and taken her dark-eye. All the ink that might be in Rosangerda whispered and yearned, and the hole in Yinii's chest felt like it could yawn as wide as the cavern.

There's no one left, she thought, loud enough to drown the susurrus of soot and char and water and flames and flood. *You must, you must.*

Rosangerda picked up her blade, and Yinii started toward her. She stopped fighting herself, stopped clinging to the edges of her. She turned inward, opening the void.

"Quill," she said. "Run."

"Yinii!" Quill cried.

But Yinii was gone.

In the heart of the spiral, all was ink.

Almost, Yinii thought. But everything that was not ink could be ink, and anything left did not matter, could be washed away— including *Yinii*. Yinii tasted the edge of it, bitter on her tongue, bitter on her brain, and sweet, so sweet. Make something from destruction. Pull truth from ruin. Burn it all down, turn it into ink.

Almost, she thought.

Half her mind saw the worktable, saw the reagents sitting on it— half her mind saw only the promise of carbon and the need to begin. She reached out with nameless, wordless longing, beckoning the wood, and it burst into bright, sudden flame.

"No," she said, "smolder." *Blacker, sharper.* The fire dimmed. "Faster. Now." Hot again, the air thinning. The fire swelled and subsided. Swelled and subsided. Charcoal oven in open air, shaped by her will.

Solvents—ink needed solvents. Water welled up through the rock, and half her mind knew that was too much, too fast, the rock would be damaged. She tried to pull less, to go slower, but there was already ink—muddy, murky ash and wet ink—curling up her skirts and it felt like cold water on a burn, such relief. She let it leap into her hands, flicked off the impurities, shedding them like sparks.

Before, the spiral was a whirlpool, a fearsome flood—a threat that Yinii could be subsumed, drowned in ink. Now—Yinii ul-Benturan was not the ink so much as the ink was Yinii ul-Benturan, even if some part of her remained adrift, outside.

This isn't how it goes, she thought, confused. She looked up at the Shrike, staring at her. Realized bare seconds had passed. Realized she was in danger. Quill was in danger. Amadea and Richa and the consort-prince were in danger.

You chose this, she told herself, over the growing chorus of the ink. *Use it.* Everything that was not ink could be ink, and anything left did not matter, could be washed away.

Wait—Quill and Richa, she made herself think, made herself look around. *Saving, not solvents.* The body before her solved both problems. She put a hand on the arm, felt the pulse of blood, the tide of water, the slick swell of fat. So many things that would burn, be ink.

The Shrike twisted, her sword shifting, and Yinii pulled the pigments from the assassin's clothes, igniting the linen and leaving behind char. The Shrike yelped, a sound so strange and far away that Yinii discarded it. She reached for the woman's throat.

Water was an excellent solvent, bad for printing, though—oil, fat, that was better, harder to pull. The sound changed to something greater, something worse, something that worked its way past the ink into Yinii's brain, the part that was still Yinii—a woman screaming in indescribable pain.

The ink building around her muttered of offal, of veins and muscles and things it didn't need, but Yinii told it of Reza Dolitha, of Tunuk, of Karimo, whom she never knew. Of Primate Lamberto and Zaverio Maschano, who were terrible too, but didn't deserve to have their lives taken.

You're taking a life, a part of her realized.

Bone black, the ink sang, *makes such a lovely shade.*

She felt the bones stand out from the Shrike's skin. Felt the carbon in them, begging to become ink. Felt it crumble under her fingers into the finest, blackest dust. Ink that had been the Shrike flowed up around her, a petticoat of midnight, discarding unusable flesh and parts behind.

"Yinii!" she heard Quill shout. She turned, half her mind aware that she'd done something abhorrent, something maybe unforgivable, or maybe heroic. Half her mind certain it didn't matter— Yinii wasn't coming back. She didn't have to choose Maqama or the archives. She didn't have to decide what she was thinking about Quill. She didn't have to think about Rosangerda Maschano. They were all only words, and she had all the ink she could ever want to write them. That beautiful boy watched her, terrified, coughing in the rising smoke, helping Richa to his feet.

"Yinii," he said. "You're not the ink."

He's right, she thought. *The ink is me.* It didn't feel like a tide or a mob or something about to run away with her. It felt like a pack of dogs on leashes—wild and wanting, but eager to please her. She could be so happy, pleased by the ink, and the ink would be so happy, if she were pleased.

She needed more ink. More water. More fire.

Ink in her nose. Ink in her mouth. "I'm sorry, Quill," she managed to say, her voice warbling. "I like you very much, but the ink can't."

CHAPTER SEVENTEEN

Rosangerda Maschano's death had been too quick for Quill to understand. One moment, the Shrike was advancing on Richa and Yinii had seized her arm. The next, the cave echoed with a throat-tearing scream, accompanied by the cracking and squelching of a body coming apart. Horror and relief flooded him like the sudden wash of ink that rose out of those broken remains.

And then there was Yinii, standing in the spiral.

Quill thought about Zoifia spiraling in the archives—like a candle to the bonfire of what was happening to Yinii. Yinii had risen off the floor several inches, buoyed by a never-ending swirl of black ink. She looked at him a moment, then reached out toward the crates on her left, the wood drained of water and ignited, disintegrating into char faster than Quill would have thought possible. Inside were bundles of rusty swords, and she crumbled these too, mixing them with the pooling water and pulling swirls of red through her midnight skirts. She drew it up her arm and smiled, like she was admiring a pretty bracelet.

This wasn't like Zoifia's spiral, and Quill was certainly not Amadea. But if he ran like he should, like made *sense*, Yinii would be doomed.

"Yinii!" Quill shouted over the cracking of stone. "Yinii, you have to come down."

She turned to him, blinking slowly. "You need to go," she said with that eerie quaver in her voice. "I have things to do. Come this way."

Drops of ink peeled off her, swimming through the air like schools of red and black fishes. She drifted out the door, down the corridor toward where the tunnel ran back toward the outside, stripping ancient soot from the ceiling and cracking rocks as she went. The smoke from the fires was growing thick.

"We need to get out!" Richa shouted. "The smoke will kill us!"

"We have to talk her down!" Quill said, coughing. "And find out if it's a tunnel."

"Quill, we have *minutes*—"

Yinii stopped in front of the storeroom Quill had hidden in. Turned. "The smoke?" she said. She frowned at them, then over their heads. She reached out a hand and the ink followed her fingers, looping and curling like strange claws.

The stone ceiling beyond cracked and shattered and collapsed, sealing off the fire—and all the Shrike's handiwork. Quill scrambled away from it, almost crashing into Yinii as he did.

"All right," Richa said, as the rocks settled, as Yinii returned to her path out of the vault. "That takes care of the fire. So a tunnel?"

"A tunnel," Quill said. "I haven't seen a surveyance or anything, but I'm mostly sure we're under the Salt Wall at this point. And there's air coming from somewhere."

"And Redolfo Kirazzi wasn't getting changeling blood from the storm-wracked sea." They reached the fork of the corridors and Richa looked down into the darkness, toward the iron door and the strange breeze. "I'll check," he said. "Can you—?"

"I'll try," Quill said. "Send Amadea if you find her." *If,* Quill thought, trying not to panic. Richa gave him a grim look and started into the darkness.

As Richa sprinted by, Yinii swept her hand up, and the ink shot through the air, dappling the wall of the tunnel with rows and rows of Khirazji hieroglyphs.

"Says Alletet, says Djutubai, says Phaseran," she intoned. "I have entered into the fire and have come forth from the water."

You are not Amadea, Quill thought, *but you are going to have to try to be.* "Yinii," he tried again. "Are you doing all right?"

She paused, her breathing audible. "I'm fine."

"You're saying 'I,'" he said, trying to remember Amadea and Zoifia. "That's good. That's some interesting work you're doing."

"Leave me alone."

He shook his head, edging toward her. "You know I'm not going to."

"I'm the ink. I want to be the ink."

"Is that how it works? I didn't think that was how it worked. You spiral and you forget yourself. You know yourself, Yinii. You're still you."

Lord on the Mountain, he hoped that was true. He moved closer, eyes on her hands moving in strange passes as though juggling the ink fishes through the air. He set a hand on her arm. "We were going to go get pancakes," he tried. "Don't you want to go get pancakes?

"I don't like pancakes."

He smiled. "We could get our own table."

"I'm busy," she said, blackened eyes boring into him.

Quill swore to himself. Why did he think he could do this? Yinii stared, emotionless, blank, as if she were waiting for a reason to end him like she had Rosangerda, and he was briefly, selfishly glad he *hadn't* kissed her if that pitiless gaze was what he got in return for flirting.

Something flickered in her features—a shift of her brows, a pull of her mouth? It was so fast he couldn't have said what happened, but in the base of his heart, he knew what it meant: *afraid.*

He knew, too, where he'd seen that face: Karimo. So many times, but in that moment, what he remembered was Karimo in Shadorma, at the huge Paremi chapter house, aware that a handsome young adept was making eyes at him and utterly, utterly petrified of moving. It felt absurd, Quill thought, remembering that moment, here, now. But it was right after he'd gone to work for Primate Lamberto, right after he'd met Karimo—it was when he'd realized Karimo understood law and system and rules and structure better than anyone, but not people, not so much.

Quill understood people better. Quill knew how to talk Karimo down, how to quiet that fear. How to remind him the most difficult part was done, and Quill was there to close the gap, to be his friend, be the fellow who talked him up when Karimo could never do that for himself.

You're good at talking to people, Karimo had said that first night. *You always sound like you care about them.*

I sort of do, Quill had said with a laugh.

Quill held Yinii's nightmare gaze. *You are good at talking to people*, he could hear Karimo say. This was talking to people. This was caring about someone.

Not flirting, you idiot—what had Amadea done? *Small things*, he thought. *Close things. Things you don't have to think about to know. Keep talking.*

"You don't like pancakes," he said slowly. "But...you love your library. You take such good care of it. All of it."

Yinii blinked, her lips parting as if she were thinking about saying something.

"You love the archives," he went on, piecing things together. "I can tell, the way you talked about the murals and the building. That matters."

"I like the ink," she said, and started to turn.

"You like the saints!" he shouted. "Is this what Saint Asla would do? Burn up all her powers without any kind of purpose?"

A flash of guilt lit up his chest—but he wasn't trying to motivate himself, chafing at the expectations of ancestors and elders. This was Yinii, whose eyes shone when she told the story of Saint Asla, whose belief burned in every word when she introduced him to the saints.

Yinii's hand slipped up to her horn, to where the salt crystal hung—but it wasn't there. "Amadea," she breathed.

"Does Amadea have your salt crystal?" he said, trying to fill up the silence. "You must have been very worried about her to give her that. It would be good if she were here, wouldn't it?" he said, trying to keep his voice calm. "Amadea's who you want in a crisis."

Yinii's mouth went small.

"Or maybe it's not a crisis," Quill said quickly. "Maybe you've got control of this, Yinii." He thought of how Amadea had said Zoifia's name over and over and maybe that was important. "You seem a lot more in control than Zoifia did. Yinii."

"I had to," she said, looking up at the hieroglyphs. "I had to save you." She looked down at the swirling ink. "We killed her."

And it took Quill a moment to realize she meant the ink. Yinii and the ink had killed Rosangerda.

"You *saved* us," Quill said. "Me and Richa and you, too, Yinii. You did this because you had to, but now you have to come back, Yinii. Please. Think of your friends. Think of your family. The archives will suffer if you don't come back."

She looked at him, puzzled. "It's ink. It doesn't miss."

"*Fuck* the books!" Quill said. "The people will miss you. *I'll* miss you. Amadea will miss you. Stavio, Zoifia, Bijan. Tunuk—you are possibly the only person in that building Tunuk adores, do you know that?"

She blinked, and for a moment her eyes went green again. "Tunuk. Quill, Tunuk's in trouble." *Blink*—black again. "Oh no. We're all in trouble."

Panic grabbed at him. "Because it might be a tunnel?"

"What tunnel?" she said. Green again, but the ink was still swirling around her. She looked up at the ceiling. "*Oh*," she said, as if understanding something. "It's not stable. So much water. Is that the problem?"

Her family were stonemasons, Quill remembered. She'd been trained to be a stonemason. And she'd collapsed the storeroom. He looked up at the cracked ceiling, the water leaking down.

This is evidence, a little part of him thought. *You can't destroy evidence. You can't make these decisions.* But he found, as he thought it, that he didn't believe it. Not after having seen the changeling shift, not after seeing how much more venom had been prepared.

"Yinii, can you . . . can you hold on to the ink a *little* bit and come with me?"

Black. Green. Black again. "I am the ink, the ink is me. I . . . I . . ."

"Stay with me," Quill said. "If you have to choose, stay with me." She hesitated, her eyes still shining black, but she turned up the tunnel where Richa had fled and headed into the shadows.

Quill followed. "Have your family always been stonemasons?" he asked. "Like Saint Qarabas, right?"

"Yes," she said, flatly.

"It's hard," he said, sprinting ahead of her. "When your family has traditions and expectations. When you want to hold on to those, but you know they aren't right for you. Look at me," he said. "I'm supposed to be a Paremi, and I've got absolutely no business doing anything more than checking contracts and scribing. But that's what we do, right?" He glanced back into the shadows. The light was growing brighter and dread pooled in his stomach. "You were pretty handy with those hammers, though."

She stopped. Blinked—*black, green.* "I shouldn't have done that."

"No, you should have," Quill said. "You stopped him killing me, I'm fairly certain. And if that's all you get from the stonemasons, that's still pretty good. But I'm wondering, Yinii, I'm wondering if you know about taking down this tunnel."

Black again, gleaming in the dim light from an exit Quill hoped hadn't existed. "Of course," she said. "We need water."

⋯ ▦ ⋯

Richa felt his way through the dark, down the narrow cave, not sure where he was going to end up. One hand to the wall, he followed it down a gentle slope, the residual prickle of smoke in the air fainter and fainter.

It couldn't be a tunnel, he thought. It *shouldn't* be a tunnel. Someone should have found a salt-sucked tunnel left by Redolfo Kirazzi sometime before now.

But suddenly the ground sloped upward, and Richa moved his hand in front of him, just in time to touch the iron doors that slanted down from the ceiling.

He fumbled with the bar across them, forcing his injured arm to move in order to get it open. A part of him was screaming that the best thing to do was to leave the damned doors closed. But he had to know.

Richa set his back against the door and heaved one side open. It landed against the ground with a clang. Richa looked across the top of the opening. He straightened. He was surrounded by forest. Over the top of the exit, through the massive trees, he could see a wide stretch of bare ground, patched with scrubby grass, running right up to the foot of the Salt Wall.

He was on the other side of the Salt Wall.

Heart pounding, he turned slowly. All around him, an ancient forest loomed, with trees so massive they would have dwarfed the aqueducts of Arlabecca, the spires of Sestina, the watchtowers of Caesura. The shadows between them were deep and secretive, but Richa's eyes were drawn to the bodies staked to the trees.

What did a shrike do? Caught lizards and beetles and maybe other birds, pinned them on thorns and brambles, and waited. *Saints and devils*, Richa swore. *Aye-Nam-Wati in her chariot.*

They were changelings. They had to be. At least the two nearest to him. They looked like people at a glance, humans, mostly. They hung like cast-off coats, patched-together pieces of a dozen different faces. This arm dark, that arm pale, this eyebrow shaggy and gray, that one bleeding into an Orozhandi horn. As if they'd died formless, but in death seized a form. Any form. Every form.

Richa stepped forward, staring. The others were ancient, little more than bones hanging on the remains of spears. But the bones had that strange glittering quality, that scintillating that made his eyes ache. The remains of nine individuals, in a rough circle around the exit, like they were a warning.

You are the monster, the changeling had said to Rosangerda. *It is you we have come for.* Looking up at the remains of the Shrike's abattoir, Richa realized he hadn't had to nudge the changeling very hard to make it hate Rosangerda.

Voices—Richa whipped toward the sound, the language that his mind struggled to place among the many he'd heard spoken. Between the trees at a distance, he could just see a clearing. An encampment. He moved behind a tree, peering through the leaves—six, maybe eight. He had a clear view of a man sitting watch, facing the Wall, a human man with golden skin, close-cut dark hair, and kohl around his eyes. He said something over his shoulder to his companions.

Human, he thought. Or human-seeming? What else would be out here?

He had to get that door closed.

Richa backed away from his vantage point and hauled on the

door. But when he went to pull it up from the ground, his injured arm screamed with pain. He tried again but only got it high enough to wedge a boot under before his fingers slipped off.

Richa found a stone within reach and shoved it under the door, wriggling his foot back out. He reached up one of the trees and carefully, quickly took the bones down, keeping his attention on the sounds from the camp. When he could, he yanked the spear free quietly and fitted it against the door as a lever.

When it got high enough, it was going to slam shut and leave him out here—and alert that camp. But an iron door meant no change-lings were getting in; so long as that door was shut everyone else would be safe.

You finish the job, he thought wryly, as he hitched the door up onto his knee. What a salt-sucked joke this was—Richa Langyun, dying while locking a door. They'd laugh in Caesura, for certain. *Sorry about the forms, Hul*, he thought, muscling the door up to his bad shoulder.

Suddenly Yinii burst through the door, still swaddled in sheets of ink, all three eyes black as pitch. Richa stepped back, just in time for Quill to come barreling out, shouting, "Yinii, wait!"

Through the trees, Richa saw the flash of movement, heard a whistle of alarm. Yinii raised a hand. A patch on the bark of the tree Richa had pulled the spear from began to weep water and resin, began to smolder. Began to crack.

"Run!" Richa pulled the spear free and pushed Yinii and Quill back through the doors. The crash of bodies breaking through the forest chased them back down the tunnel.

"I need to take the water," Yinii said, in a strange singsong way. "Quill told me."

"What are you doing to her?" Richa demanded. "You were going to calm her down, not make her into a fucking weapon!"

Quill blinked at him, startled. "It's not like that. She can collapse the tunnel."

"Well, she has to now!" Richa shouted. Shadows moved near the exit. Voices calling down unfamiliar words—challenges, queries.

And then a tentative, "Redolfo?"

"Whatever you're going to do," Richa shouted to Quill and Yinii, "do it *now*."

"Here," Yinii intoned, stopping where the tunnel began to curve upward. She reached up toward the ceiling as Quill and Richa ducked behind her. Shadows played across the open door, as if the changelings were moving nearer, blocking the dappled green light that shone through the trees.

The ink curled off Yinii's fingers, and as before, the stones above shattered, earth collapsing behind them as she pulled out the water, but this time the sides pulled in too, as if something were pushing through the earth—and something was. Great roots poked through the wall, one of the ancient trees, dragged through the earth, weeping water and resin and beginning to burn. The dirt came with it, filling the end of the tunnel and completely blocking the exit.

"Cedar," Yinii whispered. "One hundred and fifty years."

"Yinii," Quill said. "All right, Yinii, stop."

But she didn't stop. The roots kept burning, kept crumbling. The whole tunnel was filling with a cloud of ink. She wasn't even speaking to Quill now, no matter how he cajoled or pleaded or insisted. The black in her eyes started running down her cheeks.

Quill looked up at Richa. "We need Amadea. We need Amadea right now."

⊷ ▰◆▰ ⊶

You have to kill them, Amadea thought, looking back at her doubles lying silent beside the collapsed body of the changeling Redolfo.

"We set a fire," Ibramo said quickly. "We burn it all."

"They'll wake before they die," Amadea said. "They'll burn alive."

"They're changelings!"

They were changelings. Monsters. Amadea knew how the stories went, how the histories read. *Once we were ten nations among countless more, ten peoples scattered across the wide-ranging world. And then the changelings appeared.*

It could not happen again. Amadea could not let it happen again.

"He's got all sorts of chemicals in here," she said, voice shaking. "You look for some sort of accelerant. Alcohol. Oils. Naphtha."

Ibramo watched her warily a moment. "What are you going to do?"

Amadea swallowed. "The rest."

Ibramo, she knew, wouldn't be able to kill them. Not up close. Not when it looked like his father, not when it looked like her. Ibramo was passionate, easy to spark into action when the moment burned hot, but this...this took a clear eye and cold knowledge and patience, and he did not have that.

And for all Amadea had realized she needed to stop pulling her mind away from her memories, she knew that she could do so when she needed to.

Shivering with the cold, Amadea knelt down beside the thing that looked like Redolfo.

His skin was chilled, his breath faint and tepid as her hand closed over his mouth, pinched his nose. She looked ahead, not down at the body—Lireana couldn't have done this, she thought dimly, even though she wished it often enough. Lireana froze. Lireana hid.

Amadea...solved problems. And that was what she needed to think about. *Gray walls. Steel panel. White frost. Black hair.*

The changeling didn't fight. He didn't stir, even as he died, the cold had stilled him so completely. But Amadea's stomach twisted when she felt the breath in his nose stop pressing and pulling his skin against her fingertips. She rolled him onto his back and set her ear close to his mouth—dead.

Now the doubles.

This was kinder, she thought, covering the first changeling's breath, even if the changelings didn't deserve kindness—this was her, dying under her own hands, in some sense. Amadea pressed the thoughts down. *White gown. Dark hair. Steel panel. Cold stone.* It felt like an eternity, hands pressed to an alien mouth that felt strangely familiar, a nose whose arc she knew too well. She stared straight ahead, shaking, until she felt it still, and moved along the line.

You cannot let them live, she thought, pushing the horror down and down and down. *You cannot let anyone see this, fear this.* She pushed that down too. *Red blood, green blood, pink crystal, black shadows.*

By the third one, the changeling's skin was warming; the air was still cool but Amadea wasn't shivering in it. As the changeling's breath stopped, she risked a look down, and the changeling's eyes flew open, bright brown and fearful a moment, and Amadea was looking into her own eyes as the life went out of them.

Amadea pulled her hands back, clasped them to her chest as her gorge rose—no, no, no.

"Amadea?" Ibramo asked. She looked back at him, a glass jug of something liquid sloshing at his side. A bright, burning stink rose on the air. "What are you doing?"

"Keep going," she said. "I have this."

She closed the changeling's staring eyes. The fourth one was going to wake. There was no denying it. So what was better? Taking its breath or making Ibramo run it through? She looked down into the still-sleeping face.

It wasn't Amadea. It wasn't Lireana. *It's not you.*

She covered its nose and mouth.

In moments, it was struggling, but the changeling was weak, still sluggish and unused to its form. Amadea squeezed her eyes shut. *You have to, you have to.*

Once we were ten nations among countless more, ten peoples scattered across the wide-ranging world. The changelings tore Khirazj apart first, one of the oldest, most stable kingdoms in the world, shattered into a civil war so fierce and protracted it made the Brothers' War look like a tantrum over a stolen toy.

One hand clawed her arm, nails biting into the skin. Amadea pressed harder.

They ground the Ronqu's powerful empire into fragments so fine that they had to rebuild themselves into something entirely different as they fled. They burned Bemina—*Bemina,* who filled the nightmares of every nation in their reach, their armies were so vast and merciless!—down to almost nothing, and the scrolls said the blood and ashes stained the rivers all the way to the sea. They scoured Aloja's high valleys and Orozhand's deep canyons. They chased the Kuali from the Red Desert and the Ashtabari down the rivers. They unmade. They exploited.

The changelings are the worst of what we are, Amadea thought as she felt herself try to scream into her palm, as tears broke down her cheeks, as blood flowed over her arm. Both hands were clawing at her, trying to reach her face. *The worst of ourselves without the pity and the pause.*

Suddenly Ibramo was there, pulling the changeling's arms down, holding her tight. Tight-lipped, drawn, he watched Amadea, silent and pleading. *Stop,* she knew he wanted to say. *Make it stop.*

Amadea shook her head and pressed down harder. *Once we were ten nations among countless more*—and Amadea knew too well that those who had survived, those who made Semilla, they did not fear less or chafe less, doubt or trust or listen to liars less. When someone like Redolfo Kirazzi could destroy so much, when a changeling wearing his face could cause all this chaos so quickly, well, another changeling invasion could end the whole world.

The last changeling stopped fighting, but Amadea kept her hands in place for long moments after, until Ibramo reached over and gently took hold of them, lifting her away from the last body. "Stop," he said. "It's done."

Amadea nodded, swallowed, kept her eyes off the doubles. "We should..." But she didn't even know how to finish that sentence.

Ibramo took his cloak, soaked in accelerant, and spread it over the bodies, in an oddly tender gesture. Amadea said another little prayer—to Saint Asla, to the Lord on the Mountain, to Aye-Nam-Wati, the Khirazji wisdom spirits, the gods and the devils, or whoever might be listening. That she'd done the right thing. That her charges, that all the empire and protectorates, would be safe. Ibramo took a fire kit from his pocket and knelt beside the bodies. They looked as if they were sleeping.

Before he could light the pyre they'd built, Quill burst in shouting, "Amadea! Amadea, are you all right?"

He stopped in the doorway, eyes clearly on the bodies for a moment, as if he could not decide what was more pressing, more terrifying. But then Quill looked up at Amadea, "It's Yinii. You have to come."

⸺ ▰◆▰ ⸺

Ink licked its way up Yinii's cheek, flowing in and out of her skin. In a dim part of her mind, she imagined drowning, but how could you drown in yourself? She could hear someone coughing, but she paid it no mind, turning from the sound to move down the passage. She sent ink skittering along the wall, leaving bits of poetry behind. She had so much—not enough, never enough—but so much, and what could she do with it? She could cover these walls with poetry. She could ink *The Precepts of Bekesa* across the stones.

Oh. She smiled and ink flowed through her teeth, that dim part of her mind thinking *bitter, bitter*. She knew what she would do. She would ink the stories of the saints across the Salt Wall. It would be beautiful.

Her hand reached for her horn of its own accord. *Is this what Saint Asla would do? Burn up all her powers without any kind of purpose!*

No, the dim part of her said.

No matter, the ink whispered. *Why does ink need saints?*

"Yinii!"

A woman's voice cut through the haze. Yinii looked—really looked—and there was Amadea, followed by some not-ink.

Half her mind balked, panicked and guilty. Half her mind surged up, raging—Amadea. Amadea was going to tell her to stop, to turn away from the ink, and she had no idea. No idea at all. Yinii was the ink. The ink was Yinii.

Amadea stopped short of her, hands held up where Yinii could see them. Yinii blinked and part of her whispered *not-ink* but part of her whispered *Quill*, whispered *Richa and the consort-prince*. "All of you get out," Amadea said. "Now. Run. It's all on fire."

"You're going to die if you don't get out too," not-ink said. *Richa*.

"We will," Amadea said. "We're following."

Yinii looked at Amadea, full of water and fat and the promise of ink. Amadea took a careful step forward as Richa grabbed Quill's arm, dragged him back into the shadows after the consort-prince.

"You should go too, Amadea," Yinii said, as the men fled, "I have things to do."

"You said 'I,'" Amadea noted. "That's good."

"No," Yinii said. "There is ink and there is not-ink. I am ink.

I can't come back. I don't want to come back. You should go, stay not-ink."

"That's not how it works, is it?" Amadea said. "That's not how it's ever worked."

"*We* know," Yinii said with a vehemence, and the ink all squeezed close around her. "Don't try to talk me out of this! You don't know! You've never known!" She swung her head around. "I need more to burn, and it's going to be you if you don't move."

Amadea hesitated, her mouth a strike of red. "You can't burn much in here. You ought to come outside."

Yes, Yinii thought, half her mind greedy, hungry, sweeping down the corridor after Amadea. The ink overtook her, drowned her thoughts, and all she saw was water and carbon and bits of metal salts. She divided it, separating solvents and shades. Everything burned and burned around her. The stones collapsed and the soot collected, even as her lungs burned from the smoke.

Maybe that's all right, she thought, her head spinning. *Maybe you die here, become the ink, because going back is so very hard.* There was no Maqama here, part of her managed. No archives either.

"Yinii." Amadea set a hand on her shoulder. Yinii flinched and ink washed up her, trying to break Amadea's grip, but it only tightened as if it were pressing the world back into her. "Yinii," Amadea said firmly, kindly, "maybe you're the ink and the ink is you—but you're so much more than the ink. So much more than your affinity."

"This is what you always say."

"I say it because it's true. More than true—I know it in my bones."

"I can take your bones," Yinii said. "I took Rosangerda's."

"You saved me, you know," Amadea said. She held up something small and pink. Not-ink. "You gave me the amulet. You found me the secrets of the changelings. What a blessing you are. You're kind and you're brave, and I know that you're scared, but every day you wake up and try a little more. Get a little braver. Find more of yourself."

Yinii opened her mouth to argue, but the ink flowed over her tongue. It tasted salty and bitter. She didn't want it. She thought, absurdly, of pancakes.

"My father's going to take me back to Maqama," she said.

"Ink doesn't have a father, does it? But you do. But, my girl, my brave, kind girl, I won't let anyone take you anywhere you don't ask to go. I promise. And I'll be with you when you tell them, if you want that, Yinii. But we have to go outside."

"I..." Yinii started. "It..." Outside was more to burn, a part of her whispered, but it was small and getting smaller.

"I think sometimes," Amadea's voice went on, a thread that led back through the smoke and the ink, "that the Orozhandi have always been the wisest when it comes to affinities. They know that it's possible to love the ink, to even be the ink, and to come back to yourself."

"Ink isn't an Orozhandi affinity," Yinii murmured.

"It's your affinity, so I disagree," Amadea said. Her arm curved around Yinii's ribs, pulling her backward and the flood of ink with her. "Madness and death aren't a certainty. Not even now. You are such a joy, and... Yinii, if you don't come back, there will be a hole in the archives that we'll never fill. Not because of the ink. Because of you."

"If you die," Yinii said. "If you stay down here, you'll die. You should run."

Amadea stopped pulling and hugged Yinii close. "Yinii, sweet, I'm not leaving you."

Triggering a spiral in alignment was as easy as drowning, while climbing out was as easy as swimming out of the rapids of a river in full flood. But this time, Yinii found when she started weeping, started wanting the way out of the ink, it opened to her, as easy as leaping from a cliff.

And about as pleasant. She gasped as she dipped away from the spiral, saw they were standing now in sight of the exit, the air hot and foul, the smoke thickening. The world hard and hot and angry.

"I don't want to go back," Yinii sobbed, clutching at the spiral, crawling back toward the darkness of the ink.

"I know," Amadea said, stroking her hair. "The world is hard and life is scary. But, Yinii, sweet girl, you're doing so well. And I'm not leaving you."

Yinii squeezed her eyes shut. The world was hard and terrifying. There were choices she didn't want to have to make, fears she didn't want to have to face, and sometimes nothing sounded so right as curling up in the ink and drowning, she felt so alone.

"Come back," Amadea pleaded.

You did this to save them. That dim part of her mind, growing louder and stronger. *You fell into the spiral to stop them from dying. You're not alone, if that's true.*

Yinii opened her eyes, looked into Amadea's, and threw herself from the cliff. Out of the spiral, back into herself, before the little whispering voice could begin again.

It hurt. Saint Asla and the salt, it hurt! She was sobbing and retching ink as Amadea dragged her from the tunnel. Amadea settled her down on the grass, but Yinii was no sooner seated than there were footsteps, and hoofbeats, and a whole army of people there.

She flinched, shivering, the sounds hammering her aching skull. She looked around and found Quill watching her worriedly, as armed soldiers flanked the entrance to the tunnel.

"Cousin," she heard a woman say. "Very glad to see you alive." Yinii blinked blearily up at a finely dressed human woman, her skin dark, her braided hair arranged around a circlet shaped like a cobra biting its own tail. The Duchess Kirazzi, she realized.

"Zara, saints and devils," Ibramo gasped. "You're a touch late."

"She came with me," another voice, crisp and brittle, said. The empress, gold around her eyes, her layered gown replaced with trousers and a tunic, a wide scarf draped around her head.

Ibramo, still panting, made a bow. "Dita, I'm so glad you got my note in time. How did the meeting with the consuls go?"

"Very well," she said stiffly. "Although they weren't pleased to be left so abruptly. One presumes they'll understand." She exhaled noisily. "You're bleeding."

"He got it worse," Ibramo said.

"Your Alojan friend had just made it to the abbey when Her Imperial Majesty arrived," Duchess Zara said. "He's in quite a frenzy. Almost crawled back off to assist us, with half his liver hanging out."

"Oh! Tunuk!" Yinii cried, her voice rough and raw. "Is he alive? Is he all right?"

The duchess gave her a kind sort of smile that made Yinii realize what she must look like, scorched and bleeding and ink-stained. "My dear girl, he'll be fine," the duchess said. "Now let us see to you."

VI

MONSTROUS PALIMPSEST

Year Eight of the Reign of Emperor Clement
Palace Sestina

In his brother's garish office, his brother's final prison, Turon Kirazzi pieces together the truth: Redolfo Kirazzi is long gone and what sits before Turon is his changeling double. There are gaps—there will always be gaps. *How?* and *Where?* and *To what end?* Turon may know his brother like no one else, but Turon wasn't there to see his escape.

The changeling Redolfo smiles up at him, smug and blithe. Ready for the noose that wasn't meant for him. Turon's stomach is uneasy.

"Do you know what you are?" he asks softly.

"Oh, what now?" Redolfo drawls. "A traitor? A disappointment? A self-centered maniac?"

"Do you know that you're a changeling?"

And Redolfo gives him such a puzzled look. "Is this some sort of parable? Are you going to preach at me?"

It doesn't, Turon thinks. It has no notion of its nature. How Redolfo managed such a thing is a puzzle Turon can't even hold in his head. He can't help but doubt; even now, doubting.

"Get me another brandy, would you?" the creature in his brother's place says.

Numb with shock, Turon retrieves another brandy and goes to the door, to the guards outside, fresh and stern in their duty. They nod, stiff, bare bows of duty. "Did you need something, csinor?"

"Could you tell me who else has visited my brother?" he asks.

The soldiers exchange looks. "Only you, esinor."

Turon hesitates, one gap closing. "Were you here," he says slowly, "when I visited before?"

The soldier shakes her head. "It's in the logbook, though. I can see who it was."

"That's all right. Thank you. I need to...I need to discuss something with my brother again. A moment."

Turon Kirazzi believes himself a moral man, especially beside his brother. But faced with the changeling wearing his brother's face, perhaps against its will, and taking his brother's punishment...he's not sure he can claim that.

It would kill you if it had the chance, Turon reminds himself, as the changeling takes the glass. He knows that down in his bones, but this, too, he can't help doubting. What the changelings want, what they wanted before, why anything in the old world happened— these are questions so huge they eclipse into inanity how Redolfo captured and contained a changeling. This one can't tell him a single thing. It's a pale copy, a monstrous palimpsest. Its secrets are all lost.

"What are you doing?" the changeling says. "Are you going to moralize at me?"

It came into this room, Turon thinks, *wearing my face*. Did it come to help Redolfo? To *kill* Redolfo? Again, there is no knowing, but Turon has heard enough stories to guess the former is unlikely. The way it turned Turon's attention to the Shrike, to the assassin who culled changelings for Redolfo—and *there* is a reason, if any, to come after this man.

And if it's here...that means Redolfo is not. Redolfo has a second chance to not destroy himself and everyone else.

But only if Turon keeps his mouth shut. Only if Turon lets the changeling die and keeps the secret of a changeling slipping—somehow!—past the Salt Wall, where it should never have been able to. They cannot even touch the Wall to climb it, after all—that it is here is a terrible emergency.

Or a fluke. A bit of luck. The blessings of Pademaki, the source of water, the source of Khirazj, the gift that flows down into Redolfo and Turon.

And Redolfo will not die, if Turon keeps his mouth shut. Perhaps that makes Turon a coward. Perhaps a traitor. But for all his brother has caused him agonies, the thought that he will not have to bear Redolfo's death is a blessing that makes him reconsider the depths of his belief.

Turon takes his cloak. It feels strange to bid the changeling good-bye and it feels abhorrent not to say farewell to his brother. He clears his throat. He looks at the wallpaper instead of the changeling.

"Redolfo, all else besides, I love you. You are a fool and a villain, but you're my brother. I wish you'd trusted me. I wish you'd let me turn your boat away from the rocks. I wish I could have stopped all this, but I am . . . I am glad you have another chance. Don't ruin it."

"I am the smartest man in any room," the changeling sneers. "I am the most daring duke House Kirazzi ever raised. I ruin nothing."

Turon bites back a response, clenches a fist around his anger. He turns to go.

"Turon?" the changeling says. "I'm sorry."

If it had been Redolfo, Turon thinks as he leaves, that would only be to twist Turon's thoughts around, to manipulate him into or out of some action. But he wonders if Redolfo fed the creature those words, or if the creature, becoming Redolfo, had known his grief, said or unsaid.

As much as he does not wish to think about it, Turon Kirazzi will weigh those two words for all of his days, and while he watches the Wall and ponders the changeling, it is a secret he will take to his death, some months after he hands his nephew a lost letter with a cryptic promise.

He should know, even now, as he walks away from Sestina, that Redolfo Kirazzi deserves no second chances.

CHAPTER EIGHTEEN

Ibramo stayed behind to secure the tunnel as the fires were dealt with and to be sure Duchess Zara's soldiers didn't find anything they shouldn't. The rest of them were guided, not to Sestina, but to Gintanas.

Protests rose and crowded in Amadea's throat as she walked through the pale yellow halls, but she swallowed them down and tried not to get lost in memories of tombs and willows, incense and porridge, and caves she couldn't decide if she actually remembered.

But one memory she held tight to. When Yinii had been settled into a day-sister's cell and sedated, Amadea fled the soldiers and the chaos to the chapel of Phaseran, Keeper of the Dusk.

Where the chapel of Alletet bustled all day and the chapel of Djutubai sang all night, dusk was a sliver, a precious hour of change, and Phaseran's dusk-given would leave the chapel still and quiet, readied for that moment. Amadea slipped inside and sat against the back wall, looking up at the beetle-headed spirit of learning, perched on their altar with one upraised finger. Phaseran was the moment of ignorance before accepting knowledge. The indrawn breath. The foot before it strikes the ground. The worm in the chrysalis. The moment of flux and change, or collapse.

It wasn't where Amadea wanted to be at all. She rested her head in her hands and tried to still her thoughts.

She only had a few breaths to herself before the door opened and Quill slipped in, looking tense and drawn. He hurried in and sat down beside her. Amadea said nothing, feeling grief, and she squeezed her eyes shut against the panic that swelled up in her. She kept her gaze on Phaseran.

"Do you want to talk about it?" he asked.

"There's nothing to talk about," she said.

Quill gave a frantic little laugh. "I can think of a few things. A small *pile* of things." He paused. "I saw. What was in the room. What you were going to burn."

"I know," she said.

"Are you all right?"

There had been four perfect doubles of her sleeping in that room—*but I'm fine*. Four doubles obviously there since long before the coup fell, trapped and slumbering and somehow aging along with her—*but I'm fine*. Four of her, dying under her hands. Burned to ashes, because of her order.

"I'm fine," Amadea said tightly.

"Horseshit," Quill said, though the vehemence he said it with was kind. "*Horseshit.* Look, I get it—you're the person that takes care of things, you're the one in charge, and everything's going *wild*. But... I don't know how anyone—including you—can see that someone made changeling doubles of them and shrug it off like it doesn't matter. So I know that I'm *not* the person who takes care of things, I'm not the one in charge, but I also don't think you have to...to just sit with that alone."

Amadea closed her eyes. "How do you know they're doubles of *me?*"

Four doubles, and never had Redolfo threatened to replace her before now...or had he already done it? And how many times?

She had fought off wondering for years if she was a convenient orphan or a lost princess, but never even thought to consider she might be a changeling.

Quill said nothing for a long time, and Amadea counted the pulses of her heart, radiating through her face. She would not cry, she told herself, her breakdown in the street outside the palace too raw, the presence of so many people too pressing.

"How old are you?" Quill said abruptly.

Amadea startled. "That's a bit impertinent."

"I don't mean to be," he said. "But—all right, you're older than I am, fair? In all those years, have you never salted your food? Or handled a nail? A horseshoe? Lord and the devils, the railings on the stairs in the archives are iron, and you've never burned yourself on those. Have you just hibernated through 'more than twenty' winters and not questioned it?

"And if somehow I'm wrong or forgot you wore gloves or anything like that, you said yourself that Redolfo Kirazzi dosed you with the Venom of Changelings, and I have to imagine if you inject changeling blood into a changeling, all you get is an angry changeling. You're only you." He shrugged. "You're Amadea Gintanas, and no one can take that."

Amadea opened her mouth to protest...but he had a point. A very obvious point. "Well," she said, turning her attention back to the altar, "now I feel foolish."

"You shouldn't," he said gently. "It's a hard thing, I imagine. Not knowing who you are. Seeing someone being you, even if they're only sleeping." He hesitated. "So...how are you?"

Amadea hesitated. "I am not all right. But I will work on it."

Quill watched her, silent for a long moment. "She told me—the Shrike—what she said to Karimo. She told him he was a changeling. That he had been tasked with destroying Semilla, which was probably the thing he cared about the most. And so he sacrificed himself."

"Oh, Quill."

"So I guess," he went on quicker, "what I'm saying is that you're not foolish for being afraid of what that might mean. You're...careful. Caring. You're a good person. Of course you're thinking about what might change if you...if you weren't." He blew out a breath. "I messed up. With Yinii. I thought I could talk her down, and maybe I was managing, but then I realized she could collapse the tunnel, and not accidentally take down the Wall over it...Is she going to be all right?"

"It will be all right. We know how to handle the spiral," Amadea said. Although, saints and devils, she couldn't recall a spiral like *that*. She thought of Yinii's intake interview—she'd assumed setting fires meant flint and poor planning.

"Don't discuss it with anyone just yet," she said. "For Yinii's sake."

Quill worried his lower lip, staring at the altar. "I used her," he said. "I did exactly what those old kings did, and I just used her. Like a weapon."

The changeling double clawing at her arm. Her own eyes staring up at her. "You did a terrible thing in order prevent worse things from happening," Amadea said. "That doesn't make it right, but . . . you know now. And . . . Yinii was altered, but she would have done it all the same if she'd known."

Quill frowned. "Wait. Could she spiral on purpose? I think she said . . . she had to. She had to do it to save us."

Cold poured down Amadea's neck. "Specialists can accidentally trigger a spiral out of alignment if they're under a lot of stress." But doing it on purpose . . . that was something different.

Not now, Amadea admonished herself. "She will be fine," she said, to Quill, to herself. "And so will we. Go take care of yourself now."

She rose to her feet, her sanctuary pierced, her fears deflated. The indrawn breath exhaled, the step taken, the sun breaking over the horizon—she didn't belong in Phaseran's presence anymore. She walked out into the garden where the buzz of bees in the dimming light, the scent of turned earth, hit her like a slap—*an earthworm on her trowel, the duchess dripping gold, the consort-princess dripping gold, the cave dripping*—and she had to sit down on a bench.

She wasn't fine. She'd known she wasn't since the visit to Fastreda, felt the edges, the depths of the vortex she'd been turning away from for years and years. She'd seen the need to move slow, to dip her toes in carefully, to find a way to understand and maybe calm the maelstrom.

But then Quill had been in danger, Semilla had been in danger, and there was no choice but to plunge into it, to tear away the ramparts, to take whatever damage came her way.

She took the salt crystal out again and turned it in her hands. She hadn't been able to remember the prayer in the cave, but now the first words rose easily: *Saint Asla, give me a measure of your wisdom, your focus. Bless me with the strength of your heart and mind.* She pressed a thumb to the sharp point of the crystal—*the pinch of the needle. "That does work quicker. Who knew? We have enough for another?"*

"Patience, my Shrike," Amadea whispered, and the memory dissolved. Something felt wrong.

Behind her, someone cleared their throat—Ibramo. She knew before she looked back, before she saw him standing beneath the portico, blood drying on his shirt. Amadea gestured at the seat beside her on the bench, and he took it.

"Beneditta went back to Sestina to send messages back to the palace, but she'll be here this evening, to ask questions."

"How much trouble are we in?"

"You, I suspect, are fine," he said. "I...Well, Dita's not unreasonable, and the threat of Redolfo returning is over before anyone got wind of it. Once we explain the details, I suspect it will merely be... a personal amount of discord for me."

"All of the details?"

She meant the changeling doubles, but as she said it, she meant the kiss too. Ibramo bit his lip and she was sure they were of one mind. He took her hand. "Only what's a danger to the people of the empire."

Which clarified nothing at all, but Amadea folded her hand around his.

"Can I see you again?" he asked. "Tell me I can see you again?"

"Ibramo, we shouldn't have—"

"I don't mean that way," he said quickly. "I'm sorry. Everything was so...I miss you," he began again. "I don't have a great many friends, at least not many friends I can be sure of. I can be sure of you."

"I broke your heart," she reminded him.

"You did what you thought was best for both of us," he said. "There is nothing so broken it can't be repaired."

Amadea leaned against his shoulder and thought what a flimsy, foolish lie it was. But she let him have it, and let herself imagine a future where they could be friends, confidants even, Sparrow and Mouse again. "I'd like that," she said, because at least that was true.

"Do you remember your father taking me from here?" she asked, watching a dragonfly flit between the beans.

"No. I remember when you came to Sestina. I remember how wild, how manic he was in the days before. Like nothing could touch him. Like he'd found the secrets of the heavens."

Or a lost princess, Amadea thought. *Or a convincing double. Redolfo is the only one who knows.* She blew out a long, slow breath. *Enough.*

Ibramo cleared his throat. "The vigilant was asking after you."

"Oh?"

"You should... I'm not saying he's your only option or anything. But... I hate to think of you lonely."

Amadea felt her cheeks burn. "He's a colleague."

"Oh!" Ibramo said, a dangerous brightness in his voice. "That's... that's good too. Friends are... good." He cleared his throat.

Amadea hesitated. "I have to see Fastreda when we get back."

Ibramo stiffened beside her. "You don't need to keep that promise."

"I do," Amadea said, "but aside from that I have to ask her something. Only her."

Ibramo looked as if he'd like to argue, like to remind her that Fastreda destroyed everything she touched. But he stopped. He slipped his hand around hers again. "I'll make sure they let you in."

Amadea didn't look for Richa right away, fearful of what he'd worked out, fearful of seeing what had happened to him. She found him settled in one of the night-brothers' rooms, bandages peeking out of his collar, his left arm in a sling.

In his left hand, though, was a piece of wood, whittled into a sort of rounded shape, the knife still in his right hand. He smiled when he saw her, and her stomach fluttered with nerves and something more.

"So I didn't ask for you to step in," she said, trying to keep her voice light as his and failing horribly, "but I appreciate you punching that changeling in the jaw so I didn't have to."

"I don't," Richa said, showing her his battered knuckles. "Good thing I'm out of the Kinship, or my cadets would never let me hear the end of it. 'Thought it was always hard to soft, Vigilant?' Should have kicked its back knee out, got it around the neck and down. But I was a *little* distracted."

Amadea bit her lip. She sat down on the edge of the bed. "I'm glad you're all right."

"Mostly," he said. He paused. "No, I don't know that I am." When Amadea's eyes went to his shoulder, he shook his head. "Not Lady Maschano—although that too. She did almost kill me and... I don't know that I'm going to sleep well thinking of how she died. But I went out the end of the tunnel. I saw the other side. There's more of them. More of someone, anyway."

Amadea frowned. "You saw more changelings."

"I don't know," he admitted. "It wasn't like when... yeah, that's another thing I won't forget. That guard turning into..." He shuddered. "There were half a dozen of them. At least one looked human. But they knew Redolfo. They were waiting for him."

Amadea folded her hands together to steady them. There were more. There were others who might carry the message back to the one who had given the changeling his orders. Back to Redolfo Kirazzi himself, perhaps.

"Let us hope the wall-walkers can flush them out," she said.

"Let's hope that's the only tunnel," Richa said grimly. He tapped the little knife against his carving. "I could show you. How to kick a changeling's knee out. So you don't need me to step in next time."

Amadea raised her eyebrows. "How do you know I don't know how to kick a changeling's knee out already?"

"Because you can't possibly be good at everything." That made her laugh, and his dark eyes sparkled. "I'll have to find somewhere to show you. I doubt the Kinship will let me use their practice mats." He smiled. "You know, that first night, when I brought Quill to the archives, I was fairly sure you were going to be some girl he was seeing, some poor thing we were dragging out of her bed, with this horrible story, and then I'd have the both of you to manage. And then you all but kicked down those doors, face like Aye-Nam-Wati breaking into Hell. Took charge of the whole mess of it. I am very glad to have made your acquaintance."

Amadea thought of Ibramo's intimations, of the deep flush they triggered. She thought of the ragged edges of the vortex of her past.

How awful it would be, to drag someone into that. How pretty Richa's eyes were.

She had no idea, still, how much he knew, how much he'd gleaned from the events in the cavern, how much he'd realize as they debriefed the empress...

"Well, I'm sorry it led to *this*," she said, pushing it all down. Not now. Especially not if she could always find out while he showed her how to drop an attacker to the ground, she thought. She nodded at the carving. "What are you making?"

"A hawk." He held it up so she could see the beginnings of the hooked face, the sweep of wings. "Assuming I don't accidentally shave its beak off there. Because they hunt shrikes."

"Appropriate," she said. "It can go in the little forest in your office."

"This monster? It'll crush anything it perches on," he said. "It's just something to do with my hands. Helps me think. The trees don't make so much mess. Except then I have a small forest of tiny trees."

"Well, if you don't want it, I would," she said. She smoothed her dress over her knees. "I have a...a collection of little animal figurines. It would be a welcome addition."

His smile changed at that, softer, less sharp and teasing. "Only," he said, "if you take it regardless of the state of its beak."

"Esinora?" a voice called from the door. Amadea straightened to see one of the hospitaler's assistants. "Would you come—now— please, to handle the Alojan...Just the Alojan."

"I am dying," Tunuk said, looming over the girl even bent over his bandaged ribs. "And no one's even come to say they're sorry about it. I would have. If *you'd* died."

Amadea stood. "Tunuk, go back to bed."

"I *will*," he said, as she ushered him back out. "Now that I know you're *not* dead. Where's Yinii?"

"Sleeping. As you should be."

"But not dead. And the Paremi? Did you find him?"

"He's in the chapel. I'll tell him you asked after him. After you've had some rest."

Tunuk stopped in the hallway, looking over her back at the door to Richa's room. "Normally," he said in a low voice, "I wouldn't mention it, because I don't care. But that man is trying to get your attention. Sexually."

The hospitaler's assistant went wide-eyed. Amadea folded her arms—beside the last day, the problem of Tunuk was a welcome one. "You are not getting out of this by challenging the bounds of polite conversation. You are going to go and lie down, and then I will talk to you." She took his arm, and he relaxed a little. "I'm very glad you're not dead."

"Me too," he said softly, and let her lead him back to his room.

— ⚎ —

Tunuk was healed enough to attend Lord Obigen's memorial in the Imperial Complex, though he was confined to a chair, his arm bandaged down to stop him from reaching and stretching the wound, and his nest-mothers kept him surrounded and peppered with questions about the guests he had brought, and whether any of them were possibly something more than friends? Perhaps?

Amadea sighed. Poor Tunuk.

"He looks like he's going to collapse into his own rib cage," Quill said to Amadea as they stood to the side of the huge ballroom the empress had granted to the Manco nest for the memorial. No one had so much as suggested it be held in the manor's front room, where the murder had happened. Tunuk looked across the room at Amadea and scowled.

"Alzari asked if we were roommates," Quill confided. "But I think she meant something else."

Amadea shook her head as she scanned the crowded room. "I can't decide if it would be easier or more difficult if Tunuk had a roommate." She accepted a glass of wine from a passing waiter.

"Do you usually give archivists roommates?" Quill asked.

"Depends. Sometimes a specialist needs supervision. Sometimes a person just needs company. Sometimes your bronze specialist and your corundum specialist elope and you have to take out a wall to keep them in the archives." She took a sip of her wine, scanned the room again. "Why?"

"Paremi don't," Quill said. "Unless you're traveling. Supposed to help you focus." He paused. "What do you do to . . . The apprenticeship, how long is it?"

Amadea tore her gaze from the memorial guests. "An archives apprenticeship? For whom?"

"Me," Quill said, sounding affronted.

"You have an oath."

"I think I have the wrong oath." He blew out a breath. "Karimo dying was the worst thing I've ever had to face. And what did I do? I went chasing wild stories and haring after suspects. I tried to brain an assassin with a broken board, and I convinced a specialist in the middle of a crisis to essentially destroy evidence."

"That doesn't mean that what the Paremi do isn't important," Amadea said. "The law matters."

"No, it means I'm not the right shepherd for it," Quill said. "When it all came out that Lamberto was corrupt, I thought, 'That's hideous. That would never be me.' But I was breaking all sorts of laws, because it was my friend. My *friends*," he corrected. "That's not that different. Not where it counts."

"But it is different," Amadea said.

"It's different for an archivist," Quill said. "Maybe I'm not a history expert, and maybe I'm not a specialist, but I'm good at talking to people. I think you could make me better at it, given the chance. And you need more people who know how. More generalists. Plus, you can't say I can't correct a catalogue or craft a ledger—that's basically all I know how to do right now." He swirled the wine in his glass, considering the ruby liquid. "Redolfo and the Shrike were paying Lamberto to do *something*. And we still don't know what."

Amadea pursed her mouth, scanning the crowd again. "We do not," she agreed. "Could you find out what, if you stayed with the Paremi?"

"I think I could argue convincingly that my investigative resources are far superior with the archives given recent results." He sipped his wine. "I think that counts as precedent."

"Only if what Redolfo was looking for were more artifacts," she said grimly.

Then, through the crowd, Amadea saw what she'd been waiting for: the Masked Empress of Semilla, speaking to Uruphi yula Manco. Without Lady Sigrittrice at her side.

"Excuse me," she said to Quill. She set her glass down on the windowsill. "I'll be right back."

Beneditta spotted Amadea as she approached. She wore a dark teal gown with a white sash of Alojan mourning, her imperial-gold mask a motif of hares chasing each other around her eyes, the spill of spring over her nose and around her mouth. Her dark eyes were hard as Amadea curtsied.

"Your Imperial Majesty," Amadea said, straightening. "Uruphi."

Tunuk's mother clasped her hand. "Amadea. I'm so glad to see you again, although of course, I wish the circumstances were different." She sighed heavily. "Thank the stars, I am not mourning a child as well as a partner, however. What *did* Tunuk do to himself?"

Amadea's smile froze. "An accident. He should tell you."

Uruphi waved this away. "Then it shall stay a mystery, I suppose. Our child has never been forthcoming." She nodded back at Quill, beside the window and staring. "Is the apprentice well?"

"As well as can be expected," Amadea replied. "I think he'll come out all right."

Uruphi adjusted the white shawl she wore wrapped around herself. "I should go talk to him," she said. "Make sure he knows he's welcome here." She gave Amadea a sidelong look. "And while I commend your respect for Tunuk's privacy, I won't lie that I'm also hoping that boy is more willing to talk. I will visit soon, my dear." The Alojan woman bade the empress goodbye and strode off toward Quill.

"I got your note," Beneditta said softly.

Amadea looked down. "Could we speak in private, Your Majesty?"

"If this is about my husband," Beneditta said, "then I don't want to hear it. I am not a monster, Archivist Gintanas, and I know there are things between you that will never be between Ibramo and me, but our marriage is a beam in the building of this empire and I will not let that collapse."

"No, Your Majesty. It's not Ibramo." Amadea took a steadying breath. "And it's important to the empire. But...you should hear it alone."

Beneditta considered her through the mask for a long moment. Then she looked past Amadea, hunting Sigrittrice, no doubt. Whatever Beneditta saw satisfied her, because with another search of Amadea's features, she beckoned her to follow.

Beneditta led her to a small, well-furnished room, the door flanked by guards, as everywhere in the palace. A little sanctuary for a quiet conversation, two chairs and a table beneath a portrait of Empress Clotilda.

"Well?" Beneditta said. "Out with it."

Amadea pressed her hands together. "There's something I didn't bring up when we told you what happened at Gintanas. About the changelings."

Fear flickered through Beneditta's eyes. "And you didn't think it mattered?"

"It's complicated and I don't think anyone else needs to hear it, necessarily." She took another steadying breath. "You were dosed with the Venom of Changelings, at the party at Lord Obigen's manor."

"No," Beneditta said firmly, "I left well before—"

"You didn't, Your Majesty. You had a bruise on your arm shortly after, particular to the injection of changeling blood. It might still be showing, if you don't believe me." Amadea swallowed. It had to be done. "Do you know if you're a changeling?"

The horror and shock on Beneditta's face was visible even through the mask. "How...Why would you say such a thing?"

"You were dosed," Amadea said, quickly. "You were at that party, you were injected the same as everyone. I think you were meant to be the capstone, the finishing touch that made this murder inarguably what it looked like.

"But the changeling blood didn't do what it was supposed to. You don't remember what Lady Maschano told you to remember—not a word of it. And the only reason I can find for that...is if you also have that blood in your veins."

Beneditta stared at her, gave her head a little shake. "You're mad. You're completely mad."

"To be clear," Amadea said, "I don't think it means...I wouldn't have told you, and you alone, if I thought it meant you shouldn't have the throne. You're still you, whatever the answer. I'm telling you because...because you deserve to know what exactly that means. Having had that stolen from me, I think you deserve it very much." She swallowed again, looked away. "I brought salt. If you want to test it now. But if you don't want to, I understand. It's not an easy question to ask."

"I think I would know if I were a changeling!" Beneditta burst out.

Amadea wet her mouth. "Maybe not. 'The Venom of Changelings is the trap of Khirazj, and the Venom of Khirazj is the trap of the changeling.' There's a compound made of non-changeling blood that...freezes them in a single form. Makes them forget what they are. Rosangerda Maschano used it on her captured changeling, trapping it in the form of her son's bodyguard. Someone might have done that to you."

Beneditta's eyes narrowed. "Who would dare..."

But then she stopped. Stilled, as if she remembered something. Swallowed audibly. "What do I have to do to make sure?" she asked.

Amadea put a hand into her pocket and pulled out a drawstring bag full of salt. She opened it in the middle of the table. "I don't remember all the imperial taboos," she said. "And I don't know what you might have been told to do or not do...You might be able to tell just touching it. That's how it's meant to work. It seems as if... well, you could have a tolerance from the sound of things, but a pile of salt might be different." She folded her hands together. "I'll leave."

"I..." Beneditta reached up and took off the mask of her office. She set it down hard, on the table. "Please stay with me. Lira."

"Don't call me that, Your Majesty."

"Then as your empress...You have no idea, do you? Look, let us just pretend a moment you are in fact my dear little cousin, still breathing, and you hold my fucking hand while I find out what else is going to be stolen from me, all right?"

Amadea blinked in surprise. "You remember...the princesses."

"Of course I remember," Beneditta said. "And whatever the truth is...I need a friend right now, so be one. Please."

Amadea reached out and took Beneditta's hand beneath the portrait of her grandmother. Amadea risked a glance up at the stern-faced empress, sneering down at this display, this puzzle she might well have engineered or maybe only encouraged, letting her sons grow to loathing. A bitter sort of anger built in Amadea, a memory of Katucia crying—Amadea pushed it away, fighting the urge to sift through her memories, to search for Beneditta or her conspicuous lack.

Beneditta spent a long time staring at the salt, her breath coming quick. She reached forward with one shaking hand and plunged her hand into the white surface.

Nothing happened. Not even a flinch. Amadea felt a flash of guilt. She started to apologize but Beneditta turned to her. "You are an archivist. Do you have a penknife?"

"Yes. But—"

"Give it to me." Amadea handed over the little blade and Beneditta let go of Amadea's hand long enough to prick her finger, to squeeze a drop out onto the plain of salt. It was red as rubies.

"I'm sorry," Amadea began, "I thought I—"

But then the little droplet began to smoke against the salt. A bead of green fire burned merrily around it. Beneditta cried out, clutched both hands against her chest in horror.

"It will be all right," Amadea said, reaching for her. "It doesn't... it doesn't change anything."

"*How?* How is it supposed to not change things?" Beneditta cried. "I am everything this empire was built to stand against! I have spent my whole reign, my whole life, convincing my people, my protectorates, that I am everything the Ulanittis have always claimed to be—the rock they put their faith in when the world ended. Everything the Fratricide destroyed, everything Redolfo Kirazzi threatened. And now? Now I find out I'm a greater enemy than either of those—"

"Beneditta." Sigrittrice's weary voice made Amadea and Beneditta both jump. "You are not a changeling." She stood behind Amadea, before a tapestry hanging that she let fall behind her, covering the door hidden there. Her golden mask came down to the soft edges of her jaw, and her silver hair was bound in a plait down one side.

Beneditta gestured angrily at the drop of blood, burning itself out in emerald sparks. "Then what is this?" she demanded. "What are you keeping from me *now*?"

Sigrittrice eyed Amadea. "You have stumbled into something very dangerous once again, Archivist Gintanas." She folded her hands in front of her. "You are not a changeling. But you are descended from them. All Ulanittis are descended from them."

Beneditta's expression turned cold. Imperial. "How far back?"

"Oh, from the earliest days of Semilla, I should say. Long before the catastrophes and the Salt Wall, if that's what worries you. We are not like *those*, and neither were our ancestors. We are meant," she went on, "to rectify the natural failings of a monarchy. We are made to be perfect, just rulers, to devote ourselves to the good of Semilla. To resist the urge of tyranny and self-enrichment. Excessive self-enrichment," she amended. "You, like every Ulanitti child before you, were locked into form and function by potions passed down from generation to generation—the 'venoms,' as Khirazj prefers it. And like every child born since the catastrophes, it was done in secret and isolation. We are not changelings and we don't need to upset our citizens by creating the idea that we are those wild, chaotic monsters."

"But you knew," Amadea said.

"Well, *someone* has to," Sigrittrice snapped. "We're born unformed— if no one knows how to solve that, then what? The secret is passed down, *carefully*. It was my uncle's before me." She hesitated. "That's... that's what happened with Appolino. I chose the wrong time. Clotilda had...she pointed her boys against each other. It was a terrible situation. He didn't take it well. He tried to strip away the locking. He went mad of it and decided he had to cleanse Semilla. That that was what was best and most just for the people."

Father and Mother, laughing maskless by the fire, playing castles. Uncle Appolino, sullen and staring, half in shadow, and a terrible feeling in her stomach—

Amadea shut her eyes. That was invented. Or new.

"Who...Who are you going to...?" Beneditta steadied herself. "You pass this role down. Who will take it from you?"

"This is Djaulia's position, once she's old enough. Fifteen or so."

"You will *not* put this on my daughter!" Beneditta said, ferocious.

"Dita," Sigrittrice said, "you need to calm down. She is what she is. You are what you are. And how fortunate for Semilla, because there is no possibility at all that a person without your skills could hold an empire like this one together. It barely manages with us!"

Beneditta shook her head. "But they're not my skills. They're an illusion."

"Their purpose and their impact is real, so I think you should reconsider." Sigrittrice set a hand on Beneditta's arm. "Many Ulanittis go to their graves not knowing. They wear the masks, not because it once erased the skills our subjects didn't have, but because that is what Ulanittis do. They govern because it is expected, not because they understand they've been charged with a duty. Shaped for a purpose. You're lucky in this—you understand what you were made for."

"I made you," Redolfo whispers. "I built you into this. I can end you just as easily." Amadea reached over and squeezed Beneditta's hand. It was a terrible thing, not knowing who you were. Knowing someone else had decided for you.

The pinch of the needle. "That does work quicker. Who knew? We have enough for another?" Amadea frowned.

"Shouldn't the venom work?" she asked slowly. "If she's only partly changeling, why didn't it work?"

"It works *partly*," Sigrittrice said. "We require a much higher dose. Of either mixture."

Beneditta sucked in a breath. "You gave me more of the venom that night."

"I did," Sigrittrice said. "We had received enough for me to know what had happened—you were delirious, and I was little better. Whatever was happening, I had to be sure our secret remained safe, and I didn't know what plans were in motion. Only that you needed to be removed from them."

"You framed Gaspera," Amadea said.

"I needed it to end," Sigrittrice said. "Gaspera had a duty once, to protect the empire. I held her to it. But now we have uncovered the true murderer, I think it's clearly more likely that she's the one who planted the poisons, don't you?"

Beneditta took back her hand, wiped her eyes. "We're going now," she announced, and fit her mask to her face once more with shaking hands. Her gaze caught Amadea's, so clouded with grief and rage and uncertainty that Amadea could offer nothing against it in that moment. Instead, she dropped into a curtsy, as Beneditta swept from the little room without so much as a word to her aunt.

Sigrittrice turned to Amadea, looked her up and down. "If I find you have breathed even a word of this, Archivist Gintanas," she said, "I will salt your name to the stones before I make certain you are dead, followed by every soul you have ever exchanged words with. Beginning with Vigilant Langyun."

"Then why not kill me now?" Amadea asked.

"We're not animals," Sigrittrice said. She sighed. "And . . . what I have observed of you . . . neither are you. You know what this would cost the empire." She turned to follow Beneditta from the room.

"What of Redolfo Kirazzi?" Amadea said.

Sigrittrice halted. "What of him?"

"You heard all the testimony," Amadea said. "You know what he was capable of, what he *is* capable of. If there is anyone that poses a danger to this empire, it's him. There is something brewing over the Salt Wall."

Lady Sigrittrice sighed. "Then it is fortunate," she said, "that it remains on the other side of the Salt Wall. Not a word, Archivist Gintanas. Not a word." She left.

Amadea stayed, contemplating the sack of salt and the pulse of her blood, wild and anxious in her veins. The drop of Beneditta's blood had shriveled into a small black dot, from which the faintest wisp of smoke rose.

Four Amadeas lying in the Kirazzi vault. He knew how to make a double, then—of Lireana Clotilda Amadea Iespera Ulanitti, or of Lira, orphan of Gintanas abbey? The salt hadn't burned her when she'd held the crystal or when she'd filled the sack. Her blood was as red as Beneditta's, not the dark green of a changeling.

But no one had ever written, so far as she knew, about hybrid changelings like what Sigrittrice described. No one knew they existed.

It would be such a simple thing, Amadea told herself. A prick of the finger. A drop on the salt. She would know.

She would know something. But not whether she was Lireana. Not where she had come from. Not what would happen if the blood made green sparks, who would suffer and who would rise. Not whether her future would change, for better or worse.

Amadea studied the salt a long moment. She picked up the penknife and slipped it back into its case, then the sack, all the loose grains of salt brushed back into it. Whatever else she was, she thought, Amadea Gintanas was a solver of problems. Here was a problem with an obvious solution: she would continue as herself.

⚊⚊ ⚌◆⚊ ⚊⚊

Quill stood beside Zoifia in the House of Unified Wisdom in the Necessary Arts, a pair of unlikely guards behind Yinii as she informed Reza Dolitha and her father that she wasn't leaving the archives after all.

"I understand why you're concerned," Yinii said carefully, "and I miss you very much, but the archives are the right place for me."

Yinii had been sequestered for two days after returning from Gintanas, but when the presence of ink had no apparent effect, Mireia was forced to agree they couldn't keep her locked up, away from books and the Orozhandi both, forever. After all, her father was visiting every day, demanding to know when they would leave. She could go, but she needed chaperoning. And *gloves*.

Donatas Ten-Scarab ul-Benturan had a disturbing habit of scowling at Quill when the reza was talking, but at least when Yinii spoke, he looked at her. Scowled at her, Quill corrected.

"Wiil'aa–adna bidah yaa reza—" Donatas began.

"Baba," Yinii said sternly, "I'm not going."

Quill looked out the window at Arlabecca, surprised at how fragile the great city seemed from this angle. This place. Was it the

Venom of Changelings burning in his brain or grief or longing or something else? The city looked so fragile, but the people—he turned back to Yinii—they seemed so strong.

Donatas glanced at Reza Dolitha. "Yinii, shashkii, we know what's best. This city's dangerous—"

"No," the reza suddenly interrupted. She was sitting propped up on pillows, a glass cap that blocked her dark-sight covering her third eye. "No, Donatas, she's right."

Both Yinii and Donatas turned to the reza, startled. "Atnashing-yii," Reza Dolitha said, all courtesy. "I will say this in the common tongue for your friends' benefit, but I say it as your reza: In my pain and grief, I have made a bad judgment. I have failed you and thereby failed ul-Benturan. That is the sorrow of the reza, the folly of the fallible, and I hope you will forgive me, and forgive my name to the saints."

Yinii clutched her gloved hands together. "It's ... it's all right."

The reza nodded sagely. "That woman, that Amadea, she came to me and told me what a great thing you did. What the ink let you do. You avenged me and you saved the empire, and therefore ul-Benturan and the saints." Yinii's cheeks burned bright, and she ducked her head. Quill exchanged a glance with Zoifia—Yinii had spoken to no one about what had happened, about the extent of her spiral. It was starting to make Quill nervous.

"You have been given a great gift," Reza Dolitha went on. "I see that now. An irony, I see best now that I am blinded to the darkness."

"You will heal," Donatas began. But the reza cut him off.

"All gifts were once the first of their kind," she said. "Perhaps, atnashingyii, you're bringing us that new gift."

"About shitting time you noticed," Zoifia muttered.

Reza Dolitha looked up. "What was that?"

"We're just glad to hear you see the value of Yinii's affinity," Quill said quickly. "She's a credit to ul-Benturan."

"Agreed." Donatas narrowed his eyes. "Yinii, waashidii hai?"

"*Baba!*" Yinii cried, blushing deeper. "*No!*"

"He's going to take *hammers* to you," Zoifia whispered wickedly as Yinii made her goodbyes and plans to visit more when the reza was better rested. Quill picked up the urn from where it had waited on a chair beside the door, and the three of them left.

"Are you ready?" Yinii asked, bundling her cloak around her despite the heat of midday.

"Are they going to let you just wander in?" Zoifia asked. "You're not even dressed for it."

Quill had shed his Paremi robes for new trousers, a green shirt, a nicely cut jerkin. He'd taken his hair down from its loop, bound it back at the neck.

"I mean, if they don't," he said, "that's the job half-done." He looked south to where the Paremi chapter house waited. "You don't have to come."

"We want to come," Yinii said. And then: "I mean, I want to come."

"I don't," Zoifia said bluntly, "except I'm not leaving Yinii, and I'm sort of curious whether you're going to make a prelate explode."

Quill held Karimo's urn carefully as they walked. While he wished Karimo had taken Zoifia out for a coffee and not been where Rosangerda Maschano could hurt him, he could almost feel his friend's ghost watching on with horror. *You don't know*, Quill thought, as if speaking to him. *You might have gotten along.*

Salt-Sealing had ended, leaving one ragged red paper streamer clinging to the edifice of the Paremi chapter house. After convincing Yinii and Zoifia to wait outside for him, Quill walked through the building, dodging hurried Paremi as he made his way toward the back door and the columbarium that held the ashes of departed scriveners.

It was not the prelate he crossed paths with first but Deilio Maschano. His robes were the everyday habit, though still impeccably tailored, and he was exiting the chapel, hollow-eyed and drawn. When he saw Quill, he halted, looking spooked.

"Brother Sesquillio," he said, all his imperious manner gone. "I . . . I had heard you were going back to Ragale. I'm glad to see . . . I'm glad you're . . . well."

"You too," Quill said. "I'm sorry for your losses." He thought of the careless way Deilio had spoken of his parents' eventual deaths in the library where his father's body had later been found—it was hard to imagine with this grief-stricken young man.

Deilio nodded. "Thank you. I didn't... I didn't know, you understand? The vigilants... they told me some things, going through... well, it's my house now, but I can't say I want it." He looked solemn. "She nearly killed you, didn't she?"

"Yes," Quill said.

"Do you... do you know..." Deilio gulped a breath, and it seemed for a moment as if he would cry, but he mastered it and continued. "I just... I wish I knew why she did it. What she was trying to achieve. You never think about why people do things, especially not your parents, but then..." He swallowed. "I just wonder what she'd say now, is all. What she wanted for me. Was it to protect me? To... to muster something? Was someone forcing her to do these things?"

Quill thought back to Rosangerda in the carriage, all her flaws borne proudly, the mask she'd worn discarded. *You have friends, brother. I don't. I have tools I keep sharp in case I have a need for them. A use, a reason.* The way she'd used Deilio as a shield. Dosed him with the venom.

He did not like to contemplate what use she was saving Deilio for.

"What do I do now?" Deilio asked, almost a plea.

The prelate came up behind him, sparing Quill an answer. "Brother Sesquillio? What are you doing here? You were meant to be going back to Ragale."

Now or never, Quill thought. "I'm not going back to Ragale. I'm staying here."

The prelate had smiled kindly, but his eyebrows rose at this. "Brother Sesquillio, I understand you've had a rather... traumatic experience, but your place is in Ragale. We have no room here at the chapter house."

"Sorry, I meant here in Arlabecca." Quill nodded to him. "I want to take a sabbatical."

"Is that allowed?" Deilio asked.

"No." The prelate frowned at him. "You can't take a sabbatical."

"Well, that simplifies things," Quill said. "I quit."

"Sorry? You what?"

"Quit. I quit the order."

"You ... you can't quit the order. You took an oath."

And he'd believed in that oath, in the rightness of it, the strength of the law. He still did, he thought, but in the pit of his belly, he also knew this wasn't the best he could do for himself or for the empire.

"Well," he told the prelate, "I'm going to leave now. If you want to tell me what the thing I'm doing is called, I'm happy to give it a different word when I write home about it."

That gave the prelate pause, even though Quill had no desire to discuss any of this with his family. Not until he knew what he was doing.

"A sabbatical," the prelate agreed. "I'll ... send a message to Ragale and ... determine precedence."

"I'll take it," Deilio said suddenly. Quill looked back at him in surprise. "I ... could use a trip through the country," the young man went on. "And I've never been to the tower. Maybe I will find it enlightening. Perhaps there's even an apprenticeship there for me." The prelate's mouth worked a moment in surprise, and Quill wondered if Deilio Maschano had ever before volunteered for a task.

"There you are, Reverend," Quill said. "All the details managed. Now, would you excuse me? I have to ... I have to take care of something."

The columbarium of the Arlabecca Paremi was a marble building, decorated as if it were a library, its inhabitants scrolls of knowledge upon its shelves. Stairs led up and down, and the long walls waited to welcome scriveners for years to come. Quill went to a corner that seemed dry and quiet and found a shelf there with space.

"You don't have to stay here forever," Quill murmured to Karimo's ashes. "But I think you deserve somewhere nice. Quiet. And I can visit here—and I'll make sure it stays nice. You deserve that. You were a great friend, and you're still a great friend—you made me realize..." He swallowed against the lump in his throat. "It's *horseshit*. It's *utter* horseshit this happened. But I promise not to be angry every time I come, all right?" He patted the top of the urn. "See you later, Karimo."

Walking away felt impossible, but Quill made himself do it, walking out into the sunshine where the two archivists waited, Zoifia whispering to Yinii, who wove her fingers together, the way she did when she was thinking.

"Finished," he said, gruffly. "Found him the best corner."

Yinii's big green eyes found his. He found himself thinking of Deilio's mother, crumbling into ink. Deilio's mother pointing a blade at his throat.

"Did you want to stay longer?" Yinii asked.

"It's all right," he said. "I'll be back."

"How was the prelate?" Zoifia asked. "Did you tell him you were signing on with the archives? I'll bet he shit ravens."

"Oh," Yinii said. "Are you? You decided."

"Don't be dense, of course he is." Zoifia gave him a wolfish smile. "Ink hasn't had a dedicated generalist in *years*."

Yinii flushed. "If you get accelerated out of the apprenticeship, you're going to be assigned to Tunuk. To be clear."

"Amadea mentioned that," Quill said with a smile. "And...yeah, I think I will."

"Come on," Zoifia said. "Let's go get buns and celebrate your impending relationship with Biorni the Scary Rabbit. I'm starving."

As she strode ahead, Quill fell into step with Yinii. "I wanted to say I'm sorry for...for what I did in the tunnels. Even if you would have done it—"

"It's all right," Yinii said, weaving her white-gloved fingers together. "It just happened. It was...I did it, you know? I didn't slip."

Quill frowned. "You don't feel like doing it again, do you?"

"No," Yinii said, shaking her head fast enough to make her charms jingle. "No, no. It's...it's not like that. I can manage."

Quill nodded and let her be. There was so much he didn't understand about affinities and alignments, so much the archives could teach him, and he felt impatient to know—but it wouldn't help anything to pick apart her assurances. Better to watch and wait and step in when it was clear he was needed.

She gave him a sweet, bashful sort of smile. "I'm glad you're staying. Not going back to Ragale, I mean."

"Thanks." He cleared his throat. "Do you want to get a coffee or something? After the buns?"

Yinii looked faintly alarmed, and she flushed. "I . . . I have to meet Amadea. It's important—"

"That's fine," he said quickly. "Maybe another time? Unless your father—"

"No!" Yinii cried. Then softer, "No. It's not that." She hesitated a second, then took him by the hand. "Ask me another time," she said, and squeezed his fingers. "Or maybe I'll ask you?"

Quill smiled. "I'd like that."

⚬ ⚬⚬⚬ ⚬

Fastreda Korotzma never much cared for people, until the glass was taken away. People were slow and choppy, and horribly oblivious— even indifferent—to the things going on inside them, which were dull, meaty, inane sorts of things anyway. They had no flow and no structure and Fastreda had no patience for them. But starved of the glass, she'd come to appreciate that people were a great deal more interesting than, for example, stone walls or wool carpets or wooden chairs or soup. She appreciated visits, and surprise visits most especially, like the little Orozhandi archivist in her white gloves. It was interesting.

At least, now, here, in the stone-and-wood room, with her leg freshly reshaped. Before would have been a very different matter, and Fastreda never forgot that.

"Well, well," Fastreda said. "Little goat-girl. Ah! And the tea." She beckoned the guards behind the archivist—or really, the tea tray. The guards were more boring than boring.

And slower than slow. Fastreda extended her glass leg—a solid, sharp spike of perfect clarity—and scraped it over the stone with a grating squeal. The guards went faster.

"Come, sit, goat-girl," Fastreda said. "Have some tea. Tell me, though, you're not here to replace my little sparrow. This doesn't make her deal."

"No," Amadea said, entering behind her. "This is something different."

Fastreda's grin grew. Very interesting.

The girl—Yinii, that was it, Yinii Six-Owl ul-Benturan, glided across the floor but stopped short of the offered seat, plucking at her gloves. "Forgive my intrusion, maqu'tajii." She pressed her hands together, against her closed third eye. "We thought...I thought..."

"We wanted to ask you something," Amadea said, remaining beside the wall. Fastreda wondered if the girl had demanded that distance.

"Yes," Yinii said, and made another bow.

"Oh? Once again, is it this room?" Fastreda chuckled to herself. She poured tea into two cups, carved out of dead, dead wood. "Sit. Or are you too frightened?"

The little dear did, quick and sharp, but still she didn't speak. Amadea stood still, only watching. How very, very interesting.

"You have a very lucky birthday, Yinii Six-Owl," Fastreda said. "In Borsya, we say the birds are the souls of the world. The messengers of the gods and the earth and the forest."

"The owl is the herald of the Night King," Yinii recited. "The bringer of prophecy."

Fastreda chuckled. "Very good. But you're not an owl, are you? No. I think my Amadea is a little sparrow. Quick and watchful and twittering." She nodded at the woman, the stranger that time had made for Fastreda. "Or when she was your age, she was.

"You," Fastreda drew the word out as she brought the tea to her lips, "I think you are the shredfinch."

"I don't...I don't know..."

"You wouldn't. I don't even know it. It lives in the Black Mother Forest. They say it's a little gray bird, very small, with red all under its wings. They say the shredfinches were born of the broken body of one of the Black Mother Forest's daughters, killed by an evil king who thought he could take the cold-magic without giving anything in return. They are small and quiet; they search the forest floor for seeds. But nothing hunts them—everything knows better than to hunt them. If you touch a shredfinch, if it flashes its bloody wings and unleashes its unholy scream, the Black Forest Mother remembers and all her terrible powers will swarm out of the darkness and into that little bird. And I don't know, goat-girl, shredfinch, if you know what the Black Mother Forest commands, but let me tell you, that's one beast no hero wants to slay." The guards left, shutting the door behind. Good.

Yinii stared wide-eyed, and Fastreda chuckled. "My mother was Borsyan, through and through. She says it's a good thing the shred-finch doesn't follow us. I say"—she pushed Yinii's cup toward her—"those are the words of someone who doesn't respect true power."

"Are you saying I'm a monster?" Yinii asked.

"Fastreda," Amadea said in warning. "Be kind."

"I don't know." Fastreda smiled at the girl. People could be just a little bit interesting, but it had been a long time since she'd met someone like Yinii ul-Benturan. "What do you think I'm saying, little shredfinch?"

Yinii looked back at Amadea, who nodded, then down at the tea, turning the cup against its wooden saucer with a serious expression. "How did you know," she said in the smallest of voices, "that you were a sorcerer?"

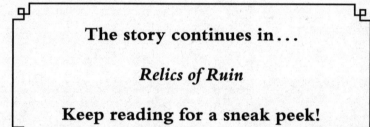

The story continues in...

Relics of Ruin

Keep reading for a sneak peek!

ACKNOWLEDGMENTS

There are three places this book began: First, in the parking lot of my therapist's office, pondering a magic system that felt like an anxiety disorder. Second, listening to the podcast *Stuff You Missed in History Class* talk about Lambert Simnel, a young Yorkist pretender who did *not* get executed or stuffed in an oubliette, despite all my expectations. Third, looking at a pile of mystery novels and knowing that I loved them, but I loved fantasy too much to change lanes.

This is how my ideas come together—random parts leaning on each other, glued together with little sticky bits until they become strong enough to stand on their own—and a great many people are to thank for helping me turn this book into something more than three ideas.

Thank you to my agent, Bridget Smith at JABberwocky, for taking the book on and also sensing what was missing. Thank you to my editors, Bradley Englert and Hillary Sames, for believing in it and helping me take the story to the next level. You guys are fantastic. Thank you to the copyeditor, Eileen G. Chetti, and the proofreaders, Janine Barlow and Manu Velasco. Thank you to Lauren Panepinto for the art direction, Lisa Marie Pompilio for a wonderful cover, and Francesca Baerald for a gorgeous map of this wild world.

Huge thanks to my brilliant friends at the No Name Writing Group—Susan J. Morris, Kate Marshall, Rhiannon Held, Shanna

Germain, Corry L. Lee, and Rashida Smith—who at various points heard about the idea pile, listened to me ramble about it until it became a single thing, told me it was fine and delightful to add things just because I loved them, and suggested excellent ways to tune it up. Thank you for being there when this felt like it would be too much, and for cheering me on when it went right too.

Endless thanks to my sister, Julia Evans, who is a rock and a whirl-wind and so much more. My life is so much better with you in it, in more ways than I can express. Thank you to my mother, Andriea, for starting me on this path long ago, and for all the help and love since.

Thank you to Ari Marmell and Ed Grabianowski, who read early drafts and kept tabs on me through the process. Thank you to all the lovely folks on the agency Slack who listened and cheered along with me during this process.

Thank you to everyone who loved my last series and messaged me asking when the next thing was coming. You were a light in a dark time, and I hope you loved this as much.

And last, thank you so much to my boys: Idris, Ned, and my darling Kevin. You three are my world, wherever we are.

extras

orbit

meet the author

Kevin Goodier

ERIN M. EVANS is the author of seven Forgotten Realms novels for Wizards of the Coast, including the 2011 Scribe Award winner *Brimstone Angels*. She is a content designer for *Idle Champions of the Forgotten Realms* and a cast member of the D&D actual play *Dungeon Scrawlers*. Erin lives in the Seattle area with her husband and sons.

Find out more about Erin M. Evans and other Orbit authors by registering for the free monthly newsletter at orbitbooks.net.

if you enjoyed
EMPIRE OF EXILES

look out for

Relics of Ruin
Books of the Usurper: Two

by

Erin M. Evans

I

The Heart of the World

Year Eight of the Reign of Emperor Clement
Unclaimed territory beyond the border of the Imperial Federation of
Semillan Protectorates

Two weeks from the Salt Wall, Redolfo Kirazzi, once Duke of
Semilla, stops to consider a crumbling map. Two weeks of walking,

he thinks, is enough time, enough space, that if Emperor Clement has discovered that the Redolfo Kirazzi hanged by this time for treason and sedition is *not* Khirazj's dashing duke but a shape-shifting changeling made to stand as his double—well, Redolfo doesn't think Clement is that clever, but he has enough of a head start to make sure it doesn't matter.

He has that two-week head start and a map from before the Salt Wall's sealing. He has four wineskins now filled with water, a sword and a knife and a coil of rope. He has four companions, among them his brother, his assassin, and his sorcerer—but really none of these, because he is also carrying a large quantity of the poison known as the Venom of Khirazj.

This he checks. He thinks there is enough left to lock two or three more changelings, to trap them in a single form and identity, to bind them to his wants. He's been lucky thus far—he's run across the creatures singly or in twos and threes. Maybe scouts, maybe outcasts—their encounters haven't been causes for conversation. He's taken over three, and with these new-made allies, he's left twice that many dead between the Salt Wall and here.

But he has no idea how many changelings might be between him and his goal.

He lays the old map on the ground before him, its surface shiny against the dust. The papyrus is thick and yellowed, the map inexact and written in ancient Khirazji, a language he has studied hard to reclaim. But if one wishes to traverse the lands beyond the Salt Wall, this is as good a guide as one can get.

"We are here," he says, and circles a place southeast of the narrow isthmus at the edge of the once lonely and distant Empire of Semilla, the seas named unfamiliar things in glyphs above and below it. An entirely different world, he thinks, one that hasn't existed for centuries.

The fourth of his companions kneels down beside him. "What's that?" she asks, pointing at the center of the map, where proud gods have been inked over a thick river, binding reeds over a blue-domed city.

"That is Khirazj," he says. " 'The Heart of the World.' "

"Is it really?"

"Maybe once," he says. But mighty Khirazj was bled dry by the changeling horde, just as all this map was: the canyons of Orozhand, the Black Forest of Borsya, the endless kingdoms of martial Bemina, and all the other birthplaces of the survivors who would become Semilla's protectorates. Diminished at the end of the world, but alive—the map is peppered with names he's only seen here, on *this* map, kingdoms and nations whose fate was to vanish utterly under the changeling menace.

"Is that where we're going?"

"Would you like to see it?" he asks instead of answering.

"Yes," she says. She traces a finger up the river path, along the glyphs there. "Pa-de-mah-kee?"

"The river's name." The first king of Khirazj—tradition holds that every king thereafter is the descendant of the river, that all the Dukes and Duchesses Kirazzi with their leashed authority are actually the children of gods. Redolfo smirks and thinks what they'll say when he returns, as if from the grave.

He hasn't got a plan—not yet—but he will. He might not have succeeded in seizing the throne of Semilla, his coup in the name of the emperor's niece crushed and his armies overtaken, but let no one ever say Redolfo Kirazzi was a man easily bested.

And let them not say that Redolfo Kirazzi was an impetuous man either—he has time now to consider what it is he really wants. Is it the throne of Semilla? Or is it Khirazj? Or is it something much greater? What a gift Clement has given him, when you think about it: this time and this space.

And when you think, really think, could one not say Redolfo Kirazzi himself might be the Heart of the World, the axis it turns on, as much as anyone? What comes next determines how the world will turn.

"Where *are* we going?" she asks. "You didn't say."

He searches the map to its limits: Orozhand, Borsya, Bemina, Semilla. The high mountains that come before Aloja, the roads that lead to iron-rich Min-Se and the glittering cities of the Datongu.

Unnamed, unknown nations, he thinks. *Changeling fortresses and monarchs.*

"Where would you go?" he murmurs.

The girl leans over the map, frowning, her hands tucked into her lap. "We should find more food. Water. More of that stuff that makes the changelings behave. They must have more of it out here than they do in there."

"Practical," he says. "Though not very imaginative." But he considers: the Venom of Khirazj and the Venom of Changelings. Two things easier to obtain out here than in there, and then... She's picked up the thread that leads through these lands to a purpose, a goal. What can he gain, after all, out here, beyond the Salt Wall, in the graveyard of the world? What advantage can he seize that Clement cannot? He traces the inked roads and smiles as he comes to an answer. A place to begin.

"Through Orozhand first," he declares, and he smiles. "That's the clearest road. Would you like to see what remains of their saints? I find myself quite curious."

She strokes the inked trade road that passes through Orozhand. *The Canyons of the Horned Ones*, the glyphs say. "I don't know about those," she says.

"Then your education continues," Redolfo says, rolling up the map.

Chapter One

Year Eight of the Reign of Empress Beneditta
The road south of Ragale, the Imperial Federation of Semillan Protectorates
(Twenty-three years later)

Blood soaked Quill's tunic as he crouched in the road. *Not again*, he thought. *Not again*.

One moment Quill had been walking through the gate to the inn of the relay station, following behind Vigilant Richa Langyun. It was late and they'd been too long talking, too much longer riding. He'd been carrying one of the boxes of documents they'd retrieved from the Tower of Parem in the city of Ragale. One moment his eyes were on the deep blue cloak of the Vigilant Kinship's uniform, the pale fur around the collar, on Richa's close-clipped black hair. His thoughts were on the boxes, the copies of the forms and filings that his former mentor had made in the last six months. Somewhere in them hid the clues to a coup, an invasion from beyond the Salt Wall.

The next moment: the shouts, the scream, the boxes falling and Richa sprinting out into the night, across the stones of the Imperial Road toward the forest. Quill chasing because he didn't know what else to do. Two men struggling as his eyes adjusted to the moonlight, and then Richa shouted, and Quill's heart nearly leapt from his chest as the moonlight caught the knife between the two men.

Suddenly, Quill was back in the home of Lord Obigen, watching his best friend brandish a knife, take it to his own throat, kill himself because he believed he was a threat to all they held dear.

But Quill watched as what he could see of the men became a tangled shadow, like a many-armed monster, the knife swallowed up in the vagaries of their shape. A scream again and they split into two, one falling, one running with Richa in pursuit.

Now: blood—Lord on the Mountain, so much blood. A tiny part of Quill hoped the vigilant would be safe and careful, even as he was trying to press the Orozhandi man's stomach back together—

It was the peddler, the man who'd been sitting against the stone wall of the relay station with an array of charms and amulets spread on a blanket before him, his curving horns adorned with many of the same amulets. Quill had bought an iron flower—a charm against changelings, something he hadn't thought he'd ever need until now—and the Orozhandi man had showed him the painted medallions of skeleton saints: Saint Asla of the Salt, the Martyr of the Wall, and Saint Hazaunu of the Wool with her spindle and date palm.

The image of the Orozhandi skeleton saint formed solid and incongruous in his mind as the man stared up at him, panting, his third, parietal eye wide, seeing the shape of Quill's body heat in the darkness.

"You must," the old man gasped. "You must..."

"Don't worry!" Quill said. "It's all right!" And in his mind, he was on the floor beside Karimo again, trying to put his throat back together, while a little part of him said, *That didn't work before. This isn't working now.*

Quill screamed for help. He must have. Where were the people in the relay station? Where was Richa? Where was the man with the knife?

"You have to... save her..." the peddler gasped.

In his thoughts he saw Yinii ul-Benturan, the Orozhandi girl he'd met in the Imperial Archives, terrible in the grasp of her magic. He saw Amadea Gintanas, the archivist superior, standing before him, saying, "I was the Grave-Spurned Princess." He saw the assassin known as the Shrike, oddly, before she was deconstructed into ash and fat, salt and water.

"Who?" he managed around his panicking brain, his hands sunk into the wet of the man's gut. "*Who?*"

The man's day-eyes fluttered open, but when he looked at Quill they did not focus. "In the woods," he said. "Upon the hill... beyond the white rocks…You must protect her." He coughed, rackety and desperate, and blood spattered from his mouth, then poured. Quill automatically reached to push it back, to hold it in, and felt the man's last breath rattle across his hand.

Quill stood up. He couldn't catch his breath. He ran a blood-ied hand through his hair, the black locks grown loose and shaggy since he'd renounced his vows as a Paremi. Where was Richa? Where were the people from the relay station?

Where was the woman he needed to protect?

Richa burst out of the woods, furious and scowling, holding a small Borsyan cold-magic lamp in one hand. "Lost the bastard," he said. He stopped, taking in Quill, the blood, the man on the road. "Shit," he said.

"We have to go," Quill said. "There's someone in the woods. A woman. That might be where the killer went. He said she's in the woods, up the hill, beyond the white rocks."

For a moment the world felt too large, the sky unable to contain Quill, to hold him down—the horror felt endless and the problem impossible and Richa was about to say, *You've been through a lot, Quill, you're imagining things, he was dying, he was raving, let's go back and send word to the vigilants.*

Instead, Richa looked away from him, toward the woods, scanning the tree line as if looking for any hint of a rise. "Come on."

They should have gone back to the relay station and gathered help. They should have taken care of the peddler's body. They should have waited for daylight when navigating the forest would be safer.

But the energy that surged in Quill to move, to do, to stop all of this madness, seemed to grip Richa just as strongly, and the younger man kept his eyes on the ghostlike patch of silvery fur as Richa moved ahead of him through the patches of gloom and moonlight, along a path Quill couldn't see. In the woods, up a hill…

The white boulders were deep in the shadow of an ancient fir tree with thick, craggy bark, but even there they glowed faintly, as if the moonlight sought them out. Richa stopped in the little clearing there. The stones were set into a steep slope.

Richa handed him the glowing orb. "Stay here."

He started to climb, scaling the smooth-sided rocks as if they were a ladder and moving up the bare earthen slope beyond. Quill looked around, suddenly aware of the possibility of the man with the knife. He moved closer to the rocks, closer to Richa. Surely the vigilant, trained in defense and dedicated to the protection of the Imperial Federation, had a knife on him? Quill had a little blade for sharpening styli.

That was how he found the gap between the rocks, and the little cave beyond.

Quill squeezed through the gap, into the space. The cold-magic lamp spread a thin bluish light around the small space. The ceiling had been dug out enough for Quill to stand up, the beams of the tree's roots protruding here and there, and the peddler had pounded the walls smooth.

There was a bed, a box full of dishes, a box full of battered books. A knife on a hook on the wall. Portraits of saints everywhere. A cushion before the largest portrait, a quiet, personal altar. The stink of a seldom-washed body.

There was no woman in the little dirt room.

Quill let out a breath. No rescue, no action—just a dead man's home, a dead man's things, the artifacts of an interrupted life. The scent of his living was fading already.

He turned, as if he could turn from the thought bodily, looking at the portraits of the saints—fleshed and skeletal—and it took Quill a moment to realize they were all the same one. The woman with the shepherd's crook and the date palm. Saint Hazaunu. In different hands and shifting styles, but the same woman.

"She is the guardian on the cliff top," the peddler had explained with shining eyes as he showed Quill his wares, not an hour before. "The eye that watches the weft, and the sentinel that guards the flock. A most holy lady."

A personal saint, he thought, remembering what Yinii had taught him. The hermit had obviously venerated Saint Hazaunu of the Wool beyond all others. He stepped closer, examining the largest of the portraits, the one that felt like an altar.

The ground beneath his foot gave a hollow *thump*.

Quill stepped back, shining the light downward. The ground was pounded dirt, but—he stomped against it again—here there was *something* beneath the dirt. A box, a chest, a wooden barrier—his imagination raced ahead, picturing some frightened hostage hiding beneath. He set aside the cold-magic light and started digging his bloodstained fingers into the dirt.

"Quill!" Richa shouted. "Quill!"

"In the cave! Between the rocks!" He found the wood quickly, swept it free to the edges. He took out the little penknife and fitted it into the uncovered groove, feeling the grit of the dirt grinding the fine edge.

"It's all right," he said to the possible girl. "It's all right."

Richa came up behind him. "Did you find—"

Quill levered the penknife up against the edge of the box, snapping the blade but breaking the wood free. He grabbed the freed edge and pulled up, scattering more dirt across the floor, and looked down into the darkness he'd just revealed.

There was, indeed, someone in there.

Only they were very, very dead.

A skeleton lay curled on its side, hands clasped before its face, as if sleeping. The bones of each browned finger glinted with caps of gold, the horn that curved away from the downturned face sparkled with charms, and fine wires wrapped the arm bones, strung with pearls.

The peddler's medallions flashed through Quill's thoughts again, the gem-encrusted faces in the Imperial Archives' Chapel of the Skeleton Saints.

In the woods, up the hill, beyond the white rocks, lay the lost bones of an Orozhandi saint.

if you enjoyed
EMPIRE OF EXILES

look out for

THE CITY OF DUSK

Book One of
The Dark Gods

by

Tara Sim

This dark epic fantasy follows the heirs of four noble houses—each gifted with a divine power—as they form a tenuous alliance to keep their kingdom from descending into a realm-shattering war.

The Four Realms—Life, Death, Light, and Darkness—all converge on the city of dusk. For each realm there is a god, and for each god there is an heir.

But the gods have withdrawn their favor from the once vibrant and thriving city. And without it, all the realms are dying.

Unwilling to stand by and watch the destruction, the four heirs—Risha, a necromancer struggling to keep the peace; Angelica, an elementalist with her eyes set on the throne; Taesia, a shadow-wielding rogue with rebellion in her heart; and Nik, a soldier who struggles to see the light—will sacrifice everything to save the city.

But their defiance will cost them dearly.

I

Taesia Lastrider had never considered herself a good person, nor did she have any intention of becoming one.

She was fine with that. Beyond the confines of her House's villa, she was freer to do whatever she wanted. Be whoever she wanted.

The last breath of summer's heat coiled around her as she shifted in the shadow of a market awning. Shoppers were buying melon juice and sarab, a clear Parithvian alcohol served with a pinch of orange-colored spice that cooled the body down. Jewelry on a nearby cart glittered in the sunlight, cuffs of hammered silver and brass sending spangles into her vision. Taesia blinked and retreated even farther into the shade.

It put her in view of the building she had been adamantly trying to ignore. But it was almost impossible to overlook the size of it, the swirling, conch-like design of shimmering sandstone, the length of the shadow it cast across the city of Nexus.

It was quite lovely, for a prison. But crack that pretty shell open, and all its filth would come pouring out, the discarded and condemned souls of Nexus's convicts.

Someone bumped into her as they passed by, and the shadows twitched at her fingertips. She was so jumpy it took her a moment to realize it was merely a common thieves' tactic: make someone paranoid enough to pat their trousers or their sleeves to know where to strike later.

An amateur trick. It didn't matter there were more guards than usual patrolling the marketplace; pickpockets would take any chance they could get.

At the next stall over, a man was prying open boxes with a crowbar, chatting with the vendor as they checked the wares inside. "Would've gotten here sooner if I hadn't been held at the city gates," the man with the crowbar said. "Guards were sniffing around me like the dogs they are."

"King's got 'em on alert." The vendor glanced at the nearest guards and lowered his voice. "Had an incident not too long ago. Some weird magic shit went down near the palace."

"What kinda weird magic?"

"Wasn't there myself, but sounds to me like it was necromancy. Folks say a buncha spirits came and wrecked shit."

"*Spirits?* Were the Vakaras acting up? I've heard they can kill with just a snap of their fingers."

This caught Taesia's attention like thread on a nail. It was well known throughout Vaega—as well as beyond its borders—that those who made up House Vakara, descended from the god of death, were the only ones who possessed the power of necromancy. It was also well known that once in a while, a stray spirit managed to wander from Nexus's overcrowded necropolis to cause trouble.

But the incident the two men were gossiping about had been different: a sudden influx of violent spirits converging close to the palace square, destroying buildings and harming those unfortunate enough to be in their path. People had been rightfully terrified—and confused about who to blame.

"No idea," the vendor mumbled. "But it was nasty stuff. Heard a man got his arm ripped clean off. Whole city's gonna be tighter than a clenched asshole from now on."

A tremor rolled across her body as Taesia turned back to the Gravespire. When the vendor beside her wasn't looking, she grabbed a glass of sarab and downed it in one go, wiping her mouth with the back of her wrist.

Citizens blaming the Houses for their troubles wasn't anything new. But the thought of Risha getting caught up in it made her want to punch something.

The shadows twitched again. Impatience crackled at the base of her lungs, made her roll onto the balls of her feet as if poised on the edge of something reckless.

"Follow me," a low voice whispered behind her.

She breathed a sigh of relief and waited a couple seconds before turning and following her brother through the market. Dante was dressed down today in a long, sleeveless tunic with a hood, the lean muscle of his dusky-brown arms on display. A few people pretended not to stare as he stalked by. Not in recognition, but in appreciation of his features despite the hood's shadow. Or maybe they were drawn to the smooth, confident way he moved, the way Taesia never seemed to get quite right.

"Did you get the information you needed?" she whispered.

"I did. We should be—"

She nearly ran into his back when he suddenly stopped. He lifted a hand for her to stay put.

She soon saw why. A couple Greyhounds had descended on a confused vendor. They were inspecting jars from her stall, dropping what didn't interest them to the ground. The vendor flinched at the sound of breaking pottery.

Taesia cursed under her breath. Although the vendor had no horns, the bluish dark of her skin and the white tattoos on her forehead marked her as a Noctan. Perhaps a mixed-race offspring from one of the refugees. Mixed blood would explain how she could stand to be in this heat in the middle of the day; most of the night-dwellers from Noctus couldn't bear it, often getting sunsick if forced to endure it for too long.

"Please, I have no contraband," the vendor said softly. They were beginning to draw spectators eagerly searching for a distraction from the heat. "These were all fairly traded within Vaega."

"We're not looking for foreign goods," one of the guards said.

His partner waved a small pot in his direction. The guard took it, sniffed, and scowled.

"Sulfur." The single word was leveled at the vendor like an arrow. "A Conjuration ingredient."

Taesia sucked in a breath. While many were eager to call the incident last week necromancy, the Vakaras had never been shy to demonstrate their magic, and their methods didn't line up with the attack. For in the ravaged spot where the spirits had congregated, something had been left behind: a cleverly drawn circle containing a seven-pointed star and a ring of strange glyphs.

Conjuration. An occult practice that hadn't been seen in decades.

The vendor shook. "I—I didn't know! I swear, I—"

The Greyhounds didn't waste time listening to her stammer. They shackled her wrists as excited murmurs ran through the small crowd they'd gathered.

"Wouldn't have bought from her anyway," someone muttered. "Anything the Noctans touch is tainted."

"Did they say Conjuration? Isn't that demon—?"

"Shh! The Greyhounds won't hesitate to haul you off, too."

"She should have stayed in the Noctus Quarter."

Taesia curled her hand into a fist. Dante grabbed her as she took a step forward.

"Don't," he said. Not a warning, but an order.

"We're responsible for the refugees."

"They're cracking down on Conjuration materials," Dante whispered. "If you interfere, think about how it'll reflect on the House."

She didn't give two shits about that. "You're saying you're all right with this?"

"Of course I'm not. But we can't do anything about it right now."

Taesia watched the guards haul away the vendor, who was trying and failing to stifle her terrified tears. Dante didn't let Taesia go until the tension left her body. When he did, she spun to face him. "Are you sure you want to go through with this? You said it yourself: We can't have anything negatively impacting the House." She dropped her voice to a murmur. "Especially considering what the Vakaras are going through. Even if you manage to find what you need, what are you going to do with it?"

"Not summon a horde of spirits, if that's what you're concerned about."

It wasn't—not really—but there was so much about Conjuration they didn't understand, since all the old texts had been destroyed.

"You want to put a stop to these scenes, right?" Dante nodded in the direction of the vendor's abandoned stall. "To not have to worry about House politics when it comes to issues like defending the people?"

She swallowed, certain her hunger for that very thing was plain on her face. "What does that have to do with Conjuration?"

"Indulge me a little longer, and you'll see." He paused, then leaned forward and sniffed. "Have you been drinking?"

"Don't worry about it."

They walked past the beehive hum of the crowd and continued on to the edge of the market, where four children were playing with a couple of dogs. A gangly man was slumped over a counter. He watched the children with an air of someone who probably should be worried about their safety but couldn't muster up the energy.

"I don't *want* to be Thana," one of the children was complaining in a nasal voice. "Thana's scary. I want to be Deia!"

"*I'm* Deia," said another child, a tall girl with dirt smudged across her face. "I'm always Deia."

"Just because you have weak earth magic doesn't mean you can be Deia every time," mumbled a boy with Mariian black skin. Judging by the crown made of twigs and sticks resting on the tight coils of his hair, he was supposed to play the part of Nyx, god of night and shadow.

"It's not weak!" With a flick of her finger, she flung a pebble at his forehead, making him cry out.

"You can be Phos instead," said the last child, likely the Mariian boy's brother. He handed the girl who didn't want to be Thana his toy wings made of fluttering leaves, which made her brighten. "And I'll be Thana. I'll put her in a cage of bones."

Taesia smiled wryly. It was common for children to play at being gods; she herself had done it with her siblings when they were younger. That was before they'd understood only one god demanded their family's piety.

Dante rapped his knuckles on the wooden counter, making the gangly man start. "Heard you have good prices," Dante said, his cautious inflection almost making it a question.

The corner of the man's mouth twitched. "Come see for yourself."

Dante glanced at the children, the dogs barking and chasing after them when they ran. "Will they be all right on their own?"

The man shrugged and headed toward the nearest alley. They were led away from the market to a building that had seen better days, with a tarp-covered window and weeds sprouting along its base. The man eased the door open and ushered them inside. A second door on the far end of the room was open, revealing a set of stairs leading down. Taesia's nose wrinkled immediately at the smell, a bitter blend of ash and pepper.

"Ruben," the gangly man called. "Customer." He left to return to the market.

A heavyset man in shirtsleeves appeared on the stairs, wiping his hands on a handkerchief. "Hello, hello. This way, please."

Dante kept his hood up as he and Taesia descended into a basement. It might have once been a wine cellar, cramped and cool. But instead of racks of wine, the place was now stocked with sacks of herbs and roots, boxes of chalk, and jars of sulfur. There was even a display of small knives along the wall.

Dante's eyes lit up the way Taesia imagined a librarian's would at finding a rare book for their collection. He began to wade through the assortment, peering into sacks and running his hands through unknown substances. Taesia meandered toward the knives and inspected one with a serpentine blade.

The man, Ruben, cleared his throat. "Let's keep this brief, yes? No guards saw you come this way?"

"Not that I'm aware of." Dante's voice was distant, the tone he got when someone tried to interrupt him. He picked up a jar and shook it, the black specks inside rattling. "What's this?"

"That would be powdered lodestone."

"And what does it do?"

403

"It's a magnetized bit of mineral, known for attracting iron. Rich deposits of it along the eastern coast."

"I'll take ten grams, as well as loose chalk." Dante paused before pointing at a nearby sack. "Throw in some hellebore root as well."

Taesia grimaced. For all his intelligence and charisma, her brother wasn't particularly skilled at pretending to be something he was not. The order strung through his words might as well have painted a broadsheet across his face reading *I'm a noble, can't you tell?*

Ruben didn't seem particularly affected by it either way. Taesia obediently held the sachet of hellebore root Dante handed to her while he tucked the vial of powdered lodestone and pouch of chalk into his own pockets. Coins exchanged hands, the clink of gold loud in the cellar.

"A pleasure," Ruben said with a sickly smile.

Taesia took a much-needed deep breath once they were back on the street. "Again, are you absolutely sure about this?"

"I'll be careful." Despite Dante's light tone, she noted the divot between his brows. He was nervous.

Spotting the tip of the Gravespire rising above the buildings, Taesia thought about the Noctan who had been hauled away and swallowed.

Nexus had once prided itself on harboring people from every country, every realm, to form an eclectic microcosm of their broad universe. Now it seemed as if they were doing their best to eradicate those who *didn't belong*, whatever that meant.

She was jolted from her thoughts when someone slammed into her and sent her crashing to the ground.

"Stop her!" someone shouted.

Taesia gaped up at the face staring down at hers. The girl couldn't have been much older than her, with lustrous black skin and a cloud of dark hair. She winked and scrambled off Taesia in a flash, slipping into the startled crowd like a fish.

Dante helped her up as a few Greyhounds ran by in pursuit. Taesia stared after the girl, rubbing a sore spot on her chest.

"You all right?" Dante asked.

"Yeah, I'm—" She checked her pockets. "She stole the hellebore root!" Not an amateur thief, then.

Dante shushed her. "It's fine, I can get by without—Tae!"

She charged after the thief with a fire kindled in her chest, stoked and restless since Dante had stopped her from interfering with the guards.

Finally, some damn action.

The Greyhounds were slowed by the crowd, but Taesia easily evaded limbs and bodies. The thief hoisted herself onto the roof of a stall, so Taesia did the same. She rolled across an awning and leapt onto the next roof, which swayed dangerously under her feet.

She lifted her hand. To anyone else, the silver ring on her fourth finger bore an onyx jewel, but the illusion broke when her shadow familiar spilled from the bezel and into her palm.

"Do something for me?" she panted as she leapt the space between two stalls.

Umbra elongated, forming a snakelike head of shadow. It tilted from side to side before it nodded.

Taesia flung out her hand and Umbra shot forward in a black, inky rope. One end lashed around the thief's wrist, making her stumble. With a sharp pull on Taesia's end, the thief crashed through an awning.

Taesia jumped down. The thief groaned and staggered away from cages full of exotic birds flapping their wings and squawking at the disturbance. The vendor gawked at them as Taesia summoned Umbra back to her ring and took off after the girl.

The last thing she wanted was for rumors of a Shade tussling in the market to reach her mother.

Taesia dove into a narrow alley to try and cut the thief off at the cross street, only to be met with an arm that swung out from around the corner. It collided with her chest and Taesia fell onto her back with a grunt.

The thief stood over her, breathless and smiling. "Well! Gotta admit, this is a first. Never stole from someone like you before."

Taesia coughed. "You punched me in the tit."

"And I'd do it again."

Taesia braced herself on the ground and kicked the girl in the chest, sending her reeling backward. "Now we're almost even."

The girl wheezed around a laugh. "Suit yourself."

Taesia sprang to her feet and charged. The thief ducked and hit her in the back, dangerously close to her kidneys. Taesia caught her arm and twisted. The thief stomped on her instep, making her yelp and let go.

"Whew!" The girl's face was alive with glee despite the dirt and sweat streaked across it. "Must've stolen something you care about."

"Not really." The shadows trembled around her, ready to be called in, but she couldn't risk it. She'd already been too careless using Umbra. "Just needed to stretch my legs today."

The girl barked a laugh as they circled. Her dark eyes flitted to the alley over Taesia's shoulder before a blow caught Taesia across the backs of her knees, sending her reeling forward.

As Taesia fell, a young woman—likely the thief's partner—ran to the nearest wall and made a broad swirling motion with her arms. Both of the thieves were caught in a sudden cyclone of wind that lifted them up onto the roof.

An air elementalist.

Cheater.

"Better luck next time," the thief called with a mocking salute. Taesia gave a rude gesture in reply, and the girl laughed before she and her partner disappeared.

A moment later, Dante burst out of the alley. "Taesia, what the *fuck*—"

"She got away."

"I don't care! I told you it didn't matter." He ran a hand through his hair, hood fallen across his shoulders. "You're filthy. We can't let anyone in the villa see you like this." He pointed a stern finger at her. "Do *not* do that again."

She wasn't sure if he meant chasing after thieves or using her shadow magic out in the open. Before she could ask, he turned and began the trek home, not even bothering to see if Taesia would follow.

Like always, she did.

The black iron gates of the Lastrider villa were manned by House guards in black-and-silver livery. But Taesia had long since figured out a path over the tall adobe wall, through the gardens, and up the rose trellis her father had built when she was a child. It was easy as a song to slip into her bedroom and change into clean clothes.

She met up with Dante at the entrance to the vaults, the underground chambers where House treasures were stored. The two of them had often played here as children. Their younger sister, Brailee, had been too afraid to stay longer than five minutes, but Taesia and Dante had made games of the thick shadows and silent rooms. As heir, Dante was the only person aside from their mother who possessed a key.

"I know you said you don't plan to call down a horde of spirits," she said as he lit a lantern and led the way down the musty corridor, "but that still begs the question of what you *are* planning to do."

"I'm more interested in the origins of Conjuration rather than using it as a conduit for two-bit necromancy."

"Origins?"

"You'll see."

Umbra slithered up her arm as Dante shoved open a door at the end of the corridor. His own familiar, Nox, began to play around his shoulders, no longer required to stay hidden. Taesia wondered if they could feel the presence of Noctan artifacts down here, a tentative link to a realm they had never seen.

Dante lit candles in the stone-walled room. It had once been used for storage but now served as his workshop. Shelves bore jars and vials waiting to be filled, and the very center of the floor was covered in a thick rug.

He pulled the rug aside to reveal a hazy, stained area where he'd practiced drawing Conjuration circles. Taesia's breath caught, remembering the events of last week, the circle with its seven-pointed star left by people the king condemned as radicals. Nox brushed Dante's cheek as it peered over his shoulder.

"So," he said. "Lodestone. Typically used for its magnetism, but there was an ancient use for this that's long since fallen out of memory." He shook the vial. "It was used as an offering for Deia."

Taesia raised an eyebrow. "If you wanted to give an offering to Deia, you should have gone to her basilica."

He smirked and pulled out a jar of sulfur. He began to mix it with the loose chalk he'd bought, and Taesia fought against the urge to sneeze. "When we talk about Conjuration today, it's always associated with one thing: summoning demons."

Demons. Cosmic beings that prowled between the realms, in the pockets of the universe only the gods could access. There were countless stories told to children to make them behave, to warn others away:

"Narizeh will come and steal your voice if you don't stop screaming."

"Never follow a woman with lips tinged black. That is Vorsileh luring you to her bed, where she will turn you into a worm once she's done with you and slurp you up."

"The sound of coughing means Celipheh has visited to spread his plague."

But Conjuration had been outlawed over two centuries ago, the grimoires and texts burned in a massive purge of all things occult in Nexus. There had never been a case outside the city; why that was, no one could say.

Taesia grimaced. "What do demons have to do with an offering for Deia?"

He gave her a loaded Dante smile, silent secrets hidden under an ocean of charm. "What we call Conjuration today is a bastardization of an ancient ritual to commune with the gods. Back in the day, priests would draw a circle to replicate the shape of the universe, add offerings unique to the god they wanted to chat with, and there you have it."

Taesia felt cold as she watched Dante draw two circles with the laced chalk, one nested within the other. She leaned against the wall and crossed her arms. "So you want to talk to the gods, is that what you're saying? Why?"

He paused, staring at the diamond he'd just drawn within the inner circle. Quietly he said, "To understand why the Sealing happened."

Taesia's fingers tightened on her arms. "And you're certain it'll work? That we won't end up with some unsavory visitor?"

His laugh was tinged with apprehension. "Not at all." He poured the powdered lodestone around the diamond, then opened a jar and sniffed its contents. "I wish we had the hellebore root, but this should be a good enough substitute."

He sprinkled something that smelled like tobacco. When he looked back up, a lock of dark hair fell across his forehead.

"I figured trying is better than sitting around feeling helpless," he said, his voice gone soft again.

A wave of fondness washed over her despite the fact she was staring at her brother across a very illegal, very pungent Conjuration circle. Dante had more willpower than she did, but they both shared the desire to *act*.

He unsheathed the small knife at his belt and cut the pad of one finger. A drop of blood, trembling and infused with ancient power, fell into the center of the circle, over the upside-down horseshoe-esque symbol commonly used for Deia.

Nothing happened at first. Taesia braced herself, Umbra nervously coiling around her neck. Dante stayed kneeling, brow furrowed. Then a steady, low hum began to fill the room, the edges of the circle glowing red.

The offerings within the circle trembled, the hum traveling up the soles of Taesia's feet until it made her molars ache. Umbra hid itself in the crook of her neck, and it took all her strength to not make a run for the door.

"Deia, we beseech you to speak with us," Dante intoned. "Please bless us with your presence."

It was one thing to visit the basilica of Nyx, the god of Noctus, the founder of the Lastrider line, and feel a hint of night-touched breeze on her face. To sense the distant stars overhead and the depth of shadows in every corner. A reminder of where they came from, and what they could do. But this was Deia, god of elements, god of life, with the power to raise volcanoes and turn entire cities to ice. Attempting to summon her in this cramped room was perhaps not the best idea.

Yet as they continued to stare at the floor, waiting—for a voice, or the outline of a body, *something*—nothing happened.

A frustrated sound wrenched out of Dante's throat as the glow died, casting them back into dim candlelight. He scored the circle with a hand, and Taesia couldn't help her relieved exhale.

"I don't know what else to do, other than try different offerings." Dante glared at the wasted lodestone. "Or perhaps try to find a different configuration of symbols."

"Even if you manage to summon one of the gods, what good would it do?"

Dante worked his jaw, the tension fading gradually from his face. "It's not just about talking to them, or asking why they sealed the realms from one another. I want..." He ran a hand through his hair. "You're going to think I'm mad."

"I already do. Tell me."

He sat back on his heels. "I want to convince them to undo it."

Taesia waited a beat. Then another. Her mouth twisted to keep from laughing.

"It's not impossible!" he argued. "If we undo the Sealing, we reopen the realms and the natural flow of the universe will be restored. We can use our godsblood for good, to prevent our realm from dying." He lowered his voice. "It'll also give the Houses leverage over the king. We can gain support from the people to take away the Holy King's authority."

It was something they had discussed before, in the privacy of Dante's study. How he admired their neighbor to the north, Parithvi, and the Parliament they had instated with more populist beliefs.

"We can actually *use* our privilege for a change," Dante said.

They sat in the possibility a moment, familiars drifting between them, a couple more shadows in a room that smelled of forbidden magic.

It sounded stupidly heroic: going against the will of the gods, wresting control of their country from a man who believed himself untouchable.

Again she thought of the Noctan refugee who had been seized in the market. Under Dante's watch, those scenes could disappear completely.

But there was one problem.

"I don't foresee myself with a political career," she said. "Once you've established this parliament of yours, what role would you give me?"

He wrinkled his nose. "Tae, you were *born* into a political career."

"Firmly without my say-so."

"Well, don't worry. Once the realms are reopened, I plan to restore the profession on which the Lastrider line was founded. I'll need someone to spearhead it."

Status came hand in hand with responsibility if you were a member of the Houses. Yet each household also had to contribute something to Nexus, to the kingdom, and to the throne in order to maintain that status. The Vakaras performed all things necromantic, the Mardovas cultivated powerful mages, the Cyrs produced and oversaw soldiers for the militia, and the Lastriders acted as inter-realm emissaries of trade.

Or at least, they had before the Sealing. Now, with resources both natural and Other-Realm dwindling in Vitae, the Lastriders worked with the surrounding countries to conserve what little was left.

Taesia felt cheated of a life of jumping from realm to realm, collecting artifacts and precious resources and exploring the wonders and dangers of other worlds. To not have to sit still. To have the freedom to go where she wished.

To not be a purposeless spare of House Lastrider, chained to a responsibility she'd never wanted.

"You're flirting with being labeled a radical for a hopeless plan," she said, though it sounded weak even to her.

He smiled at the greed suffusing Taesia's expression, his eyes glimmering with the same thrill she knew must be mirrored in her own. "But are *you* willing to flirt with it?"

Taesia glanced again at the forfeited circle. Dante wouldn't delve into something he didn't think was for the greater good. Dante believed in a better world, and she believed in Dante.

"Absolutely."

Follow us:

/orbitbooksUS

/orbitbooks

/orbitbooks

Join our mailing list
to receive alerts on our
latest releases and deals.

orbitbooks.net

Enter our monthly
giveaway for the chance
to win some epic prizes.

orbitloot.com